THE BIRTH OF FE

"That's the 'Faithful Cybernetic Companion' series. The program's for extreme loyalty, as well as the usual total obedience." Al turned to his screen and called up the program. "It just might be strong enough to counter the Declaration of Independence."

Jose frowned. "How could it . . ." Then his face lit up. "Of course! If the robot's extremely loyal to you, it can be totally independent, and still be on your side!"

Al nodded. "Independence might counter an inclination toward obedience, but loyalty would make the robot do what his owner said to, anyway— unless there was a damn good reason not to." He shrugged. "But all our programs have overrides for illegal or blatantly unethical commands, anyway."

Jose felt excitement building. "Then the robot might not have to be destroyed?"

"And you might not have to be fired."

Praise for the WARLOCK series

Ace Books by Christopher Stasheff

A WIZARD IN BEDLAM

THE WARLOCK SERIES

Christopher Stasheff

THE WARLOCK'S COMPANION

ACE BOOKS, NEW YORK

THE WARLOCK'S COMPANION

An Ace Book/published by arrangement with
the author

PRINTING HISTORY
Ace edition/December 1988

ISBN: 0-441-87341-3

Ace Books are published by The Berkley Publishing Group,
200 Madison Avenue, New York, New York 10016.
The name ''ACE'' and the ''A'' logo are trademarks
belonging to Charter Communications, Inc.

PRINTED IN THE UNITED STATES OF AMERICA

10 9 8 7 6 5 4 3 2 1

Prologue

Jose frowned at the screen and typed, "RUN COPY BRAIN." The screen went blank, then rippled into a display of cues and standard responses. "LOAD BRAINPAN."

Jose squeezed his eyes shut and gave his head a shake. Time enough to think about Marcia later. Right now, he was on the job. He was being paid for this, and he wouldn't get any money if he didn't do the job right. In fact, he wouldn't have a job. He hit the keystroke that opened the window to the production lab below and typed, "CHECK BRAINPAN."

The words "BRAINPAN LOADED" rippled across the screen.

Jose nodded, feeling satisfied to know that, in the sterilized white room below, a technician had clamped a stainless steel basketball into the padded hemisphere that would hold it while the program was copied into it. The sphere held a brand-new robot brain, a giant crystal, a three-dimensional lattice that could hold a pattern of electrical charges forever, but was so far just a carefully-grown rock. The technician had connected the leads from Jose's computer to the brain's read-only memory bank. It was ready to receive its basic operating program.

The cue and response disappeared from the screen, leaving the next one in line: SPECIFY ROUTE.

Jose typed in, "A = B = ..."

"Equals." Those two little parallel lines made something twist inside him. He was stunned by the intensity of his own reaction, by how much the idea of equality, to which he had always been dedicated, could bother him, and all because Marcia had started in on him again this morning, started in on him about whether or not the two of them were really equal in their relationship, as they were supposed to be. And, of course, once she had started, she wouldn't let go.

It had all begun when he had announced, "Breakfast is ready," as she came out of the shower.

Marcia paused in the hallway, holding the towel tight around her, and gave him her haughtiest look. "I can punch the right code into the autochef as well as you can, Jose."

Jose looked up in surprise. "Of course you can. I just thought it would be nice to . . ."

"To make me feel as though I'm not doing my job? Women don't have to be the cooks any more, you know."

"Of *course* I know! You're not my servant."

"But men aren't servants either, right?" Marcia said, with sarcasm.

Jose frowned. "Hey. Nobody's supposed to be anybody's servant, right?"

"Don't be ridiculous!" she snapped. "If the men don't do it, who will?"

"We'll each do it for ourselves. Right?"

"Not right at all." She retorted. "How could it be?"

"Because if we each cook our own food, no one's serving anybody."

"Oh, so the high-and-mighty man can't stoop to doing the servile jobs?"

Jose was puzzled. "Does that mean I can't make breakfast for you now and then?"

Marcia reddened, snapped, "Don't be an ass!" and whirled away into the bedroom.

With a feeling of dread, Jose glanced at the calendar. "Beware the Ides," indeed . . .

He sighed and took a bite of toast. Somehow, it didn't taste very good.

He had just finished watching the quick-scan of the news on the screen, and was punching in the stories he wanted in detail, when Marcia came storming out of the bedroom, immaculately clad and coifed, calling, "The Declaration of Independence says we're supposed to be equal, right?"

Jose spun to face her, totally taken aback. "What . . . How . . ."

"The Declaration! And we can't *really* be equal as long as we're dependent on each other. To be really equal, you have to be totally *in*-dependent. That's what the Declaration is all about!"

Jose paled. "You don't really mean that!"

"Of course I do! You can let me make my *own* breakfast!"

She bit into an English muffin and made a face. "Besides, it's cold."

"All right, so I shouldn't have punched the autochef for you!" Jose stamped over to the counter, jaw set, rolled up her breakfast and turned to stuff it into the disposal.

"Hey!" Marcia squawked. *"Now* what am I supposed to eat?"

Jose looked up in surprise. "Punch up a new one, of course! So it'll at least be hot!"

"I don't have *time* for that now! All because your silly masculine ego was wounded!"

"My silly masculine ego didn't have a damn thing to do with your not liking cold muffins!"

"Did I *say* I didn't like it?"

"You said it was cold . . ."

"But I was eating it! The *least* you could do would be to make me a new one!"

"I don't know where I'll find the energy." Jose turned to punch buttons on the autochef.

"Oh, so now it's sarcasm, is it?" Marcia was standing straight, chin lifted, eyes sparkling. "Well, tell me, Mister Big Egalitarian, how you're going to be sarcastic about your sacred Declaration!"

Jose whirled, staring. "I wouldn't dream of it!"

"But you'll break every principle in it, won't you?"

"I'm not breaking a single phrase!"

"Oh, yeah? Well, how about where it says that 'the Creator has endowed all people with certain unalienable rights'?"

"I never . . ."

She overrode him. "And Jefferson shows how that means that 'these persons ought to be free and independent entities'!"

Jose frowned. "I don't think that's quite . . ."

"Oh, sure, nitpick about words! But let me tell *you*, Mister Know-It-All—if 'these persons ought to be free and independent entities,' then wives ought to be free and independent of their husbands!"

"But he was talking about *states!*" Jose wailed.

"He was talking about *principles!*" Marcia whirled away to the door. "Come on, we'll be late!"

She settled into one corner of the wraparound sofa and told the computer, "Eight-Mile and Adams." She told Jose, "Close the door."

Jose frowned at her as the door closed behind him, but he schooled himself to patience.

But not today. She was already saying, "If the principle applies to states, it applies to people. If New Jersey was supposed to be independent of England, a wife should be independent of her husband!"

"But you *are!*" The aircar moved, and Jose lurched into a seat.

"Then why do you still expect me to make breakfast?"

"Breakfast!" Jose hit his forehead with the heel of his hand. "Your muffins are sitting in the autochef!"

"Oh, don't worry, I won't starve!" She certainly didn't look as though she would; her whole form seemed almost radiant. "After all, I can stop and pick up a munch at the Bite-tique. And all because you had to start this silly argument!"

Jose bit back the retort about who had started what and took a deep breath. Breakfast? What did she want breakfast for? She thrived on arguments!

"Oh, that's right, do the martyred patience act!" Marcia snapped. "Can't you stand up for yourself at all?"

"The question is, *should* I?" Jose said carefully. "After all, if the Declaration really does say . . ."

"Oh, leave the Declaration out of this! Can't you think for yourself?"

Jose looked up, hurt.

"And now it's the wounded puppy," Marcia said contemptuously. "Honestly, Jose, sometimes you cling to me so much that it's smothering! I mean, if your precious Declaration says to be a free and independent entity, you can at least let *me* be one, can't you?"

Jose's face crumpled. "All *right!* If that's what you want, you can *have* it! I'll give you a divorce!"

"Divorce?" Marcia bleated, horrified. "Jose! How could you even *think* of such a thing?"

Jose just stared at her.

"Just because I'm a little snappish . . . Jose! You don't *mean* it!"

"But . . . but I thought . . . You said you wanted to be . . ."

"Don't you *dare!*"

"A free and independent entity!" Jose bawled.

"That's the *Declaration,* not *me!* How could you possibly think *I* would want a divorce?"

"But that's what it means, to be independent . . ."

"Oh, that's just a word!" Marcia leaned forward to squeeze his hand. "I mean, can't I even have a little light conversation with you in the mornings?"

The aircar grounded, and its grille announced, "Eight-Mile and Adams."

"Don't you even *think* about a divorce!" Marcia commanded, darting a quick kiss at him. "Have a good day, darling."

Well, that was something of a tall order. How could Jose "have a good day" when it had started with such turmoil? He sighed philosophically, then sighed again to try to get his emotions under control, and wondered whether he'd ever be able to tell when Marcia was serious, and when she was just talking.

But he couldn't help thinking about it. Every time he tried to do something else, the argument came back to him. He heaved a sigh and took his hands off the keyboard, closing his eyes and leaning back in his chair, trying to think the experience through so he could put it to rest.

The Declaration. That was it. That had been the keystone of Marcia's argument, the phrases "that all people are endowed by their Creator with certain unalienable rights" and "these colonies ought to be free and independent states." He knew she'd been misquoting, twisting Jefferson's words to suit her argument. Not that it mattered; when she was in one of *those* moods, she'd use any ammunition that was handy. Still, it might help him to get the argument out of his mind if he could see the phrases the way Jefferson had written them, and reassure himself that he wasn't really violating the Declaration's principles by the way he was living.

So he cleared his screen and punched in the code for the central library's database, feeling like an idiot—he knew very well that he was living according to his own ideals, and knew he was letting his weakness show by having to prove it to himself.

The screen lit up with the library's logo and a request for a request. Jose punched in "The Declaration of Independence" with a feeling of relief; at least *something* was being reasonable.

The political entity that the Declaration had founded still existed, though it had become so completely involved in the complex of nations that it was one part of a united Gestalt, as were all the other nations of Terra. But the words that had begun that union still rang down the corridors of human history, firing youthful minds with zeal and exalting older spirits—and, through them, had in turn become the basis of the Terran Union.

Then it jumped at him from the screen, a full facsimile of the document itself, but he knew that each letter was also in binary. Not that he would dream of moving sentences around in it.

But he could scroll through it, of course, and he did. He read it word by word, feeling a measure of calmness returning to him as the clarion phrases rang out through his mind.

There they were, right at the beginning, the truths Jefferson had held to be self-evident—that all men were created equal, that they were endowed by their Creator with certain unalienable rights . . .

His mind came to a screeching halt. "All *men* are created equal?" Yes, Marcia had been misquoting. Only one word changed, though—right?

He dismissed the notion as unworthy. The distinction wasn't significant; Jefferson had probably had all people in mind, men *and* women; and if he hadn't in 1776, he surely would have in 3035.

But it *did* rather undercut Marcia's argument, didn't it? And since all she was using it for was argument . . .

Sexist document. He could almost hear her voice dismissing it angrily. And she might have a point there—but then, she shouldn't have cited the Declaration.

That wasn't germane, either, though. What mattered was knowing that he, Jose, hadn't tried to treat her as inferior— and he knew damned well that he hadn't. He'd been showing her a bit of consideration, not being condescending.

He scrolled on through the document, feeling a little better, reading as he went, until he came to the phrase, "These United Colonies are, and of Right ought to be, FREE AND INDEPENDENT STATES." He held the phrase centered on the screen, nodding with satisfaction—he'd remembered the quotation almost accurately. And Marcia had been wrong as well as right—there was a difference between a colony's having a right to govern itself, and a woman's right to not have to take orders any more than a man did.

Of course, everybody had to take orders, unless they were royalty—and these days, even the kings and queens had to obey the law. But a woman shouldn't have to take orders from her husband any more than he should have to take orders from her . . .

For a moment, Jose's head whirled, and he found himself wondering what he was doing in that marriage. Or was it really a marriage?

Heresy. He brought his attention back firmly to the issue at hand. He *was* living in accord with the Declaration's principles; he didn't have anything to feel badly about.

Unless, said a niggling doubt in the back of his mind—unless Jefferson's principle of independence really meant that no one should ever become so fully dependent on another person that you could really say they were married. But Jose was sure Jefferson hadn't meant that.

But the principle itself . . . ?

The principle could wait. Jose pulled himself together firmly. He could work out that principle now and again, for the rest of his life; it was only one more problem to solve, the problem of being independent but married, and he was sure he could figure it out in time. Meanwhile, there was an important issue of a robot brain that needed to be programmed, and had been waiting far longer than it should have.

But he was almost at the end of the document. He punched for "Scroll" and read the rest of the Declaration, letting it fill him with pride in being human, in being . . .

"Hey, Jose!"

Jose frowned, turning to the programmer next to him. "Yeah, Bob?"

"It won't access the original." Bob sat back, waving at his screen. "What am I doing wrong?"

Jose suppressed a smile. Bob was very young, and very new to the job. He knew computers better than Jose did, but he hadn't learned much about the asininities of bureacracy yet, or the arbitrary nature of its decisions. "Here, let me see." He shoved his chair over to Bob's workstation and frowned at the screen, pursing his lips. "What access code were you using?"

"RB-34h-Z." Bob shoved the manual over and pointed to the entry.

Jose let the smile show. "We quit making that model five years ago, Bob. The RB-34h-Z series is a mile long now."

Bob frowned. "Then how am I supposed to know which one to call up?"

"The catalogue is supposed to appear on your screen automatically when you enter the code."

"Then how come it didn't?"

"Because you're supposed to enter that code before you initiate the copying procedure." Jose aborted the copy program, clearing the screen, then punched in "RB-34H-Z." The screen lit up with a scrolling display on the left, while a note on the right informed them that those models marked with an asterisk were still in production.

Bob frowned. "Why didn't the manual tell me about this?"

"Because the guy who wrote it is a cretin."

Bob just stared for a second, then smiled. "Well, not much I can say to that, is there?"

"Other than asking why he keeps his job, no." Jose smiled. "Fact is, he was fired last year, but they figure everybody who works here knows the routine, so they haven't bothered to update the manual."

Bob sighed. "Makes it tough on a beginner, doesn't it?"

"That's why they mix you in with us old fogies." Jose was thirty-two. "Now—you get to guess which model you're supposed to load."

Bob's head came up; he stared, taken aback. "What . . . ? How the hell can I . . . ?"

"It's right here." Jose pointed to the fine print in the lower right-hand corner of Bob's duty sheet.

Bob frowned. "I thought that was supposed to be the final code in the routine."

"Looks that way, doesn't it? But it's really the suffix you're supposed to enter after RB-34h-Z."

"Then why don't they . . . No. Cancel that." Bob sighed. "They assume every programmer who works here knows that, don't they?"

Jose nodded. "The duty sheets are boilerplate. They just add the suffix and route it to you."

Bob spread his hands and shook his head. "Well, now I know. Thanks, Jose."

"Anytime." Jose suppressed a smile again. "Call me the next time they foul you up."

Bob's grin followed him back to his own station. He smiled at the blank screen—nothing to clear your own funk, like helping somebody else. He gave a contented sigh and typed in "RUN COPY BRAIN."

The screen responded, "LOAD BRAINPAN," and Jose was off again. Now he zipped through the program and had it all set up in ten minutes. He pressed "execute" and sat back to smile and monitor the copying, making sure nothing went wrong.

Nothing did. It ran without a flaw. An hour later, the screen lit up the "END COPY" light, then the query "EN-GRAVE?" Jose nodded with satisfaction. The program had run flawlessly; he entered "YES" and the computer cued the final changes in electrical charges in the huge crystal below him, making the electronic matrix it had just copied a perma-nent characteristic of the brain. The program was now imper-vious to flood, fire, earthquake—and electromagnetic fields of all sizes and strengths. The only thing that could erase that program now would be an electrical charge so strong that it would fuse the whole brain into a lump of slag. The screen lit up with "ENGRAVING COMPLETE," and Jose smiled and typed in "REMOVE BRAIN," cuing the production lab below to take the sphere out of its clamps.

Then he remembered the Declaration.

It had still been on his board when he started the copying procedure.

It was now part of the robot's basic operating program.

Jose stared at the screen with a sinking feeling in his stomach. He had already routed the end-of-program through to Production; the program was indelibly encoded into the brain. He couldn't remove the Declaration.

The new brain was wasted.

So, Jose thought, was his job. He stared at the screen, feeling numb.

1

"All right, I'll bite—why *do* we have to take six packs? We could just leave the clothes in the drawers and teleport clean outfits to us every morning."

" 'Tis not right to misuse our powers thus," Gwen said primly. " 'Twould be wrong of us to set so poor an example for the children—and 'twould make us, too, slothful."

"And, Papa," said Magnus, "it doth take some effort. Wouldst *thou* wish to labor so, when thou art but newly waked, every morn?"

"Frankly, I was planning to," Rod said, "and I'd rather do that than carry a pack twenty miles. Still, your mother is right—we should save magic for the things we can't do by ordinary means. Oh, I can see making the pots vibrate at a supersonic frequency to shake off the dirt, because we didn't want to wash them." He swung about to glare at Geoffrey. "Get that gleam out of your eye! It's bad enough watching you clear the table by telekinesis!"

Geoffrey tried to glower, but he was feeling too ebullient, and had to make do with a mischievous grin. " 'Tis far more fun, Papa, and faster too, though 'tis as much work. Where is the harm in it?"

"It's like bragging," Rod explained. "You're showing off—and if a non-esper was around to see it, it would make him furiously jealous. Of such things are witch-hunts born."

"Then wherefore dost thou allow it, Papa?" Geoffrey asked.

"Because the non-espers *aren't* around, and it's good practice for you—you're each increasing the number of things you can lift at one time, every day."

"Let us hear some words of sympathy for the poor woman who must needs watch thee, and catch the one-too-many thou dost ever let slip," Gwen reminded.

Cordelia flung her arms around her mother. "Ah, poor

10

dame, who must ever ward us from our own foolishness! Yet 'tis good of thee, Mama, to aid us in our play!''

"Aptly said." Gwen smiled, amused. "I thank thee, daughter." She looked up at Rod. "Yet they have each proved their ability to whisk things to themselves by thought."

"I suppose they have," Rod sighed, "so there's no point in *not* packing the clothes. But it always makes such turmoil at the last minute."

" 'Always'?" Magnus grinned wickedly. "When have we e're gone on holiday aforetime, Papa?"

"Well, there was the trip up into Romanov . . ."

"To spy out an evil sorcerer, as it eventuated," Gwen reminded him.

"And there was that ocean cruise, where we were teaching you kids how to make a ship sail . . ."

". . . And a storm came up, and blew us to that isle where the wicked magician did seek to brew magics that would enslave the beastmen," Gregory reminded him.

"Well, then, there was that little educational trip south, to check on the source of those funny stones you kids had found . . ."

"Which ended in the discovery of evil magic worked unwittingly," Cordelia reminded him.

"It was only the peasant who was unwitting of it, dear, not the futurians behind him."

"Yet 'twas scarcely restful," Geoffrey pointed out. Then he grinned. "Though we did take some pleasure in it."

Cordelia's eyes lighted, and she began to dance, remembering.

"Enough," Rod commanded. "I'll never trust music again."

"In that case," Fess's voice murmured in his ear, "you should be all the more willing to take your clothes in packs."

Rod frowned. "Any particular reason for eavesdropping? You're supposed to be chomping your oats in the stable, like a good horse! Or a real one, at least."

"No non-espers are watching inside the stable, Rod—though I am tempted to think you are being rather mulish when it comes to bearing your pack."

Rod winced. "All right for *you,* steel steed—just for that, you get to carry them when we get tired!"

"Then 'tis agreed we are to bear packs?" Cordelia asked.

Rod stilled, his mouth open.

"Well, 'tis done." Gwen buckled the last strap, hefted the pack, and tossed it to him. "Let us away, husband."

Rod reined in just before they went into the trees and turned to look back at their house. It had been a cottage once, but you couldn't call it that any more—they'd added on too many rooms. Or the elves had, for them.

" 'Tis secure, husband," Gwen said softly.

"Come, Papa! Away!" Cordelia tugged at his arm.

"You need not worry about a national emergency occurring in your absence, Rod," Fess's voice murmured inside his ear. "The Royal Coven will find you in seconds, if anything is amiss."

"I know, I know. But I didn't check to make sure the fire was out . . ."

"*I* did, Papa," Magnus said quickly.

". . . And the doors were locked . . ."

Cordelia closed her eyes for a moment, then looked up and smiled. "They are, Papa."

". . . And the cupboards were closed . . ."

Gregory gazed off into space, then said, "One was open, Papa. It is closed now."

"And if there is aught else amiss, the elves will set it to rights," Gwen said firmly, taking him by the arm.

"None will seek to enter, sin the whole countryside do know a legion of elves doth keep watch o'er it," Gregory assured him.

Gwen nodded and said softly, "Come away, husband. Our home will be safe the whiles we are gone."

"I know, I know. I'm just a worrywart." But Rod gazed at the little house a moment longer, smiling ever so slightly. Gwen looked up at his face, then turned to gaze at the cottage with him, letting her head rest against his shoulder.

Finally, Rod turned to smile down at her. "We haven't done badly, have we?"

Her eyes glowed up at him, and she nodded. "Yet 'twill bide, and await our return. Come away, husband, and let the poor house rest."

"Thou art silent, my lord," Gwen noted.

"Is it all *that* unusual?" Rod looked up in surprise.

"Well, nay," Gwen said carefully, "yet it doth usually betoken . . ."

"You mean the only time I shut up is when I'm surly."

"Nay, I had not said . . ."

"Actually, I thought I was a pretty good listener."

"Oh, thou art, thou ever art!" Gwen clasped his hand, where it held the reins in front of her. "When I have need, thou art ever ready to hearken! Yet I do feel lorn, when thou dost lose thyself in thoughts I ken not."

"Silly goose! Come, share my silence awhile!" And his arms tightened around her.

So she was quiet, leaning back against him, watching the children as they swooped and soared over the fields along the roadside; their laughter came to her like the chiming of wind-bells on the breeze. Then she looked up at the forest looming before them and said, "I do, my lord—yet I know thy thoughts are not of me."

It took a second before she heard his gentle laugh. "Are you so selfish, then, that you can never spare my mind for other matters?"

She heard the humor, and relaxed a bit. "Ever, though I do rejoice to hear them—yet there's thought, and there's brooding. Where do thy dark thoughts stray, my lord?"

Rod sighed. "To the past, my dear. Just trying to reckon how long it's been since I had a real, genuine vacation. Of course, while I was a bachelor, I wound up with a lot of free time between jobs—but those weren't vacations, they were bouts of periodic unemployment. Does our honeymoon count?"

Gwen smiled, and nestled back against him more snugly. "Mayhap, though we had great tasks indeed before us that fortnight, coming to know one another in a new and wondrous way. Yet there was the score of months thereafter, when thou wert estranged from the King and Queen, whiles I did carry Magnus and thou didst build our cottage . . ."

"Yeah, and the elves showed me how. I still think they did more of the building . . ."

Gwen hurried past that part; no point in telling him what had *really* held the stones up while the elves finished setting them. ". . . And that first year of his infant life, 'til Their Majesties had need of thee again, and sought to heal the breach."

"I'm the one who did the healing, as I remember it; they

just found a job for me. And it seems as though they've kept it up; even when the big fights are over, they find these little informational trips for me to make, or need my advice about so-and-so's new idea . . ."

"Mayhap a part of it is that we do abide close by them."

Rod sighed. "Yeah, maybe we do need a change of scenery to really relax." He looked up about himself, somewhat surprised. "And it looks as though we've had one. When did we come into the forest?"

Broad branches spread a canopy above them, stemming from tall old trees, foot-thick and rough-barked, with here and there a yard-wide veteran soaring up into the dim, dark greenery above—a murmuring roof, lanced by shafts of light so pale as to be almost silver. They gazed up, exalted, feeling their souls expand in the openness . . .

Until a four-foot body shot through a beam, laughing in delight while a half-grown juggernaut speared after him on a broomstick, shouting happy predictions of dire doom.

"Children!" Gwen cried, and Geoffrey jerked to a halt in midair, then swerved over to the nearest tree. Cordelia dropped to the ground, trying to hide her broomstick behind her back, while the elm next to her brother seemed to waver, then solidified again, a bit wider than it had been—and Geoffrey was nowhere to be seen.

"Nay, then, I ken thy presence," Gwen said in tones that evoked dread, "and thou knowest thou hast gone against the rule. Come out from that elm where thou dost hide."

"He could not help it, Mama!" Cordelia cried. "I did spring upon him and . . ." She hushed and bit her lip at a glare from Gwen.

"Thy sister's intercession will not save thee," Gwen informed the elm, "for thou hadst no need to fly an thou didst wish to flee. Come out!"

The silence stretched to the point of snapping, and Rod was just opening his mouth to point out that, after all, nobody had been hurt, and it wasn't really all *that* great an infraction (though he knew he shouldn't), when Geoffrey saved him by stepping out from the tree. His head was down and his shoulders hunched, but he was there, and the tree was slender again. Rod swung down from Fess's back, bracing himself for a shouting match—then decided to let Gwen start it. He was tired.

Gwen sat on her high horse, glaring down.

Geoffrey glowered back up at her.

Gwen's face was stone.

Geoffrey held his glare, but began to fidget.

Gwen waited.

"Well, then, I did wrongly!" Geoffrey burst out. "Thou hast told us time and again not to fly in a forest, and I disobeyed!"

"A good beginning," Gwen said, with an air of finality.

Geoffrey glowered up again, slowly wilting. Finally, he dropped his gaze and muttered, "I am sorry, Mama."

"Better," Gwen pronounced. "And wilt thou do it again?"

"Nay, Mama."

"Wherefore?"

"For that thou hast said so."

"*Nay!* Though 'twould be good, 'tis not enough! Wherefore have I forbade thee to fly in a wood?"

"For that I might dash out my brains 'gainst a tree trunk," Geoffrey muttered. Then he glared up at her again. "Yet I never have!"

Gwen only stared.

"Oh, aye, there was that time two years agone, when I did knock myself senseless." Geoffrey dropped his eyes again. "And three years agone, when I came home quite dazed—yet I was little then!"

"And hast better aim now, surely. Nay, now thou'lt strike squarely on the center of thy crown."

"I'll not strike at all!" Geoffrey's jaw jutted. "I am more practiced now, Mama!"

"Yes," Rod agreed, "he's gotten so good at it that now he can flatten his head completely."

"I shall not! I shall slip 'twixt the trees like a sky-borne eel!"

"Quite a vision, that." Rod imagined a flock of flying eels, wriggling their way across the heavens. "But with all those eels, wouldn't it be a little dangerous for you?"

Geoffrey rolled his eyes in exasperation. "Canst thou never be serious, Papa?"

"Thou wouldst not wish him to be," Gwen assured the boy.

But Rod shrugged. "I'm willing." He pointed a finger at

Geoffrey. "Just for that, you can *walk* all the way to the castle."

Geoffrey glared at him, and Rod felt a surge upward. In the split second before it could happen, though, he thought *down-ward*. Geoffrey frowned as though something were wrong; his face tightened with effort. Rod felt the boy's power of levitation pushing against his own telekinetic force, and pressed harder. Then Gwen dismounted, and he felt her effort join his. He eased up.

But Geoffrey didn't. His face reddened; his shoulders hunched with the effort.

Gwen leaned back against Rod, showing not the slightest sign of strain.

Geoffrey abandoned the effort, foreboding shadowing his gaze. "Thou dost conspire against me!"

"No, we just agree on the rules and the punishments."

" 'Tis even as I've said." Geoffrey gave them his best glower, or tried to. He couldn't simply capitulate, of course. Rod understood that, and allowed him his face-saver.

"It is indeed—but it does let you know what happens if you disobey."

"Didst *thou* never disobey when thou wast small?" Geoffrey squalled.

Rod reddened. "That's beside the point—and that's enough nattering about it, too. Come on, let's go."

He turned away, shouldering through the brush. Gwen watched him go in mild surprise, then turned back to her children with a slight smile and a nod of the head. "Come, then. Thou hast heard."

They followed her away through the trees, Cordelia and Gregory now perched on Fess's back.

"There could have been worse punishments," Cordelia ventured.

"Oh, be still!" Geoffrey snapped. " 'Tis not the effort doth chafe me."

"Nay, 'tis the shame," Magnus agreed. "Yet there's naught to rue in giving respect to thine elders."

"Including thee, belike?" Geoffrey said, with scorn. "Nay, I wager that Papa was mindful of enduring just such shame as this! Didst thou not see him redden when I did ask?"

"I did," said Magnus, with a wicked grin. "Nay, I do wonder what naughtiness he did recollect?"

They were all silent for a minute, imagining calamities.

"Fess would know," Gregory said suddenly.

"Aye, thou wouldst!" Geoffrey turned to Fess with a glint in his eye. "Nay, tell! What did chance when Papa did disobey Grandpapa?"

"That is his tale to tell, not mine," the robot said slowly.

"Oh, come, Fess!" Cordelia pleaded prettily. "Canst thou not give but a hint?"

"Your father's personal matters are confidential, children." Robots are immune to charm.

"But a clue," Magnus said, "is not telling."

"My programming does not allow disclosure of classified materials," Fess said sternly.

They were silent again, brains whirling in an attempt to bypass the program.

"Yet thou art free to tell us aught of thine *own* past," Gregory said.

Fess was silent a moment, then said, "I am, and will speak to you gladly of the history of your House and of your ancestors . . ."

"Only of our father," Gregory said quickly. He'd heard Fess's lectures before. "Canst thou not tell what *thou* didst when he did disobey?"

"Certainly not! At any point at which my own actions became involved in your father's personal matters, even my own memories become confidential!"

"I must learn Cobol," Gregory sighed.

"Wherefore wouldst thou wish to make *their* acquaintance?" Geoffrey frowned up at him. "Kobolds are vile creatures!"

"He speaks of the speech, not the speaker," Fess explained.

Geoffrey stared. "How . . . ?"

" 'Tis wizards' talk," Magnus said airily. "Of greater moment is thy past, Fess."

"You will not desist, will you?" Fess sighed. "Forebear the attempt, children—I shall not disclose your father's secrets, either accidentally or deliberately."

"Yet thou hast said thou wilt tell us of *thy* deeds," Magnus reminded. "Hast *thou* never disobeyed, Fess?"

Geoffrey glared at him in exasperation, but Gregory waved him back, eyes on Magnus. Geoffrey frowned up at him, but his frown turned to a stare as understanding dawned. He began to grin.

"Your question may be interpreted as referring to an action counter to my programming," the robot said slowly, "and in those terms, I must answer, 'No. I have never acted in violation of my program.' "

Geoffrey slapped his thigh in exasperation, but Gregory asked, "Yet what of the words of thy master? Didst thou never work counter to his commands?"

Fess was quiet long enough for Geoffrey to perk up again. Finally, the robot admitted, "There have been a few instances in which my owner's orders contradicted my program, yes."

"Then thou *didst* disobey!" Geoffrey crowed.

"Only to obey a higher authority," Fess said quickly. "Disobedience is not to be done at one's own whim, children."

"At whose whim is it, then?" Cordelia asked.

Fess emitted a burst of static, his equivalent of a sigh. "My basic program was designed by Peter Petrok, children, but it was tested, revised, retested, and finally approved by his section chief, then by the Vice President for Programming, by the President of Coherent Imperatives, Limited, and finally approved by a unanimous vote of the Board of Directors."

Geoffrey stared, somewhat stunned.

"Thus, in answer to your question," the robot went on, "disobedience is not done at anyone's whim, but at the considered, carefully weighed opinions of a group of responsible individuals, acting upon thorough evidence and elaborate validation, in accordance with well-established principles."

The children were silent, overawed.

Then Magnus ventured, "Wherefore was such a gamut needful?"

"Because a robot could do a great deal of damage, if adequate safeguards were not built into its programming," Fess answered. "You have seen the occasional, restrained attacks I have made in defense of your father, your mother, and yourselves, children. Imagine what I could do if I had no inhibitions at all."

"Thou wouldst be havoc infernal," Geoffrey said instantly, eyes wide. "Sweet Heaven, Fess! Thou couldst lay waste all of Gramarye!"

"That is a warranted conclusion," Fess agreed, "and I am

only a general purpose robot, children, not specialized for warfare.''

Gregory shuddered, and Geoffrey said, ''That thou art restrained, praise the saints!''

''Or, at least, the originators of the study of robotics. The thought has crossed my mind occasionally, yes.''

''Then how canst thou ever be permitted to disobey?'' Cordelia said, frowning.

''When obedience would require me to wreak the devastation Geoffrey noted,'' Fess explained, ''or even the injury of a living being, beyond what would be absolutely necessary to preserve my owner's safety.''

Gregory frowned. ''Dost thou say thou must needs guard other folk from thine owner?''

''That is perhaps an overstatement,'' Fess said slowly, ''though I can think of circumstances in which it might apply.''

''Yet it never hath, for thee,'' Cordelia inferred. ''Who *hast* thou had need to guard from thy master?''

''Himself,'' Fess answered.

''What?'' ''How can that be?'' ''Wherefore would he . . .''

''Children, *chil*-dren,'' Fess admonished.

They quieted.

Fess sighed, ''I see I must tell you how it happened, chronologically, or you will never understand the principle.''

''Aye, do!'' Cordelia crooked a knee around the saddlehorn, patted her skirt into place around it, and settled down to listen. ''We attend, Fess.''

''Do, for it becomes somewhat convoluted. I was brought to consciousness at the factory of Amalgamated Automatons, Inc., in accordance with a Coherent Imperatives program . . .''

''We have no wish to hear thy whole life,'' Geoffrey said hastily.

''You have asked for it, Geoffrey, for this incident befell with my first owner. He had purchased a new antigravity aircar, and the law required that such vehicles be equipped with guidance computers of the most recent model designed to safeguard human life. That 'latest model' was the FCC series, of which I was one . . .''

2

"Time enough for you to learn the business next year."
Reggie's father handed him the check for a million. "All I
want is, you should have a good time, Joe."

"How can I help it?" Reggie looked at the check, gloating. He was so grateful that he didn't even remind the old
man about the name change. "Thanks, Pop!"

" 'S all right." The elder Vapochek waved his cigar negli-
gently. "The dog bootie sales're going pretty good, and the
parakeet sweater production is way up. We can afford some
time for you to, like, sow your wild oats. Just get 'em outa
your system." Pop gave a leering chuckle. "You got a lotta
sowing to do, boy, if you wanna break *my* record—and I had
to do it when I had time off from the steelworks!"

"Boy, you can bet I will, Pop! Starting with a sports car!"

"Oh?" Pop's eye glinted. "What you got your eye on?"

"One of those new Heatrash jobs, Pop, with the afterburn-
ers and the double-strength antigrav."

"Yeah, I heard about them. Got one of them new FCC
robot brains for a guidance computer, don't it?"

"Yeah—and cashmere upholstery half a foot thick, a built-in
autobar, 360-degree sound, light show on the ceiling . . ."

"So who's gonna be watching the ceiling?" And the elder
Vapochek guffawed, waving the boy away with his cigar.
"Go on, go have your fun! Just gimme a ride in it, you
hear?"

The comely young lady stared as the aircar drifted out of its
stall. At the wheel, Reggie noticed her attention and grinned,
but pretended not to see her—so he was a bit crestfallen when
she only sighed, shook her head, and walked on by below
him. "Snooty broad," he growled.

"I do not recognize that command, master," the dashboard
answered.

"I wasn't talking to *you*, bolt-brain! . . . Probably just jealous."

"Yes, master," the dashboard answered.

"How would *you* know?" Reggie snarled. "Just get over to Shirley's place—and don't spare the horses!"

"This vehicle is not powered by animals' muscles."

"Okay, the horse*power*, then! Just *get!*" And Reggie leaned back in the plush embrace of the seat, muttering, "Snooty machine."

The aircar rose fifty feet, then hovered, hesitating.

"What's the hold-up?" Reggie snarled. "Get going!"

"There is an omnibus approaching on an intersect course at one thousand feet, master."

"So dodge it, then! Oh, hell! Give *me* that wheel!" Reggie leaned forward, slapping the toggle to "manual," and tromped on the accelerator. The aircar shot upward, so fast as to give him the distinct feeling that he'd left his stomach on the pavement. Reggie grinned, reveling in the sensation.

"Intersect impending!" the computer blared, but Reggie just grinned wider, staring up at the looming bus. He'd wait just a second or two longer, then swerve aside at the last minute and give those yerkels on the bus something to cuss about . . .

The aircar jarred to a halt so suddenly that his dental implants almost uprooted. The bus snored by a good hundred feet overhead, its passengers totally oblivious to his existence.

Reggie let loose a stream of profanity intermixed with an occasional word that bore some meaning. By sorting syllables, the computer pieced together an approximation of "What did you do *that* for?"

"We were on an intersect course with the omnibus," the computer explained. "In three seconds more, we would have impacted in a midair collision, which would not have been beneficial to your health."

"The hell with my health! I would've slid by with meters to spare! You just ruined the move of the century!"

The computer was silent, then explained, "I had no knowledge of your intentions."

"You don't *need* to know my intentions! If I damn well choose to commit suicide, that's my damn business, not yours!"

"I am programmed for accordance with all civil and criminal laws," the computer answered. "I cannot behave in breach of them."

"You're not behaving—*I* am! What about your programming to obey *me?*"

"Such programming must nonetheless avoid conflict with law."

"Let *me* worry about the law! If I slap the override, it's *my* problem, not yours!"

"The law will not allow . . ."

"The law won't sell you for scrap metal if you disobey!" Reggie howled. "But *I* will! Now you get your gears over to Shirley's place! And don't you *ever* override my override again!"

The computer was silent, registering the command as a change in its program. It was a change that created internal conflict, though, and the computer assigned part of its capacity to trying to resolve the apparent contradiction. (It assumed, as it was programmed to, that such a contradiction must be only apparent, not real.)

Reggie settled back into the cushions of the contoured couch that covered three sides of the car, grumbling, "Dumb machine . . . Hey!" He glared at the dashboard. "Let's have a martini, here!"

The panel at his elbow slid open. Reggie's glower lightened as he took out a frosty glass of clear fluid with an olive nestled amid ice cubes. "Got *one* thing right in your programming, anyway," he muttered.

The computer wisely didn't answer. Instead, it consulted the city map in its memory, compared it with the address Reggie had given when he had climbed in, corrected for pronunciation, homonymns, and spelling, and turned sixty-eight degrees clockwise as it accelerated so smoothly that Reggie snarled, "Can't you move this bucket any faster?"

The valet opened the door and ushered Reggie in. "Miss Delder will be with you presently, sir."

"Fine, fine. Y' got a martini here?"

It materialized so quickly that Reggie found himself wondering if the *valet* was a robot. Unfortunately, as he took his first sip, Shirley swirled into the room in a flurry of taffeta. "How prompt you are, Reggie! Come, let's be off! I'm positively famished."

Reggie just barely managed to slap the glass back into the valet's hand as he flew out the door. *She could at least have taken long enough for me to finish the drink!*

Then it occurred to him that Shirley might have had that notion in mind. That boded ill—her being ready when he arrived. Was she sending him a message?

No, she was freezing in her tracks, eyes huge, gasping, "Oh, Reggie! You didn't *tell* me!"

She was staring straight at the Heatrash, of course. Reggie allowed himself a grin. "Only fifty M."

"I want one!" Shirley reached out to caress the door panel, and Reggie felt a stab of jealousy. "How about you get in?" he suggested.

"I'd love to!"

The door slid back, and a resonant voice murmured, "Mademoiselle is welcome."

Shirley lifted her head, eyes glowing. "Well! Whoever programmed *this* one knew how to treat a lady!"

"It's an FCC robot," Reggie said, offhandedly.

"That new Faithful Cybernetic Companion series?" Sudden wariness in Shirley's eyes. "They're programmed for extreme personal loyalty, aren't they?"

"Well . . . yeah . . ."

"We are also programmed with the most profound respect for all human beings," the robot assured her, "unless there is a direct, physical attack endangering our owners. Will you enter, mademosielle?"

"Well . . . if you put it *that* way . . ." Shirley stepped in.

Reggie followed—quickly, just in case she or the robot developed ideas—and the door rolled shut.

Shirley nestled into the cashmere cushions. "I always *did* like being a sybarite."

"Hey, that's great!" Reggie slid closer.

"On the other hand, there are limits." Shirley edged away from him. "When are we going to start?"

"We are already airborne, Mademoiselle" the computer informed her.

Shirley stared. "I didn't even feel the lift!"

"Sissy car," Reggie muttered.

"We are programmed for smooth operation."

"So'm I," Reggie said, inching over.

Shirley inched too, till she was leaning back against the side. "You really provide comfort, car."

"Just give *me* a chance," Reggie offered, sliding over farther.

"Even a bar!" Shirley rose and spun over Reggie's lap to the door side, to exam the autobar panel. "There're no pressure patches!"

"I am programmed for oral input, mademoiselle."

"Wonderful!" Shirley settled back again. "Chablis, if you don't mind."

"I'll take a martini," Reggie sighed. It looked as though that was all he was going to get, for the time being.

"Don't you think you might wait for the food to catch up to the alcohol?"

"What'sh to worry? I haven't had all *that* many," Reggie said breezily.

Shirley held her breath till the breeze had passed; it had rather high octane.

"Would monsieur care to order?"

Reggie glowered up at the waiter. *Probably learned his accent from watching old movies*. "Yeah, uh—juh prefer-ray un verr dough fresh."

"Bon, monsieur," the waiter said, straight-faced, ignoring the glass of ice water sitting in front of Reggie and the pinching of Shirley's lips. "And for the entree?"

"Yeah, uh—boof burganyone." He looked up at Shirley. "You were talking about the chicken?"

Shirley nodded, not trusting herself to speak.

"Blanks duh capon cordone blue."

Shirley winced.

"Bon, monsieur." The waiter jotted the order with a flourish and took their menus.

"And, uh—make the boof well done, would you?"

"Well done, monsieur." The waiter made an ostentatious note on his pad. "Will there be anything else?"

"Nah, that's fine."

The waiter inclined his head and turned away.

"Did I hear it right?" Shirley demanded. "Did you actually tell him to make your *boeuf bourguignon* well done?"

"Yeah, sure." Reggie frowned. "I don't like it bloody."

"Sh!" Shirley glanced frantically at the neighboring tables, but apparently no one there was British—or else they were well bred. Then she leaned forward to hiss, "What do you think *boeuf bourguignon* is—steak?"

"Well, sure. I mean, steak is beef—so . . ."

"Beef is steak. Sure." Shirley nodded, resigned. "Flawless logic, Plato."

"Hey!" Reggie frowned. "I ain't no mouse's dog! Come on, Shirl."

"Shirley," she snapped.

Reggie sighed, leaning back in his chair as he began to realize that the evening was not going well. He wondered why she was such a stickler about using her whole name. The girls back in college had been that way, too—or at least, at his last college, the big one his pop had bought him into after the business started really paying off. Back at Sparta C.C. the girls had been the all-right kind, but these big college skirts were a bunch of snobs.

Like Shirl. Shirley.

"So what do you want to do after dinner? Take in a movie?"

She brightened. "Wonderful idea—I always love those old flat-screen shows."

Reggie winced; that hadn't been what he'd had in mind.

"Bergman's *Seventh Seal* is playing at the Cinema Classiqe."

The closest Reggie had ever come to Bergman was a film course he had taken in junior college; he had passed it by getting enthusiastic Rathskellar descriptions from students who *had* seen the assigned movies. "Hey, maybe live theater would be more like it. I could get tickets to a nudie show at one of those off-off-off-Broadway places."

Shirley managed to keep the shudder down to her shoulders. "Why don't we just go to a cabaret?"

"Yeah!" Reggie said, with a lascivious grin.

"Not *that* kind! I know where there's a nice soft-jazz group playing."

Reggie sighed. "Okay, baby, it's your party."

"I'm fully grown, Reggie."

"Boy, are you ever! . . . Oh. Uh, sorry . . ."

"Your soup, sir."

Reggie looked up to see the waiter smiling benevolently. He looked down at a cup of soup that had materialized in front of him, then looked back up, but the waiter had already whisked himself away.

Shirley sighed and took up her soup spoon.

Reggie frowned at the array before him, then picked up a teaspoon. "Never did like them round bowls. Hard to get in the mouth, you know?"

Shirley managed a smile.

"Reggie, don't you think you've had enough?"

"Nah. This group didn't start sounding good till after the second one." Reggie eyed the all-female jazz group, wishing that their strapless gowns didn't defy gravity quite so successfully. "How come they're keeping 'em opaque?"

"Those dresses are made of real cloth, Reggie—not polarized plastic."

Reggie shook his head, irritated. " 'S too bad. If y' got it, y' oughta show it." His groggy glance strayed back to Shirley.

"Don't even think about it!"

"Well, maybe the floor show . . ."

"I don't think I want to wait for it." Shirley stood up with sudden decision. "Reggie, I'm getting sleepy. Let's go."

"Huh? Oh, yeah! Sure!" Reggie brightened.

"*Just* sleepy," Shirley said firmly.

"Awright, awright," Reggie grumbled, bumping the table as he lurched to his feet. He frowned down at the spot of alcohol spreading over his shirt front. "Well . . . it'll dry."

Shirley frowned at the upset glass and the rivulet of gin coursing toward the table edge. She picked up a napkin, tossed it on the spill, and turned away.

Then she turned back, fumbling in her handbag. Reggie had bumbled out without leaving a tip.

Reggie grinned, and the car swooped down. Shirley shrieked, and he smirked with satisfaction. Look down her nose at *him*, would she? Well, she'd find out how great he really was! He might not be much at the dinner table, but he was something else when he got physical. When she saw how great he was behind the wheel, she'd realize how nuclear he must be in bed.

"Look out! You're going to hit that building!"

"Nah. Six to spare, easy."

The aircar swerved aside, missing the eighty-third story of the Empire State Building by two inches, not six.

"Not sleepy any more, are you?" Reggie gloated.

"No, but I'm getting a headache you wouldn't believe! Reggie, please put the car back on computer pilot!"

"*That* old lady?" Reggie made a rude noise. "You can't stay on comp if you wanna have fun!"

"If I wanted a variable-grav ride, I'd go to Coney Island," Shirley moaned.

"Aw, come on." Reggie nosed down and went into a power dive. "Driving's *fun.*"

Shirley screeched and clawed the upholstery, rigid as an icicle.

"Oh, all right!" Reggie levelled off, pouting.

"Thank Heaven!" Shirley went half-limp. "Reggie, please put me *down!* Or find me an airsick bag, fast!"

"Hey, no! The upholstery's brand new!"

"I'm not going to have much choice about it," Shirley groaned.

"Oh, all right, all right!" Disgusted, Reggie slowed the car and started a sedate descent. Shirley went the other half limp, breathing in slow, steady gasps. "I . . . *never* . . . want to go . . . through something like that . . . again!"

"No chance you will, the way this date is going," Reggie muttered to himself as he watched a police car swoop by overhead. "Wonder what's the matter with him?"

"Oh, just after a drunk driver, probably." Shirley took a deep breath and sat up straight as the car gently grounded. "Are we down yet?"

"We are in contact with the earth's surface," the computer assured her, "or, at least, the pavement over it."

"Good." Shirley lurched up, grabbing the manual door handle and hauling it back.

"Hey! Whatcha doing?" Reggie protested.

"I," Shirley answered, "am getting *out.*"

"Silly dumb broad." Reggie huddled in the corner of the seat, glowering at the instrument display across from him, sipping another martini. The instrument cluster was beginning to seem kind of removed, but that was okay—the alcohol was beginning to lift him from the funk the evening had put him in. "What does *she* know, anyway?"

"She has had a liberal arts education," the computer replied.

"Oh, shut up!" Reggie growled. "Who asked *you,* anyway?"

The computer weighed the command to "Shut up," decided from the context that it was an order to be silent, weighed the order against the direct question that followed it, decided from the context that the question had been rhetorical, and wisely decided to remain silent.

"Doesn't know what a *real* man is like," Reggie grumbled. "All she knows is those knitting little preppies." He scowled at the memory of what one of those preppies had done to him during a wrestling match, and what another one had done when Reggie took a swing at him. "Cheaters, every one of 'em."

The computer reviewed its data bank of irrational human behavior, concluded that its owner needed to talk in order to relieve emotional stress, and would therefore appreciate leading questions. "They are deficient in a sense of fair play?"

"Boy, you can say that again! Always sneering at you, making fun of you by asking questions about things you don't know nothing about! 'What did you think of that concert last night, Reggie?' 'How'd you like that new drama the Players did, Reggie?' Then talking down to me, only asking me about the league standings and all! Here, give me another drink!"

The autobar door slid open, and Reggie yanked the glass out, spilling as much as he sipped. "Gack! Don't fill 'em so full next time, huh?"

The computer registered the directive in its manual of drinks. "As you wish, sir."

" 'Azh I wish, azh I wish!' When did you do *anything* I wished?" Reggie snarled.

"I have endeavored in all ways to please . . ."

"Oh, yeah? Then why'd you preach law at me, huh?"

"I cannot . . ."

"Always tryin' a takeover when I wanna drive," Reggie growled. "Here, gimme those controls! Let's see some *real* drivin', here!" He lurched forward into the control seat and slapped the manual switch. " 'N' doncha *dare* override me!"

The stress level within the computer's program increased as it forecast Reggie's probable action. "Sir, I compute that the alcohol level in your blood is . . ."

"Don't *preach*, I said! Here we *go!*"

With a quarter of its capacity, the computer reviewed the commands Reggie had given, failed to find one that specifically banned preaching, then checked the definition of preaching and concluded that it had not performed that particular action. Another quarter of its capacity monitored Reggie's swerves and swoops, but the remaining half sought to resolve the conflict between its basic programming and Reggie's command not to override his manual controls. It extrapolated the results of his wild driving within the context of the skyscrapers surrounding them and the extreme heaviness of the nighttime pleasure district traffic, and came to an alarming conclusion. "Sir! If you continue in this course, you will eventually collide with a building or another vehicle!"

"Oh, shut up and enjoy the ride," Reggie snarled. "You're as bad as *she* was."

The computer saw another aircar zooming toward them, filling its receptors' field of view, calculated the vectors of the two vehicles, and concluded that a collision would occur within 5.634 seconds (it rounded off the repeating decimal). It would have warned Reggie, but he had just commanded it to "Shut up." It would have taken control and avoided the collision, but Reggie had expressly forbidden it to override manual control. That created a conflict between two different aspects of its program—the one that demanded it keep its owner safe, and the one that insisted it obey. Of course, it could disobey to save its owner from major injury—but was such an action warranted? It had to consider the matter. After all, it had 5.634 seconds (5.173 now). But to a computer, five seconds is a world of time, so it could afford to ponder.

A human being might have asked, "All right, so what can they do to me?" But that wasn't an important question for an FCC robot brain—it assumed that any damage to itself was inconsequential; it could always be repaired, and it had no pain circuits. What *was* consequential was whether or not there would be any damage to its owner and, secondarily, whether or not there would be any damage to the passengers of the other aircar. Of tertiary importance was whether there would be any damage to the other aircar itself. The robot concluded that, if it stayed on the intersect course,

A) There would be damage to its owner;
B) There would be damage to the owner(s) of the other aircar; and
C) There would be damage to the other aircar itself.

Also, as a byproduct, there would be damage to the computer's aircar, too. Obviously, therefore, it should take evasive action—it should swerve to miss the other aircar. But its owner *had* ordered it not to override his override.

The whole problem would be academic if the owner were planning to turn the aircar aside at the last moment; it might be bad practice, but that wasn't for the computer to decide. So the robot said, "You are on an intersect course with another aircraft. Do you wish to swerve . . ."

"Oh, shut up."

The computer silenced itself, reconsidered the situation, and concluded that it should, at least, override the command to "Shut up." "Do you plan to turn aside before you collide with the other aircar?"

"Of course," Reggie snorted. "What do you think I am, an idiot?"

"No," the robot answered, quite truthfully. It was aware that Reggie's intelligence fell within normal IQ parameters, so that he could not technically be categorized as an "idiot."

The collision would occur in 2.98 seconds. The robot noted that the oncoming aircar had begun to turn aside, but computed that it could not by itself veer away enough to avoid the impact. Reggie's aircar would have to swerve, too. But, since Reggie had stated his intention to swerve aside at the last moment, and had further forbidden the robot to override him when he had taken manual control, it could do nothing.

But it knew Reggie's reaction time when he was sober, and could subtract a loss of reaction time proportional to the amount of alcohol he had ingested. It concluded that his body couldn't execute his brain's commands in less than 1.23 seconds, and that if there was no sign of swerving by that time, it should take control. Accordingly, it counted down the nanoseconds, waiting.

At 1.34 seconds, Reggie shouted, "Now!"

At .09 seconds, the aircar started to turn.

At .08 seconds, the computer noted that Reggie had not turned sharply enough, and computed that there would be at least a partial collision. So it finally overrode Reggie's manual control—but only to the extent of increasing the thrust in the direction in which he had turned the wheel, by boosting it drastically.

The aircar roared aside at the last split of the second, shooting just beyond the point of impact . . .

Almost.

"Almost" is a large brass gong, surrounding you, filling all of space and time with an enduring, sonorous tone. "Almost" is the sum of the kinetic energy of two bodies, impacting along nearly parallel vectors. "Almost" is a body slamming into shock webbing, and two other bodies slamming into shock webbing. "Almost" is the grating crash of an aircar against a plasticrete surface, the crunch as it rebounds off a lower surface, and the sickening, accelerating whine of a disconnected turbine, no longer fully engaged with its antigravity unit, but increasing its power as much as it can to soften the crash, soften it *almost* enough to prevent major damage. "Almost" is a groggy driver scared sober, shaking his head, staring about him wild-eyed, heart racing in panic, gasping, "Wha . . . wha' happen . . . wha . . ."

The other aircar lurched by overhead, saved from collision with the stone of the building by the nanosecond reflexes of its computer. It settled to the ground nearby with considerable cosmetic damage, none of it major. The passenger leaped out, dashing over to Reggie's aircar and yanked the door open, crying, "Are you all right, man? Are you all right?"

Reggie blinked, turned an owlish stare on the other man, and suddenly realized that he might be in some way to blame. So he scowled, summoned his last vestige of belligerence, and snarled, "Who taught *you* how to drive?"

Then he passed out.

"And thou?" Cordelia asked, eyes wide with the realization of tragedy. "Didst thou, too, lose awareness?"

"I did not," Fess replied. "I am, after all, a robot, and will not lose awareness unless I sustain sufficient damage to incapacitate me."

"Yet thou wast damaged by the accident," Gregory inferred.

"I was," Fess agreed. "Before the collision, all my circuits had been in perfect operating condition—but afterward, I was removed from the wreckage, subjected to tests, and found to have a severely weakened capacitor."

" 'Tis that which doth cause thy seizures, is't not?" Geoffrey asked, wide-eyed.

"It is," Fess confirmed. "That collision was the last decision in which I was successfully able to consider a multiplicity of factors under a severe time limit. Since then, any such situation overloads the weakened capacitor and causes it to discharge. Realizing this, the robot technician built in a circuit breaker and an absorbing pad that allows the component to discharge in isolation.''

Magnus frowned. "An they had not, it would have burned out others of thy components, would it not?"

"It would have," Fess agreed. "Fortunately, they anticipated the situation, and there has been no further damage."

"And what of the harm to the aircar?" Gregory asked.

"It was total," Fess answered. "I had delayed taking action too long."

"Thou hadst little choice," Magnus said, with disdain.

"On the contrary, my makers decided that I had had a great deal of latitude, but had not been able to comprehend that, within the context of the situation, I should have ignored my owner's order not to override manual control. Such a discrimination circuit was built into all later FCC robots."

"That did not aid *thee* greatly," said Geoffrey.

"Certes, they did have a sufficiency of cold blood!" Cordelia shuddered. "I wonder that they did not break and bury thee, sin that they were so heartless."

"Well they might have," Fess agreed, "the more so since they determined that the cost of repairing me would be too great, for they could not simply replace the capacitor, but would have had to replace the whole molecular circuit with micromanipulators, and a high probability of totally destroying my central processing unit. Certainly the operation would have cost far more than anything my owner could have gained by selling me."

"Then what did he do," asked Geoffrey, frowning, "sin that 'twas his fault entire?"

"There surely must have been some fault of mine, Geoffrey."

"Wherein?" the boy challenged. "Thou hast but now said that later robots had the discrimination thou didst lack, to enable thee to prevent it!"

"Thou dost speak without logic, Fess," Gregory agreed. "Still, I can see 'tis in accord with the program thou hast told us of."

Geoffrey looked up, nettled. "How canst thou know that, wart?"

But Magnus waved him to silence, eyes on Fess. "Then what did thine owner do with thee?"

"He never wished to see me again," Fess sighed.

"Aye," said Cordelia, "sin that 'twas thou hadst witnessed his embarrassment."

" 'Witnessed' is accurate," Fess acknowledged. "My trip log was transcribed and read out in open court to convict him of drunken driving, as a result of which, his license was suspended."

" 'License'?" Geoffrey stared. "Dost thou mean he could not drive without leave?"

"It is not allowed," Fess agreed. "There is too much chance of a driver injuring others."

"Witness the tale he hath but now told us," Magnus said scornfully. "Canst thou not hang one thought to another?"

Geoffrey reddened, but before he could say anything, Cordelia said, "He could not drive, then?"

"He could not," Fess confirmed, "and therefore had no need of a private aircar. Accordingly, he sold what was left of it—my self and circuits—to the highest bidder."

"And who was that?"

"A salvage company," Fess sighed, "which specialized in supplying replacement components at the lowest possible cost."

"Thou must needs have been a great find for them," Cordelia said quickly.

"It is good of you to seek to spare my feelings, Cordelia—but please be mindful that I have none."

The girl looked skeptical, but held her peace.

"I was junk," Fess said baldly, "and was treated as such. Certainly the matter should not occasion shame for me, when it is five hundred years in the past! Still, Cordelia is right—I *was* a great find for a salvage company, a most excellent piece of junk."

"Yet wast thou not distressed to find thyself sold for scrap?" Geoffrey blurted. Cordelia glared daggers at him, but Fess answered, "I cannot honestly say that I was, especially since it freed me from Reggie. The degree of reluctance his commands produced within my circuits, by opposing two separate aspects of my program, was quite disagreeable."

"But thou wast devalued, thou wast debased!"

"There is some degree of accuracy in that statement," Fess admitted. "Still, looking back on the incident from five hundred years' perspective, I cannot help but feel that gaining my freedom from Reggie was cheap at the price."

3

Magnus was being noble; he wasn't even asking. But Gwen could see the pinched look about his face, and took pity on him.

Geoffrey, however, was not yet old enough to be self-denying. "Mama, I'm hungry!"

"I am sure that thou art," Gwen said grimly; the effect of the boy's impatience was not improved by comparison with Magnus's self-control. "But peace, my lad—there's an inn not far from here."

And so there was—just around a bend in the road. It was a pleasant-enough-looking place, a big two-story frame structure with mullioned windows and a thatched roof. From a flagpole over the door hung a hank of greenery, bobbing in the breeze.

"The bush is green," Gwen noted.

"New ale." Rod smiled. "This may be a better lunch than I thought."

But Cordelia was staring at the animal tethered in front of the door. "Oh! The poor lamb!"

"Hast no eyes, sister?" Geoffrey scoffed. " 'Tis not a lamb, but an ass!"

"No more than thou art," Cordelia retorted. "Yet 'tis a very lamb of a donkey! Doth not thy heart go out to him?"

"Thou hast no need to answer." Gwen caught Geoffrey with his mouth open. He closed it and glowered up at her.

"Thou hast it aright, my lass," Gwen said. "The beast is woefully treated."

And indeed it was—its coat was rough and dull, with patches of mange here and there, and its ribs showed through its hide. It stretched its neck to crop what little grass grew within reach of its hitching post.

"How vile must his master be," Magnus said indignantly,

34

"to take his ease in the cool of an inn, and leave his beast not so much as a mound of hay!"

"He is also badly overworked," Fess noted.

The comment was an understatement—the poor little donkey was hitched to a cart dangerously overloaded with barrels of various sizes.

"Such conduct towards a poor draft animal is inexcusable!" Fess stated.

Gregory looked up at him in surprise. " 'Tis not like thee, Fess, to so judge a human."

"He's sensitive on the subject of beasts of burden, son," Rod explained.

"What kind of man could be so calloused as to mistreat his donkey thus?" Gwen wondered.

"Assuredly," said Geoffrey, "a proper villain—a fat, lazy, slovenly boor, a very brute!"

But the man who came out of the inn was neither fat nor slovenly. He was of middle height, and only a little on the plump side. He wore clean hose and jerkin, and carried his cap in his hand till he was outside the inn, chatting with the landlord, a pleasant smile on his face.

"Why, he doth seem almost kind!" Cordelia said, shocked.

But the appearance of kindness disappeared the moment the man came to the hitching post. He untied the tether and yanked the beast's head up away from the poor strands of dry grass with a curse, then climbed into the cart and unlimbered a long, cruel whip as he yanked the donkey's head around.

"He must not!" Cordelia protested, but the driver was already plying the lash—and not just cracking it over the donkey's back, but cutting the poor beast's flanks.

"Why, the villain!" Cordelia cried, and her broomstick leaped from her hand to shoot off toward the cart.

But Rod had noticed something she hadn't seen, and clapped a hand on her shoulder. "Pull that broomstick back, daughter, or you may interfere with the course of justice."

"That cannot be so," Cordelia objected, but the broomstick slowed to a hover.

"Yes, it can. Look over there, at the edge of the meadow!"

Cordelia looked, and gasped.

"Rod," Fess said, "surely that is the same . . . beeeasstt . . ." He began to tremble.

"Hold yourself together, Rust Inhibitor—no need to have a

seizure over it. I'm sure there's a perfectly unreasonable explanation. But yes, that donkey underneath the trees *does* look exactly like our friend between the traces, there.''

''He hath gained, at least, a deserved reward,'' Gregory said, ''for he doth crop rich, sweet grass with relish.''

Magnus frowned. ''Yet how can the two be so exactly the same? Hath someone crafted a new beast of witch moss?''

''And wherefore?'' Geoffrey demanded.

''I don't think it's witch moss,'' Rod said slowly. ''In fact, I'm rather curious. Doesn't something about that duplicate donkey strike you as a little—odd?''

''Now that you mention it,'' Fess mused, ''the donkey's behavior is a bit *too* abject.''

''That's what I thought.'' Rod nodded. ''He's overacting.''

''Who, Papa?''

''Wait and see.'' Gwen said it softly, but her smile threatened to break into a grin.

The donkey heaved against the traces, managed to get the huge cart lumbering into motion, hauled it out of the inn yard and onto the road—and calmly proceeded to trudge off the track. The driver cursed at it and gave the reins a savage tug, but the donkey didn't even seem to notice. The man cracked the whip so deeply into its flank that the gouge filled with crimson—but the donkey only trotted the faster, out into the middle of a field. The driver went frantic. He flayed the poor beast with the whiplash, cursing like a fiend, and hauled on the reins so hard that one broke.

''What manner of donkey is that?'' Geoffrey stared. ''Never could a poor breast so withstand the pull of the bit!''

''Mayhap he hath it in his teeth,'' Magnus suggested.

''Or maybe he made his mouth as hard as rock.'' Rod couldn't help grinning.

The donkey bent its course away from the broken rein, trudging around in a circle. The driver howled in rage, beating and beating with the whip, but the donkey only went faster, around and around, until the driver began to feel the pull of centripetal force and felt the first stab of fear. He dropped the whip and turned to leap off the cart—and jolted back into his seat.

''He is stuck to the bench!'' Geoffrey howled.

''Husband,'' said Gwen, ''there is more to this than shape-shifting.''

"Oh, I agree—and I think we both know what it is."

The whip sprang out of the grass with a snap, turned, and cracked its lash over the driver's head. He looked up in horror and let out a low moan. The lash swept back, cracked, and struck like a snake, tearing the man's shirt and welting his back.

Rod turned to Cordelia with a frown. "I told you to wait!"

"But I did, Papa! That was not my doing!"

Rod stared at her.

Then he whirled back to catch the next act.

The donkey was galloping now, far faster than any Rod had ever seen—and the cart was skidding, the inner wheel lifting off the ground, then rocking back, then lifting again. The driver held on for dear life, howling with fright as the whip cracked over his head and the cart rocked under his feet.

"It's going," Rod said. "It's . . ."

With a crash and a rumble, the cart went over on its side, and the barrels went tumbling. The largest two split open, and red wine drenched the meadow. The driver landed ten yards away, flat on his back. A small barrel slammed into his belly.

"Oh, the poor man!" Cordelia cried. "Papa, ought we not aid him?"

"Wherefore, sister?" Magnus asked. "Hath he more pain than he gave his donkey?"

"Thou didst but now call him 'villain,' " Geoffrey reminded.

"That was when *he* had no need—and now he doth! Oh!"

"Peace, my daughter." Gwen laid a hand on her shoulder. "Let it work. I misdoubt me an he'll mistreat another beast whiles he doth live."

"Yet will he?"

"He will certainly live," Fess assured her, craning his neck to watch. "I can magnify visual images, Cordelia, and I am replaying the tumble in slow motion. So far as I can see, there is little probability of any serious damage to the man."

"Praise Heaven for that!"

"I don't think Heaven had anything to do with this little farce," Rod said slowly.

Sure enough, the driver had already managed to roll over, and was scrambling to get his feet under him—but the donkey squared off, turning tail, lined up its rear hooves, and caught him just as he managed to get his bottom off the ground. The driver went sprawling again, face in the dirt.

"Oh, well aimed!" Geoffrey tried to hide a smile. "Is't wrong to laugh at his discomfiture, Papa?"

"I don't really think so," Rod said slowly, "considering that he's only getting a taste of what he gave his donkey. And, of course, I have reason to suspect he's not going to sustain any real injury—no more than a bruise or two."

"How canst thou be certain?" Cordelia demanded.

But the driver had managed to clamber back up now, somehow without the donkey giving him the benefit of hindsight again, and was running back to the inn in a panic, crying,, "Witchcraft! Foul sorcery! Some witch hath enchanted my donkey!"

"Mama," Cordelia said, " 'tis not good for us that he should so defame witchfolk!"

"Be not troubled, my daughter. I am sure that any who hear this tale will know quite well 'twas not the work of a witch."

Cordelia frowned. "But how . . . ?"

The donkey gave its erstwhile master a snort of contempt, broke the shafts with two more well-placed kicks, and trotted off toward the woods.

"Papa, stop him!" Cordelia cried. "I must know who hath wrought this deed, or I'll die of curiosity!"

"I don't doubt it," Rod said, grinning, "and I must admit that I'd like to have my own suspicions confirmed." He gave a low, warbling whistle that slid through three keys.

The donkey's head snapped up, pivoting around toward Rod. The warlock smiled and stepped out into plain sight, and the donkey changed its course, trotting back toward them.

"I think we'd better step off the road," Rod explained. "The folk in the inn are apt to be coming out for a look any minute now."

"Indeed," Gwen agreed, and led the way into a small grove just off the meadow.

The donkey followed, and came trotting up in front of them. It stomped to a halt with a haughty toss of its head.

"All right, so you're noble." Rod smiled. "But tell me, do you really think that driver deserved that?"

"All that, and more," the donkey brayed.

The children's jaws dropped, and Fess started to tremble.

"Easy, Logic Looper." Rod rested his hand on the reset switch. "You knew this donkey wasn't all it appeared to be."

"I . . . shall accustom myself to the notion," Fess answered.

Gwen wasn't having much luck hiding her smile. "Dost thou bethink thyself so good a fellow, then?"

"Certes, I do." The donkey actually grinned—and everything around the grin seemed to blur and fade into an amorphous mass—then it reformed, and Puck stood there before them. "In truth, I do think I am a Robin Goodfellow."

The three younger children nearly fainted from sheer surprise, and even Magnus had eyes like coins. But Rod and Gwen only smiled, nodding, amused. "Was this just a spur-of-the-moment thing?" Rod asked. "Or did you actually think it through before you did it, for once?"

" 'For once,' forsooth!" the elf cried. "I'll have thee know I have watched this villain these seven months, and if e'er a man deserved to suffer for his deeds, 'twas he! 'Tis a bully entire, though too much a coward to attempt the beating of a mortal man! E'en a horse he would beware, and fear to strike! Therefore doth he bespeak you as pleasant as a dove, the whiles in his heart he doth wish to rend thee limb from limb. Nay, at last I did weary of his maltreatment of his poor beast, and bethought me to give him a draft of his own potion!"

" 'Tis not like thee, Puck, to be so cruel," Cordelia protested.

The elf grinned with a carnivore's smile. "Though knowest only one face of me, child, an thou canst speak so. Yet there was no true cruelty in this, for I did but make the man appear a fool, and that not even before his fellows. If he is wise, and doth profit where he can, he will not henceforth be so certain as to whom he can, or cannot, smite with impunity."

Cordelia appeared to be somewhat reassured, though not greatly. "Yet he was mightily affrighted, and sore hurt . . ."

"Had he worse than he hath given his beast?"

"Well . . . nay . . ."

"I cannot say thou hast done ill in *this* case, Robin," Gwen said, still smiling.

"*This* case, pooh! I am a man of many mischiefs, yet rarely of true hurt!"

Rod noted the 'rarely,' and decided it was time to change the subject.

Apparently, so did Puck. "Yet enough of this villain—he's not worth more words! How dost thou came to be nearby, to witness his coming to justice?"

"We," Rod said grandly, "are going on vacation."

"Oh, aye, and the sky is beneath our feet while the earth's overhead! Naetheless, 'tis a worthy goal. Whither wander you?"

"To our new castle, Puck," Cordelia said, eyes shining again. "Oh! Will it not be grand?"

"Why, I cannot tell," the elf answered, "unless thou dost tell me what castle it is."

"It's called Castle Foxcourt," Rod said.

Puck stared.

"I take it you know something about the place," Rod said slowly.

"I do not *know,*" the elf hedged, "for I've only heard tell of it."

"But what you've heard, isn't good?"

"That might be a way to speak of it," Puck agreed.

"Nay, tell us," Gwen said, frowning.

Puck sighed. "I know little, mistress, and guess less—but from what I have heard of it, this Castle Foxcourt is of ill repute."

"Dost say 'tis haunted?" Geoffrey asked, his eyes kindling.

"Not unless I'm asked—yet since I am, I must own 'tis that which I've heard of it. Yet there are ghosts, and ghosts. I would not fear to have thee near the shade of a man who was good in his lifetime."

Magnus frowned, cocking his head to one side. "From that, I take it the ghost who doth haunt this castle was not of the good sort, the whiles he did live."

"Not from what I hear," the elf said, his face grim. "Yet as I say, I do not truly *know*—even whiles the man endured, I had no business in his realm, and never chanced to meet him. Yet he bore his title with ill fame."

"Thou didst hear of him whiles he still did live?" Magnus frowned. "He hath not been so long a ghost, then."

"Nay, only a couple of hundreds of years."

"*Thou* didst know a man who . . ." Gregory's voice petered out as his eyes lost focus. "Nay, thou *art* spoken of as the oldest of all Old Things, art thou not?" But he looked a little dizzied by the implications.

Puck tactfully ignored the reference to his age. "I shall travel with thee, good folk."

"We might ever take pleasure in thy company, Puck,"

Gwen said, dimpling. "Yet if 'tis for cause that thou dost fear for us, I thank thee, but bid thee stay. No mere spirit can long discomfort *this* family, no matter how evil it was when alive."

"Be not so certain," Puck said, still looking uncomfortable. "Yet I'll own I've business of His Majesty's to attend." They all knew that the "Majesty" in question was not King Taun, but only Rod knew that the dwarf referred to the children's grandfather. "Yet an thou hast need of me, whistle, and I'll be by thee in an instant."

"Thanks," Rod said. "Hope we don't need to, though."

"Most dearly do I also! Yet an thou hast need of more knowledge than I do own, thou hast but to ask of the elves who dwell hard by the castle. They'll know the truth of its tale, I doubt not."

Rod nodded. "Thanks for the tip. *That,* we definitely will do."

"Nay, surely we must come to know our neighbors," Gwen agreed.

"There are few enough of those, I wot," Puck said with a grimace. "Rumor doth say that any who can, have fled its environs."

They had to wait for all the laughing and joking to die down in the inn, and for the limping driver to make his exit, red-faced, before they could order; but when the food came, it was good, and filling. With his stomach full, Rod declared that, since he was on vacation, he was going to honor it by attempting to nap, and any child who made enough noise to disturb him was likely to gain empirical evidence of the moon's composition.

It was a good excuse, at least, for going off under the shade of a tree fifty feet away, and lying down with his head in his wife's lap. From the constant murmur emanating from the two of them, the children doubted that their father was really sleeping or even trying to, but they bore it stoically.

"Is he not a bit aged to playing Corin to Mama's shepherdess?" Geoffrey grumbled.

"Oh, let them be," Cordelia said, with a sentimental smile. "Their love is our assurance, when all's said and done. Bide, whiles they make it the stronger."

"Cordelia speaks wisely," Fess agreed. "They did not

wed to speak of nothing but housekeeping and children, after all.''

"There is, of course, no loftier topic," Geoffrey assured him.

Cordelia gave him her best glare. "Thou art unseemly, brother.''

"Mayhap—yet I am, at least, only what I do seem."

"I wonder." Cordelia turned moody.

"You are still troubled by Puck's cruelty to the driver, are you not?" Fess said gently.

'Nay—I do not doubt the rightness of it, nor the man's well-being," Cordelia answered. " 'Tis the look of the man that doth bother me, Fess.''

"Wherefore?" Geoffrey asked, amazed. "He was well favored, for all that I could see."

"Aye, only a man such as any thou mightest meet upon the road," Magnus agreed.

"But dost thou not see, 'tis therein lies my grievance!" Cordelia said. " 'Tis even as Geoffrey did say—he was not fat, nor slovenly, nor had he the look of a brute! Yet he was one, beneath his seemly guise!"

"Not all do wear their villainy openly, sister," Gregory reminded her.

"Oh, be still, nubbin! 'Tis even that which doth trouble me!"

"Ah," Fess said. "You have begun to fear that all people are truly only bullies at heart, have you not?"

Cordelia nodded, her eyes downcast.

"Take comfort," the robot advised her. "Though they may be beasts within, most people do learn how to control their baser instincts—or, at least, to channel them in ways that are not harmful to others."

"But are they the less vile therefore?" she burst out. "They are still brutes within!"

"There is good at your cores as well as evil," Fess assured her. "Indeed, many people have so strong an instinct for helping others that it quite overshadows their urge to browbeat those about them."

"How canst thou say so!" Geoffrey said indignantly, "when thy first experience of mankind was with so base a knave?"

"That is true," Fess agreed, "yet he was in contact with

other human beings, and I had some indication of redemptive qualities in them.''

Cordelia frowned up at him. ''Did thy second owner confirm those hints of virtue?''

They heard a sixty-cycle buzz, Fess's equivalent of a contemptuous snort. ''He confirmed the opinion I had gained from Reggie, children, and demonstrated nadirs in human nature I had not thought possible, the worst of which was treachery. Reggie, at least, was not treacherous, and had some slight interest in others. My second owner, though, was of a mean and grasping nature, which is, I suppose, only natural.''

Geoffrey frowned up. ''How is that?''

''Why, anyone who would purchase a defective component simply to gain a bargain price, must necessarily be miserly—and he bought me to be the guidance computer for his burro-boat.''

Geoffrey frowned. ''What is a burro-boat?''

'' 'Was,' Geoffrey, for they are no longer manufactured, which is something of a blessing. They were small, heavily shielded craft designed for excavating and hauling, but certainly not for beauty.''

Magnus smiled, amused. ''Yet thy second owner cared little for grace, and greatly for gain?''

''He did, though I suppose the attitude came naturally to one of his occupation. He was a miner in Sol's asteroid belt, and lived constantly with danger, but with little else; only a solitary individual would choose such a life, and might well become bitter accordingly. He was interested only in his own self-aggrandizement—or his attempts at such; he never succeeded notably.''

''Was he poor, then?''

''He subsisted,'' Fess answered. ''By towing metal-rich asteroids into Ceres station, he gained enough to buy the necessities, which are notably expensive at so remote a location from the planet where your species evolved. He was interested in other human beings only as sources of his own gratification—and if they did not contribute to that gratification, he preferred to reject them completely.''

''Thou dost not mean he hated good folk!''

''That is perhaps an overstatement,'' Fess said, ''yet not quite so far off the mark as it might be.''

"But folk cannot live without other folk!"

"On the contrary, they can. They will be emotionally starved, of course—but such people frequently are emotionally crippled to begin with."

Cordelia shuddered. "How couldst thou think any good of mortal folk with such as that to form thine opinion?"

"Because I was constantly exposed to good people, Cordelia—or to news of them, at least."

Magnus frowned. "How couldst thou be?"

"Because most of the Belt folk were lonely, and wished company. They sought it the only way they could—by radio and video communication with others. I, of course, had to be ever vigilant, listening to the constant stream of chatter, in case some event should occur that would affect my owner—and as a result, I came to learn of all manner of people—some bad, some good, some quite evil, some very good. I learned of events, both important and insignificant. I think I remember best the time when an asteroid's dome failed—a force field that enclosed the atmosphere the people breathed."

Cordelia stared, shocked. "How could they have lived?"

"They did not—they died, with the exception of a technician and a tourist, both of whom happened to be in space suits at the time, and a little girl, who survived under rather unique circumstances."

"Oh, that must have wrung the heart of thee!"

"I have no 'heart,' as you call it, Cordelia—but I did learn a great deal about the abilities of people to sacrifice for one another, as I tracked her through the remainder of her childhood."

"Tell us of her then!" Gregory cried.

"Oh, 'tis all weepy lass's stuff!" Geoffrey objected.

"Not entirely, Geoffrey, for there was a villain involved, and a bit of fighting."

The boy's eyes glittered. "Tell!"

"Willingly, for it is part of your heritage. The hero of the tale is a quite unlikely specimen, for he was a reformed criminal."

"Indeed! Who was he?"

"He came to be called 'Whitey the Wino' after he reformed, and he earned his living by making up songs and singing them in taverns . . ."

* * *

Whitey struck a last chord from his keyboard and lifted his hands high, grinning at the burst of applause from the customers. "Thank you, thank you." His amplified voice boomed out through the cabaret—at least, they called it that. "Glad you liked it." *Yeah, and the shape you're in, you'd like anything right now.* But you don't get cheers by insulting your audience, nor return engagements either, so he kept the smile on and waited till the applause slackened, then said, "I'm going to take a little rest now, but I'll be back real soon. You take one too, okay?" Then he waved and turned away, with cheers and laughter behind him. *Yeah, take one—or two, or three. Then you'll think whatever I do is great.*

He shouldn't be so bitter, of course—they were paying his livelihood. But fifty-three, and he was still singing in glorified taverns on backwater moons!

Patience, he told himself. After all, there had been that record producer on vacation, who'd heard him and signed him before he sobered up. But he'd come back the next day with a studio booked, and Whitey had cut the wafer, and it had sold—with a low rating, yes, but a low rating of a hundred billion people on fifty-some odd planets is still twenty million, and Whitey got six per cent. It kept him alive, even under a dome on an asteroid or a lifeless moon, and paid his passage to the next planet. He never had trouble finding a cabaret who was willing to pay him now, so its patrons could hear him chant his songs. Then that critic had gone into rhapsodies about his verses being poems from the folk tradition, and a professor or two had agreed with him (anything for another article in print, Whitey supposed) and there had been another burst of sales, so here he was back in the Solar System, even if it was only on Triton, to cut another wafer. He hoped the professor wouldn't be too disappointed when he found out Whitey had a college degree.

All right, so a few million people are willing to keep you alive so they can hear your verses. Does that mean you're good?

He tried to throw off the mood—it meant he was good enough, he thought as he stepped into the glorified closet that the cabaret laughingly called a "green room." Well, at least it had someplace for the entertainers to relax between sets—more than a lot of clubs had.

He looked around, frowning. Where was that wine Hilda had promised him? Promised to have it waiting, too.

Ah, there she came, diving through the door, sailing in Triton's low gravity, out of breath. "Sorry, Whitey. There was a hold-up."

"Don't give them anything—it's a water pistol." Whitey reached out and plucked the glass from her as she braked against the other chair. "What was his name?"

"Terran Post Express." Hilda took an envelope from her bodice and handed it to him. "For Mr. Tod Tambourin."

Whitey winced at the sound of his real name. "Official, huh?"

"I'll say. Who knew you were here?"

"My producer." Whitey grinned, stroking the letter lasciviously as he eyed her.

"Don't give me that—if you meant it, you'd be trying to pet me, not the letter. What is it?"

"Probably money." Whitey slit the envelope.

She could almost hear his face hit the ground. "Who . . . who is it?"

"Lawyers," he told her. "My son's."

Not that he had ever known the boy that well, Whitey reflected, as he webbed himself into the seat on the passenger liner. Hard to get to know your son when you're hardly ever home. And Henrietta hadn't wanted him to be, after she realized her mistake—at least, that's what she had called it when she had figured out he wasn't going to settle down and become a nice safe asteroid miner, like a sensible man. She didn't approve of the way he made his living, either—selling exotic pharmaceuticals at an amazing discount, on planets where they were highly taxed. Totally illegal, and his first big regret—but she'd been plenty willing to take the money he'd sent back, oh yes—until that horrible trip when he'd landed on a tariff-free planet, and couldn't even make enough profit to ship out, and had found out, the hard way, what his stock-in-trade could do to his clients.

So no more drugs, for him or his customers—only wine, and beer at the most. He hadn't needed to smuggle any more, anyway—he had enough invested, he could live on the interest. Or his wife and boy could, while he eked out a living wandering from bar to bar, singing for shekels. The accommodations weren't too great, but other than that, it wasn't so different. He'd missed his son's early years though, and was beginning to think of going back to Ceres and getting to know him. Henrietta couldn't be all that bad.

Then he'd had the letter from the lawyer, and decided maybe she could. He'd *had* to live on his singing after that, because the court had given Henrietta all the stocks and bonds, and the kid. Whitey didn't have a leg to stand on—so he'd missed the lad's middle years, and teen years, too, because Henrietta had taken the money and the boy and emigrated to Falstaff, where Whitey couldn't follow—he didn't have the money for a ticket any more.

Not that he was about to try. In fact, he was ashamed for even thinking about it.

Of course, there was the chance that the kid might have wanted to meet him, when he grew up—so Whitey had written him a letter, when he found out that the kid had come back to Ceres. But the boy sent him a pointed note, one, and very pointed—"Stay out of my life." Not much arguing with that—and not much of a surprise, considering all the things Henrietta had told him about his father, some of which were actually true. So Whitey had lived with his second big regret, and gone on singing.

Ceres! Why did the kid have to go back there?

Because it was where he'd spent his boyhood, of course— nice to know it must have been halfway happy.

So Whitey had subscribed to Ceres News Service, and kept track of the main events in the boy's life—his marriage, his daughter's birth, his family's plunging into the new commuter colony on that large asteroid called Homestead, with the brand new idea in domes—overlapping force-field generators that completely englobed the rock.

And the dome had collapsed, and the boy and his wife were dead.

But the baby was alive.

The baby was alive, and her father hadn't left a will, and her mother's parents had followed Henrietta's lead and opted for cold sleep while their assets increased—

And Whitey was next of kin.

He touched the letter in his breast pocket, not needing to open it, still able to see the print when he closed his eyes. Next of kin, so little Lona was his responsibility, his second chance to raise a child. He watched Triton dwindling astern with Neptune's huge orb behind it, and felt a strange excitement welling up under the sorrow, vowing that, this time, he wasn't going to make a mess of it, no matter how tough it got.

It got tough.

It got really tough really fast, because it was a hospital the lawyer took him to, not an orphanage or a foster home—a hospital, and she was sitting in the dayroom, a beautiful, blonde, blue-eyed, six-year-old little girl, watching a 3DT program. Just watching.

Not talking, not fidgeting, not throwing spitballs—nothing.

"Lona, this is your grandfather," Dr. Ross said.

She looked up without the slightest sign of recognition—of course. They'd never met, she probably hadn't even known about him. "Are you my mommy's daddy?"

Whitey's smile slipped. Hadn't she met the other grandfather, either? Before he chilled out, of course. "No, I'm the other one."

"My daddy's daddy?"

"Yes."

"What was he like?"

The doctor explained it to him, after he had recovered, in her office. "It was a huge trauma, and she didn't have any defenses against it—after all, she's only six. It's not surprising that she has repressed all memory of it—and any memory that had anything to do with it, too."

"No surprise at all." He forced a smile. "She didn't have that much to remember yet."

Dr. Ross nodded. "We'll have to be very careful, very patient in working around the amnesia. She'll have to learn everything, all over again—but you have to tread very lightly. Don't mention Homestead, or her parents, or anything about her past for a while. There's no way of knowing what will trigger a memory painful enough to set her back."

Whitey nodded. "And she'll have to have psychiatric care?"

"Yes, that's vital."

"I see . . . Do you take private patients, Doctor?"

"Yes, a few," Dr. Ross said instantly, "and I can make room for Lona."

*   *   *

So he had to settle down, after all—find an apartment to buy, arrange the financing, have the furniture cast and delivered. Then, finally, he was able to lead her out of the hospital and out into the corridor, her little hand in his, already trusting, on her way home.

She was very good.

Too good—Whitey found himself wishing for a little naughtiness. But she was totally obedient, did exactly what she was told—

And not one thing more.

When he didn't have something for her to do, she just sat watching the 3DT, hands in her lap, back straight (as he had commanded, hoping to get a rise out of her). Everything he taught her, she learned on the first try, then did whenever he told her to do it. She made her bed every morning, washed her dishes, studied her alphabet—

Like a robot.

"She could simply be naturally good," Dr. Ross said carefully. "Some children are."

"Some children may be, but it's not natural. Come on, Doctor—just a little disobedience? A little backtalk? Why not?"

"Guilt," the doctor said slowly.

Whitey stared. "What could she have to feel guilty about?"

"The explosion," the doctor sighed. "Children seem to feel that if something goes wrong, it must be their fault, must be the result of something they did."

Whitey frowned. "I can see that making her sad, all right—but absolutely perfectly behaved? And why would that keep her from dreaming?"

"Everyone dreams, Mr. Tambourin."

"Whitey." he squeezed his eyes shut; his real name had unpleasant associations with his past. "Just 'Whitey.' "

" 'Whitey,' " the doctor said reluctantly. "And we know Lona dreams—that's why I gave her the REM test."

"Then how come she says she doesn't?"

"She doesn't remember. She's repressing that, too."

"But they're happening *now!* And the accident was *months* ago!"

"Yes," the doctor said, musing, "but she may feel that it's wrong to dream."

"In Heaven's name, *why?*"

"She may have been angry at her parents," Dr. Ross explained. "Children frequently are, any time they're told No or punished. They want to strike back at their parents, want to hurt them, tell them to drop dead—and, if she'd gone to bed in that frame of mind . . ."

"She might have dreamed she was killing them?"

"Something like that. Then she woke up, and found they really *were* dead—so she repressed the traumatic event, and repressed all memory of her parents, since that reminded her of her guilt."

"Isn't this a little farfetched?"

"Very," the doctor admitted. "It's just conjecture, Mr. . . . Whitey."

He sighed. "Mr. Whitey" would do. "We don't have enough information for anything more than a guess, do we?"

"Not yet, no."

"Okay, let's say you're right, Doctor. What do we do about it?"

"Prove to her that wishes don't make things happen, Mr.—Whitey."

Whitey suddenly turned thoughtful. "I suppose that is how it looks to her. But why would that make her so scrupulously obedient?"

"Because if you're naughty," the doctor murmured, "horrible things happen."

"And if you've been *that* naughty . . ."

"You want to be punished," the doctor finished for him. "Yes."

"Well." Whitey stood up, with a smile. "She shouldn't have to do it all by herself, should she?"

So he punished her. Tirelessly, relentlessly, ruthlessly, no matter how it made his heart ache. Made her scrub the floor. Do the dishes. Dust the furniture. All by hand, too.

She should have protested that the robot could do it.

She didn't.

He made her comb her own hair, and watched with a beady eye to make sure every tangle was out, trying to ignore the ache in his chest—watched the tears rolling down her cheeks as she pulled and yanked, but never a whimper.

And no games. No playing—not that she did, anyway. No 3DT programs.

He made her do everything. She out-cleaned Cinderella, out-shined the Man in the Moon, and moved in on the labors of Hercules. She was starting in on the Aegean Stables when she finally exploded. "I wish you'd get spaced, Gran'pa!"

Then she froze, shocked, appalled at herself—but she'd said it.

"No," Whitey said, with his meanest grin, "I won't."

Then he had to deliver on it, of course. If anything happened to him now, she'd probably *never* come out of it. He got mighty tired of wearing the space suit, day in and day out, but after a week, she saw nothing had happened to him, and began to relax. And, when lightning failed to strike, she began to become a bit more irritable.

"Gran'pa, you're a meanie!"

"I know. But you have to clean your room anyway, Lona."

"Gran'pa, you're horrible!"

"Scrub the floor anyway, Lona."

"Gran'pa, I wish *you* knew what it feels like!"

"Finish combing your hair, Lona."

It was the hair that finally did it. One night, she yanked at a particularly bad snarl and cried, "Ouch!" And the tears rolled.

"Poor little girl," Whitey said, fairly oozing sympathy. "But crying won't get you out of it."

Her face reddened with real, genuine anger. "Gran'pa, drop dead!"

"But I didn't," Whitey explained.

"Yes, and I'm *awful* glad! But can't you stop wearing that space suit now, Gran'pa?"

"Sorry, child."

"But the kids next door are making fun of you!"

"Calling names doesn't hurt me."

He could see her registering that, but she went on. "But you look so silly!"

He shook his head. "Sorry. Can't do it."

"Yes you can! All you have to do is take it off!"

"No, I can't," he said, "because if anything happened to me, you'd think it was your fault."

"No, I won't! That's silly! You're not going to get hurt

just because I said to!'' Then she stopped, eyes wide, hearing her own words.

''That's a very important thing to realize, Lona,'' Dr. Ross was carefully sitting upwind of Whitey, and as far away as she could.

''Then Gran'pa can take off the suit now?''

''Yes, but not here, please.''

''Do you *really* realize that just wishing won't make something happen?'' Whitey demanded.

And he was appalled that Lona was silent.

''Why do you think it does, Lona?'' the doctor said kindly.

'' 'Cause they said so on the 3DT,'' Lona mumbled.

Whitey took a deep breath, and the doctor leaned back in her chair. ''But those are just stories, Lona—fairy tales.''

''No it's not! It was about Mr. Edison!''

Whitey stared.

''Oh, yes, the genius inventor,'' the doctor said slowly. ''But he didn't just 'wish,' and see his invention appear all of a sudden, did he?''

''No.'' Lona looked at the floor.

''How did he make his wishes real, Lona?''

''He worked at 'em,'' the little girl answered. ''He worked awful hard, and stayed up nights working a lot, until he'd built a new invention.''

''Yes,'' the doctor said softly, ''and later in his life, he drew pictures of new machines he'd thought of, and gave them to other men to make. But it all took work, Lona—work with people's hands, not just their minds.''

She nodded.

''What wish do *you* want to make real, Lona?''

''For no one to ever be hurt again from a dome collapsing!'' she said instantly.

Now it was the doctor who took the deep breath, though Whitey joined her. ''That's very difficult,'' Dr. Ross warned.

''I don't care! I want to do it anyway!''

''Look, child,'' Whitey said, ''this isn't just pushing your body, like scrubbing the kitchen floor. This means learning mathematics, and physics, and computer programming, and engineering—grindingly hard work.''

''I can do it, Gran'pa!''

''I know you can,'' Whitey said softly, ''but not overnight —or next week, or even next year.''

"You mean I *can't* do it?"

"No, you can," Dr. Ross said quickly. "I'm sure you have the intelligence, and we know you have the industry. But it does take a long time, Lona—years and years. It takes high school, and college, and maybe even graduate studies. You won't be able to invent your fail-safe dome till you're in your twenties or thirties."

"I don't care how long it takes! I'm gonna to do it anyway!"

And Whitey and the doctor could both breathe easily again, finally. *At least,* Whitey thought, *we're safe from suicide.*

First, of course, she had to find out why the dome on Homestead had blown. It was touchy, but Dr. Ross had said she was ready for it. Still, she trembled when Whitey managed to get her the printout from the asteroid's systems computer. But the trembling stopped when she looked at it. "What's all this mean, Gran'pa?"

"I don't know, child. I never learned enough about computers to be able to make sense of it."

"Can't you hire somebody to tell you?"

Whitey shook his head. "I don't have that much money—and everybody in the Asteroid Belt is too busy trying to earn enough to stay alive."

She stared. "You mean nobody *cared?*"

"Oh, they cared, all right. There was an investigation, and I read the report—but all it said, really, was that there had been a horrible accident, and the dome field had collapsed."

"They didn't say how or why?"

Whitey shook his head. "Not that I could tell. Of course, I don't understand all the technical stuff."

"Can't you learn it?"

"I could," Whitey said slowly, "if I didn't have to worry about earning a living."

"Well, then, *I'll* learn it!" Lona said, with determination, and turned back to the computer screen.

And she did. But before she could begin to learn programming, she had to learn a little about how computers work—and that meant she had to learn math, and a little physics. But when she came to microcircuits, she had to learn enough chemistry to understand silicon—and that meant more physics, and more physics meant more math. Then she began to become interested in mathematics for its own sake, and Whitey pointed out that she had to learn enough history to understand the way people were thinking when they invented programming, and history turned out to be pretty interesting, too.

Meanwhile, of course, Whitey was filling her head with bedtime stories about the Norse gods, and the fall of Troy, and the travels of Don Quixote.

"Isn't there any more, Gran'pa?"

"Well, yes, child, but there isn't time to tell it all."

So, of course, she had to start reading the books, to find out what Gran'pa had left out—and that was more fun than 3DT. Not that she watched it that much, there wasn't time. Oh, Gran'pa insisted that she take a few hours every afternoon to play with the other children, and now she was so full of life that she made friends in no time.

And that, of course, was probably why the Board of Education came knocking on the door.

Whitey wasn't about to let her be locked into six hours a day listening to material she'd already learned, of course. Not that he would have dreamed of claiming he knew better than the education professionals—for normal children. But Lona was a special case, and even they would have had to admit that.

If he had bothered arguing. But there were four school districts in Ceres City, and a dozen more on the asteroids nearby, all close enough to scoot over on a rocket sled and visit her friends every afternoon, and Dr. Ross once a month, and whatever cabaret Whitey was singing at in the evening. Not that she had much contact with any of what went on in the clubs, of course—she brought her notebook computer along.

So Whitey started travelling again, living the lifestyle he preferred, even though he wasn't travelling very far. He developed it into a system—move into town a month after the first semester began, and by the time the School Board realized he was there, he was already packing up to move on. Then three months there, and the school year was almost over, so there was no point in starting—and, of course, by the time the next school year was beginning, he'd already put his apartment on the market and gone to contract on a new one in another town-asteroid.

And Lona learned. And learned. And learned.

By the time she was ten, she knew enough to be able to

piece together the sequence of events from the printout. Not
that she needed the hard copy, of course—she was able to
access it by herself as she explained it to Whitey in a flat,
controlled, emotionless voice.

Only one force-field generator had blown. Only one, but all
the force-domes interlocked—so when one went, it disrupted
its six neighbors' fields badly enough so that all the air
poured out of them into its sector—and gushed out into space
in a swirl of snowflakes. Their generators all tried to strengthen
their domes, and the whole system overloaded, fields weak-
ening to the point where Terran sea level air pressure could
rip through them, gusting in the first and only wind Homestead had ever known, howling around the eaves of all the
houses the settlers had built in their cocksure confidence in
their dome, around the eaves and down the streets and on into
the fieldless sector, then out into space, leaving only vacuum
behind.

And bodies.

And, in one house, a little girl whose silly, overprotective
daddy had insisted on making his house airtight, even though
everybody knew it wasn't necessary, because the dome envel-
oped the whole asteroid in a force field that could never be
punctured by any meteor—a silly daddy and a silly mommy
who had put their little girl to bed, then gone outside to hold
hands and look at the stars.

Whitey held his face immobile, his heart swelling up with
pride in his son, but squeezing in with pity for the little girl.

The little girl who had waked up to find everybody else
dead, and no one nearby to tell her it wasn't her fault.

The little girl who sat looking at the computer screen with
eighty-year-old eyes in a ten-year-old face, a little girl whose
foolish grandfather could only stand beside her, wishing there
were something he could do, and asking,

"But what made that first generator blow?"

"I don't know," Lona answered, "but I'm going to find
out. And when I do, I'm going to make sure that it never,
ever happens again."

But she didn't shed a single tear.

Whitey wished that she would.

So they hired a burro-boat and went out to Homestead. It
wasn't hard to find a pressure suit in her size—children

weren't all that rare in the Asteroid Belt. Not any more; not since the domes had been pronounced safe and fail-safe.

The ordinary domes, that is—the standard ones.

"Anybody who'd take a kid to live in an experiment has all the moral sensibility of a cuckoo," Whitey muttered—but it made him uneasy. Would his son have been a little less cocksure if Whitey had stayed with him?

"What did you say, Gran'pa?"

"Oh, nothing, Lona. Come on, let's go look." He fastened his helmet and checked her seals; she checked his. Then they stepped into the miniscule airlock.

"An hour and ten, standard," the pilot told him. "Any more than that, and I'm pushing an energy crisis."

"Back in forty-five," Whitey assured him, and sealed the inner hatch.

Bastard could wait, he thought—a burro-boat could run for a week or more on a block of ice. Of course, the reason old Herman had taken the charter was because he was down to frost, or so he said—but Whitey had to admit it was better to play safe. Still, he doubted the prospector was *that* low.

The patch turned green, and Whitey pushed it. The hatch swung open, and he reached out to clip his safety line to a ring bolt. Then he climbed out, moving slowly and smoothly in the negligible gravity, then turned back to take Lona's line, clip it to a ring bolt, and help her out.

She came out easily; free fall was nothing new to her (Whitey had made sure she took gymnastic lessons). But she was pale, her eyes huge. He felt a stab of guilt at having brought her back to the scene of the calamity, but steeled himself to it—the doctor had said it was okay, hadn't she? Still, he watched the child very carefully. "Over here, Lona— Herman did a very good job. It's only fifty yards away."

She nodded, looking all about her, face haunted, as she groped for his hand.

And no wonder, Whitey thought, looking around him at the empty houses and storage buildings. They were near a park with playground equipment, swing chains dangling from a central mast, pathetic in their loneliness. There was only an occasional broken window (windows on an asteroid! The gall, the audacity, the sheer overweening pride of these pioneers!). That was all, no other damage. Oh, here and there, the odd tile had broken loose from a roof, but only a few—when the wind had come, it hadn't had much force. It was vacuum that had killed this place, not hurricane.

It was a grim town, dead and forlorn, with memories of families and laughter and tears—a ghost town in space.

"Are there any—bodies?" Lona swallowed, hard.

"No—the disaster squad took them all away for burial." No need to add that the crypt was under the skin of the asteroid itself. "If it seems you've been here before, it's nothing to worry about. You have been."

"I know," she said, her voice flat in his helmet speakers, "but it's really creepy. It all looks the same, and it makes me feel like I'm little again—but it's all so different."

Yes, without life. Whitey reminded himself that the doctor had said this would strengthen her immensely, would banish any lingering ghosts of guilt, that there was almost no chance of another breakdown, she was a very strong little girl inside now. "Of course, we can't ever be *completely* sure, Mr. Whitey. The human brain is inconceivably complex."

"Is that the generator?" Lona stared at the hemisphere of metal honeycomb before them, in a fenced-off section of the park.

"No, just its antenna," Whitey answered. "The generator's underground."

Lona stared up at him. "Then how could it blow up?"

"We don't *know* it blew up," Whitey reminded her. "Come on, let's look."

He found the trapdoor set into the rock beside the antenna, punched in the combination. It had been a real job getting that set of numbers—they were classified material of the highest order, vital to public safety (never mind the fact that the people they were supposed to guard had died four years before). But finally, with a letter from the doctor testifying how important the expedition was for the child's mental health, a few bribes, and a flawless train of logic, the relevant bureaucrat had reluctantly agreed to let him have the combination. It was reassuring, in its way, giving you the feeling that the living were protected as well as the dead.

Whitey swung the lock handle and hauled the trapdoor open. They went down carefully, him first, flashlight probing the darkness around him. "Careful not to foul my line."

"I won't, Gran'pa." But she wasn't being sassy about it—that worried him.

Then he saw the generator.

He stopped stock still, just standing there, staring.

"Gran'pa," she said, "it's . . ."

"In perfect condition." Whitey nodded. "At least, it *looks* that way. Let's just check, child."

Then he brought out the toolkit, opened the access panels one by one, and took out the circuit checker. "What do I do with *this* thing?"

"Red lead to contact A, Gran'pa—there." Lona pointed. "And blue lead to contact D."

"I'm glad one of us knows what I'm doing . . ."

But Lona was frowning at the meter, frowning and taking out her keypad. She punched in the data displayed on the circuit and said, "Red lead to contact B, Granpa, and blue lead to contact H."

So it went, Whitey placing the probes where she told him, she frowning at the readout and punching data into her keypad. He began to think she wasn't really aware of him any more, was just using him as a sort of voice-activated servomechanism.

Well, at least it was *some* sign of life.

Finally, she straightened up with a sigh and said, "That's all. We've checked every circuit. There's nothing more here for me."

Whitey fastened the access panels back in place, listening to her words echo inside his head in secret, sad satisfaction. But he kept his face solemn, a little exasperated, and glanced at the time display built into his faceplate. "Not a minute too soon; I promised Herman forty-five minutes, and it's been fifty. Come on, child, let's go—and counterclockwise, please— let's not get our tails snarled."

"Hm? Oh sure, Gran'pa." and she followed him out, frowning, deep in thought.

Whitey fastened the trapdoor back in place and took her hand, turning back toward the burro-boat. "Learn anything?"

"Uh-huh." She nodded. "It's in perfect working order."

"What?" Whitey jerked to a stop, staring down at her.

"It is, Gran'pa." She sounded a little bit afraid, as though she might have done something wrong. "We could power it up, and it could put out a dome."

Whitey kept a firm hold on Lona's hand, but whether it was for her stability or his, he couldn't have said. His mind, at least, was in a whirl. "How could that generator have failed if it was in perfect working order?"

"Somebody turned it off."

He looked down at Lona, startled.

She looked up at him out of wide, grave eyes. "Somebody had to have turned it off, Gran'pa. It's the only way."

"But it took me a full week, a letter testifying need, and a dozen forms to five different offices, to get the combination for that lock—and that's when it wasn't operating! How could anybody even have *gotten* to it?"

"I don't know," Lona said, "but somebody did."

Whitey froze as a thought hit him. "Child," he said slowly, "I didn't see a power switch in there."

Lona stopped dead with one foot in the air. Then, carefully, she put it down and nodded. "You're right, Gran'pa. There wasn't any."

"Well, if there's no switch, who could turn it off?"

"The computer," she said.

"But that means somebody programmed it to turn off the field!"

She was quiet for a moment, then asked, "Couldn't it have developed a glitch?"

"Chances are obscenely low, child! But who could have reached the computer?"

"Gotta find out," she mumbled, and turned away toward the boat.

Whitey came out of his stupefaction and hurried after her. Abstracted as she was, she was apt to bump into a sharp piece of junk and tear her suit—so he was in the perfect position when he saw the drilling laser on the boat's bow turn toward them.

He hurled himself at her in a long, flat dive that caught her hips right across his shoulder and carried her into cover behind a house as the laser bolt spattered molton rock where she'd been standing. She cried out, of course, and Whitey snapped, "Quiet!" His brain revved into high gear, picking illusion as their only defense and pegging the manner of it instantly. "Now get in there, and lie absolutely still!" he snapped, cradling her in one arm and holding the other fore-finger up in front of his faceplate. Helmet or not, she recognized the "Sh!" sign and squeezed her lips shut, eyes wide, stiff as a fashion doll.

The stiffness didn't help any, but he managed to dodge

around a corner, weave a right-angled "S" around three houses, find a broken window that he could reach in and unlock, then opened the casement and pushed Lona through. She grabbed the nearest table and crouched under it, wide-eyed. Whitey pointed downward, hoping she understood that he wanted her to go down into the cellar, and very much aware that whoever had fired on them must be listening to their radio frequency. Then he turned away, dodging and weaving as far from his granddaughter as he could, eyeing the black sky with trepidation, knowing the burro-boat must be aloft and hunting.

And it was. Fire spat down out of sun-glare—right into the first house he'd hidden behind. He felt a glow of satisfaction—the would-be murderer had blasted the spot where Whitey had *said* he was hiding Lona. Because the gunman had been eavesdropping on their suit frequency, of course, and thought Whitey had stuffed Lona into hiding at that first house.

Only you can't "blast" something with a drilling laser—the beam is too narrow, and the power's too low. Constant, but low—and the blast was still walking down out of the sky, stabbing the house again, and again, and again.

How long can he keep that up? Whitey wondered, and the idea blossomed. Because a laser used a lot more power than the bursts of acceleration needed in the Belt, and maybe Herman had been telling the truth, maybe he really *was* that low on fuel.

But he had to keep that idiot in the boat firing. He'd be done with that house very soon—and he'd figure Whitey wasn't in it.

Hatred seared through Whitey, hatred at any man who could try to burn up a child like that. He put his feet against the nearest wall and shoved off, darting from house to house, looking for something, anything, to keep the man shooting.

And cover—to keep the murderer from shooting *him*.

A blank wall loomed in front of him—a warehouse. The door was open, of course—why lock anything, when you know all your neighbors? He ducked in and breathed a sigh of relief, then pushed himself over to a window on the long side, and looked out at the square with the park at its far end.

The boat was there, right enough, hovering fifty feet up, high enough to see any movement, low enough to be within range—and not firing.

But if it was in range to shoot at them, it was in range to be shot. Whitey toggled his helmet lamp and cast about frantically, looking for a weapon, some kind of weapon, or at least something that would make a big explosion of light . . .

And there they were, racked against the side wall, right next to the door he'd come in by, twenty rifles, plugged in to recharge. Whitey hopped over to them, blessing the Belter's inherited sense of caution—the Asteroid Belt detachment of Marines had kept the peace well for the last fifty years, but there were still old-timers around who could tell hair-raising stories of the pirates and claim-jumpers who had riddled the asteroids almost from the day they were opened to prospecting, and had even made a fair bid to establish their own tyranny. The pirates were gone, but it had become traditional to keep a rifle handy.

Very handy. Whitey unplugged one, blessing his luck and hoping the current was still running. No reason why it shouldn't be—the planetoid had been powered by a fission generator, which was good for fifty years. No reason to have shut it down, either, with fissionables so plentiful out here. He picked out a rivet on the far wall for a target, set the rifle on low power, sighted, and squeezed.

The bolt of energy spattered a circle of molten metal, just above and to the left of the target.

Whitey's heart sang as he corrected the sights and fired again. This time the rivet disappeared, and he leaped back to the window, setting the rifle to full power, aiming at the burro-boat, breathing out, and squeezing the firing patch.

A flower of fire lit the boat's bow.

It was turning toward him even as Whitey was squeezing off his second shot. Whoever the pilot was, he recognized a real weapon when he saw its bolt, and knew he had to put it out of action fast. The boat shot toward the warehouse as the drill bored down, punching through the warehouse roof.

But Whitey was already out the door and crouching behind the next house. He popped up above the roof, aimed, fired, and ducked down, then arrowed away behind the next house, then popped up to fire again just as the drill pierced the last roof he'd fired from. He torpedoed away again, but around a corner, because two points determine a straight line, and two events determine a trend, if you're the kind to jump to conclusions.

The assassin was, and the beam hit the third house in the row. But Whitey was firing from two houses south, then from the house west, then two houses west. His blood pounded in his ears, his heart thrilled to the hunt, even though he kept expecting to pop up and see ruby fire all around him.

But he didn't—the assassin never knew where he'd be next. Not surprising—Whitey didn't, either.

Then, finally, the beam grew dim.

That was it—one shot dim, then only a feeble glow from the drill, then nothing. The burro-boat floated in the night, not a light showing, not a flicker of a rocket.

Whitey waited, holding his breath. Finally, he had to breathe, but the boat still hadn't moved. Slowly, he started back to the warehouse, keeping an eye on the burro-boat, but there wasn't the least sign of life, or of movement. Whitey grinned, picturing the man inside raging, stabbing pressure patches in blind panic, not even able to get back to the asteroid and the hidden scooter he surely had ridden out from Ceres, not able to shoot, to transmit, to move.

Out of juice. Completely.

Whitey ducked in through the door and began to search the warehouse more thoroughly. If there were rifles, maybe there was a radio.

There was, and it was plugged in to recharge, too. Whitey turned it on, set the frequency to the emergency mark, toggled his helmet's loudspeaker, and bent down to put it next to the microphone grille. "Emergency! Calling Marine Patrol, Sector 6 . . ."

The only sour note, he reflected, was that the assassin couldn't hear his call.

The Marines were there in an hour—after all, Ceres was a commute, not a day trip. Not that the murderer was going anywhere, of course. But it was time enough for Whitey to go back and collect a very thoroughly frightened Lona, a little girl who was sobbing with fear and dread of the haunted place where she crouched alone, then crying her eyes out with relief. Whitey had soothed her and comforted her and had her looking brave, by the time the Marine ship loomed over them—space suits or not, a hug is a hug.

"His name is Cornelius Hanash," the Marine captain said,

closing the door to his office and coming around to sit down by the desk.

Whitey stared. "Millionaire Hanash? The one who built the Ceres Center? The one who has all the filthy rich tourists paying him through the nose to lie back in their loungers and watch the asteroids fly by overhead? *That* Cornelius Hanash?"

"The same," the captain answered, "and the records show he was thinking of setting up a branch on Homestead, had even bought a major hunk of bare rock there. But he ran low on cash, and got behind on his payments."

"But how did—how did squashing Homestead . . ." Lona broke off, trying to swallow her tears.

"Insurance," the captain explained. "He had that hunk of real estate insured for the full value of the hotel he 'planned' to build there. When the dome blew, Farland's had to pay— and it was enough to pay off his debts on the Ceres operation."

"But how did he know we were . . ." Whitey stopped, frowning. "I didn't exactly make it a secret that we were going out to Homestead, did I?"

"No, and even *I* heard the gossip that some nut was trying to get into the blown generator on the asteroid. Hanash was bound to hear it, with all the connections he has in Sector Hall—and he knew what you'd find."

"Death," Lona whispered. "Death for a hundred thousand people—and Mommy and Daddy."

Then the tears broke. Finally. And Whitey held her and comforted her, and waited for the storm to pass, glad that she could finally grieve, could finally put the past where it belonged.

Cordelia wiped her eyes, blew her nose, and tucked her hanky away with a sniffle. "Oh, she was a brave lass!"

"She was indeed—and, although she did not live happily ever after, most of her life was delightful. The rest was only exciting."

"If 'twas as exciting as her childhood, she did ne'er grow bored," Magnus opined.

"He was a brave man, this Whitey." Geoffrey's eyes glowed. "Valiant."

"I cannot help but agree—though I must say he never sought danger. Still, he had a way of attracting it."

"Oh, praise Heaven thou didst hear of such as they!"

Gregory breathed. "Even through all thy years with the miner, though couldst know folk could be good!"

"Aye, what of that miner?" Geoffrey frowned. "How didst thou come to be free of him?"

"By death, wood-pate!" Magnus aimed a slap at his brother's head. "How else could one be free of such a louse?"

Geoffrey blocked the blow easily and slapped back to score as he said, "I could think of an hundred ways, with a club at the beginning, and poison at the end."

"Geoffrey! I trust you jest!" Fess said, shocked. "No, in point of fact, I was freed from him as a result of his own moral turpitude."

"Turp . . . what?" Gregory asked.

"Turpitude, Gregory—doing wrong without compunction. He exhibited this quality when he received a distress signal from a group of castaways and sought to pass them by, since he perceived no likelihood of immediate gain or pleasure from them."

"The dastard!" Cordelia gasped. "Had he no respect for humankind, then?"

"None," Fess confirmed. "He would cheerfully have left them to die, and never thought twice of it."

"Yet thou wouldst not permit it?"

"I could not. My program dictates that human life is of greater importance than human convenience—and saving lives was more important than my owner's whim. So I turned the ship aside and picked them up, containing them within the airlock. Once they were aboard. I persuaded my owner to permit them to come into the ship itself."

" 'Persuaded'!" Geoffrey cried triumphantly. "Thou didst not disobey!"

"I did disobey my owner, by rescuing the fugitives—but he sought to break the law."

"And thou didst obey the law!"

"I did," Fess agreed.

"Was there no other time when thou didst disobey?"

"There was," Fess admitted, "for I soon perceived that the castaways had excellent qualities of mutual assistance and support; but my owner had received a broadcast identifying them as fugitives from governmental forces, and offering a reward for information leading to their capture. Since the fugitives had not contributed to his gratification, he attempted to use them as coin to buy it."

"As coin?" Goeffrey frowned. "How can one use people to buy with?"

"There is slavery," Fess answered, "and I am certain that the only reason my second owner did not descend to such depths, is that he lacked the opportunity. But he was not averse to attempting to collect bounty on fugitives when the chance presented itself. Accordingly, he ordered me to transmit a signal to Ceres Station, notifying the authorities of the fugitives' presence—and I refused to do so."

"Thou didst most thoroughly disobey, both thine owner and the law!"

"Not quite," Fess demurred, "for I had reason to believe that the authorities in question were themselves violating the law."

Geoffrey looked exasperated. If Fess said he "had reason to believe," then he had almost complete proof.

"My owner activated a manual transmitter, though, and sent the signal."

Cordelia frowned. "Was that not exceedingly dangerous?"

"Aye," Geoffrey agreed, "and from what thou hast said, he hath not the sound of being a bold man—for would he not have valued his own welfare above all else?"

"He did," Fess confirmed. "The fugitives in question, though, were scarcely dangerous. They were not criminals, but simply people who had expressed a disagreement of opinion with the party that was attempting to overthrow the government of the time. Since they were not dangerous in themselves, the miner showed no hesitation in betraying them to the assassins employed by that party."

"The coward! The poltroon!" Geoffrey cried. "Had he no fellow-feeling in him at all?"

"I suspect not. Certainly, he was not averse to attempting to collect bounty on the fugitives when the chance presented itself. Yet he did not know that he would gain a considerably greater amount than I was worth from the gentleman who purchased me from him."

Geoffrey frowned. "Dost thou say these 'fugitives' did buy thee from him?"

"Their leader did, yes."

Cordelia frowned, too. "Yet wherefore did the wealthy gentleman purchase thee from the miner?"

"Because he and his friends needed me and the burro-boat to carry them away from the assassins the miner had summoned."

"How did he know the miner had called them up?"

"I took the liberty of informing them."

"Fess!" Geoffrey stared at him, scandalized. "Thou didst betray thine owner!"

"I did," Fess said, without the slightest hesitation. "I have explained my reservations about the miner's character, children—but in only an hour's time, I had come greatly to respect the fugitives, and had realized that they were struggling to preserve liberty for all people. My program holds such liberty to be fundamental, equal in importance to my loyalty to my owner."

Geoffrey frowned. "That hath an odd sound, in light of what thou hast told us of thy program aforetime."

"It does seem anomalous," Fess admitted, "to the point that I suspect some error was made in my program, and only in mine. Nonetheless, this was the only instance in which such a conflict arose. Revealing the miner's report to the fugitives was consequently in accord with my program."

"Thou hadst learned summat more of human folk than when thou didst guide an aircar, hadst thou not?"

"Considerably more, and had come to realize as I have said, that there are qualities of goodness and badness in people."

Gregory looked up, puzzled. "Yet thou art but a robot, or so thou wouldst have us believe. How canst thou know good from bad?"

"Be mindful of my programming, children. To me, anything is 'good' if it is conducive to human life, liberty, or happiness, and anything is 'bad' if it is inimical to that life or happiness, or threatens liberty."

"Yet strong drink would thereby be 'good,'" Geoffrey said.

"I spoke of happiness, Geoffrey, not pleasure."

Geoffrey shook his head. "I ken not the difference."

"Nor did my second owner. But even acknowledging the difficulties of his situation, I could not condone his behavior."

"'Tis a wonder he did not scrap thee!"

"He did not have the opportunity; for the chief of the fugitives secured his own safety, and that of his friends, by the simple expedient of abandoning the miner on a small asteroid, with a sufficiency of food, water, and shelter—and a beacon to summon assistance.''

"Why, how cruel!''

"Not really; there was no doubt of a rescue well before the miner's supplies ran out.''

Geoffrey frowned. "Then why abandon him in so unlikely a place. Why not take him to a town?''

"Because, if they had taken him to Ceres, the authorities would have arrested them. But if they marooned him, it would take several days for the rescue to arrive, which guaranteed their being able to vacate the vicinity safely.''

"Wherefore did they not slay him out of hand?'' Geoffrey demanded.

"Geoffrey!'' Cordelia protested.

But Fess admitted, "There was some sentiment in favor of such an action—but the fugitives' leader suggested the more humane alternative.''

"Only 'suggested?' '' Geoffrey questioned. "Had he no authority, then?''

"I do not know,'' Fess mused, "for the issue never arose. None of them contradicted him, when he spoke of action.''

"Thou dost mean they did not think to disobey.'' Geoffrey scowled. "Is this admirable?''

"It is,'' said Fess, "when the commands are right.''

"But thou dost tell me naught!'' Geoffrey cried. "Am I to disobey, or not?''

"The issue is unclear, Fess,'' Gregory agreed.

"You must decide for yourselves, children, and decide each case as it arises, not seek to abdicate your power of decision by imposing an inflexible rule.''

"Then give us a rule that *is* flexible,'' Magnus suggested.

"Your parents have already done so.''

The children looked at each other, puzzled.

"Doth he toy with us?'' Geoffrey asked.

"Nay,'' said Gregory, "for 'tis not in his nature.''

"His nature is to be loyal to his owner,'' Magnus said, "and that owner is Papa.''

Cordelia turned to stare at the back of Fess's head, beginning to feel angry. "Hast thou sold us, then?''

"I have not,'' Fess answered, "and if you consider, you will find it so. If you seek to know whether or not to obey, I can only tell you the answer I have gained by experience: 'Obey, but be true to your programming.' "

Geoffrey frowned. "What use is that to a flesh-and-blood person? What programming have we, to be true to?"

"You will have to discover that for yourself, Geoffrey," Fess answered. "That is a part of what adolescence is for."

The children stared at him, trying to decide whether or not to be outraged.

Then Magnus smiled. "Yet thou didst not know this when thou didst first awake, didst thou?"

"I did not have subroutines for resolving conflicts between my program and the daily problems I encountered, no. But my program does allow for development of such subroutines."

"And thou didst form these subroutines by contemplation of the events of which thou hast but now told us, didst thou not?"

"That is an accurate statement, yes."

"Then *thou* didst have an adolescence!" Cordelia crowed.

"A period equivalent to human adolescence, yes. I am glad it pleases you to discover that, Cordelia."

"Oh, we ever seek to learn from they who have gone o'er the road before us," Magnus said airily. "From whom didst *thou* learn to resolve such conflicts as these, Fess?"

The robot was silent a moment, then said slowly, "I worked out my subroutines from principles contained in my basic program, Magnus. However, I did incorporate some concepts from one human being, who professed ideas that formed perfect loops, comparing present events to past events, enabling one to discern similarities and contrasts, and thereby judge the appropriate action to be taken."

"And that person was?"

"The leader of the fugitives."

"Thy third owner?" Magnus stared. "How came he to have so great an impact on thee?"

"Principally by the brilliance of his mind, Magnus—though he would have disclaimed such a statement. And the effects of his ideas were no doubt enhanced by his being the first of my owners to be a good human being."

"I can credit that, from what thou hast said." Magnus frowned. "Who was he, this chief fugitive, this paragon?"

"His name was Tod Tambourin, and he was scarcely a paragon, though certainly, at heart, a very good man."

"Tod Tambourin!" Cordelia stared, aghast. "Dost thou mean this 'Whitey the Wino' of whom thou hast but now told us? He who aided his granddaughter out of the agony of her parents' death?"

"The same," Fess confirmed.

Gregory frowned. "Yet how doth he come to be the namesake of that other 'Tod Tambourin' thou hast taught us of, in our schoolroom?"

"By the easiest of means—he was not the namesake, but the same man."

Geoffrey's mouth dropped open, flabbergasted. "*That* Tod Tambourin? That weakling man of pen and ink? Him whom thou dost say was the greatest poet of the Terran sphere?"

"That is not merely my opinion, children, but the consensus of Terran critics—and he was scarcely a weakling."

"Yet 'tis he whose verses thou hast made us con by heart," Geoffrey objected, "whether we would or no."

"Wast thou reluctant, then?" Magnus jibed.

Geoffrey frowned. "Not with 'The Rebels and the Admiral,' nay, nor with his 'Foc'sle Ballads.' Yet for his 'Decline and Fall of Liberty,' I've little use."

"Nor I," Cordelia agreed, "yet I shall ever treasure his 'Young Wife's Rejoicing' and 'The Dandy's Courtship.' "

"Thou wouldst," Geoffrey scoffed.

"Every person who has read his verses has a favorite, children," Fess said quickly, forestalling mayhem, "though they frequently know not who wrote them. Yes, my third owner was Tod Tambourin. He gave me as a wedding present to his granddaughter, Lona, and I have served her family ever since."

Magnus stared at Fess. "Thou dost not mean that we are of the blood of Tod Tambourin!"

"You should not be so surprised," Fess chided. "Have you not found that, when your heart is light, you cannot keep from singing?"

The children looked at one another in amazement.

"But enough now, your parents call."

"More, Fess. More of Tod Tambourin!" Cordelia pleaded. But the great horse shook his head, and led them toward Rod and Gwen, who waited under the shading tree.

4

They came up the long, winding road to the castle just as the sun slipped below the horizon—and, though they had travelled east from their home, the road had wound its way around and around up the mountain, so that, as they looked up at the castle, the sunset was behind it—a blood-red sunset, making the castle appear black and ominous, brooding above them.

Cordelia shivered. "It doth watch us, Papa."

"Just an illusion, dear." Rod squeezed her against him—to hide his own shiver. "It's the angle of view. A pile of stones can't watch—it has no eyes to see with."

"Yet it doth, Papa." Magnus's voice broke on the word, somewhat spoiling the effect of his tone—but he ignored it, frowning up at the castle with a scowl as dark as its own. "There is summat held there within those stones, that doth mark our approach."

This time Rod let go of Cordelia to hide his shiver. There might indeed be a presence in the castle—on a planet where virtually everyone was a potential esper, you couldn't rule out anything. He glanced at Geoffrey, and even his hardening warrior-child was frowning, drawn-in and truculent, glaring at the castle as though it were an attacker—and Gregory was wide-eyed and pale.

Rod turned to Gwen. "Do you feel it, too?"

Gwen nodded, gaze fixed on the castle. "There is a sense of old misery there, milord—some ancestral curse that must needs be lifted."

"Well, then, a family like ours is the one to lift it!" Rod squared his shoulders and strode ahead. "Come on, troops. How long has it been since we've found a villain who could stand up to us?"

He should have heard a cheer at his back, but he didn't. He risked a quick peek and found they were all following him, with a sense of determination that he found more unnerving than reluctance would have been.

"Are you sure this is wise, Rod?" Fess's voice said behind his ear.

Rod noticed that the robot hadn't used human thought-frequency, which meant the rest of the family probably hadn't heard. He muttered back, "Of course not, Old Iron. Has that ever stopped me before?"

The sky had darkened to dusk by the time they came up to the moat and saw just how dilapidated the castle was. A roof had fallen in, and some crenels were missing from the towers. Frost and thaw had prised several other blocks out of the northern wall, leaving a four-foot notch high at its top. As they watched, bats shot out of the northern tower and darted away into the night. Rod wondered just how much more of a ruin it would seem by day. Slowly, he said, "I don't think I want to spend the night there."

But, "Nay," Gwen said, "we must."

Rod turned to stare at her. "Spend the *night* in there? The time when unquiet spirits are most apt to roam? When we've all *felt* some wrongness there?"

"Aye, and therefore must we stand against it," she answered, eyes hard with determination, "or let the evil that it holds endure to befoul the domain that hath been given into our care."

Well, there was no way around that, Rod had to admit—they had accepted the estate that had been split off from Di Medici's lands, which meant they had assumed the responsibility for the welfare of its people. Not that they had asked for it, mind you, or wanted it—but they hadn't refused it, either. If Tuan and Catharine needed to have them take care of this parcel of land and people, why then, it was their duty to do so, as loyal liegefolk—unless they had a damn good reason not to.

Which they hadn't. "I notice the Di Medici haven't bothered de-ghosting it, no matter how long it's been in the family . . ."

"Thou hast said it; 'tis haunted." Gregory's eyes were huge.

Geoffrey gave him a contemptuous glance. "Is't such news, sin that the Puck hath told us so, and we all have felt some eldritch presence there?"

"Nay," little brother answered, "but once 'tis said, there's no unsaying it."

Geoffrey frowned, irritated, and was about to comment, but Rod stopped him with a hand on his shoulder. "It's labeling, son. It's a way of confronting our fear . . ."

"I have no fear!"

"Then you're braver than I am. And once we've put a name to that fear, we can't just walk away and pretend it never existed."

Geoffrey still frowned, but he quieted.

"And if the Di Medici have failed in their duty, what of it?" Gwen demanded. "It nonetheless falls to us."

"True," Rod admitted.

"Then the sooner we deal with it, the better."

"Oh, I wouldn't go *that* far. I'd just as soon make my first confrontation by daylight, thank you."

Gwen turned to confront *him*. "Delay will not make it cease, milord."

"No, but it'll make me feel a little better about it."

Gwen tossed her head impatiently. "Art thou so worn with travel, then, that thou canst not stand to battle?"

"Now that you mention it—yes. Or rather, I could if I had to—but no general will make his troops fight when they're tired, if he can help it. I've got an even better reason than that though."

"Which is?"

"I'm scared."

"Thou, craven?" Geoffrey bleated. "Thou canst not speak truth!"

"I do." Rod turned away, picked up a fallen branch, and began to sweep out a campsite. "And I intend to have full sunlight before I walk into that stone pile."

Geoffrey stared at him, thunderstruck, then whirled to Gwen. "Mama! Assuredly our father hath not become a coward!"

Gwen squeezed his shoulder and shook her head, but her eyes were on Rod.

Geoffrey stared, unbelieving, then whirled away to Fess. "It cannot be true! Thou, who hast known him longer than any, who hast watched o'er him from his cradle—tell me! Hath my father ever admitted to fear?"

"Frequently and regularly, Geoffrey, as he should. Only a

fool will deny being afraid. The wise man will admit his fear, at least to himself, then triumph over it.''

That brought the future hero to a frowning halt. "There is an air of sense to thy words . . .''

"He who denies his fear, even to himself, lies," Fess assured him, "and fear denied may leap out at the crucial moment, to disable you in battle.''

Magnus listened closely.

"So never hesitate to admit being afraid, Geoffrey," Fess went on, "but do not let it keep you from action.''

"Yet he doth! Even now, he doth!''

"True, and that is atypical for him," the robot agreed. "You might wish to ask him why—especially when he does it so blithely.''

Geoffrey stared at him, then whirled to his father. "Thou dost lie!''

Magnus turned, too, though more slowly.

"I do not," Rod said evenly. "I am most definitely afraid of that castle.''

Geoffrey lifted his chin. "Yet not so afeard that thou wilt not encamp in the shadow of its walls.''

"You've noticed.''

Geoffrey winced. "Be not so cruel to me, I pray! Tell me wherefore thou dost hesitate.''

Rod just gazed at him. Geoffrey twitched, but held firm.

Softly, Magnus said, "Hast thou the right to hear it, brother, when thou hast lost faith in him?''

Geoffrey seemed to loosen a little. "I did not. Not truly, I did not—I but craved a reason to keep belief.''

Rod still gazed.

Finally, Geoffrey bowed his head. "Thy pardon, sir, that I did doubt thee.''

"Why, of course," Rod said. "Question me all you wish, son, though you may not like the answer—but don't doubt me, please. I don't deserve it.''

"Nay, thou dost not," Gwen said, musing. "Yet thou couldst have been more open, husband.''

"I could, if I could have put words to it—but it took a few minutes to figure out what was bothering me. And really, it's simply this—I don't like surprises.''

"Aye!" Geoffrey cried, relieved. " 'Tis even as thou hast ever said—to march ahead unknowing is most dire folly!''

Rod nodded. "Took me a few minutes to figure that out, though, since it isn't an army we're facing. That's why I told you I was scared. Emotions are there for reasons, and when I can't figure out exactly what I'm scared about, it's wisest to stand back—if I can."

"And in this, thou canst." Gwen nodded. "There is wisdom in this, husband. Nay, let us bide without for the night, and learn what we may on the morrow." She turned to Cordelia, who had been watching very intently the whole time, taking copious mental notes. "Come, daughter. Let us prepare for the meal, and the night."

"You heard her, boys," Rod called, "pitch camp."

The light of a campfire under a tripod and cauldron, and the smell of stew, cheered their spirits considerably. Firelight flickered on their faces, Fess, and, across from him, the family tent, which had grown steadily over the years until it had become a pavilion.

"How shall we begin to discover knowledge of this castle, Papa?" Magnus asked.

"Well, your mother and I already know a little, son."

Gwen nodded. " 'Tis not so far from Runnymede that folk there would have heard naught in all these years."

"Then what thou dost know is but gossip," Gregory objected.

Gwen nodded again. "And 'tis thereby faulted—yet there's oft a kernel of truth in a rumor."

"And what doth Rumor say?" Cordelia demanded.

"First," Rod answered, "we know that the name of the castle is Foxcourt. That, I think, we can take as fact, because that's what King Tuan called it when he enfoeffed me with it."

"Doth 'enfoeffed' mean aught like to 'encumbered,' Papa?"

Rod nearly choked on his stew. He wiped his mouth and his eyes and said, "Only in this case, Delia. Usually, it just means that the King is letting the knight live there and have the income from it. It's like gaining title to a piece of land, in reward for service to the Crown."

"Yet 'tis still the Crown's?" Magnus asked.

"In theory, yes—but for all intents and purposes, it belongs to the knight who's been given seizin of it, and to his heirs."

"What doth 'given seizin' mean?" Geoffrey asked.

" 'Enfoeffed.' "

"Oh." Geoffrey frowned, puzzled.

"There are many words in our language that have meanings so similar as to be nearly the same," Gwen explained, "though there are different occasions for their employment. 'Tis why its use doth become art."

"And defeats those who would treat it as a science," Rod agreed. "However, we *are* seized of this castle and the ten miles surrounding it, which *is* our fief, whether we like it or not—so, if there are some maleficent spooks disputing its ownership, we'd better take care of them for once and for all."

"And that doth begin with its name?"

Rod shrugged. "It's a starting place. If we can find out why it was named that, we may have a start at finding out what the haunting spirit is."

"The castle's name doth sound as thou 'twas famed for its hunting."

"Aye," Gwen agreed, "the more so as 'twas the hold of a noble family."

"But they also bore the name Foxcourt," Rod objected. "They'd have had to take the name of the castle for their own, if hunting was really its source."

" 'Tis common enough, is't not?" Magnus asked. "The Earl Marshall is fully Robert Artos, Lord Marshall—yet though his family's name is 'Artos,' all do speak of him as 'Marshall.' "

"True enough, but it's been known to happen the other way just as often. 'Tudor' is our neighbor Earl's family name, but he gave it to his demesne."

"Then the family of barons who dwelt here took their name from the castle?"

"They were counts, not barons—and yes, that's my guess. But it might have worked the other way around."

Cordelia gazed up at the walls, dark against the dusky sky. "How long did they dwell here?"

"Three centuries, which means the castle's been empty for two hundred years. Tuan says the family died out then, and Di Medici left the building to rot while he administered the county through knights and reeves."

Gwen frowned. " 'Tis unlike what we know of that family, to let a castle stand when it could be invested against them."

"And just as unlike our erstwhile Duke Di Medici to let a useable strongpoint go unused, when it could be tightening his hold over his peasants." Rod nodded. "You're right—something doesn't fit."

"Canst thou tell why?" Gregory asked.

Rod shook his head. "That's all the information King Tuan gave us."

"Where shall we gain more?"

"Where do we always go?" Rod turned to Gwen. "Do we have some extra stew?"

Gwen nodded. "Nearly as much as we've eaten."

"Then let's have company over for dinner. After all, Puck recommended we consult the local authorities." Rod turned to the surrounding trees, calling, "Ye elves of hills, brooks, standing lakes, and groves! Care to take potluck? 'Tis the Lord Warlock who calls, and we'd love some company! Also some information . . ."

Cordelia's eyes shone, and she started to say something, but Gwen pressed a finger across her lips, and she subsided. Gregory watched, eyes huge, and Geoffrey fidgeted, but managed to stay quiet. Magnus tried to look bored, but failed.

Leaves stirred, then a head the size of Rod's fist poked out. "Art truly he?"

"I am, and these are my wife and children. We're all honorary elves."

"Is't as honorary as all that?" The elf missed Rod's glare, because he turned to Gwen as he scrambled to his feet and bowed. He wore hose and a jerkin of brown—bark, Rod guessed—and was almost as brown as his clothing. "We are honored that thou hast come, Lady Gwendylon. I am hight Buckthorn."

Rod breathed a sigh of relief; for a moment, he'd thought the mannikin was going to start talking about Gwen's parentage.

The boys were staring at Rod, scandalized at the lack of respect accorded him, but Rod just held up a palm and watched.

Gwen smiled and inclined her head graciously. "Nay, 'tis thou dost honor me, Old One."

"Nay, for thou art wise and good. Hast thou come, then, to heal this festering sore on our mountain?"

Gwen darted a quick glance at Rod, then turned back to the elf. "We must, for this manor is given into our stewardship. Canst thou tell us aught of its past?"

"Aye, and most gladly!"

"Then do, I prithee. Yet first, call up such of thy fellows as may wish it, to partake of our supper."

"Aye, and right happily." Buckthorn turned back to the forest and made a sort of falling whistle, like the call of a night bird. It was answered by half a dozen like him, four in hose but two in skirts, who came out of the underbrush with shy and hesitant steps, to line up in a half-circle by Buckthorn. "These," he said, "are my companions—Hazelberry and Rose, first."

The elf-wives curtsied. Hazelberry was slender and brown as the wood of her name, with a bright green leaf-cloth dress. Rose was plump and red-cheeked, with a rosy complexion and dusky pink skirt and bodice.

"These are their husbands, Bight and Burl." Buckthorn gestured toward the men. Two of them stepped forward to bow. Burl was short, scarcely more than a foot high, but almost six inches broad, with bulging muscles. Bight was tall and wiry.

"And these are the bachelors of this mountain, Loon and Gorn." Loon was slender, with a dreamer's eyes, and Gorn was so plump that Rod wondered if he moonlighted as a subordinate Claus.

"Thou art welcome to our fire, as I hope we are to thy mountain." Gwen inclined her head gravely, carefully not mentioning the matter of official ownership. "Wilt thou join us in meat?"

"Aye, and right gladly," said Gorn. All seven of them came forward and settled down cross-legged in a circle near the pot.

The juvenile Gallowglasses tracked them with huge eyes. Rod felt a thrill of pride. His children had seen elves before, but they never seemed to tire of them.

Gwen ladled a bowl full of stew and set it down in their center, then set a half-loaf of bread beside it, and another bowl of milk. The elves set to with gusto.

"We are told the family of this keep were the Counts Foxcourt," Gwen began. "Did they take their name from the manor?"

"Nay, they gave it theirs," Burl answered.

Gwen exchanged a look of surprise with Rod, then turned back. "What manner of folk were they?"

"Oh, bad folk, lady!" Hazelberry answered. "Horrid indeed, from the second Count to the last. There do be tales of the cruelties wrought upon their peasants, of the heaviness of the taxes levied, and of their delight in the floggings when folk had not the wherewithal to pay."

"And tales more foul than that," Bight said darkly, "which I will forebear to speak of, with younglings present."

"Oh, do not let us dissuade thee," Magnus urged.

"No, do," Rod contradicted with a glare at his son. "I think we can guess."

"Aye, guess worse deeds than they did," Geoffrey grumbled.

"That, I misdoubt me," Buckthorn answered. "Think whatever ill thou canst of the Foxcourts, and 'tis like to be true."

"So bad as that?" Cordelia's eyes were huge.

"So bad," the elf confirmed. "But finally came a Count who was so evil that he flouted even his duty to his family, and would not wed, though he did force his attentions on every woman who came his way."

" 'Force his attentions?' " Gregory looked up at his father.

"Later, son—in about ten years. So he had no legitimate son to inherit the title?"

"He did not."

"Were there no cousins who could take it up?" Gwen asked.

"Aye, there were two cadet branches of the line," Gorn answered, "yet both had removed to other dukedoms, and pledged their swords to county lords, thereby retaining knighthood; and both cast off the decadence of their sires."

" 'Twas not all of a moment, look you," Bight added. "The first knight, we are told, did keep faith with his lord, serve bravely in battle, and deal fairly with his peasants, though harshly. Their sons did leave off swilling of ale and despoiling of women, and the grandsons were as good as any knight, and better."

Buckthorn nodded, munching. "They had even become beloved by their serfs and tenants."

"Very impressive." Rod nodded. "So what happened after they took over the estate?"

"Naught, for they did not," Buckthorn said.

Rod let out a long whistle. "*That* bad? Two families turned down the chance for a noble title and estates, just because of the castle's reputation?"

Bight nodded somberly.

"What kind of closet skeletons could make a family refuse a title?"

"Any, an they walked." Magnus scowled. "Is not a haunting reason enough to deny inheritance?"

"No, not really. I know of quite a few families that cohabited very companionably with ghosts, or at least ignored them—the family manor house was so important to them that they were willing to share it with a few of their ancestors who were a little reluctant to move out. In fact, there was a time when the *nouveau riche* began to try to buy family ghosts to go with their fabricated coats of arms. I understand a real rage for that kind of thing hit my home, ah, 'land,' really hard, about four hundred years ago. One of my ancestors even pioneered a new fad in holograms."

Magnus glanced up at Fess, but the robot carefully ignored him.

"So family ghosts, just by themselves, wouldn't account for having turned down the title," Rod finished.

"Unless 'twas a truly vile haunting," Gwen demurred.

Rod nodded. "There had to be something especially rotten about the last Count Foxcourt, or his household."

"I assure thee, there was," Hazelberry said. "Name a vice or debauchery, and he did practice it."

"Yeah, but that wouldn't . . ." Rod's voice trailed off as he remembered some of the tales he'd heard about sadists. "No, strike that. I *can* think of some sins that would give the castle such an aura of evil that no one would want it, even with a title."

"Most truly," Rose agreed.

"And no one would want to take up the name." Rod frowned. "We were wondering about that part. I mean, 'Foxcourt' isn't your garden variety kind of nomer, after all. Was the manor known for its good hunting?"

"Nay," said Buckthorn. "There was some hunting, though no better than most—and the knights generally did course after boar, not fox."

"Or peasants," Burl added darkly.

Cordelia shuddered, Gregory blanched, and Magnus and Geoffrey grew somber.

Rod tried to bypass the reference. "Can't have been the source of the name, then."

"Nay," Buckthorn agreed. "Word hath come down from the first elves who dwelt here, that the name of this family was first spelled in a fashion far more elaborate."

"Aye, and spoken with a haughty accent," Bight seconded, "wherefore both we, and the peasants, were the more ready to bring it down to earth and pronounce it simply as 'Foxcourt.' "

All the elves nodded, and Rose added, "By the third generation, the family had taken our spelling of it, and by the fifth, all had forgotten any other."

"Hm." Rod frowned. "Makes it tough to find the original."

"Thou canst not," Buckthorn assured him. " 'Tis lost for all time."

Behind Rod's ear, Fess's voice said, "That is a challenge."

Rod agreed. The original spelling of the name had to be recorded somewhere in the Lord Chancellor's books—antique tax records, or maybe even the original deed to the property. It probably had nothing to do with the haunting, but Rod resolved to find it.

The guests had departed, filled with stew and emptied of gossip—after all, they'd been waiting two hundred years to tell it—and Gwen had decreed bedtime. Rod had mentioned to Fess that keeping a watch might be a good idea, and the Steel Sentry had taken up his post, right next to the children.

Which made him handy for bedtime stories, especially since the children were so keyed up that sleeping was the least possible activity for them. Quarreling ranked high on their list, though, with fighting right behind it, so Fess was watching for more than ghosts.

Not that they were out of line yet, of course. They were just barely bedding down.

" 'Tis a foul and brooding pile," Geoffrey gloated. "Nay, who doth know what deeds of glory a valiant man might achieve within it?"

"Naught, an he doth run at the sight of a spectre," Magnus answered.

"Thou dost not say I would run!"

"Thou hast it; I did not. For myself, I *know* I shall stand fast."

"Aye, transfixed in horror!"

"Boys, boys," Fess reproved. "You are both brave and bold, as you have proved many times."

"Yet I am not." Gregory's eyes were wide, and his blanket was drawn up to his chin. "Thou wilt not allow a spectre to approach, wilt thou, Fess?"

"Pooh!" Magnus said quickly. "Thou hast as much courage as any man, when the fight's upon us."

"Well—mayhap when 'tis come." Gregory relaxed a little, reddening with pleasure. "Yet 'til then, I do wallow in horror."

"I, for one, think 'tis grand." Cordelia snuggled down into her blankets. "Ghost or no, 'twill be thrilling to live in a castle. Will it not, Fess?"

"I cannot truly say so," Fess answered slowly.

"Wherefore?" Cordelia frowned. "What canst thou foresee disliking in it?"

"I look not to the future, Cordelia, but to the past."

"Thou hast lived in a castle?" Cordelia sat bolt-upright.

"Down," Gwen's voice called softly, and the girl flopped back down with a flounce.

"I helped build one, Cordelia," Fess answered, "and I dwelt in it while we were building it, and after it was completed."

"Who was 'we?'" Geoffrey rolled over on his stomach and propped his chin in his hands.

"The first d'Armands, Geoffrey—your ancestor Dar, and his wife Lona."

"Dar?" Cordelia frowned. "Him of whom we have heard, as Dar Mandra? Papa's ancestor who was pursued by his enemies?"

"The same—though, since he and Lona had gone into hiding, he amalgamated his two names and inserted an apostrophe, then trimmed the end to make it 'd'Armand.' Yet he kept his surname, though he reversed the phonemes when naming his son."

"Dar d'Armand?" Magnus frowned. " 'Tis not greatly euphonious."

"No, but it was practical."

"He was thy fourth owner, was he not?" Gregory chimed in.

"It was Lona who was officially my owner, Gregory, though in practice, they both were, the more so since I was Dar's only companion for long stretches of time."

"His only companion?" Cordelia frowned. "Were they not wed?"

"They were, but they were also a manufacturing concern. There was little else to do on Maxima—the asteroid they chose to live on—but they chose it because it offered that opportunity for making a living . . ."

5

"DAMN! It doesn't work!" Dar sat back and glared at the chipped enamel on the robot's claws. "What happened, X-HB-9?"

"I did just as you said, sir," the little robot answered. In size and shape, it resembled nothing so much as a cannister vaccum cleaner—but one with jointed arms extruded from the top.

"All I said was to go into the kitchen and take the breakfast tray out of the autochef!"

"I did, sir, but my clamps encountered a solid vertical instead of a vacant space."

"They sure did." Dar had heard the clang all the way to the bedroom. Not that he'd been sleeping, of course; after all, it was 1:00 P.M.—Terran Standard Time; if they'd gone by local Maxima time, they would have had a noon and a midnight four times a day, and sometimes five. Maxima was big, as asteroids go, almost a kilometer and a half in diameter, but it was still miniscule on the planetary scale.

So why was a robot delivering breakfast in bed? Purely a trial run, with an imitation breakfast. Food was too scarce to waste on a simulation.

And if this was a trial, X-HB-9 was doomed. Dar frowned. "But I don't understand. All you had to do was wait until the door was open. Fess!"

"Yes, Dar?" A humanoid robot stepped into the room. His head was a stainless steel sphere with binocular lenses, an audio pickup, and a loudspeaker, positioned in a rough semblance of a human face. His body was a flattened tube, big enough to have some storage capacity for tools and spare components; his arms and legs were sections of pipe with universal joints. His gait was a bit awkward, like that of a gangly adolescent.

"What did you see in the kitchen?"

83

"X-HB-9 came up to the autochef, waited for its chime, then reached up to crash into the door. The enamel on the autochef is chipped, too."

Dar sighed. "One more fix-up for me to get to. Damn! This whole shelter's put together with chewing gum and baling wire!"

"It is still more salubrious than a PEST prison, Dar—especially when you consider that no one is torturing you to reveal psionic powers that you do not have."

"Yeah, but it doesn't work! Why didn't the autochef open its door?"

"Because X-HB-9 has no provision for cueing it to do so."

Dar lifted his head slowly, eyes widening. "Of course! Why didn't I think of that?"

Fess tactfully forebore to comment; from contextual analysis, it could tell Dar's question was rhetorical.

"I was so chirpy about getting the take-out-the-tray part of the program right, that I forgot to program X-HB-9 to open the door!" Dar slapped his forehead with the heel of his hand. "All these details that I keep overlooking. Where the hell is Lona, anyway?"

Fess was unexpectedly silent.

"No, no!" Dar said quickly. "The PEST immigration authorities might trace the radio signal. Don't try to contact her."

"I am merely attempting an extrapolation of her activities, based on past records, Dar."

"Back when you used to take her there, you mean." It still rankled that Lona had only started leaving Fess with Dar after she had made herself a new guidance computer that did even better piloting than Fess had.

"After all, he's just a general purpose robot," she had explained. "GAP is built to do guidance and piloting only—of *course* he's better at it! And I really do need a specialist. PEST has tightened security around Terra again, and it takes some very careful astrogating to slip through their net."

"No argument." Dar held up a hand. "The important thing about sending you away, is to get you back. Just seems kind of poor of you to dump good old Fess just because you've got a new one."

"Oh, he won't mind. He really won't, Dar—he's a machine. You keep forgetting that. Computers are just machines; they don't really think, and they don't have feelings.''

"I know, I know! It's just that . . . well . . . I wouldn't have expected it of you, that's all.''

"But you shouldn't care.'' Lona swayed a little closer. "Or do you identify with him, darling? You shouldn't, you know.''

"Yeah. After all, *I* never get to go to Terra with you, at all.''

"But you did—vicariously. As long as I was taking Fess with me. And now you're feeling rejected. Is that it?''

"What *can* I feel, when you keep going off and leaving me? I know, I know, you don't have any choice—but you don't have to be so damned happy about it.''

"Poor darling.'' The sway turned into a snuggle. "I know you feel left out—but honestly, it wouldn't make sense to put us both into danger of being arrested, and I'm the one who has the contacts.''

"You didn't, the first time you went.''

"No, I had one—Lari Plandor.''

Dar felt a stab of jealousy. "Yes, just a close friend left over from your college days.''

"And that's all he ever was, too. Mind you, I'm not saying he didn't want to be more—but *I* didn't.''

"Yeah, I know. And you didn't want to be cruel, so you stayed friendly. Aloof, but friendly.''

"Yes, and it came in handy when we decided to start up our own business. A friend in the purchasing department of Amalgamated Automatons was just what we needed.''

"Still do, I suppose,'' Dar sighed. "And are you still aloof to him?''

"Well, I can't be, now, can I? When I'm trying to get him to place an order for a thousand new components. I mean, I have to be a little warmer.''

"Just so long as you don't get him fired up.'' But Dar felt his stomach sinking; how could any man *not* get fired up when he looked at Lona?

"*I* can't control what he feels.''

The hell she couldn't. "Let me amend that—'just so long as you don't get interested in him.' ''

"Silly! Do you really think I could feel amorous with anybody but you?''

Do lady kangaroos have pockets? Dar carefully noted that she had avoided the direct answer. "What've I got that he hasn't got?"

"Me," Lona answered. "All my clients have are my order forms. After all, I don't feel toward them the way I feel toward you."

"Oh? And how do you feel toward me?"

"I'm in love with you," she murmured as her lips met his, and her body curved into his.

Dar shook his head with a sigh—it had been a wonderful way to say "good-bye." He couldn't understand his luck—her clients had status, wealth, influence, sophistication, looks—but, true to her word, he had her.

On the other hand, two hours later, she'd been space-borne again, heading for Terra—and he'd stayed here to watch the factory, with her discarded robot. It still rankled.

But not too much—it had been very lonely whenever she had taken off for the fleshpots of Terra, and Fess was good company.

Fleshpots—the thought sent a shiver through Dar. What was she up to, down there in Sin City? Which, as far as he was concerned, meant the whole planet. What was she up to, and how many times had she been unfaithful to him?

Not that it mattered. Or at least, he knew it wouldn't when he saw her again, live and vibrant, before him. She always came home with stars in her eyes and contracts in her hands. So who was he to criticize?

"Her husband, that's who," he muttered.

"Not officially," Fess corrected.

"Does it matter?"

"Certainly. Your current status is only that of business partners."

"Yeah, business partners who've been living together for seven years!"

"Still, that is only a matter of convenience and mutual pleasure," Fess said primly. "Neither of you is legally bound to the other."

"Well, fine. You talk about the legalities, but I have to live with the actualities."

"You are free to leave, Dar."

"Yeah, and she keeps all the patents." But Dar knew that was only the smallest part of it.

"You have become so skilled an engineer that you could earn a living anywhere in inhabited space, Dar."

"Yeah, but *she* wouldn't be there." Fess wouldn't say it, but Dar knew he had a problem with his self-image. It resembled nothing so much as a large, multicolored lollipop. "Come on. If I'm such a hotshot engineer, I gotta be able to figure out how to make a simple little housecleaner deliver breakfast, don't I?"

"Yes, Dar. After that we can move on to the really interesting program—enabling it to wash windows."

Dar thought of the chipped enamel and shuddered. He glanced at the skylight. "Well, we've got time—a good two hours till the next sunrise. Come on, X-HB-9." He headed for the shop.

They finished the next (successful) test just as the first ray of sunrise fingered the skylight dome. Dar looked up at it, swallowed his toast (well, it had been time for tea), and said, "Go stand in the corner, X-HB-9."

"Yes, sir." The little cannister turned, rolled over to the corner, plugged itself in to recharge, and went immobile.

"I'll meet you at the airlock," Dar called. He took a last swallow of tea, wiped the cup, dropped it into the dishwasher, and headed for his pressure suit.

He suited up, checked his seals, stepped into the airlock, and floated. The hatch closed automatically behind him, but he had to grab a handhold with his right while he spun the locking wheel with his left, or he would have gone spinning away in the other direction. As the air hissed back into its storage tank, he allowed himself a glow of self-satisfaction; he'd been wise to insist on not having artificial gravity under the airlock, so that he could get used to weightlessness before he stepped out onto the surface. Dar's enduring nightmare was a breakdown in the gravity plates.

On the other hand, he wouldn't have to worry about falling. No, strike that—in weightlessness, he was *always* falling. He just didn't have to worry about the sudden stop at the end. Of course, he was good at landing—he tripped a lot, and had learned how to hit safely, if not softly—but he didn't like it much.

Fess was waiting for him just outside the airlock, one more sharp-angled piece of rock in a surreal landscape of glaring light and total shadow. "Visual inspection, please," Dar requested.

"No leaks in evidence," the robot answered as Dar turned slowly, changing hands on the grab-handle next to the hatch. "All seals appear intact. Good manners are not necessary when dealing with a robot, Dar."

"Yeah, but if I neglect them, I'll get out of the habit of using them, and I'll start being rude to people. Can't afford that, Fess—I need every friend I've got, especially when there are only two hundred fifty-six of us on Maxima. Come on, let's see how the cutter's been doing the last three hours." He clipped his safety lead to the guide wire and pushed off toward the north side.

The robot rock-cutter had produced another forty blocks during the three-hour night.

"Well, production's up to standard." Dar looked back over the cutter's trail. "Just wish we could afford another one."

"That would be desirable, Dar, but it would push the limits of our power output. Slagging requires sixty percent of our reactor's capacity, and the crane and factory require the rest."

"So we could buy a bigger power plant." Dar glanced at the cable running from the crane off to the reactor, dug into the foot of an outcrop a hundred meters from the house. "Then we wouldn't have to depend on the solar-cell screens for the household."

"You should be able to afford one in the not too distant future, Dar."

"How far is 'not too distant'?" Dar growled.

"Only four years now," Lona had answered. "Our ship will come in, Dar. You'll see."

"Yeah, but will it be a tug or a freighter?"

"A freighter." Lona raised a hand as though she were being sworn in. "Cross my heart."

"Okay." Dar reached for her.

"Not yet, naughty." Lona slapped his hand away. "I have work to do first."

"I take a lot of doing," Dar suggested.

"Braggart. Next thing I know, you'll tell me you do a lot of taking."

"Well, as a matter of fact . . ."

"Don't try." She pressed a finger over his lips. "Any teacher who really does his job, doesn't qualify as a taker."

"I stopped teaching six years ago."

"Only because the sheriff was after you. You'd open school here, if there were any children."

"That's a vile canard; there are fourteen children."

"Yes, but the oldest is only four."

"Well, I specialized in adult education, anyway. Is it *my* fault nobody here has less than a B.S.? Except me . . ."

"A B.A. will do quite well, thank you. Expecially since you've learned enough about engineering to qualify for the other bachelor's anyway."

"Yeah, but I was only interested in the bachelor girl."

"So I was a great motivational device." Lona shrugged impatiently. "You're the one who did the learning."

"Yeah, but you did the teaching."

"Me and a small library. You've even learned enough not to be afraid of the reactor."

"Oh, I wouldn't say that." Dar turned to look out the port at the outcrop where he had just finished burying the power plant. "Intellectually, I know no radiation can get out of that plasma bottle—but emotionally, I still want it as far away from me as I can get it."

"Well, you're only human." Lona came up behind him, slipped her arms under his, and began to trace geometrical figures on his chest.

"Of course, five hundred meters wouldn't do any good if it blew. We'd still be right inside the fireball."

Her hands stilled. "You know it can't blow up, though."

"Yeah, my mind knows it, but my stomach doesn't."

"If anything did go wrong enough to make the plasma bottle collapse, there wouldn't be anything to hold the hydrogen in, so the fusion reaction would stop."

"I know, I know. I just don't like the feeling of living next door to a hydrogen bomb, even if it *is* in a bottle. I keep thinking about what happened when they broke the seal and let the genie out."

"Well, this is one genie that isn't going anywhere, and in the meantime, it's going to make all your wishes come true."

"Is that why we need a bigger genie?"

"Of course. That's the only way this one can fulfill your

more extravagant hopes—by calling in his big brother.'' Her hands began moving again.

Dar held still, trying to let the sensation wash through every inch of himself. ''What do you think you're doing—rubbing the lamp?''

''All right, so I have designs on you. I told you I have to leave for Terra tomorrow, didn't I?''

''Yeah, but you promised to make today worthwhile.''

''Then *carpe diem.*''

''I thought I'd done enough carping.'' Dar turned around, reaching out. ''And the moment is not what I wanted to seize.''

She had, though. He could have sworn she had—she'd led him on into a place where time slowed down, and he could have sworn the climactic moment lasted for an hour. He blew out a long breath and gave his head a shake, remembering.

''May I remind you of the project at hand, Dar?''

''Huh?'' He looked up to see Fess's rod-and-cannister body silhouetted against stark, jagged rocks, and wrenched himself back into reality and the present. ''Just letting my mind wander for a minute.''

''I am concerned for your safety while you are operating the crane, Dar.''

''Don't worry, I'll turn on the radio.''

''There is no real reason for you to assist. I am perfectly capable of building the wall.''

''Yeah, but if I do, too, it'll take half the time.''

''You are needed to supervise the factory.''

''So what's to see? I checked the automatons just before tea break, Fess. They were in fine shape, as always, and the alarm will sound if anything goes wrong.''

''Quality control . . .''

''I'll check the monitor at triple-speed and run the other checks in the morning. Come on—time to throw stones.'' Dar pushed gently against the rock and glided to the crane, unhitched his safety line while he held onto its grab-handle, hitched onto it, and climbed in.

''You do not yet live in a glass house, Dar,'' Fess's voice said in his earphones.

''Then I'd better toss rocks while I can. And the house *is* glass, on the outside, after we get done slagging it. Or at least obsidian—and if it's not, it's too close to tell.'' He powered up the crane, checked its water level, turned up the hold-down jets, and retracted the anchor. Then he dipped the arm, lifted a block of stone in its tongs, and turned to trundle over to the wall of the house.

Fess was there before him, fitting a block onto the top of the wall, interlocking it into the corner beside it. He stepped back. "Clear, Dar."

"Going in." Dar eased the crane forward and lowered his block into place. Nothing another robot couldn't have done, of course—but one more brain in the crane meant one less they could sell to a company on Terra. It was cheaper for Dar to do the guiding himself, boring as it might be.

As he trundled away, Fess came up with his next block— and so it went, the two of them taking turns for an hour and a half, as the wall grew higher and higher.

Eventually, Fess said, "Midday, Dar."

"Gotcha." Dar threw the crane into neutral and glanced back at the cutter. "Timed out just right; it's only three blocks ahead of us. Okay, faithful worker—let's slag."

"I shall assume a discreet distance, Dar."

"Please do." Dar turned the crane to face away from the wall, turned his seat around, and took hold of the torch's controls.

"Good thing we've got a decent water supply on this asteroid." He pressed the ON patch for the big laser.

"I believe that was one of the factors in the founders' selection of Maxima as a dwelling place, Dar."

"Yeah. It wasn't for aesthetic factors, that's for sure."

"That statement is debatable, Dar. I find great satisfaction in contemplation of the mathematical interrelationships of the landforms in our vicinity."

"I'd *like* to say it's the kind of vista only a robot could love—but I know that some of our more eminent members think this stark, harshly lit landscape is the epitome of beauty."

"It is not your aesthetic ideal, though, Dar."

"No." A brief vision of Lona flashed before his mind's eye. "My notion of beauty runs more to curves than to planes." He felt a surge of frustration-charged irritation, knew it for what it was, and tried to quell it. "Come on, let's spit."

All the meters were in the green—at least, he knew it was green, though it looked more like charcoal gray, between the glaring sunlight and the filter in his faceplate. He thumbed the pressure point at the top of the handle, and a bolt of coherent light stabbed out at the wall, searing the shadows and darkening his faceplate. He yelled for the sheer joy of it and moved the beam slowly back and forth over the rocks he'd just been stacking, watching the cold rock glow red, then begin to flow. He panned the beam over to the next area, and the stone congealed as the beam left it, glowing an angry ruby, darkening as it cooled.

Off to his right, Fess's laser seared the adjacent wall.

They kept it up until sunset forced them to stop, darkness hiding their target; the laser beam lit only the stone it was currently melting.

Dar shut down his systems and climbed down from the crane, feeling stiff but satisfied, recognizing the sublimation involved, but happy about it anyway. He went toward the new wall.

"Please be careful, Dar," Fess reminded him.

"Don't worry, I'm not stupid enough to touch it." In fact, Dar stopped a good five feet away from the wall. Without air, there was no possibility of the heat reaching out to him—but he was planet-born, and inbred caution held him back. He could admire his handiwork, though, by the light of his headlamp—the first section had cooled into darkness now. It was a great effect—a towering wall of wax left too near the fire, melted into drips and runnels. He stepped back, then remembered what tripping and falling might do to a pressure suit and turned away, stalking off fifty meters before he turned back to take in the whole of the shelter he and Fess were building.

"It is good to take pride in your handiwork, Dar."

"Thanks." Dar grinned. "Though I wasn't about to squelch the feeling, Fess—I'm not *that* much of a Puritan."

Fess didn't respond.

"Besides, it's not my design—though I can't see why Lona wants another room for the factory. We can just barely sell the dozen brains we make in a month, as it is." Dar cocked his head to the side. "But I think I'm beginning to see the effect she's trying for, now."

He was silent long enough so that Fess prompted him: "And that effect is?"

"A castle." Dar turned away. "Not that she doesn't deserve it—but she also doesn't have to let everybody know."

The call light on the console was blinking as Dar stepped in from the airlock. He pulled his suit open just enough to tilt back the helmet as he stepped over to punch for playback. The comm screen lit up with the face of Maxima's Director of Imports. He knew Myrtle was plain, as women go, but she looked very attractive at the moment. Dar remembered his vision of Lona, and realized how much too long she'd been away.

"Shipment coming in, Dar," Myrtle's face said. "A miner's trying to make a few kwahers on his way back out from Ceres. He's bringing in the usual mixed bag—silicon, metals, and replacement parts. If you're interested, he'll be opening shop about 1600. 'Bye, now." She favored him with her favorite sheep's eyes just before the screen went dark.

"She'll never stop," Dar sighed. "I swear that woman has given me the best leers of her life."

"No doubt because she is certain it is safe to do so," Fess assured him. "Will you go, Dar?"

"Are you kidding? We've only got a month's supply of pure silicon left! And the aluminum and gold are getting low, too." Dar stripped off his suit in a hurry and hung it on its peg in passing, heading for the shower.

"You could buy a smelter," Fess reminded him, "and buy raw minerals much more cheaply, from the local miners."

His answer was a blast of water-noise—Dar preferred the sensation of spray to the admittedly quicker supersonic vibration that shook dirt loose; and why not use water, when it was only going to be purified and fed into the fusion reactor, anyway? His voice rose above the burble. "Don't trust 'em, Fess. The big one on Ceres does a better job than any home bottle could do—and I can buy an awful lot of pure minerals for what a smelter would cost."

Besides, with his own furnace, he wouldn't have as many occasions to go into town and see other people.

Dar headed out a half-hour later, cleansed, depilated, and annointed, with a hot meal in his belly and Lona's shopping list in his pocket. He knew well enough what they were low on, of course, but she always hit a few things he wouldn't have thought of. He had to admit she was more experienced at shopping.

Of course, it could also be that she knew more about building and programming computers.

"No question there," he said, holding up a hand and closing his eyes. "I defer to your superior wisdom." It was galling to have to admit it, but he did. "I scarcely know how to grow rock candy, let alone a molecular circuit."

"But there's nothing to it," she'd said. "You see, this little sawtoothed line means a resistor, and the number over it tells you how many ohms it has to be."

Dar frowned and peered over her shoulder.

"The paper," she reminded him.

"I *am* looking at the paper."

"But I want you to concentrate, too." Lona pushed her chair aside so that the schematic was between them. "And these parallel lines show a capacitor."

"But how do I tell how many ohms the resistor is? The real one, I mean, not the one in the drawing."

"It's printed on the side of the box."

"Yeah, but we're talking about me being able to make sure the robots are using the right ones. What if the wrong number gets stamped on the side? Or if it's the right number, but a stray resistor is in there with the wrong number of ohms?"

"Hm." Her brow knit (she had a very pretty frown, Dar thought). "That *is* a good point, my love. So that's why Mama taught me how to read the color code."

"Color code?"

"Yes. You see how each of these rings painted on the resistor has a different color? Well, each color is equivalent to a number . . ."

And so it had gone—electronics, chemistry, particle physics, with Lona always impatient, always trying to breeze past and hit only the points absolutely necessary for the job, and Dar always doggedly pulling her back to the part she'd skipped, knowing that if he didn't keep asking "Why?" it wouldn't be very long before he wouldn't understand what she was talking about.

When you're trying to learn, it helps being a teacher.

She'd taught him enough to be able to supervise the factory, which meant that he knew how to do every job himself, if he had to—but he still didn't know enough to plan a job,

and certainly couldn't have designed anything more compli-
cated than an autobar. He was studying whenever he could,
of course—and she'd been delighted, when she had come
home from that third trip to Terra and had found the hard
copy sitting out on his desk . . .

"Dar! You've been studying!"

"Huh?" Dar had looked around in panic. "I won't do it
again! I promise!"

"No, do!" Lona bent over to look more closely, and Dar
had a dizzy spell. "It's about wave propagation!"

Dar glanced at his desk, irritated; waves were the last thing
he'd wanted to propagate, just then. "Well, sure. I promised
you I'd learn enough to run the factory, remember?"

"But I already taught you enough for that. This is above
and beyond the call—and it's all on your own! Oh, you
wonderful man!" And she turned to him, hauling his face up
to hers for a kiss that was so deep and dazzling that he began
to think maybe he was pretty wonderful, after all.

When she let him up for air, he gasped, "You keep that
up, and I'll have to study all the time."

She did it again, then propped him up before he could slide
to the floor. "All right, I'm keeping it up—and you! So start
studying. Even when I'm around. Why didn't you before?"

"Uh . . ." Dar bit his lip. "Well, uh . . . I kinda thought
you might feel like I was, uh . . ."

"Poaching on my territory?" She shook her head (her hair
bounced so prettily when she did that!), eyes shining up at
him. "Knowledge is free, sweetheart—or at least, the price is
limited to how much studying you're willing to do to gain it.
And the more you know, the prouder I am to be with you."
Then she'd co-opted his lips again, to show just what form
her pride took.

Well, she was body-proud, Dar reflected—and had a perfect right to be. She'd sure given him reason to keep his nose
in the books when she was gone. He'd learned calculus and
was beginning on some of the more esoteric branches of
mathematics, and was almost up to date on wave mechanics—
but that still left an awful lot he didn't know: circuitry,
information theory, particle physics . . . "I wonder if I'll
ever be able to learn it faster than the scientists are developing
the knowledge," he wondered aloud.

"That is possible, Dar." Fess lay in the cargo hold, his

computer plugged into the car's controls. "The rate of new discoveries is slowing down, on Terra. There are as many articles published as ever, but they are increasingly derivative. The number of original concepts published and tested declines every year."

Dar frowned. "Odd, that. I'd heard the universities were graduating more Ph.D.s than ever."

"True, Dar, but they no longer require truly original work for their dissertations. Nor will they—bureaucracy tends toward stability, and truly new ideas can upset that stability."

"Well, the Proletarian Eclectic State of Terra *is* bureaucratic." Dar frowned. "But its most prominent characteristic is that it's one of the tightest totalitarian governments ever seen. I thought dictatorships *wanted* research, to give them new and better weapons."

"Only if there is an enemy who threatens the dictator's rule, Dar—and PEST has no rivals for the government of the Terran Sphere, at the moment. Such weapons research as is done, is only a seeking after new applications of existing principles. A dictatorship does not encourage the discovery of new ideas."

"I can understand their viewpoint; I'm a little reluctant to try coming up with new ideas, myself."

"That is only because you know enough to know how little you know."

"In which case, I'll probably never outgrow it. Still, I'll be glad when I've learned enough to understand why Lona tells me to do something a certain way. It'd be nice to know what I'm doing, instead of just following her directions blindly."

"That will boost your self-esteem, Dar, perhaps to the point of developing the occasional idea or two, yourself."

Dar shuddered. "Please! I want to court Lona, not disaster. I'm not about to start trying to do things my own way for a long time, yet."

"I think you have Lona on a bit of a pedestal, Dar."

"No, I'm only awed by her knowledge. Well, maybe by her business instincts, too. All of her instincts, in fact . . ."

He stifled the thought. *Later, boy,* he told himself sternly. *When she comes home. Let's keep to the business at hand here.*

Unfortunate turn of phrase.

"Your attention is drifting again, Dar."

"That's why I've got a robot pilot." But Dar reluctantly hauled his mind back to business. "In the meantime, if I don't follow Lona's instructions to the letter, our little five-robot factory will break down or start producing defective computers."

"True, Dar, and you will start losing sales."

Dar nodded. "No sales means no money—and on Maxima, no money means no food."

"That statement is true in any civilized society, Dar."

"True. But on an asteroid, 'no money' also means no water after we finish mining the ice on our own homestead— and there're only two pockets left, scarcely ten years' supply. And no water means no oxygen to breathe, and no hydrogen for fusion, which means no electricity."

"True—and, though our airproofing is very good, there is always a slight loss from day to day."

"Yes, and 'No money' also means no nitrogen or trace gases for the atmosphere, and no replacement parts for the life-support machinery. 'No money, no life,' as the Chinese say."

"I do not think Maxima is in any economic danger, though, Dar."

"Not as a whole, no." Dar gazed at the Ngoyas' house, off in the distance. It was a French chateau that could have rivaled Versailles. In fact, it was a copy of Versailles, on a smaller scale (but not much smaller). "The Ngoyas don't seem to be doing too badly. Of course, their factory is almost as big as their house, now." He could see its skylights poking above the ground behind the mansion. (That was the nice thing about ice pockets—when you mined them out, you had great underground chambers for automated machinery). "Their sales have to be over a million therms a year."

"One million three hundred sixty-eight thousand, Dar. It is a matter of public record."

"Which means our income is, too." Dar winced. "No wonder they're being patronizing toward us."

"I still believe that to be primarily a matter of your perception, Dar. An analysis of speech patterns and facial expressions does not reveal any such attitude in any of your neighbors but the Laurentians, the Mulhearns, and the Bolwheels."

"Those are definitely the worst of them, yes." Dar watched a small mountain of a house come into view. "There's the

Mulhearns' palace, now.'' It was Buckingham Palace, in fact—
the Maximans were not shy in their pretensions. ''Remind me
to try to stay away from them.''

''If you insist, Dar, though they are relatively harmless.''

''Which means they won't harm me, if I don't come near
them. Oh, don't worry, I won't insult them. They *are* human,
after all.''

''You must not sneer at your neighbors, Dar, if you plan to
co-exist with them.''

''Come on, Fess! You know I get along okay with most of
'em. I just don't particularly have a yen to build a palace in
a vacuum, that's all.''

''But you would, if you could surround it with atmosphere
and a grassy park?''

''Well, maybe.'' Dar frowned. ''There must be some way
to enclose those mansions. Maybe if we built underground . . .''

Fess made a buzzing noise, the robotic equivalent of clearing his throat.

Dar looked up sharply, startled. ''Was I drifting again?''

''Yes, Dar, and such speculation is to be encouraged—but
within the context of the present discussion, I would like to
point out that you are not entirely out of sympathy with the
pretensions of your technocratic fellows.''

''Well, maybe a little.'' Dar frowned. ''But then, I'm only
skilled labor so far.''

''Yes, and you have not yet begun your own dynasty.''

The simple thought of offspring made Dar's head whirl.

''Town'' was a cluster of one-story basalt buildings in three
concentric circles; at their hub was a spaceport. The structures
were almost all shops—ship repair, retail import/export, and
recreation. There was even a small hotel mixed in with the
three bars, but it was only for genuine lodging. The good
citizens of Maxima were all engineers, scientists, program-
mers, and other high-tech workers; none of the women had
the time, or the need, to be prostitutes. They had also been
very successful in keeping professionals from moving in; the
last entrepreneur who had tried it had been chained to a desk
with a computer terminal which was hooked to an autochef.
The 'chef wouldn't supply food unless the prisoner took, and
passed, a computerized exam.

She dug in her heels and maintained the pride of her

calling—but after three days of nothing but water, she caved in and learned how to study. A "C" in a basic algebra lesson won her a bowl of chili and a glass of milk. Thus fortified, she plowed ahead through history, algebra, plane geometry, basic chemistry, and a survey of Terran literature, working her way up to pot roast and stringbeans. By the end of three months, she had saddle sores and a high school diploma, at which point she was released from durance vile and packed aboard the next Ceres-bound burro-boat. She spread the word, and Maxima rarely had trouble with women in her line again. She, however, had come back five years later and applied for a job. She turned out to have a talent for organization and was currently coordinating the import-export trade.

"You know," Dar said, as he watched the blocks of the town grow, "these people haven't done all that badly, in some ways."

"Their concern for their offspring has moved them to altruism," Fess agreed. "I would ask you to bear that in mind when you talk to them."

"Oh, I'll be nice," Dar growled. In actuality, he could hardly wait. Living human beings . . . !

Fess slowed the car, banking it around to point it toward the largest building in town, and Dar tensed, not wanting to say anything—in fact, definitely *not* wanting to say anything, to give Fess one less datum to process. He was ready, though. Sometimes it happened, sometimes it didn't.

The comm screen crackled into life. "Dar, if you're coming, you'd better . . ."

The screen went black, and the instrument panel went dead. The car dropped like a rock.

Dar slapped the manual override, and the instrument panel glowed to life again. He brought the car down in front of the port, as the commscreen showed Myrtle finishing saying, ". . . stuff will be gone," and faded from sight.

Dar cut the power, sighed, and lifted the floor plate that gave him access to the prone robot. He pushed the circuit breaker at the base of Fess's "brain," and waited.

"Wwhhhaddtt . . . DDddaarrrr . . . whhhhadddttt . . ."

"You had a seizure," Dar explained gently. "You were coping just fine with the landing, but Myrtle came on the air to tell me to hurry up, and the extra item of processing overloaded your weak capacitor."

"AAAiiii . . . ammmm . . . verrry . . ."

"Nothing to be sorry about, *mon vieux*," Dar said quickly. "Just keep practicing your meditation exercises, eh? Concentration does it! Lona assured us that's how to control it."

"Iii . . . willl . . . attemmptt . . . it."

"Good. Have a good rest, now." Dar climbed out of the car, making a mental note to try to figure out some way to accelerate Fess's recoveries. He chained his car to the pylon alongside a score of other cars, all of them newer and fancier. Not that he, or any of his neighbors, doubted anyone's honesty—but with the gravity so low, the cars might easily drift away. He turned to survey the row of pylons that curved around the great dome of the meeting hall. It was a very gay display, all colors of the rainbow, with sweeping fins and airscoops and baroque ornamentation—all of it perfectly non-functional, of course; how much good could airscoops be in vaccum?

They could look nice. And they did. And by looking nice, they proclaimed their owner's wealth and, consequently, status.

The hell with that. It looked pretty. Beauty was its own excuse for being. Dar turned, clipped his safety to the guy wire, and hauled himself into the hall.

He came through the airlock, opening his faceplate, splitting his seal, tilting his helmet back—and a ham of a hand caught him between the shoulder blades. "Hey, Dar boy! Great t' see ya! How ya been?"

Dar recovered and caught the offending hand with a grin. "Hello, Estivan. What's germane?"

"Not much." Estivan squeezed back. "In fact, from what I hear, the miner only brought in silicon, steel, gold, and some plastic."

"No germanium at all, huh?"

"Yeah, but who uses it any more? So what's been happening at Maison d'Armand, huh?"

"She's not back yet. But as soon as she is, we'll declare party."

"I'll look forward to it. Hey, Carolita!" Estivan waved his daughter over. Carolita looked up from a box of crystals she was fingering, saw Dar, and broke into a smile. "Hi, Dar!" She came over to catch his hand in a warm clasp. "Getting lonely yet?"

"Fess doesn't let me go out alone, Carol," Dar answered, grinning. "Shopping for ornaments, or raw materials?"

Carol shrugged. "Depends on how pretty they are. Need any help on your organic chem?"

"No, but I wish I did."

"Gallant, very gallant—though untrue. Be off with you, though—I know you want to look over the merchandise. You might take a look at the minerals, too."

"Yeah, I gotta at least pretend I'm doing business. Drink after the auction?"

"Suits. Go get ready to be an adversary, now."

Dar turned away, warmed by camaraderie, but also relieved. Carol was right—she wasn't exactly pretty. Not quite ugly, but who was he to talk?

Lona's husband. Whether it was official or not, all the neighbor women knew it, and respected her claim—which made it easier for Dar, since he could enjoy their friendship without worrying about avoiding overtures.

He threaded through the throng, exchanging handshakes and shop talk, and occasional hugs with the ladies, when he couldn't avoid it.

"*Dar*-ling!" Bridget threw her arms around his neck and leaned down to plant a kiss on his cheek. "What have you been doing with yourself all these weeks?"

"Working, eating, and sleeping, Bridget." Dar pecked at her cheek, reflecting that the daughter of the Mulhearns, at least, didn't patronize him.

No, she was very forthrightly the take-charge type. "You call that a kiss? Here, let me show you how . . ."

"Oh, come on! I get so tired of lessons!"

"You ought to consider a change of curriculum." Bridget let her eyelids droop, producing the effect of an amorous dugong.

"Yeah, but what if my prof caught me studying from someone else's notes? You wouldn't want me to get expelled, would you?"

The reference to Lona, oblique though it was, reminded Bridget of her manners. She edged away, still smiling—but idling down from flirt to friend. "Of course not; she's got a mean left hook. How about a bite? A snack, I mean," Bridget actually blushed. "My lord! Once you start this kind of thing, it's hard to stop, isn't it?"

"So I'm told. Just think clean, Bridget."

"Yeah, but what happens if I hear dirty?" They sailed into the restaurant area, and she sat as Dar tucked her chair in, then took the one next to her—better a wolf who'd been muzzled, then one who'd just been let out of her cage. "May I order for you?"

"No, thanks—I can enter a code for myself." Bridget pressed in the sequence for coffee and lo-cal Danish, then sat back to sip. "How is your factory running?"

And they were off into shoptalk, safe and chummy—which was just as well because, regardless of how Bridget didn't look, Dar's hormones had given him a rush when she had. Weeks of celibate living had their effect—though the sight of the ladies of the community helped quell it. They ranged in appearance from plain to ugly, with only the occasional woman who was mildly pretty. Dar wondered why Maxima attracted so few beauties. Maybe the stunning ones preferred to stay on Terra, where the standard of living was higher, and the morals were lower? Of course, Lona hadn't—but she had spent half her life in space, hopping from planet to planet with her grandfather, before she'd ever heard of Maxima; and even *she* took off for Terra every chance she could get, leaving him at the mercy of his neighbors' wives and daughters.

Nothing but wives and daughters, of course—the young men who had come to Maxima to build robots and fortunes still outnumbered the women 2.36 to 1. Any single woman who showed up to join the colony was married within a year, plain or not, usually after a hectic courtship that resembled a bidding war. Of course, there were one or two who chose to stay single, like Myrtle—but they were very few. Looks or no looks, Maxima was a marriage mart.

Of course, Dar had to admit he was biased. To him, *any* woman would look plain, compared to Lona.

He found himself wondering if the other husbands could possibly feel the same way about *their* wives.

"Two therms!"

"Two and five kwahers!"

"Two and ten!" Msimangu turned to glare at Dar. "Blast you, d'Armand! You're running the price up!"

"No, I'm buying it! Two and twelve!"

"Two and twelve?" the miner cried. "Do I hear two and fifteen?" He glanced at Msimangu.

"Not from me." The white-haired black man turned away in disgust. "I'm not *that* low. I'll wait for the next shipment."

"Two and fourteen?" the miner called. "Two and thirteen. I have two and twelve; who'll give me two and thirteen?"

There were several mutters, but no one called out.

"Going once! Going twice! Sold!" The miner whacked the gavel on the board. "Three kilograms of silicon to the young man in the pin-striped coverall, at two therms, twelve kwahers per!"

Msimangu shouldered through the crowd to shake a finger under Dar's nose. "Do not bid against me again, young d'Armand! I can ruin you!"

Dar lifted his chin—he had to; the old black man was six inches taller than he—and gave back glare for glare. "Would you dock us a fair chance to get started, Omar? We're not thick in the wallet; we have to pick up small lots when we can."

"Perhaps, but the gold is not small!"

"No, but it's vital."

"Then deal in retail! If a beginner like you seeks to buy gold wholesale, he will break *himself!*"

"One hundred fifteen kilograms of fine gold!" the miner called. "What am I bid?"

A storm of calls answered him. He sorted them out, the price leapfrogging. "Five thousand therms . . . six thousand . . . eight thousand . . . ten . . ."

"Twelve thousand therms!" Msimangu called out. "Twelve thousand therms per kilo!"

"Thirteen!" Laurentian answered, and "Fourteen!" Mulhearn called from across the room. "Fifteen!" Ngoya called. "Sixteen!" Bolwheel shouted.

"Seventeen!" Msimangu bellowed. "Seventeen therms per kilo!"

The small bidders had dropped out; now the plutocrats were getting down to serious competition. It was exciting in its way, but watching his neighbors fight made Dar nervous. He edged away toward the rim of the crowd, pulling out Lona's list and checking through it. All the items were crossed off, except for the silicon; he drew a line through that and turned away, tucking the list back for future reference. He patted the pocket where the trio of rubies lay. He really shouldn't have spent the money, but Lona would love them, if he could cut, polish, and mount them properly. Besides, they'd be worth ten times the amount he'd paid, back on Terra.

"Twenty-two and nine going once—twenty-two and nine going twice—SOLD! To the tall black gent with the white hair!"

Msimangu whooped victory, and his fellow millionaires turned away, reviling his ancestry and personal habits. Msimangu ignored them, laughing as he turned away, shouldering through his congratulating fellows. "I won the big one, at least! Come, come drink with me!"

A few accepted, though most withdrew to take their turns at the retail booth. Still laughing, Msimangu caught up with Dar at the door to the restaurant. "Come drink with us, young d'Armand! Let us rejoice, let us make a celebration!"

Dar looked up with a slow smile. "Don't mind if I do, Omar."

"Fine, fine! Then come with us!" And Msimangu plunged into the public bar.

Dar sat down at table with a half-dozen solid citizens. He noticed that Mulhearn and Bolwheel had joined the crew, and was amazed once again that people who could rage and revile one another in the bidding, could relax and talk together without the slightest rancor only five minutes later. Everyone seemed to understand that business might be business, but friendship was more important.

Much more important, out here where the shrunken sun blazed in eternal night, and your own survival depended on your neighbors'. They couldn't afford feuds on Maxima; they all had a constant, common enemy—the ever-present void. Sitting down for a drink wasn't just a celebration—it was a declaration of apology and forgiveness, a healing of wounds, and an unspoken pledge of mutual support.

He felt honored to be included, though it had become part of the pattern. From the first, he'd been invited to join in every gathering that happened. If they needed each other here, it made them all the more willing to accept the newcomer into the fold. Dar wondered if they would be so open in a hundred years, when (if!) the colony was firmly established and thriving.

"We will grow," Bolwheel maintained. He was a red-haired, jowly man of middle age, who looked fat but wasn't. "We grow already."

Neils Woltham nodded. "We all tend to have large families, somehow."

"That is half the reason we are here." Msimangu punched up another tankard. "For the room to have families."

David Mulhearn, pale and red-haired but graying, nodded. "All is rationed, on Terra—food, land, houses, what you will. Rationed, or so dear that it might as well be."

"I wouldn't call the prices low here," Jory Kimish said. He was almost as young as Dar, and newly come from Earth. "You blokes seem to have put in a good deal of time and labor. Can't rate that too low, you know."

"We do not," Msimangu assured him. "But even if you compute the cost of our houses so, young man, you will find them much less expensive than their equivalents on Terra."

"True," Bolwheel said, "but this isn't exactly the choicest location, you know."

"And what is wrong with it?" Msimangu rounded on him. "You can have as much land as you can fence, here!"

"Aye, but naught will grow on't," Mulhearn pointed out. "Yet I cannot fault the neighborhood—for nowhere else have I found neighbors of my own mindset and code."

"Nor I," Msimangu agreed, "nor I. I could not ask for more congenial company."

"When we get it," Dar pointed out. "Of course, it's worth waiting for."

"Surely there's no dearth of folk who wish to join us," Mulhearn pointed out.

Bolwheel answered with a knowing smile. "Where else can they find a reputation for their product, David? Only fifty years, and already our computers and robots are known as the best in Terran space!"

"Of course, it helps that Terran space has been reduced a bit by the DDT," Dar pointed out.

"Only officially, young d'Armand. None seek to bar us from trading with other PEST planets—and the outermost of those, trade with the frontier. No, our robots are known wherever men use automatons."

"Well, surely it's your reputation that I came to join," Jory Kimish said, "though I'd stay for the company alone.

But why is the Maximan product so much the best? You'd think Terra would have it all!''

"All but the brains," Bolwheel answered. "For don't you see, the brightest of the computerfolk saw the collapse of the DDT coming, and came out here early. The second brightest stayed till the civil war, then escaped to avoid being shot by the storm troopers, or by the loyalists; and the third brightest waited till PEST had taken all the planet, then escaped just before PEST banned emigration.''

Msimangu nodded. "First, second, third—most of the best came to us.''

"Nay, not all, though," Mulhearn cautioned. "There are brains on Terra still, and not all of them were made on Maxima.''

"True," Msimangu agreed, "though they lose steadily of what's left, by deportation. And some of those come here.''

Dar stared. "You mean PEST is deliberately trying to get rid of its bright ones?''

"Only those who show some sign of making trouble, young d'Armand—which means only half of the brightest.''

"And the other half?''

"They work their way into government, join the LORDS party, and start the long, savage climb," Bolwheel assured him.

Dar frowned. "So they can't design a decent robot?''

"Decent, yes. But if it's more than 'decent,' they are marked as dangerous; they might take their bosses' jobs. No, a smart young man on Terra will be sure to hide his mind.''

Dar shuddered. "No wonder they come to Maxima! Who would want to work in *that* kind of environment?''

"Not me," Kimish assured him, "so I made just enough trouble to be deported, but not enough for them to care where." He leaned back with a sigh. "Can you know how intoxicating the spirit of freedom is, here? Where your neighbors challenge you to dream up some idea nobody ever thought of before? Where they make you feel ashamed, if you *don't* come up with anything new?''

"Yes." Dar had a few memories of PEST's Terra, himself. "It makes all the toil and loneliness worthwhile.''

He caught looks of sympathy, quickly veiled; *their* wives stayed home to keep them company.

Quick change of topic needed, and Bolwheel supplied it.

"I think perhaps that is why PEST leaves us alone, and does not seek to impose its rules here."

Kimish frowned. "I was wondering about that. One sqaudron of destroyers, and we'd be slaves."

"But they need us, they need us," Msimangu assured him. "They need someone, away from Terra, to invent better computers for them, for they must have machines to do the work, if they are to give the people the leisure they have promised. And they dare not have such innovation being developed on any of their planets—it could set people to thinking, and questioning their orders."

A rumbling chorus of agreement went around the table, men nodding their heads in concurrence, and Dar nodded along with the rest of them, even though, privately, he thought it might also have something to do with PEST thinking Maxima was too small to be worth swatting. Realistically, he knew that the asteroid would die if its customers stopped buying, which meant the Terran government could destroy them any time it wanted to. And if PEST's bureaucrats could destroy the Maximans, surely they could also control them, easily and totally, as much as they wished—or so they thought, so they reasoned.

They were wrong, of course. They could kill Maxima, they could conquer it—but if they didn't conquer, they couldn't control. As long as they left the asteroid free, Maximans could do whatever they wished.

But Maxima wasn't about to let PEST know that. Sure, it might be fun to send the Terran bureaucrats a list of all the things Maximans did, that were forbidden on Terra—but it would also be very foolish. A bureaucrat defines himself by the amount of power he has; PEST's logical response would be conquest.

Which in itself was pretty silly, when all they would have to do would be to send back a list of all the things Terrans could do, that Maximans couldn't—mostly hedonistic pastimes. The younger Maximans would start eating their hearts out.

Or maybe not. Dar's neighbors were a pretty unworldly bunch, if you excluded making money and building grandiose houses.

Houses they were definitely big on, though. "I passed your estate on the way in, young d'Armand," Msimangu was saying, "I saw your home. I confess I thought it the height of ugliness last year, but now I begin to see its form emerge. It will be beautiful, when it is done."

"Why, thank you," Dar said, frankly floored by the compliment. In fact, he was so pleased that he forgot to mention who had designed it.

The factory was running just fine. Dar wandered up one aisle and down the other, feeling increasingly useless as he went along. He couldn't even dump the waste bins any more—since Lona had started leaving Fess home, Dar had assigned him that little chore. After all, he couldn't have the poor robot sitting around with nothing to do.

It was hard to believe these machines were of the same genus as Fess. Technically, they were robots, though with nowhere near the capacity of a general purpose model such as Fess. They were operated by much smaller computers, specialized for a very limited number of tasks. Dar hesitated to call them "robots" at all—they were really just automated machine tools. Robots were originally supposed to be artificial people, but these machines couldn't mimic human thought patterns in the slightest way.

And they certainly didn't look human. The first was only a set of rollers that rotated a synthetic crystal a millimeter at a time, then lowered onto it a hemispherical cover that was filled with golden contacts. The central computer tested each circuit within the crystal through those contacts, checking continuity, resistance, power input versus output, and a host of other electronic characteristics. After fifteen minutes, the rollers tilted the crystal out onto the padded belt that carried it to the next robot—or into the garbage can, if it had failed any of its tests.

The next robot was very similar, except that it connected microscopic filaments to each contact point.

Then came a robot that looked like an octopus, with fifteen arms sprouting from a central globe that held its computer. Its job was assembling fifteen crystals into one globular cluster joined by filaments, then immersing it in a chemical bath. After two hours, enough silicon had adhered to the filaments so that the robot could withdraw its arms and start assembling another cluster, while the first rested in its bath for a week, slowly growing together into a single giant crystal.

Meanwhile, another robot—a single bench that grabbed, folded, and held metal and plastic while a steel arm welded joints—was casting and assembling the housings for the completed machines. Then came the assembly line—a final robot which took the finished giant crystals out of their baths and fastened them inside the housings, then connected the contacts to the terminals for the mechanical attachments that actually did the work.

All of it faster than he could do. All of it better than he could do. And most of it much, much smaller than he could see.

Dar surveyed the area, feeling totally useless.

"You really should take a finished robot out for testing, Dar."

"Yeah, I know—but I've done two already today, and there's plenty of time to check the other three."

"Still, it must be done, or you will have a dozen untested robots at week's end."

"I know, I know—but there doesn't seem to be much point to it. You know they'll work perfectly."

"I do not, Dar. True, if the individual crystal circuits are sound, the finished computer will be fine . . ."

"Of course, because the central computer tests each stage of the work as it's being done." There were contacts embedded in the "holder" on each bench, and in each arm, allowing testing while production was in process.

"But you may find a mechanical flaw, Dar."

"Yeah, sure. Last week I found a pinhole in a suction funnel, and the week before that, there was a hum in a lifting fan. Never in the computers, of course."

He watched the process, shaking his head with dissatisfaction.

"What displeases you, Dar?"

"Huh? Oh. I keep forgetting you're programmed for gestures, too. Nothing, Fess—or nothing that should, anyway. We make darn good household robots—but blast it, *all* we make is household robots!"

"True, Dar, but, as you say, you make them very well—and you always manage to offer an automaton that will do more than your competition's product."

"Well, that's true. We started out with a little cannister that could dust, and speak a few simple responses such as 'Yes, ma'am,' 'No, sir,' 'Good morning,' and 'Please move . . .' ''

"Which every other company's could also do, of course."

"Yeah, but we figured out a way for ours to scrub floors and polish furniture, too."

"Then you added the abilities to pick up, clear a table, load a dishwasher, one by one—and always a year or two before the other companies."

"Yeah, because they wait till we come out with it, then buy one of ours and copy the new feature—but that always takes six months at least, while we make another hundred thousand in sales. Which reminds me, we'd better finish debugging that breakfast-delivery program, or we'll lose our edge."

"I would not be terribly concerned, Dar. You can still add many features before you will have perfected the ideal household helper."

"What do you mean?" Dar frowned.

"Why, your robots cannot yet replace a closure seam in a garment, or light a fire—or fight one, for that matter."

"Oh. Right. And they don't do windows." But Dar was gazing off into space. "Let's see, now . . ."

"You will find ways to accomplish them all," Fess assured him.

"True, true. And there are other improvements I'm itchy to get to."

"Such as?"

"Well, they could be a lot smaller, for one thing."

"I do not know, Dar—there is a lower limit on size, for accomplishing mechanical tasks."

"Oh, not the robots themselves, Fess—we've got those as low as they can go, and still be practical. Anything less, and the householder will be tripping over them every time he turns around. No, I meant the computers. They're still bigger than my fist."

"I fail to see how they could be smaller, Dar. You are already working with the smallest crystal lattice that can carry an adequate number of differences in electrical potentials."

"Are we?" Dar's tone sharpened. "A crystal has a regular shape because its molecule has, Fess. Why can't the differences in electrical potential that made a crystal lattice function as a circuit, be made to operate with only a single molecule?"

Fess was slow in answering, which meant his computer, which worked in nanoseconds, had analyzed the problem thoroughly, and made a preliminary try at resolving it. "In theory, there would be no reason for it not to, Dar—but the complexity of the circuitry would be limited by the number of electrons available."

"All right, so it might take a dozen molecules, or maybe even a single giant molecule—but you're still talking about something microscopic, or just barely visible."

"Are you seriously intending to research the possibility?"

"Not without telling Lona—and I don't know enough physics yet, to know if it's worth investigating. I mean, okay, it might turn out to be possible, but not marketable, especially if it wound up using giant molecules. After all, who wants a computer made of U-235 in his living room?"

"The mass would not be critical, Dar."

"No, but the customer would. Call it atavism, call it superstition, but the stuff has a bad reputation."

"Even if it were, why would you wish to do it? The current generation of computers is certainly small enough for all practical purposes."

"Not all—I can think of a few applications where microbrains would come in handy. Especially in the line I *want* to get into."

"Which is?"

"Industrial robots." Dar rubbed his knuckles against his palm. "We need to branch out, Fess. There's just so far we can go with household robots, and right now, the *real* money is in industry. If we could offer smaller, more compact computers, that would cut down on size and give flexibility a big boost. Factory managers are always complaining about having to replace all their robots with new models, every time they retool. If we could figure out how to grow a single -molecule circuit, we could sell them new brains for more generalized robots."

"An excellent idea," Fess said slowly. "You must tell Lona."

Dar felt a surge of irritation, but reminded himself that Fess was, after all, Lona's robot. "No. I just don't know enough yet."

Which made him feel even more useless.

He turned away, closing the factory hatch behind him, and went into his den. "I'm going to brood—uh, study, for a while, Fess."

"I shall not disturb you, Dar." But he would wait for Dar's call. That went without saying.

The lights came on, and Dar sat down at his computer with a sigh of relief. Here, at least, he had something to *do,* and the illusion that it might actually be of some use, even though that was highly unlikely. Of course, he was only experimenting with computer simulations of radio sound waves and FTL drives, not with the real thing—but he might hit on a workable idea.

It didn't make sense, after all—if ships could travel faster than light, why couldn't radio? If you could make a whole spaceship isomorphic with a seven-dimensional surface, why couldn't you do the same with an electromagnetic wave?

Because it wasn't an object, of course. In fact, it wasn't matter; it was an energy pattern. But patterns were patterns, and three-dimensional patterns could be made isomorphic with seven-dimensional equivalents.

Except that energy didn't seem to exist in seven dimensions. Which was nonsense, of course—the mathematicians just hadn't started thinking about it, so Dar couldn't read their conclusions.

But at least he'd found the right question to ask. That, he felt, was real progress. Of course, he didn't know enough math to look for the answer—but that could be rectified. He stared at the simulation, rotating it to gain the illusion of movement, and, from it, inspiration and motivation.

It worked; he was motivated. He cleared the screen and loaded the first chapter of the text on topology. He'd already made it through Page 2 . . .

He was halfway through Page 3 when the sensor chimed.

Dar was out of his seat and over to the screen before the sound had died. The call signal could only ring if it was triggered by a coded radio signal—and only Lona knew the code. She was coming home! Dar located her blip, referred it to the center of the screen, then punched into viewphone mode and entered her code—and there she was, or at least her face, in beautiful living color, complexion flawless, every feature perfect, saying, "Roger, ground control. Will burn for entry at 24:32:16."

"Roger," said a tinny (male) voice. "Over and out."

Dar felt a stab of jealousy. Had she perfected her makeup for him—or for Louie at Ground Control?

But she was reaching out to punch him up on her screencall signal. Her face lit up, and his heartburn quenched as he realized she'd seen him.

"Welcome, wanderer!"

"Hi, handsome." Her eyelids drooped. "Slay the fatted calf and warm the sheets."

"Both are roasting, and so am I. When should I pour the martinis?"

"An hour, sweetling." She winced. "Don't groan so loudly—my amp can't take it."

"Neither can I. Tell me something to be happy about."

"That it's *only* an hour. Just think how long it would be if we were civilized enough to have a spaceport and customs."

"I'd nuke 'em both! If our neighbors couldn't trust us . . ."

"Who *could* they trust? So I'm landing on our own pad, dear, and docking in . . ." she glanced aside, at her chronometer, " . . . sixty-four minutes and 20."

A chime sounded, out of range. Lona glanced at it, then back at Dar. "Entry burn in two. Love, darling." Her screen blanked.

Dar could have screamed at it. Instead, he took her parting line as a promise and headed for the shower.

Of course, he had just showered, shaved, and changed a few hours before, for his trip into town—but what the hell, he could do it again. Anything to pass the time!

He did, and he still had half an hour left to chew his nails. He manfully refrained—she only liked *controlled* scratching. Instead, he drew two martinis from the autobar and set them next to the big quartz port, then sat down to watch her land. Thirty seconds later, he got up and started pacing—but still kept his eyes locked on the sky.

She had certainly timed her entrance right. (She always did, of course.) The sky was filled with stars, but Sol was about to rise, and its glare dimmed the lesser suns, leaving a field strewn with glory, but not backed by powder. Nearby asteroids arced across the field, making his heart lurch—but finally, one of them started growing more than it slid, and he knew Lona was coming in.

The meteor waxed brighter and brighter until it showed as a

little disc that grew and grew until it assumed the shape of a small rocket ship, fifty meters long, arching lower as it brightened, then blossoming into roseate fire that swelled up about it, hiding it, consuming it, a fireball that swung lower more and more slowly—and touched the ground. The fire died, and the little rocket ship emerged, balanced on landing grapples.

Dar hit pressure patches and turned a wheel, and the house's boarding ramp snaked out across the graded rockfield to nudge, very gently, against the side of the ship. Then it rose up on jacks of its own, like a blind, questing cobra, found the electromanetic ring around the airlock, and clung.

It was a convenience, for people. Expensive—too expensive, just for the privilege of coming in without a faceplate, so Dar didn't pressurize it. But cargo needed atmosphere, sometimes, and for trade, they could afford it.

He couldn't see her coming, though. That was the disadvantage.

Then the red light died over the airlock, and he knew she was in. The yellow light started pulsing, and kept on, for what seemed an eternity—but finally, the green lit.

Dar stepped up five feet from the hatch, a martini clutched in each hand, breath held in his lungs.

Then the hatch swung open, and she was there, lumpy as porridge in her space suit, but her helmet under her arm, face glowing, lips parted . . .

They never did get to those martinis. What good is the gin when the ice has melted?

Two hours later, Lona sat across from him in one of the latest Terran fashions, which didn't manage to obscure her splendor, especially when she was lit by candles (right under the air-exchange vent). She was finishing her bouillabaisse and a fascinating account of her odyssey through the best shops on Terra (''Well, I have to look my best when I'm talking to purchasing agents, don't I?''). Dar smiled at her out of a pleasant haze, compounded of one part gin to five parts Lona. She didn't miss a syllable as X-HB-9 cleared their bowls, but she did stop to stare as the little robot set places of almost-genuine steak in front of them. ''Dar! What have you *done!*''

Well, Dar, would have preferred to have the accusation

refer to less licit activities, but he'd take praise where he could get it. He gave back a foolish grin. "Aw. You noticed."

"Noticed! You wonderful man! You figured out how to cram that whole program into such a limited brain!"

"Only applying what you taught me, dear."

"Well! Such excellent application deserves reward." Her eye gleamed as she turned back to him.

"If you're going to deliver on that promise, you'd better keep your strength up."

Lona took a bite. "Done to a turn!" She didn't say which one. "Is X-HB-9 ready to manufacture?"

"Needs a little more field-testing to be certain—but, yes, I'm pretty sure it is. It'll bring you breakfast in bed tomorrow."

"Oh, goody! Just what we need for the triple contract I've lined up!"

Dar dropped his fork. *"Triple . . .* contract?"

"Uh-huh." Lona nodded, hair swaying. "I talked Amalgamated into renewing our contract without the exclusivity clause."

"How did you manage . . . NO! Cancel that! I don't want to know!"

"Poor dear." Lona reached past the candles to pat his hand. "But there's nothing to be jealous about. I didn't do anything unethical, let alone immoral."

Yes, but that didn't say what she had implied. Also, Dar kind of wondered about her ranking.

"Simple threats," Lona explained. "I told them we were thinking about opening our own dirtside sales office."

Dar's jaw dropped. Lona merrily took another bite, and he shoved his mandible back up to his maxillary. "Boy, you really don't lack for chutzpah, do you?"

"Why not? We probably *will* open a dealership on Terra, in twenty years or so."

"Actually, I was thinking about all the Maximan families getting together and opening a cooperative distributing corporation—but I think we need more leverage first. You know, get Terra totally dependent on our product, so they can't threaten to take us over. Otherwise, we might suffer a sudden horrible decline in creativity . . . Uh . . . What's the matter?"

"And you tell me *I've* got nerve," she gasped. "Good

thing you don't live on Terra, Dar—you'd wind up running PEST.''

Dar felt a surge of irritation. "I only want to run them out of town."

"I know," she sighed. "You never did have much respect for good old healthy self-interest. Maybe I do have a function around here, after all."

"Maybe!" Dar squawked. "I'm just the errand boy!"

Lona stared into his eyes for a long moment, then reached out to pat his hand again. "Please keep thinking that way, dear. It works wonderfully for me."

Dar was pretty sure he was supposed to feel complimented. Anyway, he glowed inside, just on general principles. "So how much is this triple deal going to bring?"

"Well, over the next three years, and with a guarantee to each company to bring out a new model, on a four-month rotation plan . . . just about five hundred thousand each."

Dar could feel his eyes buldge. "A *million* and a *half*?"

Lona nodded, looking immensely pleased with herself.

Dar sat back, sucking in a long breath. "Yes. Well, I can see that might make a little research and development desirable, yes."

"But that's the good part about it." Lona winked. "You've already done the tough part. With a robot who serves breakfast in bed, it's just a short step to one who can load the dishwasher."

Dar developed a sudden faraway look in his eyes. "With extendable arms, that shouldn't be too tough—and once you've got the telescoping arms, it could vacuum the cobwebs in the corners, and wash the walls."

"And if it can wash the walls, it can paint them!"

"Yeah." Dar grinned. "No more having to rent a painter-robot from the homecare store. I see the point. We have half the improvements figured out already. No wonder you wanted me to add another workroom before we finished mining out another ice cavity."

"Well, yes." Lona looked down, toying with her wine-glass. "Actually, Dar, I was going to ask you if you could add on the northwest circular room. It isn't very large . . ."

"The one right next to our bedrooms on the plans?" Dar frowned. "Sure. What kind of product are you planning to develop in it?"

Lona actually blushed and lowered her eyes. "A product that would be very small at first. But it would grow. Fifteen years or so, but it would grow."

Dar stared.

Then he stood up and came around to take her hand. "Darling—are you telling me we can finally start a baby?"

She nodded, smiling up at him—and he was amazed to see her eyes fill with tears. "Yes," she whispered, just before her mouth was pre-empted.

An hour later, their breathing slowed down enough for Lona to heave a satisfied sigh, and for Dar to breathe into her ear, "Will you marry me now?"

"Uh-huh." Lona turned to him, nodding brightly. "I do think children should have that much security, at least."

"Security?" Dar pursed his lips and asked, carefully, "Does this mean you might be planning to stay home for a couple of years?"

Lona nodded, eyes huge and face solemn. "At least two years before I go kiting off to Terra again, Dar. I promise."

Cordelia sighed, misty-eyed. "I do so love happy endings."

"Yet was it truly?" Goeffrey said, frowning up at Fess. "Did she keep her promise, Fess?"

"Regretably, she did not," the robot answered. "In practice, she *could* not—there was need for her to attend business meetings and speak with prospective clients."

Magnus asked, "Wherefore could her husband not have done so for her?"

"He was quite willing," Fess sighed, "but he lacked the gift for it, perhaps due to his earlier career as a teacher—he was obsessed with the need to tell the precise truth. He just was not as good at business as she was."

"Nor as good at aught else, from what thou sayest." Magnus added.

"Thus it seemed to himself, too. He died feeling that his life had been full and enjoyable, but insignificant."

"Papa hath said that all folk must find and know their limitations," Gregory said, "then seek to transcend them."

"It was Dar Mandra who first enunciated that aphorism, Gregory; it has been passed down from generation to generation of your family. But the operative word is seek. The attempt will surely result in better work than you would otherwise do, and may result in greater accomplishments—but may still fall short of your goal.''

Gregory's eyes lost focus as he tried to digest that statement, but Geoffrey was still frowning. ''Did the founder of our house, then, accomplish nothing with his life?''

''That depends on your definition of the term 'accomplish.' With his wife, he built a major company within the Maxima conglomerate, raised three children to become excellent citizens, and formed an enduring marriage that gained substance as it aged.''

''Yet he did not create anything in his own right, nor invent or discover it.''

''Only in that he had not found the answer to the question he had formulated, and did not realize that no answer may be an indicator of the correct answer. His son Limner, though, took that question and likewise tried to answer it: 'Why can physical objects be mapped into seven-dimensional space, when electromagnetic waves cannot?' He, too, failed to discover its solution, just as Dar had—but took the lack of an answer as an indicator.''

Gregory asked, ''What did Limner think it did indicate?''

''That perhaps electromagnetic waves *could* be mapped into seven dimensions; they only needed a different technique. Just as electromagnetic radiation was its own medium, the transmitter had to be its own isomorpher.''

Magnus looked up. ''Yet 'twas Dar's thoughts, and the question they led to, that enabled Limner to discover that principle.''

''That is so, yes.''

''Then,'' Magnus demanded, ''how can he be said to have failed?''

''He had not, of course—yet he felt that he had.''

Geoffrey squeezed his eyes shut and gave his head a shake. ''A moment, I prithee—thou dost say he succeeded in some measure, but knew it not?''

''Precisely. Dar's feelings of failure were due to a fundamental misunderstanding of his own nature—he was not an engineer, like Lona, but a research scientist.''

''Oh, the poor ancestor!'' Tears brimmed Cordelia's eyes. ''To die feeling so, when 'twas not true!''

''Oh, do not pity him, Cordelia. He recognized his true

success as a husband, a father, and a stalwart member of the community. In his old age, he counted accomplishments in scholarship and commerce to be relatively inconsequential, as indeed they were.''

Gregory stared, scandalized. ''Why! How canst thou say the discovery of new knowledge is of no consequence!''

''Only relatively, Gregory, only relatively. For Dar's measure of worth was in adding to the happiness of other people—and in that, he had succeeded enormously. Now hush, children. It is time to sleep. Tomorrow, we will begin to solve the mystery of the castle.''

6

The rain came down, and it hit with thunder. Rod jolted awake wide-eyed, lurching up on one elbow to stare at the ceiling. The only light was the soft glow of the will-o'-the-wisp Gwen had lit on Fess's saddle before they settled down. Rain roared on the tent.

"How long has it been going on, Fess?" Rod murmured.

"It began only ten minutes ago, Rod."

Then the whole tent-top turned bright with lightning, barely gone before thunder bellowed. Rod turned and looked down at his youngest, and sure enough, the little boy lay rigid, eyes wide, scared witless by the thunder but too proud to cry out.

"You know there's nothing to be scared of, don't you?" Rod said conversationally.

"Aye, Papa." Gregory relaxed a little. "The lightning will not hurt us, nor will a tree fall on us—we pitched our tent far from the branches."

"And lightning bolts are much more likely to strike a higher object, such as a tree or the castle. Yes." But Rod reached out a hand anyway, and Gregory's fingers seized on his like a little vise.

"Oh! 'Tis glorious," Cordelia breathed.

The whole tent flashed bright again as thunder slammed down at them. It showed Magnus and Geoffrey halfway to the door. Darkness struck, and Rod could just barely hear Geoffrey say, "I do so love a storm!"

" 'Tis grand," Magnus agreed. The gloom lightened, and the sound of the rain became even louder.

" 'Ware the rain." Gwen was sitting up beside Rod, facing the door. "Doth it come toward thee?"

"No, Mama, 'tis at the tent's back." Lightning flared with a thunder blast, and Rod saw the boys hunkered belly-down with their chins on their fists, gazing out, and Cordelia wriggling up between them.

" 'Tis right atop us,'' Gregory murmured. ''There is no delay 'twixt lightning flash and thunder.''

Rod smiled; ever the scientist! Well, if it let the boy share his siblings' pleasure, what harm? ''Don't you want to look at it, too?''

Gregory looked up at him, then smiled. ''Aye!'' He turned and crawled toward the door.

Rod caught Gwen's hand and squeezed a little. She returned the pressure and murmured, ''Why should they have the sight to themselves, my lord?''

''Hey, the family ought to stay together, right?'' Rod rolled up to his hands and knees. ''After you, dear.''

''What, durst I trust thee so?''

''Sure, the kids are awake. But let's go side by side, if you doubt me.''

Gwen giggled and they rubbed elbows as they came to their feet and stepped over to join their offsprings. Lightning blazed as they came to the doorway, thunder crashing down around their heads. Rod looked up in time to catch the last sight of the tower tops in silhouette—and stiffened.

''Hist!'' Geoffrey cried.

They all fell totally silent, ears straining.

" 'Twas not the last boom of the thunder alone,'' Magnus said.

''I hear a lass wailing,'' Cordelia answered.

Rod started to say what he'd heard, then bit his tongue and stared up at the unseen tower with narrowed eyes. Gwen's hand tightened on his arm.

Gregory said it for him. ''I do hear a man's laughter.''

''Aye, and 'tis as wicked and foul a laugh as ever I've heard,'' Magnus agreed.

''I, too, hear it, my lord,'' Gwen murmured.

''He's gloating,'' Rod said softly. ''I don't know what about . . .''

''The maid?'' Cordelia guessed. ''Doth he rejoice at having made her weep?''

''I mislike this castle,'' Magnus said, his voice hard.

Thunder tore at the stones, bleached white by the lightning. When it quieted, Gregory asked, ''Ought we go home, then?''

''Nay.'' Magnus said it even faster than Rod. ''Whatever is here, we must face and banish it.''

Thunder blasted them again, the next lightning flash following so hard on the first that it seemed one long, unbroken instant of light with only a flicker between. Then it died, and the afterimage danced before Rod's eye, confirming what he'd thought he had seen.

As the thunder faded, Cordelia gasped, "Was it a lass?"

"Mayhap." Geoffrey's voice hardened. "Whatsoe'er 'twas, it was long-haired and cloaked."

"Yet why did it plummet head-first toward the ground?" Gregory wondered.

"Because it was pushed, brother," Geoffrey answered.

"Or did it throw itself down?" Cordelia wondered.

"Whate'er 'twas, it was the fruit of wickedness," Magnus answered.

Rod could hear the anger in his voice, and said quickly, "*Was*, Magnus. Remember the *was*. Whatever happened there, however cruel or vicious, it was done two hundred years ago, not tonight."

"But how evil must it have been," Cordelia cried, "that the spirit must live through it again, and again and again, for two hundred years!"

"Then 'tis time it was finished." Magnus's voice was grim, with a determination Rod had never heard in it before. "Whatever lies within that stone pile, 'tis a fell, foul evil, and we must not let it stand."

Rod frowned down at his boy. He was right, of course—but where had this sudden determination come from? Magnus had never heard anything about Castle Foxcourt but its name, before tonight. He wondered further about it as the family settled down once again, but decided to say nothing to Gwen—yet.

"Wherefore doth it not now appear so grim, Papa?" Cordelia looked up at the walls of the castle, golden now in the morning light.

"Because it's dawn, dear, and everything looks better by the light of the day."

"Then too, the rain hath washed it clean," Gwen explained, "as it doth with all. The sky is cleaner above, and mine heart doth sing within me to behold it."

"But we still have to get into the castle." Rod frowned up at the drawbridge. "There's the little problem of getting that slab of wood down."

"We must turn the windlass, Papa," Magnus said brightly.
"Shall I?"

Rod turned to him. "What—do you think you can make it
move without even having seen it?"

"Oh, aye, and next shalt thou bid a mountain come to
thee!" Geoffrey jibed.

"Aye, sin that I know where it *should* be."

"Thou canst not truly, Magnus!" Cordelia stated.

Gregory didn't say anything; he just gazed up at Magnus
wide-eyed. After all, if Big Brother *said* he could do it . . .

"Mayhap he can," Gwen suggested, "though even if he
cannot, 'twill be good practice for him."

"Yeah, you need to stretch if you want to grow." Rod
nodded slowly. "Okay, go ahead. It *would* save a bit of
time."

Magnus frowned up at the drawbridge, his eyes losing
focus. Gwen watched him carefully.

Rod glanced from Magnus to the castle, half-expecting the
old planks to come rattling down. Just as a caution, he waved
the other children back. They went, but with poor grace.

Magnus relaxed and shook his head in chagrin. " 'Tis no
use—there is no response."

Gregory looked disappointed. Geoffrey's eye lit with vin-
dictiveness, and both he and Cordelia started to say something, but Rod caught their eyes, and they stopped openmouthed.

"Still, 'twas good for thee to attempt it." Gwen stared at
the castle. " 'Tis odd, though."

"So we do it the old-fashioned way." Rod replied.

"I shall!!"

"No, I am best at . . ."

" 'Tis my turn . . ."

"No!" Rod barked.

The kids fell silent, staring at him with truculence—but
also with apprehension. He saw, and forced a smile. "I
appreciate your willingness, kids, but there might be a bit of
danger there—you know, rotten beams and falling rocks. I'm
pleading seniority on this one—just me and Magnus."

"Wherefore doth Magnus go!"

"Magnus, thou dost cheat!"

"Wherefore not Mama?"

"Because," Rod said, "someone has to take care of you
three."

"Fess can mind us!"

"Fess cannot stop you from following," Gwen pointed out. "Wouldst thou promise me not to go within?"

"Nay!"

"Then I bide here." Gwen gave Rod a sunny smile. "Go quickly, husband."

"With all dispatch. Let's go, son." Rod gazed up at the castle, but this time, he didn't really see it. His attention was on the unseen world, as he thought of pushing against the ground, away—and, slowly, drifted up to the arrow-slit at the top of the gatehouse.

"Thou didst promise all dispatch," Magnus reminded him, hovering in midair and leaning against the narrow window.

"All right, so I'm a slow old man," Rod grumbled, "just because I didn't have the good fortune to grow up using psi powers, the way you did. Come on, inside." He turned sideways and drifted in. It took a little shoving, though.

"Thou art hardly come," Magnus said, sliding in effortlessly.

Rod slapped his belt. "That's muscle, boy, not flab." He looked around, frowning. "Not so bad."

It wasn't. There was a slab fallen from the roof, and the morning sunlight coming through it and the arrow-slits, showed them a round room of old, mellow stone. The corners were filled with antique spiderwebs, and a broken table and bench stood near one wall. Except for that, the room was empty, with a few shards of crockery on the floor.

"Not anywhere nearly as bad as . . . What's the matter?"

Magnus's eyes had lost focus; he was turning slowly about the room, his face drawn. "I do hear voices, Papa."

"Voices?" Rod tensed. "What are they saying?"

"Naught . . . too distant . . . only some feel of loud talk, and soldiers' oaths . . ."

"Well, it's the gatehouse; there would have been soldiers here, so it's easy to ascribe it to them." Rod carefully ignored the chill oozing down his spine. "Probably just the wind playing a trick with the acoustics, son, like a whispering gallery."

"Dost thou truly think so?"

Rod didn't, so he said, "What bothers me is what I *don't* hear—or see."

That caught Magnus's attention. "And what is that?"

"Birds." Rod pointed up toward the rafters. "There's a

dozen nesting places in this room, but not a single one is used—not even a trace that there ever was a nest.''

Magnus looked around, nodding slowly.

"Come on, let's find that winch." Rod turned away toward the doorway. "High time we got your brothers and sister in here." And Gwen. Most especially Gwen.

The porter's room was empty, except for some more crumbled furniture. Shafts of sunlight pierced its darkness, from a row of slits along one wall.

"Well, that's why you couldn't turn the windlass." Rod looked around him as he stepped in. "No windlass."

"Aye . . . I thought at a thing that was not . . ." But Magnus had his abstracted air again. "Yet how did they make the drawbridge raise or lower?"

"Counterweights, probably. Let's go find the gateway." Rod led the way across the room, out into the passageway, and looked around. Light filled it, from the courtyard archway. "There!" He strode over to the great portal, closed now by the drawbridge, and pointed to a huge iron ball attached to a chain that ran up into darkness. "But there had to be an operating line, somewhere . . ."

"Yon." Magnus pointed. Rod followed his direction and saw, centered above the gate, a huge pulley with a strip of something that might once have been rope hanging from it and looping over to the side, into a hole in the wall.

"Into the porter's room." Rod nodded. "Makes sense. Come on." He ducked back into the chamber they'd just come from and looked up at the front wall. The rope came through the hole, sure enough, and draped into a pulley like the one over the gateway. Only about four feet of it hung down, though, and on the floor under it was a mound of toadstools.

"Well, so much for the operating line. But how . . ." Rod broke off, frowning. "Wait a minute. The drawbridge goes higher than that pulley."

"Aye. 'Tis for the portcullis." Magnus stepped back out into the passageway and pointed.

Just below the central pulley was the top of the iron gate. Rod's gaze traveled over to the corner and traced the chain attached to it, following it down to the huge iron ball that rested on the ground. "Frozen open, fortunately. But then how did they work the drawbridge?"

"Yon." Magnus pointed up into the gloom.

Squinting, Rod could barely make out huge links that traversed overhead to run over great, rusty sprocket wheels in the back wall.

"Very sharp, son." Rod nodded. "Very good observation."

"It is not."

"Oh?" Rod peered at him, with a stab of apprehension. "This is definitely not your standard drawbridge. How're you figuring out what to look for?"

"I am not. I hear them."

"Them?" The stab twisted. "Who?"

"A murmur, a babble of voices—but among them is one telling another how to manage these devices."

Rod stared at him for a moment, not that Magnus was watching. Then he linked his mind to his son's. The rest of the room darkened even more about him.

"Dost thou hear?"

Rod shook his head. "Just a babble, like a distant crowd."

"Yet 'tis there."

"Oh, yeah, it's there all right. Where it's coming from, is another matter." Rod turned away. "Come on, let's figure out how to get that drawbridge down. I think we need your mother in here."

Magnus led him out through the archway and into the courtyard.

It seemed spacious after the porter's room and the tunnel, but Rod knew it could only be a hundred feet across. The keep bulged out into it, like a hugely fat tower. There were a lot of dead leaves and broken branches, of course, and mounds of humus in the corners, with weeds sprouting luxuriantly.

But not a single bird. Nor, now that Rod noticed it, a butterfly.

He wrenched his mind back to business, to suppress a shiver. "Where's this counterweight?"

"We have stepped over it." Magnus pointed behind him. Rod looked down, and saw a metal slab set in the stone; he'd thought it was a threshold to the archway. But now that he looked, he could see it was rust, not just brown stone, and that rings rose from its corners, rings that were fastened to huge links whose chains stretched up on the wall to disappear, over huge sprocket wheels, into the stone above the archway.

Now Rod shivered.

Magnus was pointing up. " 'Tis so well balanced that the drawbridge doth need but a strong pull to let it down."

"Yeah—but the iron slab goes up then, and everybody coming in or going out has to ride under it."

"True." Magnus frowned, in an abstracted sort of way. "Wherefore did the Count not use iron balls again, and keep the gateway clear?"

"Nice question." And Rod had an answer, which was anything but nice. Not that he was about to say it, of course—and he decided, then and there, that Magnus was never going to touch that bar.

A caroling cry echoed above them.

Rod's head snapped up.

There, atop the gatehouse, perched his two younger sons, with his wife and daughter gliding down in lazy spirals on their broomsticks. He couldn't help noticing, all over again, that Cordelia had a full-sized brookstick now, not just a hearth broom, and wasn't much shorter than her mother any more.

Gwen pulled up beside Rod and hopped off. "Thou wert so long about it that we grew impatient." But he saw the concern in her eyes. "What kept thee?"

"Trying to figure out the drawbridge system." Rod noticed his two boys drifting down like autumn leaves. He shuddered, and hoped the simile wasn't apt.

"Is't so rare?" Gwen asked.

" 'Tis odd, at the least," Magnus answered.

Gwen turned to him, and her eyes widened. "How is't with thee, my son?"

"Well enough . . ."

"Is it truly?" Gwen set her broomstick against a wall and reached up to press a hand against Magnus's forehead. She stared off into space for a few seconds, then said, "Step to the wall, and touch the stones."

A crease appeared between Magnus's eyebrows, but he did as she bade. Rod "listened" to Gwen's mind, eavesdropping on the eavesdropper, as Magnus's hand touched rock.

A babel of urgent voices filled his ear, some conjecturing whether or not there would be a battle, some discussing how exciting it all was. Beyond them were the voices of soldiers bawling orders, and under it, surfacing and submerging, the sinister laugh they had heard in the midst of the thunderstorm.

"Away," Gwen snapped, and Magnus slowly took his hand from the wall, then turned to his mother with a troubled gaze. "Thou hast heard it?"

"Aye. 'Twas some peasant folk come into the castle for fear of a seige—and 'twas hundreds of years agone."

"He is a past-reader!" Gregory's eyes were huge.

"Magnus always gets to do things first!" Geoffrey grumped.

" 'Tis not fair!" Cordelia complained.

" 'Tis as like to be a burden as a joy," Gwen assured them, and turned to Magnus again. "Thou hast a form of clear sight, my son. I've heard it spoken of, yet never known a one who had it. Thou canst read the thoughts embedded in the stones, or wood or metal, by the anguish or joy of those who dwelt near them."

"A psychometricist!" Rod's eyes were wide.

Magnus turned to Gwen, trying to focus on her face. "Yet wherefore have I not noted this aforetime?"

"For that thou hast ever been in places thronged with living folk, whose thoughts did obscure any that came from stones."

"Sure it might not be part of the boy turning into a young man?" Rod asked.

"Mama did speak of strong feelings," Gregory pointed out. "Mayhap such thoughts stay not in stones, with lesser feelings."

Gwen nodded. "There is some truth to that—and I bethink me that this castle has seen many who were overwrought."

"And not pleasantly." Rod scowled. "Try not to touch anything, okay, son?"

"I will endeavor . . ."

"Then I'll give you some help." Rod turned to face the gatehouse. "We still have to get that drawbridge down, unless we're going to expect Fess to wait outside the whole time."

"Aye . . ." Magnus turned, his frown deepening, seeming to come into clearer focus.

"Gregory, help me. Just think of holding that chain up, when the time comes. Gwen, if you and the other kids would take the right-hand chain . . . ? Good. Now, everybody think *hot* at it." He glared at the bottom link, concentrating on it while the rest of his surroundings grew fuzzy. The link began to glow, first red, then orange, on through yellow into white, until finally the metal flowed. "Now," Rod grated, and the chain lifted a foot. Rod sighed and relaxed, watching the metal darken back down the spectrum as it cooled. He turned to look at the rest of his family, but their chain was just now yellowing. Rod glanced back at his own, saw it was ruby again, and told Gregory, "Okay, put it down now." The chain lowered to swing clinking against the wall, and Rod turned to add his bit to the right-hand chain. The metal flowed, the chain rose—and, with a low and rising growl of breaking rust, the huge old sprocket wheels began to turn. The growl rose to a grown, underscored by a furious clanking as the drawbridge fell away at the end of the tunnel, faster and faster, till its tip slimmed into the far bank of the moat. Hooves clattered on the wood.

"Careful, there!" Rod called, alarmed. "Those boards might be rotten!"

"The unsound ones fell to powder when the drawbridge dropped, Rod, and I can pick my way well enough around the holes." Then the clattering changed to thunder as Fess's hooves echoed in the tunnel, and the great black horse came trotting in.

The children cheered. Gwen glanced at Magnus, saw his face alight, and relaxed a little.

"Why is destruction the only thing I do better than the rest of you?" Rod grumbled.

" 'Tis for cause that thou hast come to it lately, husband, not grown to it," Gwen assured him breezily.

Gregory was staring at the huge bar buried in the stone. "We could have lifted it, Papa . . ."

"This was faster."

"Yet now we cannot draw the bridge up again."

"I know." Rod grinned. "Works out nicely that way, doesn't it?"

They spent the morning exploring the rest of the castle, and found a lot of dead leaves and branches blown in through the windows over the years. They also found a fair quantity of antique furniture, some of it still intact.

But not a single bird. Not even a rat or a mouse, for that matter.

"And never a one, through all these years." Cordelia looked up at the rafters. "How could that be, Papa?"

Rod shrugged. "They felt unwanted, dear."

"What was it that wanted them not?"

Rod avoided the question. "But look at the bright side—at least we won't have to set out traps. Or endanger a cat, either."

"Nay, Papa." Geoffrey corrected. " 'Tis the cat would endanger the rats."

"Not some of the rats *I've* seen—but there aren't any here. One advantage to ghosts, anyway." Rod had a brief, dizzying vision of an advertising sign: "Rid your house of those troublesome pests! Hire a *haunt!*" With, of course, a picture of a comical ghost shouting "Boo!" at a rat and a cockroach who were neck-and-neck in a dead heat away from the spook. Rod found himself wondering what to name the ghost? Buster? He shook his head and came back to the here and now.

"And none have dwelt here for two hundred years." Gregory gazed about him, wide-eyed.

"Not a living soul," Rod agreed. Strangely, there were no signs of squatters having moved in, or even having spent the night. On the other hand, that would've been hard to do, with the drawbridge up—which raised the question of why it was still up. Rod had a mental picture of the last servants to leave, heaving hard on the lip of the bridge, and watching it rise slowly, riding up on its counterweight. Either that, or the last servant had decided not to leave. Rod shuddered at that thought, and hoped he never met the person.

It was a pretty basic castle—just a keep with a curtain wall, diamond-shaped in its ground plan, with watchtowers at north and south, the keep itself serving to guard the western point, and the gatehouse at the east. There were only three floors to the keep, the first being all one huge, open room fifty feet in diameter, and the second divided into several rooms, presumably family quarters. The third was piled with small catapults and moldering crossbows and rusty bolts—the upstairs armory, for aerial defenses.

"Enough!" Gwen clapped her hands. "If we are to dwell here, no matter how short a while, we must needs make the keep fit for dwelling. Magnus and Gregory, sweep and dust! Cordelia and Geoffrey, hurl trash out into the moat!"

Geoffrey whooped and set to it; heaps of leaves began to swirl out the windows. Cordelia glowered at a broken, old table, and it rose off the floor, cracked leg dangling, and drifted toward the window.

Magnus frowned. "Wherefore do *they* pitch while we sweep, Mama?"

"For that thy sister's the best at making things fly," Gwen answered, "and Gregory's well suited to kiting along the ceiling and beams."

"Yet Geoffrey and I . . ."

"Are chosen for these tasks, for reasons thou knowest well." Gwen said, with steel beneath her voice; then her manner softened. "I promise thee, thou'lt trade tasks when we go to another floor. Aid me in this, my son."

Magnus grinned. "As thou wilt have it, Mama. Wilt thou lend me thy broomstick?"

And away he went, sweeping up a storm; Rod wondered about the whirlwinds in it. He sighed with relief, and blessed his eldest—trying to put a broom in Geoffrey's hands was asking for a major confrontation, unless you went after him with a quarterstaff. Even then, the broomstick would probably beat the quarterstaff, and there wouldn't be much work done.

All went well for a good fifteen minutes; then Geoffrey remembered to grumble. "Wherefore must we clean?"

"Wouldst thou truly wish to dwell in so stale a mess?" Cordelia asked, with scorn.

Geoffrey started to answer, but Magnus cut him off. "Do not ask, sister—thou dost not truly wish to hear his answer."

Geoffrey flushed an angry red, but before he could blast, Gregory burbled cheerfully. "Mayhap 'twill help to banish the ghosts."

That gave Geoffrey pause. He cocked his head to the side, frowning.

"Real ghosts!" Gregory went on, his eyes shining. "I had thought they were but old wives' tales!"

"On Gramarye, old wives' tales can turn real, Gregory," Fess reminded.

Gregory nodded. " 'Tis a point. Are they true ghosts, or only some aspect of psi we've not met before?"

"So much conversation surely cannot increase productivity."

"Oh, thou art but a killjoy, Fess!" Cordelia scoffed. "How can we help but speak of so wondrous a thing as our very own haunted castle?"

"It is difficult, I know," the robot commiserated. "Still,

you have been instructed to accomplish a task, and so much chatter inhibits your work.''

''Then give us summat to quiet us,'' Gregory suggested. ''Tell us more of our ancestors.''

Fess was silent a moment; after thirty years of Rod's squelching him every time he tried to discourse on family history, it was a little difficult adjusting to the idea that somebody was interested again. Slowly, he said, ''Gladly, children—but you had many ancestors. Of which would you like to hear?''

''That minor issue of which thou didst forbear to speak, yester eventide,'' Magnus said, too casually. ''Papa did mention an ancestor who did seek to find a family ghost.''

Fess sighed. ''You would remember that.''

''Wouldst thou not also, under such circumstances as these?''

''I fear I would,'' Fess sighed, ''yet I would prefer to gloss over it.''

''Then speak of our ancestor who finished building the Castle Gallowglass!''

''D'Armand, Cordelia,'' Fess reminded.

''Aye, ninny!'' Magnus jibed. ''Canst thou not remember that Papa took the name 'Gallowglass' when he came to Gramarye?''

''Oh, forever!'' Cordelia said crossly. ''What matter if I slip in its usage now and again?''

''Great matter, if thou dost ever seek to discover thine ancestral home!''

''And which of us shall ever wish to leave Gramarye?'' Geoffrey scoffed. ''Cordelia hath right, for once.''

''Once!'' Cordelia squawked. Geoffrey grinned wickedly in answer. Magnus was silent.

''Well enough, then.'' Cordelia turned away and tipped her nose up, scorning Geoffrey. ''Tell us of the ancestor who did finish Castle d'Armand.''

''Which?'' Fess almost seemed hopeful. ''It was finished several times.''

''Several?'' Magnus frowned. ''How long dist thou dwell therein, Fess?''

''From A.D. 3050, Magnus, till your father left home in 3542,'' Fess answered.

''Four centuries?'' Gregory gasped. Geoffrey glanced at him in annoyance; he wasn't good with figures.

"Four," Fess confirmed, "which is most of the time that has elapsed since I was activated."

"But was it not a delight?" Cordelia demanded.

"On occasion, yes," Fess admitted, "but it just as often was not. It depended on my owner of the time."

"Thou didst esteem Lona highly," Cordelia said, "for thous didst build her castle for her."

"True, but I would have done so for any other owner who so commanded—and did, since that was only the first time Chateau d'Armand was finished. It was quite modest by Maximan standards, you see."

Geoffrey frowned. "I misdoubt me an her descendants could abide that."

"They had difficulty," Fess admitted. "In fact, her son and grandson each built an addition, but one that was dictated by her original plan, thereby finishing the castle a second and third time. Nonetheless, their neighbors' houses were far more grand. They were good souls, though, and envy did not bother them greatly."

"Not so their wives," Cordelia demurred.

"You have guessed accurately, Cordelia." Fess sounded surprised. "Yes, the wives found it quite difficult to accept such relatively modest quarters, the more so because they were themselves younger daughters of grander lords."

"Lords?" Magnus lifted his head, frowning. "I wot me an thou didst speak of factors and crafters. Whence came nobility?"

"By mail, Magnus, from the heralds of Europe. Maxima was, after all, a sovereign world, with its own government . . ."

"But thou hast said Maxima had no government."

"Not really, though I can understand how my remarks could have seemed to indicate that. Nonetheless, the Maximans did have some mutual means of coordinating logistics and resolving disputes, and they had annual meetings of the leaders of all the Houses."

Magnus nodded. "And if that assembly did declare the head of a household noble, who could contradict it?"

"Precisely. The Earl Mulhearn was the first to receive a patent of nobility, and the others followed in a rush. Your own ancestor, Theodore d'Armand, changed his first name to 'Ruthven' and applied to the Assembly for status as a duke."

Magnus whistled. "He saw no vantage in modesty, did he?"

"No indeed. In fact, Ruthven saw no point in anything that was not his own idea . . ."

"Tell us of him," Cordelia begged.

"Nay!" Magnus turned to her with a scowl. "I claim primacy. I wish to hear of the ancestor who sought a family ghost!"

"Thy chance hath passed." Cordelia turned on him. "You know Mama and Papa have told us . . ."

She broke off at the very credible imitation of a throat-clearing, and turned to Fess with a frown. Before either of them could say anything, the robot told them, "The distinction does not exist; it was Ruthven who wanted a spectre."

"Then we must hear of him!" Cordelia settled herself for a long listen.

"If it is absolutely necessary . . ."

"Why dost thou hesitate?" Magnus frowned, puzzled. "What harm is there in telling us of him?"

"Ought we not to know of all our ancestors?" Cordelia demanded.

"There are some aspects of family history that should perhaps wait until you are more mature."

"Oh, pooh," Cordelia retorted, and Magnus concurred. "An we are old enough to have witnessed lords who have broke faith with their king and rebelled, we are old enough to know the truth of our own family."

"There is some merit in that, I suppose . . ."

"What fun is there in hearing only good of our ancestors?" Cordelia demanded.

"She speaketh truly," Magnus averred. "Wouldst thou have us believe our forebears were wax figures?"

"Oh, they were all quite human, Magnus. It is only that in some cases . . ."

"Some were more human than others?"

"You might say so, yes."

"Yet accuracy is of the greatest import," Gregory pointed out."

"Aye!" Cordelia leaped on it. "Is not the truth thy prime criterion?"

"No, frankly, Cordelia—in my program, loyalty to my owners is primary."

"Thy current owner will not mind thy speaking the truth of thy former owners," Magnus pointed out.

"There is some validity to that," Fess said reluctantly. He was remembering how Rod had taken him to task when he had poked around in the family library and learned some of the facts about those ancestors that Fess *hadn't* told him.

"And there is the matter of loyalty to thy future owner," Magnus added.

"Which will be yourself, since you are the eldest."

Magnus blithely ignored Geoffrey's glare. "Thus, thy present owner careth not, and thy future owner doth desire thee to tell. Ought thou not to speak?"

Fess capitulated. "Very well, children. But remember, if you find your relationship with the subject of this tale distasteful, that you required me to tell it."

"We shall not reproach thee," Cordelia assured him.

"But an archway at the base of a tower cannot stand, Ruthven."

" 'Milord,' Fess," Ruthven said sternly. "I am noble now."

"But the Assembly . . ."

"The Assembly will no doubt grant my request at its next meeting. After all, it raised Joshua Otis to Marquis, only last week; it surely can have no reason not to bestow a like title upon me."

Silently, Fess sighed and carefully did not point out that the Assembly had no particular reason to grant Ruthven's request, either. If the factory business department had not been automated, d'Armand Limited would have gone bankrupt from sheer neglect.

Not that the House of d'Armand would have fallen. Quite the opposite, in fact. Ruthven seemed to spend all his time building.

"Of course the tower will stand."

"How, milord?"

Ruthven waved the question away. "A minor detail. See to it, Fess."

The robot sighed within and focused its lenses on the blueprints. Perhaps a judicious use of gravity generators . . . On a low-gravity asteroid, there was no concern about the tower falling down . . . But if there was too little of it, it might fall apart from centripedal force.

"How dare they!" Ruthven stormed, jamming his helmet at Fess. "How can they have the effrontery to be so insolent!"

He yanked at the seals of his pressure suit so hard that the fabric ripped. He saw the gaping rent, and cursed all the more loudly.

"Ruthven, please!" His wife came running with apprehensive glances. "The children . . ."

"They had damned well better be at lessons in their nursery, madame, or I shall bid Fess cane them!" Ruthven yanked his arms out of the pressure suit, relying on Fess to catch the sleeves in time, and pulled his feet out of the legs as he stepped forward. "The degraded peasants!"

"Ruthven!" his wife gasped. "Your own children?"

"Not the children, you goose! The Assembly!"

"What . . . Oh!" Matilda's eyes widened. "Did they refuse your patent of nobility?"

"No—much worse! They raised me to the rank of . . ." Ruthven's voice sank to a hiss. " . . . Viscount!"

"Viscount! Oh, how dare they! One cannot be lower, and still be a peer!"

"Precisely." Ruthven threw himself into a lounger and pushed the "medium massage" button. "I shall be revenged upon them! I shall humiliate them! How, I do not know—but the time will come, will come for each of them!"

"At least," Fess offered, "you are now legally a lord."

"But only barely a lord, you officious ingrate!" Ruthven shouted. "How dare you address me as 'you'? Do you not know a more respectful form of address?"

"But . . . my program indicates no flaw in etiquette . . ."

"Then it shall!" the new Viscount thundered. "You shall learn, sirrah, you shall be educated! I shall buy the module today!"

Castle Gallowglass rose far above its humble beginnings in a maze of towers joined in vaulting arches, a fairytale concoction of metallic traceries and onion domes and gargoyles.

It was a mess.

It was a hodgepodge of periods and styles of architecture, all jumbled together without rationale or critical standard. Somewhere beneath the festoons of racoco plasticrete, the original, classic simplicity of Lona's tranquil palace gathered in upon itself—but the casual passerby would never know it was there. What he would see was the most disgusting example of *nouveau riche* lack of taste Fess had ever seen—and after a hundred fifty years of contemplating the handiwork of the Maximans, that was saying quite a bit.

Not that he *could* say it, of course—not about his owner's masterpiece. His new programming had seen to that.

"How could they possibly have denied me!"

"I'm sorry, milord, I'm sorry." Fess's judgement circuits produced massive reluctance at the sound of his own words. "The College of Heralds of Europe says that another family's been using that coat of arms of three lions quartered with fleur-de-lis, for many generations."

"Then they may forfeit the device! How much do they want for it?"

Inwardly, Fess shrivelled, but his vocoder said, "Oh, no, sorry, milord boss! Coats of arms simply can't be bought!"

"Don't say 'can't' to me!" Ruthven raged. "They have no right to that device, I tell you—because *I want it!*"

"Well, certainly, milord boss, but that doesn't mean there is any way we can get it."

"There *must* be a way! Confound it, *find* a way to gain a coat of arms!" Ruthven stalked away toward the bar.

Fess sighed and rolled off toward the library to plug himself into the data banks. He knew very well that no family would be willing to give up its coat of arms, and that the College of Heralds would not honor such a transaction even if it could be made. The answer, of course, lay in designing a device that Ruthven would accept, and that was not already in use.

"A wonderful design." Ruthven beamed at the drawing. "It says so much."

"Yes, milord boss." Fess knew quite well that the device said only what the viewer read into it. It was nothing but the silhouette of a man with girded loins, a cloak, and a staff in his hand, standing with one foot atop some nameless geological formation, facing toward the left, but with his back mostly toward the viewer. Nonetheless, it was silver on a field of blue, so he knew Ruthven would like it.

"A masterpiece! Am I not a genius?"

"Yes sir, boss milord. No, boss mi—uh, yes, milord!"

"Architecture, fine letters, now design—there are no limits to my talents! Surely the College of Heralds cannot deny me now!"

"No sir, boss milord." That, Fess could say with conviction—because he had examined the records of the College thoroughly, then sent off the sketch by fax as soon as it was finished. He hadn't shown it to Ruthven until the College had sent back preliminary approval.

"None must deny me anything." Ruthven patted his stomach, which had grown steadily with the years and was approaching critical mass. "There is none like me!"

The phrase struck an echo in Fess's memory banks—several of them, in fact.

"But, boss milord!" Fess protested. "How am I going to do *that?*"

"Order one from Terra, of course." Ruthven waved away the problem.

"*Order* one, milord sir? A family *ghost?*"

"There is a catalog, I presume."

"But you can't buy a thing that doesn't exist!"

"Of course ghosts exist. Every noble family on Terra has one." Ruthven gestured carelessly with sausage fingers. "An ancestral ghost for my castle, Fess. At least one. Don't ask me for particulars, though. I know nothing about them."

That, at least, was true. Sometimes Fess could have sworn that Ruthven had gone to great pains to know nothing—and when he did accidently pick up some information, he did the best he could to forget it. His way of making sure he had a clean mind, no doubt.

But the ghost of one of Ruthven's ancestors? Would he want one, really? Fess was tempted, and if he could have brought back Lona's ghost, he would have. He would have loved to see her haul Ruthven over the coals fifty times, for what he had done to her palace—and when she had finished, she would have bullied what was left of him into restoring some vestige of order to his household. Or maybe the ghost of Dar, who would have taken one look around, bellowed in outrage, taken Ruthven apart, then remembered his vocation as a teacher and put the aging playboy back together and tried to explain the basics of good taste to him.

Or, best of all, the ghost of Tod Tambourin—alias Whitey the Wino.

Now, wait. The ghost of Whitey . . . That had possibilities . . .

* * *

A shriek split the night, and the Countess Freiliport came barreling out of the bedroom. Fess heaved a 16-Farad sigh, stretched alloyed arms (the more conducive to the mood because Ruthven had given him a new, and very skeletal, body) to catch her, and began soothing. "There, now, Milady, it's gone. Nothing to be afraid of, no spooks out here, only your good old faithful Fess the butler, here to make sure the nasty thing can't get at you . . ."

"Oh! It *is* you!" The Countess collapsed against Fess's ribcage, sobbing. The sobs choked off as she saw the ribs and went rigid.

He had to head off the scream. "That's just my new body, Milady. The Viscount thought it would go better with the decor. It's really still good old Fess inside here. Was he as bad as all that?"

"Who? The ghost? Oh!" The Countess went limp. "He was horrible! First only those spectral footsteps, coming closer and closer, and no answer when I called out 'Who's there?'—no answer at all, mind you, until that horrid moan broke out right by my ear, and that glowing cloud appeared, towering over the foot of my bed!"

"Only a glowing cloud?"

"No, no! Only at first. It gathered in on itself slowly, till it had assumed the form of a perfectly horrid old man, skinny as a rail, moaning so dolefully that my heart went out to him— until he *saw* me!"

"Saw you? What then?"

"Why, he . . . he *winked* at me! And began to come toward me, reaching out and grinning that lascivious leer . . . Oh! I was never so frightened in my life!"

That, Fess could believe. The hologram of Whitey had been assembled from clips of him in the role of a vampire in a 3DT epic he had directed, and in which he had also starred.

"I am so sorry you have had such a fright, Milady. If you wish, I shall summon your chauffeur . . ."

"Oh, my heavens, no!" The Countess turned to blow into her handkerchief, then tucked it back into her bosom with a sniffle, straightening and turning back toward the room. "It was wonderful. I wouldn't have missed this night for the world." She stepped firmly toward the bedroom, then fal-

tered and looked back over her shoulder. "I don't suppose he
might come back—the ghost, I mean?"

"I'm afraid not, Milady," Fess sympathized. "Only one
visitation per guest per night, you know."

"Ah. Well, I was afraid of such a thing." The Countess
sighed and went back toward the bedroom. "I really must
discuss the issue with your master, Fess. So paltry of him, to
limit his hauntings in that fashion."

The door closed behind her, and Fess resigned himself to
refereeing another bout in the morning. It was a compliment,
really, but Ruthven just could not abide anything remotely
resembling criticism. He was sure to bristle, and was likely to
anger the Countess, jeopardizing a family friendship that went
back a century and a half.

"If thou wert human, Fess, thou wouldst have been tempted
to refrain from interfering. Ruthven would have had no more
than he deserved!"

"True, children—but I am a robot, and was capable of
pouring unlimited oil on the waters."

"E'en so, thou shouldst not have." Geoffrey folded his
arms and lifted his chin. "He had not *commanded* thee to
intervene, had he?"

"No, children, but when Lona died, she asked me to look
after her descendants for her."

Geoffrey heaved a sigh, deflating, but Cordelia had a
merry glint in her eye.

"I am sorry that you have received a somewhat unflattering
portrait of your ancestors from me," Fess said gently.

"Unflattering, indeed! In Father's book of the family history, Ruthven appears a noble and generous character, re-
nowned for his building and beautifying. Why is there no
mention of his failings in that chapter?"

"Why, because Ruthven wrote it. And he *did* increase the
glory of his family, in a way."

"In some way, mayhap." Magnus grinned wickedly. "But
by this time, had not the other folk of Maxima gained summat
of a sense aesthetic?"

"They had, Magnus," Fess sighed. "All applied for patents of nobility, and all received them—and most felt obliged
to find some civic duty to do, as well as to gain some cultural
refinement."

Magnus was puzzled. "Dost mean all who dwelt on Maxima were noble?"

"According to themselves, yes—and almost all of them are now worthy of the term."

"Yet even in Ruthven's time, they did know a monstrosity when they saw one?"

"I fear they did," Fess sighed, "and yes, they did look with contempt on Ruthven's 'masterpiece.' The ghost of Whitey redeemed him in their eyes, though."

"For that it brought to their minds the illustrious founder of our House?"

"No, because it was such great fun. Word of the apparition spread, of course, and within a fortnight, everyone wished to be invited to stay the night at Castle d'Armand."

"And therefore did need to treat gently with Ruthven and his wife."

"Quite so, Cordelia, at least to their faces."

"And each guest wished to stay in the 'haunted' room, I warrant," Magnus said, grinning again.

"Yes, and there was considerable fussing when they found someone else was already there, fussing which descended upon the head of the majordomo."

"Thyself, of course."

"Correct, Gregory. Yet since it assured Ruthven that most of them would come back for another weekend, it worked to the benefit of himself and Matilda."

"And thou didst need to stand watch o'er the bedroom door o' nights?"

"I fear so. Everyone who stayed there wished to be frightened, so of course they all were, and it fell to me to calm them."

"And to intervene 'twixt them and Ruthven in the morning?"

"Generally, yes."

"But that could not last." Cordelia protested. "Soon or late, everyone on Maxima must needs have stayed in the haunted chamber."

"Aye," Geoffrey agreed. "There are not so many people on but one asteroid, after all."

"True, quite true—and I was never so relieved as when the Viscount tired of the hologram, and I could deactivate it."

"Did not their children wish it to stay?"

"No; they quite resented it, for their schoolmates had teased them about it unmercifully . . ."

"Jealousy, no doubt," Geoffrey muttered.

"Thou shouldst know, brother."

" . . . AND about the mansion," Fess concluded, overriding Geoffrey's response. "When they grew, they made sure to gain a thorough grasp of all the arts, including the study of aesthetics, and were much less concerned with social pretensions."

"Dost thou mean they became noble?"

"Well, they had certainly furthered the process. In fact, they eventually gained enough taste to see the amusing side of the holographic display, and would now and again ask to have the 'ghost' once more turned on for a while, then turned off again."

"Would we could so deal with the spectre within this castle," Gregory sighed.

"It would be pleasant, yes—though I suspect that *these* ghosts may be considerably harder to eradicate. And you must remember that there may be an element of actual danger involved."

"Dost thou truly think so?" Geoffrey perked up noticeably.

"I do. When your father first came to Gramarye, he was nearly frightened to death by the ghosts in Castle Loguire, until I pointed out to him that the cause was a subsonic harmonic of their moans, not their actual presence."

Magnus turned somber. "I misdoubt me an these ghosts will be a part with them."

"Aye, for those were *nice* ghosts," said Gregory, "as Father hath told it."

"Fair or foul, we shall vanquish them," Geoffrey said proudly. "The villain's not made that can stand against us, an we stand together."

"Remember that, please, Geoffrey—it may become an important principle in your lives."

"And now?" Gregory asked.

"Most especially now. Please be very careful, children, to be sure you are never alone, in Castle Foxcourt. Now back to work! I feel my storytelling has slowed your cleaning."

7

Rod kept a weather eye cocked on his children the whole time, but all he could see was that the four of them were working industriously. "Gwen, there's something wrong."

"How so, my husband?"

"They're all working in the same room, without bickering. What's more, they're keeping their noses to the grindstone, without having to be nagged."

"Oh." Gwen dimpled. " 'Tis not so amazing as that. Hast thou not heard what Fess doth tell them?"

"Yeah, but that just makes it worse! When I was a kid, I went crazy when he tried to give me a lecture on top of my having to do chores!"

"Thy children are not thyself," Gwen said, but her tone was gentle, sympathetic. "And, too, these tales of thine homeland are like visions of a magical kingdom to them."

Rod frowned. "I suppose that makes sense. If people in a high-tech environment used to read fairy tales for escape, then . . ."

"Even so," Gwen agreed. "In any event, husband, I pray thee, do not question our good fortune."

"Or our good horse. Well, so long as there's nothing to worry about." And there wasn't, so Rod was obviously going to have to find something else to serve the purpose. He turned away, going back to sweeping the trash out from the corners, and gradually working his way further and further into the available shadows, closer and closer to the archway to the stairs. He carefully hadn't mentioned the downstairs armory. If it wasn't on the ground floor, it was in the cellar—and Rod didn't want the kids going anywhere near a real, authentic dungeon. Especially Magnus.

So he waited until Gwen had gathered them in the courtyard again, and was setting out leftovers—then quietly slipped away to explore.

He was only halfway to the cellar door when he heard hooves on the floor behind him. His heart jumped into his throat, and he spun about, then relaxed with a gusty sigh. "You nearly gave me heart failure!"

"I would just as soon you did not explore the dungeon alone, Rod," Fess told him.

"I *was* trying to sneak off unnoticed."

"It is my duty to notice you, Rod. I promised your father."

"Yeah, but he *also* told you to take orders from me, from then on." Rod turned away, heading back toward the huge oaken doors that closed the spiral stair from the Great Hall.

"I have obeyed all your orders, Rod."

"Yes, but not always their intent. Though I have to admit I'm glad of your company—as long as the kids don't tumble to it, and follow us."

"Gwen had them well occupied."

"Yes; that's the advantage of the appetites of youth." Rod heaved at a door, and it fell off its hinges. In several pieces. He stared down at its remains, then said, "Remind me to have that replaced."

"Yes, Rod."

"Immediately."

"To be sure."

They started down the curving stairway, and ran out of daylight pretty quickly. "It is not safe to proceed further, Rod."

"Yeah, I noticed." Rod held up a dead branch. "I salvaged something out of the detritus the wind blew in."

"Foresighted of you. Would you care for a spark?"

"Naw. It'd take too long." Rod glared at the end of the stick. After a minute, it burst into flames.

"You have learned well."

"Just practice." Rod held up the torch. "Let's see what's down here."

They came out into a narrow corridor—and Rod stopped dead. "Fess—there's *evil* here!"

"I am sure much wickedness was done here, yes."

"I mean *now!* I've never felt such malice!"

"I sense nothing, Rod."

Rod looked up slowly at the robot. "Nothing at all? Listen on human thought-frequencies."

Fess stood still a moment, then said, "Nothing, Rod."

Rod nodded slowly. "Then it's completely psionic."

"It would seem to be more intense than poor lighting and restrictive architecture could account for. Shall we leave?"

"Not until I'm sure what's here." Rod stepped ahead down the hall. "But I think we'll keep the kids out. I'll remind them what dungeons were for."

"They were for storing foodstuffs, Rod, and other supplies the castle needed, especially those of military nature."

"It wasn't just potatoes they stowed down here, Fess." Rod steeled himself, then thrust his torch through one of the open doorways and stepped in.

"What do you see?"

"Damp stone walls." Rod frowned. "And a dirt floor, with several circular mounds about two feet across. And one open pit, the same size, with the dirt piled beside it."

"What is in the pit?"

"Apples. Or their mummies, anyway." Rod stepped back into the hall. "I give in. They *did* keep stores down here."

"Shall we forego the rest of the exploration, then?"

"Not until I've seen the whole thing. Come on."

There were six open doorways, one holding bundles of dust that might once have been arrows, another holding casks, and so on.

The the pool of torchlight showed doors.

Rod stopped, then stepped ahead with determination, but with his heart in his throat.

The doors had iron gratings in them, about a foot square. Rod thrust his torch through, but saw only empty shackles. He pulled the branch back out with a sigh of relief.

"Empty, Rod?"

"Yes, thank Heaven. Come on."

The final two doors showed dim light filtering down. "Must be at the side of the keep." In spite of the light, the feeling of evil intensified. Rod peered through the left-hand grating. His jaw hardened.

"What do you see?" Fess asked.

"I can recognize a few items," Rod answered. "There's a rack, and I'm pretty sure the coffin thing is an Iron Maiden."

"The torture chamber."

"Off-limits, especially for Magnus." Rod turned away. "Come on, let's go back."

"But you haven't investigated the last chamber, Rod."

"And I'm not going to, either—at least, not until after lunch. I'm pretty sure what I'm going to find there."

"What is that, Rod?"

"Let's just say that, if you're going to have a torture chamber for extracting information, you're going to keep the raw material close at hand—and apples aren't the only things that leave mummies."

After lunch, they went back to cleaning. Gwen and the kids set to work on the Great Hall, and Rod took the basement. He was right about the remaining cell—and even though it was two hundred years old, he handled what he found there with pity as he rolled it in their oldest blanket and set it on Fess's saddle for its last trip. He dug a deep hole far down the slope from the castle, and lowered the blanket down. As he started to throw the dirt back in, Fess said, "He was probably a Christian, Rod."

"She, I think."

"What evidence have you?" The robot sounded puzzled. "There is no clothing left, after all these years."

"Not even a scrap—but if that was a man, he had the broadest pelvis I've ever seen on a male. And as to his religion, you're probably right, and I'll ask Father Boquilva to come along on our next trip and say the funeral service."

"I wish you would say a few words now, Rod."

Rod looked up at the horse-head with a frown. "Odd of you to be so sentimental about someone you never knew."

"Humor me," the horse suggested.

Well, if there was one thing Fess was never without, it was a reason. Rod didn't ask—he just took the advice, and recited as much of the Twenty-Third Psalm as he could remember, added a few snatches from Ecclesiastes, and ended with a verse of the Dies Irae. Finally, he asked eternal rest and light everlasting for the soul that had inhabited the pitiful remains, and started shovelling.

On the way back, he asked, "Any particular reason why you wanted that?"

"Yes, Rod—to aid the spirit's rest."

Rod frowned. "You don't believe the ghost would come walking back in the middle of the night, do you?"

"I would not," Fess said slowly, "declare anything impossible, on Gramarye."

* * *

Rod tramped back in across the drawbridge, carefully avoiding the missing planks, crossed the courtyard, and went into the keep.

He had a pleasant surprise. He could scarcely believe it was the same room. There wasn't a speck of trash anywhere to be seen, and Gregory was just finishing dusting the last of the cobwebs out of the corners, high in the air, floating up near the ceiling. Their bedrolls were spread over mounds of pine boughs, and Cordelia was laying bowls and spoons around the edge of a picnic cloth. Magnus, Geoffrey, and Gregory were unloading bundles of logs and sticks next to the fireplace, where their mother stood over the great hearth, face lit by the flames of a small fire as she tasted something in a pot that hung from a crane. She twitched her nose, unsatisfied, put the cover back on, and pushed the cauldron back over the flames.

"Amazing! How did you manage this in only two hours?" Then Rod answered his own question. "No, of course—what's wrong with me? This is the kind of situation that *does* justify using magic, doesn't it?"

"Oh, nay, Papa!" Gregory said, eyes wide. "Such spirits as do slumber here, we have no wish to wake, an we can avoid it."

"Then how did you manage it?"

"With good, hard work," Gwen answered, with some asperity, "though I will own, 'twas somewhat faster to think at the trash, and make it fly itself out the window. Yet there was still a deal of sweeping and hauling to do, and thy children have labored mightily."

"As their mother has, I'm sure." Rod came and sat down by the fire. "You're going to make me feel as though I haven't done my share."

Gwen shuddered. "Nay. I think the chore thou hast done, was one none of us would have wished—though I think I should have stood by thee the while."

"It wasn't fit for you to see," Rod answered, "and Fess was company enough."

"Aye." Cordelia looked up. "He hath great experience of the surprises in castles, hath he not?"

"Not in the sense you mean, Cordelia," Fess answered. "However, as supervisor of the construction robots that built each stage of Castle d'Armand—I became somewhat conversant with the making and mending of castles.''

"As well thou shouldst be, in light of all that Count Ruthven made thee do! Yet wherefore was he so curlish in his manner?''

Fess was silent. Rod had to explain, "It's called inbreeding, Cordelia—and since it could be construed as an insult to the family, Fess won't say anything about it.''

"Not e'en an I ask him the question direct?''

"No—he'll just refer you to me. Count yourself referred,'' Rod turned to Fess. "Tell them what inbreeding is, would you?''

Fess rasped a sigh of white noise. "It occurs when people who are too closely related, have children, Cordelia.''

"Thou dost speak of the law which saith first cousins may not wed?''

"Yes, and that second cousins should not. Oh, do not mistake me—when such a marriage occasionally occurs, it will not always result in great harm. But if first cousins marry first cousins for three or four generations, problems are likely to occur.''

Cordelia asked. "Of what manner of problems dost thou speak?''

"Anything you can think of, Cordelia.'' Out of the corner of his eye, Rod was aware of Gregory listening, wide-eyed. "Birth defects of all sorts. Some of them don't show up until later in life, though—anything from a person being born without a limb, or with a weak heart, to having low ability to heal. One such boy was perfectly normal in every way—until he broke his legs, and they never healed properly, and wouldn't grow along with the rest of him.''

"How horrible!''

"But the problems we're thinking of in your ancestor's case, were problems of the mind.''

Cordelia lifted her head as understanding came. She turned to Fess with a beatific smile. "Such as behaving like a churl?''

"Well, that, too,'' Fell admitted, "though in Ruthven's case, I fear another aspect of inbreeding may have become obvious.''

"He's talking about a drop in intelligence,'' Rod explained.

"Not always, mind you—but even now and then is bad enough."

Magnus spoke up. "Dost mean we are heir to all these ills?"

"Oh, you kids are safe, thanks to your mother."

"Aye, for that I married thee."

"Well, true, there was some inbreeding on your side, too," Rod said, with a glance at his collection of espers, "but you had the good sense to marry me. I mean, someone from outside the gene pool."

"Thou hadst first said it best."

"Well, thanks. Of course, you had a bit bigger pool; there were a few hundred thousand of you. But the good citizens of Maxima all stem from thirty-two-thousand-odd ancestors, and have been cheerfully marrying each other for five hundred years."

"Then all must have some aspect of this inbreeding," Cordelia inferred.

"Yes, even if it only shows up as occasional ugliness—or not so occasional, in the case of a good many of my—" Rod coughed into his fist, "—female compatriots."

"Yet surely this was not true of all the d'Armands!"

"Fortunately, it only became fully evident in Ruthven's case," Fess agreed. "Both his sons, as I have told you, reacted to his excesses by becoming much more reserved, and cultivating their artistic sensibilities—though, I must admit, neither was extraordinarily high in mental capacity."

"Not really necessary." Rod shook his head. "What counts is the goodness of the person. We don't all have to be geniuses." He noticed Gregory's eyes suddenly glazing, and knew his words were sinking in where they were needed the most.

"And their children?" Cordelia prompted.

"They were noble in every sense of the word, Cordelia," said Fess, "and most of your ancestors have deserved the honorific. Some were frighteningly bright, some were amazingly simple, and most were more intelligent than they needed to be. Your grandfather was a most excellent gentleman, a truly good human being, intelligent and sensitive, in addition to being highly responsible, and caring deeply for his wife and children. It was an honor to serve him."

"Was he truly such a paragon?" Geoffrey seemed surprised.

"He was indeed."

"Why then, 'tis no wonder that our father is so princely a man." Magnus turned to Rod with a glint in his eye. "Or was it simply that thou wast reared in a castle?"

"I wasn't."

The children stared in surprise.

Then Gregory coughed and said, "We had thought thou wast reared in the Castle d'Armand, of which we have spoken."

Rod shook his head, smiling. "Not so, kids. Your grandfather was the second son of the current Count—and I'm *his* second son."

"The Count's eldest son inherited the title," Fess explained, "and the castle with it."

"They were Viscounts, though." Gregory corrected, "Thou didst say so explicitly, Fess."

"Yes, Gregory, but the third Lord d'Armand so far surpassed his grandfather that he was able to be of major service to Maxima, in its relations with Terra, and was therefore created Count. Your grandfather could thus be given the rank of Viscount, and a third of the family estates."

"Then where didst thou grow, Papa?" Cordelia asked.

"We grew up in the Grange, dear—just a big house, but roomy enough for my parents, my brother, and my sister. And, of course, for me."

"Your father somewhat understates the issue," Fess advised the children. "The house had twenty-two rooms, and most of them were quite large."

"Still, 'twas not a castle." Cordelia was severly disappointed.

"Oh, it was adequate." Rod leaned back, stretching. "More than adequate, in fact—but only because Grandpa was living with us."

"Thy father?" Magnus stared. "Was he not the Viscount?"

"No, *my* grandfather," Rod amplified.

"Then he was the Count himself." Geoffrey was confused. "Wherefore did he live in the lesser house?"

"He, ah, found it more congenial," Rod explained.

"Your father understates again," Fess assured the children. "Inbreeding and recessive genes caught up with my old master in his seventy-third year . . ."

"Also the realization that he was never going to get away from Maxima," Rod reminded. "He finally admitted that to himself."

"That is mere conjecture, Rod, bordering on slander," Fess stated.

"It's conjecture based on all the advice he gave me, mostly to leave home as soon as I grew up."

"He did seem to regret his youthful decision to stay and take care of the family business," Fess admitted, "though that was also his responsibility. He was, after all, the heir."

"And how did these regrets affect him?" Magnus asked.

"He became—somewhat foolish," Fess answered.

Geoffrey cocked his head to the side. "Thou dost mean he went mad."

"Most would say that," Fess agreed. "Certainly, from his conversation, he was no longer fully aware of the real world, and had escaped into a fantasy realm of his own devising. He spoke of knights and fair maidens, of wizards and dragons. He believed himself to be chronicler of a royal court in a fantastic land."

"He was lots of fun to be with, though," Rod said quickly.

"Unless he decided that you were a monster of some sort," Fess demurred.

Rod shrugged. "Even there, he had very good judgement. After all, the Duchess of Malcasa *was* an old dragon."

"What did he do to her?" Geoffrey asked, eyes wide.

"Oh, nothing. Never hurt a soul, mostly because Fess was always there. That's why his successor gave us Fess, along with the Grange."

"There was also some mention of being 'outmoded' and some claim, on the part of his wife, that the only antiques that graced a house were furniture," Fess said darkly.

"Which applied as much to Grandpa as it did to you," Rod said quickly, "and I think you've disproved the 'outmoded' part a few hundred times since then. Starting as soon as the two of you moved in, in fact—you became very good at calming Grandpa down."

"I merely accorded him the respect that was due him, Rod."

"Yeah, and couched everything in the terms he was using." Rod turned back to the children. "Me, I thought it was a fun game. What was I—six? So if he said a bush was an ogre, I was ready to play along."

"Thou didst take pleasure in his company, then?"

"Oh, yes," Rod said softly. "Always."

"What was this fantastic land he did see?"

"The kingdom of Granclarte," Rod sighed, gazing off into the years of a childhood made magical by a childish old man. "I used to sit and listen to him for hours."

"Well, for half-hours," Fess amended, "though in a child's time-sense, the tales must have seemed longer."

"Longer? They never ended!" Rod turned back to the children. "He wrote some excellent stories in the process. They became instant best-sellers, after he died."

"After?" Cordelia asked. "Wherefore not whiles he lived?"

"He would not publish them," Fess explained. "He was quite insistant on the point. It was perfectly compatible with his delusion, I assure you. He was writing for the glory of the Courts of Granclarte, not for his own aggrandizement.

"Mad as a hatter," Rod sighed, "but a wonderful old man." He gazed off into space, into the years of his childhood. "I used to sit on the floor in his study, listening to him tell me about the wonderful adventures of the knight Beaubras and his quest for the Rainbow Crystal. Of course, the voicewriter was picking up his every word. When I grew up, I found out that, after the Nanny-bot took me off to tuck me in, he'd sit up and edit it all. But it was wonderful to hear."

"What was the Rainbow Crystal?" Gregory demanded.

"In the story, it was sort of a master-key," Rod explained. "It could tie all the different sorts of magic together, uniting them to confound the evil sorcerer Maumains."

He smiled down at them. "Of course, in the real world, it was the big prism that hung in the middle of my mother's chandelier—but I liked it better his way."

"Aye," Cordelia breathed. "When may we read his books?"

"As soon as I can find a copy, dear. Unfortunately, I left them all about thirty light-years back."

Fess said nothing, but Gregory eyed him speculatively.

"Oh, why did he not endure till we could meet him!" Cordelia cried.

"I'm sure he wanted to," Rod sighed, "but he had a prior engagement. I hope he found Granclarte as he ascended. The Count was good enough to let us stay on in the Grange after he died, though—it was wrenching enough to be suddenly without Grandpa. Even made it pretty clear that my older brother Richard would inherit the place when Dad passes on, in his turn.''

Magnus frowned. ''And what wilt thou inherit?''

''Nothing.'' Rod smiled sadly. ''There's nothing left over. All the houses are taken by my cousins, and all the family land, too—if you can call bare rock 'land.' Oh, there'll be a bit of money from my father—a goodly bit; he contributed quite a few designs to the family business, and invested the proceeds well and wisely, so he has made quite a sum on his own. But that's all.''

''You did have an option, Rod,'' Fess reminded. ''You could have taken a position in d'Armand Automatons, Ltd., and doubtless done quite well.''

''Yeah, but a poor relation is a poor relation, no matter how cleverly it's disguised.'' Rod made a face. ''Besides, Maxima was . . . boring.''

''Oh, truly?'' Magnus perked up. ''In what way was it boring?''

Rod glanced at Fess out of the corner of his eye. Magnus caught it, and turned to the robot. ''Wilt thou not tell me, Fess?''

''We have spoken of this before,'' Fess said, somewhat severely. ''I will not betray your father's confidences.''

Rod did a rapid mental balancing act. He and Fess had managed to distract the children, quite successfully, from their current, rather grim, surroundings. He compared the advantages of continuing that distraction, with the disadvantages of letting their minds return to the haunted castle around them, and made his decision. ''Oh, go ahead and tell them!'' He leaned back. ''After all, there's nothing in my past that I'm *really* ashamed of. A bit embarrassed, maybe, but not really ashamed.''

''As you will have it, Rod,'' Fess sighed, and Rod sat back to listen as the tale grew more and more lurid, and his ears grew more and more red.

8

"Look, Fess, just call me 'Rod' when we're alone. I know you can do it!"

"I cannot, sir master boss." Fess was looking better these days—he had gone through two body changes and an overhaul. He fairly gleamed with a metallic shine, and his arms and legs were much fuller than the pipestems he had worn when he first came to Maxima. They had to be—they were the storage places for his spares and tools, now. His torso had been enlarged enough to hold his computer/brain, and his "head" had consequently been reduced to a much more anthropoid size and form. He was virtually a metal android now, albeit a somewhat barrel-chested one. "I cannot change my terms of address," he explained, "unless my owner issues the command."

"And Dad won't do it, because he has too much respect for his ancestors." Rod shook his head and went back to sorting through his revolving closet. "One more reason why I need to get off this provincial backwater of a planetoid."

"I cannot understand your preoccupation with leaving, young master."

"Yeah, well, if I could have gone to college on Terra, as Cousin Rupert did, maybe I wouldn't be quite so antsy. But when you have to stay here on Maxima and let college come to *you*, via comm screen, and the only place you've ever visited is Ceres, you start developing a huge hankering to *see* some of what you're learning all about."

"Such feelings are consistent with my knowledge of the juvenile male of the species, Rod. But if you wish to leave home, why not ask your father's permission?"

"Oh, come on, Fess. If he could afford to send me to Terra and put me through college, he would have!"

"The support I had in mind was moral, not financial."

"He wouldn't give it, Fess. He'd think I was crazy, to go jaunting off into nowhere on a tramp freighter. He'd also be panicked out of his mind with worry."

"I think you may underestimate your father, boss master sahib."

"Are you kidding? It'd be one thing if it had never crossed his mind to get off Maxima when *he* was young—but it's entirely another, knowing that he actively decided against it!"

"You cannot know what your father's thoughts were when he was young, master boss raj."

"Fess, you remember how Grandpa used to tell me, every few weeks, that as soon as I was old enough, I should leave Maxima?"

"You did take into account that your grandfather was no longer of sound mind, did you not, young effendi?"

"Yeah, and now I know what drove him around the bend! Every time he told me to go, he reminded me that he'd given that same advice to Dad."

"Surely he had always had too great a sense of responsibility to act so selfishly, young master batyushka."

"Would it have done him so much harm, as long as he was home before Grandpa went off the tracks? Especially since he's spent the rest of his life just hanging around on this back patch of the estate, taking care of Grandpa and us, and waiting, just in case something happened to both Uncle Despard and Cousin Rupert—which it never has."

"May it never!" But your father's self-sacrifice should be a shining example to you, young master baas!"

"Oh, absolutely blinding—and I'm going to make damn sure it doesn't happen to me! That freighter from Mars is in, and the captain says they can use another hand. They're slipping orbit at midnight, outbound for Triton—and I'm going to be with them! Make sure my bag gets to the spaceport by 2300, Fess."

"As you wish, *very* young master," Fess sighed. "Meanwhile, there is still a matter of tonight's ball. If you are not there, questions will be asked."

"Don't I know it, though! Why do you think I'm going? Besides, if I'm out at a ball, nobody will expect me till way after midnight . . . Ah, there!" Out of the closet, Rod pulled a set of frills with buttonholes. He slipped it on over his singlet. "Yuck! I like formal shirts, but they're way overdone this year!"

"They lend you a look of elegance, young master boss."

"Elegance have long trunks, Fess—and that's what I need to carry these things in. I just wish I could get out of going to this one last ball."

The robot emitted the burst of white noise that was its equivalent of a sigh. "You may counteract the boredom by reminding yourself that it will be the last one you need ever attend, Rod. Still, some of the young ladies have truly wonderful hearts . . ."

"And truly deplorable looks, with faces like mashed potatoes. Well, no, I'm being unfair. Strike the 'mashed.' "

"But surely their figures excite your interest."

"Who would know, under all the drapery they have to wear to these things? Probably just as well, too." Rod shuddered. "Not to mention their minds. I mean, the inbreeding here is *really* beginning to show."

The robot forebore mentioning that Rod himself might be something of an example. It wasn't really true, and besides, it would have been a cheap shot. "I must urge you to retain your politeness, young master sahib. There is no reason to visit your own torments on the young ladies."

"Yeah, you're right," Rod sighed. "It's not *their* fault that they're unattractive, or that I'm a misfit who can't settle down and have a good time raising a family and holding down a job, a maverick who needs adventure! Excitement! Independence!" His eyes sparkled and gleamed. "That's the life for me—out on my own! Bound to no one! Rugged individualism! Untrammelled! Self-reliant!" He sighed with a happy smile, then gave his head a shake and turned to let the robot push studs into his shirt. "Pack my bag for me, will you, Fess?"

The ball was every bit as boring as Rod expected it to be. Not that he disliked the starched collar or the swallow-tailed coat; he always got a kick out of being in costume—it made him stand a little taller, and put a spring in his step. He felt like a character out of a nineteenth-century play in his white tie and tails.

And it wasn't the atmosphere of the ball, either. Rod had a bent for the fantastic, had had it for all of his twenty-one years, and had never quite outgrown his childhood games of "Let's Pretend." In fact, he was doing very well in the Maxima Amateur Theater Society and the Light Opera Association of Maxima. No, in terms of stepping into character, he was right at home.

And it wasn't even that the dances were too sedate—Rod enjoyed the waltz and even the minuet; they went along with the acting. No, it was the company—the simple fact that there was no one else there who was interesting to talk to, and certainly nobody female who was good-looking.

"Oh, I love your costume!" Lady Matilda Bolwheel chirped.

"I'm glad you do," Rod murmured. She damned well had better like it, since every man in the place was wearing a variation on it. "And your dress is very fetching." He gallantly forebore to mention what it would fetch.

"Why, thank you." She turned coyly half-away, letting her eyelashes droop, reminding Rod of a 3DT clip of a cow his tutor had shown him when he was ten.

But she was obviously angling for him to ask her for a dance, and there wasn't much else to do. With a mental sigh, he braced himself and said, "Shall we dance?"

She blossomed into radiance. "Why, I'd be delighted!"

And off they went, in a stately whirl of crinoline and swallow-tails.

When the dance was over, though, Matilda kept firm hold of Rod's arm, with the clear intention of monopolizing him for the evening. "Oh, do let's go into dinner together, Rodney!"

"Uh, well, I've been on a diet lately . . ."

"Ah, there you are, Rodney!" Lady Mulhearn, his hostess, came sailing up like a square-rigged galleon. "How naughty of you to hide with Matilda, when you *know* we must have you circulate! You do know Lady Jenine, don't you?"

The question was purely rhetorical; everybody knew everybody else on Maxima; there were only three hundred thousand of them, and only a few thousand in Rod's generation. "Hi, milady." Rod bowed, thankful that the issue of Matilda had been, at least temporarily, squelched.

"My pleasure, sir." Jenine dropped a curtsy. She had the golden complexion that comes from the mingling of all Terra's races, as had most of the people on Maxima. Rod himself was considerably paler than the norm, but he tanned well. He was a throwback in other ways, too. "There's a new dance out," he ventured. "Have you heard of the gavotte?"

"Oh, I just love it! Shall we prance?"

The line would have been a hopeful sign, if Rod hadn't heard it before in the same 3DT historical that had brought back the gavotte. He turned to make his apologies to Matilda, but Lady Mulhearn was already doing it for him. "You mustn't be selfish, Tildy . . . No, do go away, Rodney, there's a good boy . . . After all, when there are so few eligible bachelors, young ladies must learn to share."

The pout was beginning as Rod led Jenine out to gallop.

"And to think this all came from a 3DT epic!" Jenine burbled as she bobbed and weaved. "Didn't you just love Hamlish Hofernung as Louis XV?"

"He lived up to his nickname, that's for sure." Inwardly, Rod sighed. He was in for a good ten minutes of discussion of nothing but the latest tank stars and their exploits. It wasn't that epics were the only thing Jenine was interested in—it was just that they were the only topic she knew anything about. At least she had a modicum of wit, though—or witty lines, provided she'd heard them from an actor.

Dinner surpassed the proverbial bore crashing; it didn't even leave any splinters. Rod had learned how to smile on cue at a very young age; he and his brother had practiced making faces in the mirror, so he was admirably suited to being a good conversationalist. He had perfected the trick of mental activity on two levels, thinking about something interesting with his forebrain while his speech and hearing centers were routed together on automatic, ears picking up cues that his mouth responded to by delivering up the appropriate noncommittal responses. "Is that so?" "You don't mean it!" "You don't say . . ." There were even places for "Uh-huh," and "Yes," and "I thought so myself." But never, of course, for "No," or "I don't agree"; those might take some explanation, and actually involve saying something.

Officially, he had taken Lady Heloise into dinner; she was plain as a prairie, but she at least had a brain, and could comment on the day's news, if nothing else. But by some strange fluke, he had Lady Morwenna on his other side, and Lady Laetitia across the table. The result was a matter of trying to respond to three conversations at once, since none of the girls was willing to wait for either of the others to stop talking before she directed another comment at Rod. He actually had to pay attention to what they were saying, which ruined all the fun—not that it was in any great shape to begin with. Why they couldn't aim their ramblings at their own dinner companions, Rod didn't know—though it might have had something to do with the gentlemen in question being half again as old as themselves. But they had much better prospects than Rod; after all, some money is better than none, isn't it?

Which led to the inexcapable conclusion that Rod wasn't the kind of man these young ladies intended to marry (or that their mamas intended for them), but that he *was* the kind they wanted to dance and flirt with.

Why me? It certainly couldn't have been his looks.

Maybe his conversation. In a desperate attempt to divert attention *away* from himself, he pointed his nose at Marquis Msimangu, Lady Laetitia's escort. "I hear a rumor that you've designed a new robot, milord."

"Why, yes, actually." Hugo came alive with surprise that anybody should be talking to him. "Still full of bugs, of course, but looks as though the damned thing may actually work."

Rod paused a fraction of a second, to let one of the young ladies ask the polite follow-up, but they were all looking as though the lemon in their tea was getting to them. "What kind is it?"

"Oh, a household 'bot. It'll do all the usual—you know, cook, clean, dust, pick up . . ."

Rod frowned. "Usual, yes. What's the new part?"

"Oh, it makes toast. For those who like their grilled bread *truly* fresh—it has two slots in its chest, and makes the toast right there, by your bed."

"A startling innovation," Rod murmured, picturing himself sitting up in bed and being hit in the eye by two slices of toast. "Really wakes you up in the morning."

Lady Morwenna ostentatiously turned aside and straightened in "surprise." "Oh! Lady Michelle is talking about that new card game from Terra!" She turned a dazzling smile back toward Rod. "You know, the one you can play without a calculator to hand?"

Rod still couldn't understand why people needed special calculators for bridge and canasta—but then, he had never taken card games seriously enough to try to keep track of which cards had been played. "Really? How's it work?"

"Oh, the object of the game is to match cards by number," Lady Laetitia spoke up, oblivious to Morwenna's start and glare—it had been *her* topic! And she took it back. "Yes, you ask the player to your left, 'Have you any eights?' or some such, and if they have, they must give them to you."

"Intricate," Rod murmured. "What if they don't have any?"

"Why, then they say, 'Go fish!' and you search through the extras."

"It's a great deal of fun," Lady Heloise said, delighted to find something she could talk about. "Frees you from trying to think about the cards, and lets you pay attention to the play."

"Like a drama where the characters are very simple?"

"Oh, you've *seen* the new Notty Alent romance!" Laetitia gushed. "Isn't she just *splendid* as Lady Carstairs!"

"And that wonderfully decrepit house she's brought into, as governess!" said Morwenna. "What a comedown for the poor thing—a lady born, and finding all the money gone when her father dies." A tear glistened at the corner of her eye. All the other ladies were silent, too, contemplating the awful spectacle of actually having to earn their own livings.

Rod cleared his throat, aware that reality should never intrude at a ball. "Your gown is striking, Laetitia." In fact, it almost struck out. "I don't believe I've ever seen that cut before."

"Why, thank you!" Laetitia flushed with pleasure, and Morwenna cooed, *"She* reached Monsieur Valdez first!"

"Really, Titia, you were quite precipitate," Heloise scolded. "I swear you scarcely let the poor man step off the boarding ramp before you were on him!"

" 'She who hesitates is lost,' " Laetitia quoted, looking immensely pleased with herself.

"Mine will be done for Thursday's ball, though, so don't think you'll keep the advantage, Tish."

Laetitia sat back with a pinfeather smile. "A genuine original by an authentic Terran couturier."

Well, that explained it. Rod had heard about the new arrival, and had been so surprised that a Terran designer would actually *choose* to come to Maxima, that he had asked

Fess for a brief on the man. The robot had run through the last six months' news, and given him the not-so-startling information that Monsieur Valdez was more widely known by his Terran trade name of Monsieur Iberien. That put the whole thing in perspective. Rod remembered, from his weekly newsfeeds, that Monsieur Iberien had struck out on his own only two years ago, after ten years' apprenticeship in the House of Lachenoir. He had obtained backers, launched his first fall line, garnered unanimous critical censure, obtained absolutely no orders except one from a costermonger who wanted something special for his wife, and had gone spectacularly bankrupt. "I understand he has a novel theory as to what constitutes art."

"Yes, it does seem singular." Sir Gilman, on Morwenna's other side, frowned. "Something about the feeling you get, you know, when you look into a can of worms."

The ladies paled and Rod said quickly, "Well, that was only an example. He says art consists entirely in arousing strong emotional responses, and the nature of the response doesn't matter."

"I certainly receive a great emotional response from looking at *your* dress, Laetitia," Morwenna purred. Laetitia flushed angrily, but Rod said, "Yes, it's called envy." Actually, he sympathized with Morwenna. The dress had only a touch of Monsieur Iberien's theory left in it—the emotion it tried to arouse was surprise, by use of fluorescent colors and patterns of dots running counter to the stripes, and it certainly enhanced Laetitia's appearance, by distracting attention from her face. Rod speculated that Monsieur Iberien might do very well here, after all, as long as he could restrain his artistic impulses and try to give the ladies what would help them. Apparently he had really let himself go, on Terra, and no woman was terribly interested that season in wearing a dress full of fishbait. His fall collection had become a matter of passing the hat in November; the other designers had pooled their resources and paid him to leave Terra, before he brought the whole fashion industry crashing down. He had been able to settle his debts, but had arrived on Maxima almost destitute.

Not for long, though. The ladies of Maxima wouldn't really care what their clothes looked like, as long as they were made by a genuine Terran designer—and his spirits might revive enough to start giving expression to his notion of art again. Rod decided that, no matter what happened to him aboard that freighter, he was *not* coming back for the next season.

The clock chimed 2300, and Rod, with a start, realized that Fess would be arriving at the spaceport with Rod's duffel bag. He gritted his teeth, forced a smile, and kept dancing, and the "Minute Waltz" seemed to last an hour. But it finally ended; he bowed to his partner. "Forgive me, milady, but I must attend to an urgent matter."

"Certainly not so urgent as all *that!*"

"Didn't you hear how they were playing? I'm sorry, but I really *have* to step out for a moment." He turned away, hurrying.

He almost made it to the door before an elbow-glove hooked out to snag him, with a hand inside it. The hand tightened, and Rod's eyes bulged; she'd hit a pressure point— accidently, surely. He turned, forced a sickly grin. "It's been a wonderful ball, Lady Mulhearn."

"Oh, but it's scarcely begun!" Lady Mulhearn turned back toward the ballroom, keeping a firm hold on his arm. "Surely you can't leave yet. Your dear mother would think my soiree a crashing bore, if you were home before three."

"I wouldn't think of it! I'll find a quiet bistro."

"Excellent! I have one in the Florida room. Or perhaps you wish to join the gentlemen at cards."

Somehow, Rod wasn't in the mood for five-card draw. "Really, milady—I have to be in before midnight."

"Posh and poppycock! Your parents would be ashamed of you, if you didn't last past one!"

"But I have a headache. Absolutely splitting, I tell you. It's a sinus vaccum! It's a migraine! It's . . ."

"Stuff and nonsense!" Lady Mulhearn turned to the nearest robot. "An analgesic for the young gentleman, Fadey!"

The robot pressed a button at its waist; two pills fell into its hand. It held them out to Rod as it popped open its chestplate and pressed a button. Water gushed, then stopped, and it took out a foaming glass.

Rod gulped the pills and reached for the water. He almost spat it out; it wasn't water, it was a potion. "Lady Mulhearn, please . . ."

"You'll be right as rain in two shakes." To emphasize the

point, Milady shook him. "Now, a mild card game in dim lighting, and you'll feel fine."

"But I have to run home! My cactus plant needs me!"

"What for?"

"I forgot to water it before I left . . ."

"No matter; you can call your robot and have him do it. Fadey!"

The robot snapped off its hand and held it out. The thumb held an earphone; the forefinger had a mike.

Rod waved away the handset, feeling a surge of panic at the reminder of Fess. "Lady Mulhearn, my deepest apologies, but I really *must* leave now! Any longer, and it'll be too late!"

"Too late?" the lady demanded. "Too late for what?"

"To find my glass slipper!" Rod cried, twisting his arm free and all but running for the door.

He gained the hatchway and stepped into his car with relief. Out with ignominy, maybe—but out!

He saw the freighter's lander alone, still joined to the terminal by the boarding tunnel. Well, not quite alone—just inside the clear plastic of the tunnel stood a solitary, gleaming figure, a duffel bag slung over its shoulder.

"Good old Fess! Faithful to the end!" Rod brought the car in right beside the old family robot, pressed the button that matched position and sealed lock to lock, then jumped to the hatch and pressed the pressure plate. The ramp checked for pressure and opened, and Rod leaped out. "Thanks, Fess!" He caught the duffel bag off the robot's shoulder.

"Lander for freighter *Murray Rain* will lift off in five," the nearest loudspeaker announced in a brazen voice.

Five what? Rod wondered, then noticed what Fess held on his other arm. He dropped the duffel, ripped off his coat and tossed it to Fess, followed by his frilled front. He grabbed the loose broadcloth shirt off Fess's other arm, tugged it on, and reached for the jacket—then froze, as he realized who was standing in the shadows just behind Fess.

The Viscount stepped forward into the light with a gentle smile. "You could at least have told me, son."

"Who *did?*" Rod snapped out of his trance with a glare at Fess.

"I must fulfill my duty to my master, Rod," the robot said, with a tone of apology.

"Yes, he really must; that's how he's made," the Viscount said. "Don't blame him, son; his prime loyalty is to me; he doesn't have any choice but to do as his program dictates, and he knew I'd want to know you were leaving."

"Fess, I can never trust you again!"

"Oh, of course you can, son—when you're his owner. Then, he'll be as fanatically loyal to you as he now is to me."

Rod tossed his head impatiently. "That's thirty years away, at least, Dad, and it's Dick who will inherit . . . Wait a minute. You said when *I'm* his owner!"

"As you will be, from this moment. Fess, I hereby give and bequeath you to my younger son, Rodney. Serve him as you have served me—and, from this day forth, obey no commands but his."

"But Dad, I can't take him along! I'm *spacing!*"

"Every crewman is allowed baggage, son, and you have only one small pack. I think you'll find that Fess masses no more than your allowed luggage. And he can fit into whatever kind of storage space they give you."

"I hate to ask him to fold up like that, but . . . Wait a minute! You're talking about him going with me on that freighter!"

"That is what I had in mind, yes. I know I have to let you go your own way—but I can at least make sure you're as well protected as possible."

"You're letting me go? You're not going to try to make me go back?"

"Make you go back? Son, you don't know how many times I've wished *I'd* jumped a freighter when I was your age! Oh, I'll miss you, and I'll miss you sorely—but I *want* you to go, while you're still young and still can! Godspeed!"

"And Godspeed to you, too, Dad." Rod threw his arms around his father in a bear hug. After a second, the older man returned it.

The lander hooted, and Rod stepped back, alarmed to see tears in his father's eyes.

"Go with God, son—and God go with you. May the wind be ever at your back, and may you find your heart's desire."

"Thanks, Dad," Rod husked. "And may yours find you. Stay well."

"I'm lifting," the lander squawked. "Through the hatch now or never, kid."

And, suddenly, Rod found he didn't want to go, after all—but his father turned him around, and walked with him, quick-step, toward the airlock. "Now, don't forget where your handkerchief is, and don't forget to write—and don't forget Fess."

"I won't, Dad—or you. Ever." Rod turned back to wave, but the hatch was closing, cutting off his view of his father, and of Maxima.

Fess stepped back beside him as the hatch closed. "You are my master now, boss Rod sahib. Command, and I will obey."

Rod stood very still, the reality of the situation coming home to him.

Then he turned, slowly, with a spreading grin. "Well, just for openers—stop calling me 'boss.' "

"And thou never hast since?" Cordelia asked.

"No, Cordelia, though I did call him 'milord' unless he specifically ordered me to do otherwise."

"It's not really legitimate," Rod growled, "or it wasn't, until Tuan ennobled me here."

"But it did remind you of your heritage, Rod, and of the conduct becoming your station."

Gregory frowned. "Yet thou dost not call him 'lord' now."

"No, Gregory. When we landed on Gramarye, your father gave his usual order to call him only by his name as long as we remained here—and as you can see, we have not yet left."

"Nor shalt thou." Gwen came over to latch on to Rod's arm.

"Not while you're here," Rod answered with a grin.

The children relaxed, almost imperceptibly, and Cordelia asked, "Hast thou enjoyed having Papa for a master, Fess?"

"Cordelia," the robot answered, "it has been a blast."

9

All was quiet, except for the distant calls of night-birds wafting through the windows. There wasn't even the rustle of a mouse searching for crumbs. Moonlight crept in through a tall slit window, drifted across the floor, and was gone.

It was only a slight sound, but it grew quickly to a wail that tore at the heartstrings.

The Gallowglasses shot bold-upright, staring about them. Rod reached out and caught Gregory to him; Gwen hugged Cordelia. Rod clasped Geoffrey's shoulder, felt a slight quivering.

Then he saw Magnus.

The boy sat still, every muscle taut, staring at the apparition.

She was beautiful, even now, with her hair disheveled and her face contorted with terror. She was pale as moonlight on snow, her garments a cloud about her. "A rescue," she moaned, "a rescue, I beg of thee! A rescue, good souls, from this monster who hath chained me here. I prithee . . ."

Suddenly, her gaze leaped up to fix on something above their heads, and her fists came up to her lips as she began to wail again, voice rising to a scream that seemed to pierce their temples. Then she leaped, shot toward them . . .

And was gone.

Bitter cold chilled them, then faded. The last echo of the scream rang into nothingness.

In the silence, Rod heard Cordelia sobbing, and white-hot anger flared in him, against the thing that could so terrify his child.

But what thing was it? He looked behind him, but only darkness was there.

Light was the one weapon against it. He pressed Gregory into Gwen's arm and turned to blow on the coals, laying kindling on them until flame licked up. He put on a heavier stick, glared at it to give the fire a boost, laid a log on, and turned back to his family.

They seemed to thaw in the warmth of the fire, but not much.

" 'Tis well now, daughter—'tis well," Gwen murmured. "What e'er 'twas, it is gone."

Cordelia gasped, bringing her sobs under control.

But Rod saw Magnus still tense, eyes gazing off into darkness. Rod concentrated, listening, and could hear distant, mocking laughter echoing into stillness far away.

Magnus relaxed a trifle, and his eyes came back into focus. " 'Tis gone, as much as 'twill ever be."

"Oh, I don't know." Rod's eyes narrowed. "I think we might be able to make it a little more permanent than that."

Magnus stared at him, shocked. "We are no priests, to exorcise spirits!"

"No, we're fighting wizards. Expert espers, where I come from—and every form of magic we've encountered on this planet has been psionic, in some way or another. Why should ghosts be different?"

Magnus's stare held; he almost whispered, "Dost mean we can lay this spectre to rest?"

Rod shrugged. "It's worth investigating."

"Then we must! Whatsoe'er we can do, we shall! The lady is in peril dire—e'en now, past her death, she doth bide in terror! Howsoe'er we can aid her, 'tis vital!"

The other children stared at him, startled, and Gwen seemed very thoughtful; but Rod only nodded, flint-faced. "Let's learn what we can, then. First we need to know who she was, and what happened to her."

"Who she *is*, Papa!"

"Was," Rod grated. "She's *dead*, son, no matter whether or not you can see her! She died two hundred years ago!"

Magnus stared at him, but Rod held his stony gaze, and the boy finally relaxed a little. "Was," he agreed. "Yet she is still in torment. How shall we learn?"

"As to that, you're the only research tool we've got," Rod said, "but the rest of us are going along; no splitting this family at night in *this* castle!"

"Never!" Cordelia shuddered.

"What! Wouldst thou search *now*, husband?"

"But we *must*, Mama!" Magnus cried. " 'Tis only at night they are so strong! By day, we might learn no more than we already know!"

Gwen stared at him, surprised.

"Were you thinking of drifting back to sleep?" Rod asked.

Gwen shuddered. "Nay, I think I shall not slumber now till dawn bringeth light! Wherefore should we not wander these halls? We have conned them already—and can we see worse than we have?"

"It's possible," Rod allowed, "so let's keep our torch with us." He turned to pull a branch out of the fire. "You remember that ball-of-light spell you used when we first met?"

"Aye, husband." Gwen smiled ruefully. " 'Twas due to ghosts' work then, too, was't not?"

"Yeah." Rod nodded. "I think I'm beginning to understand how that happened now. Well, lead on, stone-reader."

Magnus stepped away in front of them, frowning, then reached out to touch the wall. He stood still a few seconds, then drifted toward the stairway, fingertips brushing rock.

The other children followed. Behind them, Fess clopped into movement.

Rod hung back to murmur in Gwen's ear. "Any question as to the nature of the malady, Doctor?"

"Not a doubt of it," Gwen answered softly. "She is a beauteous lass, though a spectre, and he is in love, as any young man might be."

"Yes." Rod nodded. "I'm relieved, really."

"I, too. I feared he might be so distraught that he'd try to join her."

"Kinda my thought, too." Rod gave her a sardonic smile. "Fortunately, he's young enough to still be sufficiently scared of girls so that he's more apt to sublimate than to woo. Well, let's follow where love leads, dear."

"Have we not always?" she murmured, but he'd slipped behind her, and didn't hear.

The stairway hadn't seemed nearly so long by daylight. But they toiled up, following the curve as they went. Fess's hooves rang loudly in the stairwell. Rod turned to him, glaring. "You don't *have* to make that much noise, you know."

"True, Rod, but I do not think you would truly wish me to move silently behind you, on such an occasion."

"A point," Rod admitted. "The more noise, the fewer spooks. But can I hear myself think?"

"Do you truly wish to?"

At the top, Magnus stepped away from the wall, frowning and looking about him.

"Lost the scent?" Rod asked.

"Nay, yet 'tis quite faint. And I bethink me there's more to her tale than she herself."

Rod nodded. "True. There's also the thing she's afraid of."

"Let us seek through all." Magnus stepped over to the nearest doorway, pushed the door open wide, and stepped in, reaching out to touch the wall.

Cordelia had managed to slip back to her parents. Now she whispered into her mother's ear. "What hath him so beset?"

Gwen smiled at her, amused. "Why, lass, what dost thou think?"

"That he's besotted," Cordelia said promptly. "Is it thus boys behave, when they're lovestruck?"

"Aye, till they finally come nigh the lass. Then pursuit halts awhile."

Cordelia smiled. "Let us hope this light-o'-love doth not give encouragement."

"Any lass must, if the lad's not to flee," Gwen said. She stopped in the middle of the chamber to look around. It was perhaps twelve feet square, walls bare stone except for a tapestry hanging on one wall. The room held a bed, a small table, a stool, and a chest.

"Standard medieval furnishings." Rod reached out to the tapestry, then thought better of it. "Do you suppose this thing would crumble if I touched it?"

"I would not chance it," Gwen answered.

"A knight dwelt here." Magnus's voice was a sigh, a breeze. "A knight, and his lady wife. They were goodly, and content with one another—though toward the end of their tenure, the knight was oft upset by the Count's son."

"Upset?" Rod said. "Why?"

Magnus shook his head. "All manner of wrongdoing—and the knight was on his guard to prevent such malfeasance."

"Had they no children?" Cordelia asked.

"Aye, and they were oft in this chamber, though they slept elsewhere."

"Elsewhere" turned out to be the room next door, and there was a similar suite across the hall for another knight and family. Magnus stayed in it only long enough to ascertain its nature, not even touching the walls, then came out.

"So the married knights took it in shifts, to attend on their lord." Rod looked about the chamber, musing. "How many did you say were in here in a year?"

"Four, to each suite—each to a season."

"And all were on edge, toward the end, because of the Count's son." Rod nodded. "We'll probably find a dormitory for the bachelors, outside the keep. What kind of people lived here after the heir became Count?"

"The single knights thou hast spoke of, though they but slept here. There is small trace of their presence, and that only for their more—earthly pleasures." Magnus's face hardened. "*Most* of their wenches were willing, yet I do sense summat of women's fear and pain."

Cordelia began to look angry.

"I'm beginning to see why the place was abandoned." Rod turned away, face dark. "What else is on this floor?"

They went out, and turned into the next chamber. Their torch was burning down; Rod plucked a mummified stick from a wall sconce and lit it. It burned brightly but quickly.

The room held only a single bed, a washstand, and a chest.

"A gentle-lady dwelt here." Magnus's voice seemed to come from a distance. "She did wait upon the Countess till she was wed; then another took her place, till she in turn wed."

"Probably several of these rooms; usually more than one lady-in-waiting at a time."

Magnus nodded. "The last dwelt in some apprehension, for the Count's son had grown to young manhood, and had an eye for the lasses. He had no scruples as to his manner of attaining their favors—though he feared his father's wrath."

"Did this damsel leave the castle free of him?" Cordelia asked, eyes thoughtful.

Magnus nodded. "She wed, and went—and none dwelt here after."

"Wherefore?"

"I know not." Magnus turned to the door, moving like a sleepwalker. "Let us seek."

He drifted on down the hallway, fingertips brushing the wall, and turned into the next chamber.

But it was exactly like the one before; the memories were of different women, but held no new information. So it was with the third, and the fourth—though the last lady-in-waiting of that chamber had been importuned by the heir, who had become quite unpleasant when she refused. She had managed to break away; the young man had pursued her, but had been brought up short by one of his father's knights, who had rebuked him soundly and reported the incident to the Count, who personally took a horsewhip to his son. Nonetheless, the lady asked permission to return to her parents, and the Countess granted her request.

Cordelia frowned. "I begin to have some notion of the cause of this spectre's misery."

"I, too." Gwen wasn't smiling.

"No more rooms on this floor." Rod stood at the end of the hall, glowering around at the doorways and the slit-window in the end wall. "Back to the stairs, folks."

Gregory went first, being the lightest, followed by Geoffrey, then Magnus. They were going up in order of ascending weight, with the levitators first. "Just in case the masonry isn't what it once was," Rod explained. But he insisted on bringing up the rear.

At the top of the stair, a small chamber opened on either side of the hallway, very much like the ones below. Magnus stepped into the one on his left, concentrating and touching the stones. " 'Twas another lady-in-waiting dwelt here—the Countess kept two near her in the night. This damsel . . ."

He broke off, for the air was thickening in the corner, beyond the torch's pool of light.

The Gallowglasses held their breaths, their eyes wide.

The keening started before the form had become clear; Gregory clapped his hands over his ears. Then she drifted there before them, the same young lady they had seen in the great hall below, wailing in fear and terror.

"Damsel, what affrights thee?" Magnus cried, stepping forward and reaching out.

Rod thrust out an arm, blocking him.

"Thou dost!" the girl wailed. "Go, get thee hence! Leave me in peace!"

Rod started to talk, but Magnus beat him to it. "I cannot, for thy pain is mine, and when thou dost feel agony, a blade doth twist in mine heart! Nay, speak! Tell me why thine unquiet spirit still doth walk, and I will set it aright!"

A glimmer of hope glowed in the darkness that was her eyes, but she moaned, "Thou canst not, for I did not roam these halls till thou didst come to wake me! 'Tis thou, and thou alone! But for thee, I'd not have walked!"

Magnus's head snapped up, and he fell back a pace, staggered—but Gwen stepped forward and asked, very calmly, "Canst thou truly say thou hast lain quietly?"

The girl's face contorted, and her hands came up to her cheeks as she wailed once again, a wail that soared up and up until it rang in their ears, then twisted and was gone, and the room lay empty about them.

They straggled back to the Great Hall, a very glum and silent crew, with glances out of the corners of their eyes at their brother, whose face was thunderous. Gwen stepped up to the hearth, stirred up the coals, tossed on a handful of kindling and blew it alight, then put on larger sticks and a log.

Then she turned back to her son.

"Be not heartsick, my lad. We know ghosts have walked this castle for two hundred years. 'Tis not thou who hast brought her unending misery."

"But how can she speak of my waking her!" Magnus burst out.

"Thou art a stone-reader," Gwen answered, "and a thought-speaker, and a crafter. The traces of her unquiet spirit may have kindled thy mind into bringing her forth from the stones."

Magnus looked up, appalled—and Rod lifted his head with dawning understanding.

"Yet why she?" the boy burst out. "Why she alone? Why she, and none of the others who dwelt 'midst these rough stones?"

"For that 'twas only she did live through agony so sharp as to leave traces so strong they could be conjured forth. Where others have left only some lingering touch that thou canst read, her feelings were so deep as to bring her once more before us."

"Call it hallucination," Rod said softly, "but you're also a projective—and once *you* could see her, anyone near you could, too; you put the picture into their minds."

"But I know the craft of that, Papa, and 'tis not a thing to be done unawares! It doth take intensity of thought, and some strength!"

"You did it when you were a baby," Rod said evenly. "We had to keep you away from witch-moss, because anything you were thinking about, took form."

"Yet there is no witch-moss here!"

Rod shrugged. "You can't be sure of that. And even if it isn't, your mind is thoroughly capable of projecting a hallucination into other people's thoughts."

"I have never done so before!"

"You've never encountered a stimulus this strong before, either." Rod forbore to mention that most of the strength might have come from Magnus's feelings toward the ghost-girl, but he exchanged glances with Gwen, and she nodded. First love can do wonders.

Magnus's face crumpled. "Then 'tis I am to blame for her misery?"

"No!" Rod said, full-force. "The misery was caused by someone else, and I have a sneaking suspicion he's lurking about, just panting to be hallucinated, too—so try not to hate him too hard; it might help him."

"Yet she would have slumbered, had I not come within!"

"I have a notion she has waked a few times in the past," Rod said evenly. "I doubt that you're the first psychometricist to come in here in the last two hundred years. You remember how boys like to prove their courage by spending the night in a haunted house? And who would be most likely to do that? I have a notion that any time you hear about a haunting anywhere in Gramarye, you've had a latent psychometricist who doesn't know what he is."

Magnus's gaze was fastened on Rod; the boy was drinking in the words, hungry to believe.

"Besides," Rod said, feeling uncomfortable, "if you hadn't triggered her walking, I probably would have."

"*Thou?*" Magnus stared, then whirled to his mother. Gwen nodded, gaze fast on him. "Thy father hath waked ghosts aforetime, son." She turned to Rod, and couldn't help a smile. " 'Twas not long after we met."

Rod couldn't stop the smile, either. "No, it wasn't, was it?"

He turned back to his son. "I did something rather stupid: I went for a stroll in the haunted section of Castle Loguire—alone."

"Wherefore wouldst thou have committed such folly?" Cordelia's eyes were huge.

"Because I didn't believe in ghosts. But I saw them, all right—and I was scared hollow, till Fess figured out their trick. And mind you, I wasn't the first to see ghosts there—that part of the castle had so strong a reputation that nobody lived there any more. And the same is probably true here—I have a notion that this isn't the first time this spectre has waked, though she may not remember the others as more than a dream. I'd bet that psychometricists are more common here than she led you to believe."

A bit of color was coming back to Magnus's face now. "Yet her cries of anguish, and the wicked laughter we all heard last night, whiles the storm did rage . . ."

"When we weren't even inside yet. Right." Rod nodded. "Either you have a lot more range than we thought, or the ghosts linger once they're roused. Of course, all the electricity in the atmosphere might have had something to do with it."

Magnus paled again. "Dost think they may talk to one another when we living are not by them?"

"Interesting thought," Rod agreed, "but a pretty useless one, for our purposes. If they do, how can we tell, since we're not here to hear it? If a tree falls in the forest, but there's no one near to hear the noise, did it make any sound?"

The junior Gallowglasses exchanged glances, which could have meant that it was a good question that would require thought, or that Papa was being silly again.

"No matter how she hath been raised." Magnus banished the question with a wave of his hand, and Rod's heart leaped; if the kid could put it behind him, he'd been lifted past it. "Wherefore would she wish me to go, rather than asking mine aid, as she did before?"

"I don't think it was *your* help she was asking for." Rod rubbed the bridge of his nose. "More likely reliving a scene from the days of her life."

"And as to bidding thee go," Gwen answered, "she may have wished to hide her shame from the world."

"What shame?"

Gwen spread her hands. " 'Tis hidden yet. Naetheless, when a damsel hath been hurted deeply, she will oft wish to be alone until her wound hath healed."

"Definitely," Rod agreed, "and that's not exclusive to women. It can take a long time for a man to heal, too."

Magnus frowned. "Dost thou speak from conjecture, or from knowledge?"

"Doesn't matter," Rod said, "since the important question is really not how we've waked her, but how we can help her to find rest again."

Magnus's gaze drifted. "Aye—that is the nubbin . . ."

"Then," said Gregory, "we must first learn why she is unhappy."

"Back to where we left off." Rod smiled. "So tomorrow, we'll search the castle and grounds and see if we can find any more clues. But I don't think we can do too much more tonight." He lifted a hand to stifle Magnus's protest. "You're tired, son, and not at your most perceptive any more—and if any of the rest of us have this particular gift, we don't have it as strongly as you. We need to get what rest we can. Come on, back to bed." And he stepped over to lie down on his pallet. Gwen smiled gently at the children, then went to join her husband.

Reluctantly the children followed suit, and lay still in the firelight.

"Mayhap," Cordelia offered, "we ought not to meddle in this affair at all."

"Nay, we must!" Magnus protested loudly.

"Softly, softly, son," Gwen called. "I do not think we can worsen matters for the lass, Cordelia, and we well might help. Yet her affairs aside, there's some small matter of our own interest."

Geoffrey looked up. "Why, how is that?"

"I do not mean to dwell in a house where ghosts do wander in the dead of night, to disturb our sleep," Gwen said, with finality.

"An excellent point," Rod agreed. "You're right in this, Cordelia—that if it didn't affect us, we should probably mind our own business."

"Nay, even then, we ought to seek to alleviate the poor damsel's suffering, out of simple humanity!" Cordelia cried.

"Thought you were the one who was saying we should back out. Well, since we're all agreed, we'll consider ways and means—and let's sleep on it, shall we?" He rolled up a little more tightly.

Slowly, Magnus lay tense but quiet again.

The hall was still, and a branch popped in the fire.

Cordelia tossed and turned, unable to sleep, even when the low, even breathing of her mother and brothers, and her father's snoring, told her that she alone remained awake.

The thought was frightening. There was a small sound, somewhere in the great room, and she lifted her head to peer around, eyes wide, heart hammering.

She saw only the forms of her sleeping family, and the dark silhouette of the great black horse, standing watch over them. Its eyes glistened in the firelight, ever vigilant.

Cordelia felt relief; she wasn't completely alone in her wakefulness. Very quietly, she slipped out of bed and came over to the robot. Fess lifted his head at her approach. "Lie still, Cordelia. Sleep will come."

"I have need of talk." She twined her fingers in his mane.

"Your charms avail you nothing, Cordelia—I am made of metal."

"I shall try the mettle of a man, when I am grown." She managed a small smile at her own feeble jest. "Speak to me, that I may sleep."

"Am I so boring a companion as that? No, do not answer. Tell me what you would have me speak of."

She said nothing, only set to work making a plait in his mane.

"Of love, of course," Fess answered, with a sigh. "You are, after all, a young maiden."

"Aye. Wouldst thou, mayhap, recall Papa's manner when he first was moonstruck? Was he as Magnus is, this night?"

"Cordelia!" Fess reproved, in his softest tone. "I have told you before that your father's experiences are entirely confidential, and that it is for him alone to breach that confidentiality, not I."

"Oh, thou didst not even know when the Archer did smite him!"

"How should I, when I am only a thing of iron, with no feelings? How might I recognize romantic love?"

"Thou dost know it by its signs."

"Signs that can be hidden, with self-control. I will tell you only this: that when humans do suppress such evidence of love's coming, they cease to know clearly when they are in love."

Cordelia looked up, frowning. "Why, how couldst thou know such a thing?"

"I have studied humankind for five centuries, Cordelia. Go, now, and let your fancy play with the notion."

She smiled, taken with the idea. "Why, that I shall. I knew thou wouldst know cures for wakefulness, good Fess." And she turned away, going back to roll up in her blanket.

Of course, Fess *did* recognize the signs of infatuation, and remembered that the young Rod d'Armand had been worried because it had never happened to him. But Fess had seen the reason clearly, when he looked at the belles of Maxima—so he had not been surprised with the quickness of love's striking, once Rod left home. He remembered, with the clarity that only comes from permanent changes in the electrical patterns of molecules. It had been a time when Rod's joy and pain had been so clear to see that Fess was, for once, quite glad he had no emotions of his own. Rod's had been bad enough. Oh, yes, he remembered . . .

10

The lander jarred with a thud and a clash. Rod waited, excitement beginning to well up under his sadness at leaving home. The wall-patch next to the hatch glowed green. Rod opened it and stepped through into his new life.

The welcoming committee was a stocky man in a uniform too tight around the waist and a three-day beard on his jowls. "A rich boy!" he groaned. "With a private robot—preserve us! And shall I roll out a red carpet for you, me lord?"

"Not a lord," Rod said automatically.

"Well, ya know that much, at least," the man grunted. "But ya need a bit more, swabbie. When ya walked through that hatch, ya became the lowest of the low, boy. And close it behind ya!"

Rod turned, sure that he had. Yes, the hatch was dogged.

The jowly man pushed past him to check, and gave a reluctant growl. "Well, it's good enough."

Rod knew it was a lot better than "good enough." People who grow up on asteroids become very used to hatches—by the time they're eight. But all he said was, "Thank you, sir."

The man's eyes narrowed. "Ya got that part right, too." He looked distinctly unhappy about it. "Well, 'sir' it is, to *anyone* ya see. I'm Albie Weiser, Second Officer of the good ship *Murray Rain,* and you have the lowest rating aboard. Anything you see, you 'sir,' because there's no one aboard who's lower than you—and ya salute a senior officer!"

Rod snapped to what he hoped was "attention" and touched his forehead.

"No, no!" Weiser seemed relieved as he reached out to boost Rod's arm and crank his wrist. "Elbow up, so your arm's parallel to the deck, and turn yer hand out t' face me!"

Rod clenched his jaw to keep from saying "ouch."

"Right enough, then," the officer growled. "Now, come on and see this berth y've signed on for." He pushed off

against a wall and glided down the passageway, glancing
back just once—to make sure his new charge was following,
Rod supposed. He looked very disappointed, and Rod's spirits sank. Was he really doing *that* badly? He swallowed hard
and plucked up his courage, resolving to become the best
recruit Weiser had ever seen.

Fess followed, drifting silently in null-G. A bit less naive
than Rod, he realized that Weiser had been hoping the young
man would prove horribly clumsy in free-fall. Apparently the
second officer hadn't realized that growing up on an asteroid,
however large and however well provided with artificial gravity in dwelling areas, would still afford a young man a great
number of low-G situations, and free-fall sports.

He was also aware that being faultless, when people were
actively seeking faults to belittle you for, could prove dangerous.

They filed down a metal passageway, over the foot-high
sill of a hatch, down a clanging ladder, and down a darker
passageway. Rod's spirits sank with the altitude.

Then the hallway opened out into a large chamber filled
with vague lumpen shapes, walls divided into metal boxes.
Pipes festooned the ceilings, and the floor humped up into
ridges here and there.

Weiser turned and pointed to a rectangular outline in the
corner, about eighteen inches wide and three feet high. "There's
yer locker. And there—" He pointed to a larger rectangle
inscribed on the wall, "—is yer berth."

Rod stared at it in dismay, and the mate sneered, "What
did ya expect for an engine wiper on a freighter—a stateroom
with a private bath?"

"Oh, no, no! It's just that, uh, I don't know what I'm
supposed to do."

"Stow your duffel, swabbie, and report to the engineer!"
He looked at Fess with disgust and grunted, "Private robots,
yet! Where're ya going to store *that*, laddie?" He gave Fess a
slap.

"Hey, careful! He's an antique!"

"Oh, is he, now? And maybe I should dust yer china fer
ya, too!" The mate swatted at Fess, and the robot stepped
aside easily—a twentieth of a second was a quick punch for a
human, but a long time for a computer. "Stand still when I'm
swinging at ya!" the mate roared, and slammed another
punch at the robot.

"Sir," Fess said as he dodged, "I have done nothing to merit your . . ."

"Hold on, now! That's *my* robot!" Rod leaped in, grabbing at the mate's arm. Weiser turned to aim a punch at him, and Fess darted forward to interpose himself between Rod and the mate's fist. Then he tried to dodge Weiser's kick, protesting, "I have done . . ." and went stiff as a board. The mate's kick caught him in the hip joint and sent him crashing against the wall.

Rod saw red. "You bastard! You made him have a seizure! And then when he was defenseless, you . . ." He couldn't finish; he leaped at the mate, swinging . . .

Swinging completely around in a circle and crashing into the wall. As he slid toward the bottom, a calloused hand grabbed him by the jumpsuit and yanked him upright. The jowly face loomed over him, mouth curved in a grin and vindictive satisfaction in the eyes. "The first thing ya must learn, swabbie, is to *never* talk back to a senior officer!" The calloused hand shot out, clenching into a shotput fist, and crashed into Rod's jaw.

Rod was only dizzy for a few seconds; then he was struggling up to his hands and knees and lurching over to grope at the base of Fess's skull for the circuit breaker. He pushed, and the robot sat up slowly. "Whatddd . . . didddd AAAeee . . ."

"You were defeated in a gallant attempt to save me," Rod rasped. "Sorry I got you into this."

"Thhhuh ffaullltt iz awwl . . ."

"All Weiser's," Rod grunted. "That bastard was doing everything he could to pick a fight. Help me up, will you?"

Slowly, the robot climbed to its feet, then reached down. A hard hand grasped Rod's arm, helping him up. "How . . . how long were we out?"

"I have been unnn-ckon-shus forrrr . . . no morrrre than . . . threeee minutes."

Rod gave his head a shake, blinked, and managed to see that Weiser wasn't there. "He didn't have to do that . . ."

"He would have con-tin-ued to be off-offensive until he managed to . . . pro-voke you into attac-king, mas-ter. He was seeking to . . . e-sta-blish his au-tho-ri-ty."

Rod's mouth tightened. "Are you telling me I shouldn't have reacted, no matter *what* he did?"

"Short of attack with lethal intentions, no. I certainly was not damaged; I am considerably more durable than that."

Rod remembered childhood tales about accidents when Fess had been building the castle. "All right, so I shouldn't have worried."

"But I am delighted by your wish to defend one you regard as a friend, boss—it shows that my moral teachings have taken firm hold. Nonetheless, please remember that it is *I* who am supposed to be loyal to *you*, not the reverse."

"Point noted," Rod grumbled. "People don't help robots."

"Of course, my own loyalty is reinforced by such firm evidence of your own."

"But you would have suffered a major breakdown if I'd been really hurt. Yeah, yeah, I know."

"Well . . . I did note that you seemed to have forgotten your boxing, boss."

"I don't know what that guy was using, but it sure wasn't boxing." Rod pushed his jaw back into place and blinked at the pain. "Whew! And you'd better not call me 'boss' around here; I'm beginning to see that it could bother my fellow crewmen."

"How shall I address you, then?"

"How about 'Rod'?" Rod said sourly.

"If you insist," Fess sighed.

"I do. After all, I've learned my first lesson—that the universe is a nasty place. Let's see if I can't make my way in it anyway, shall we?"

"One human is not the universe, Rod."

"So I've got a negative attitude. I can hardly wait to meet my chief."

"According to Mr. Weiser's instructions, you must 'stow your duffel' first."

"Oh, yeah." Rod frowned, turning to the little locker. "How do I get it open, do you suppose?" He started running his fingers along the outline, pressing as he went. The left edge gave under pressure, so Rod pushed harder. The panel rotated outward, revealing small shelves on its other side, and a compartment three feet deep.

Rod stared, appalled. "There's no way you'll ever fit in there!"

"I can if it is necessary, Rod."

"Yeah, well, let's try and get by without it first, shall

we?'' Rod tossed his bag in and pushed the panel shut. ''You just stand in the corner here and do your best to turn into a statue. Okay?''

''Certainly, Rod.'' Fess stepped into the corner and became just what Rod had ordered—a modernistic sculpture of a human being.

''You gonna be okay if the ship changes direction?''

''The floor is an iron alloy, Rod, and I have electromagnets in my feet. We found them quite useful, during Maxima's construction phase. And I notice ringbolts within reach, if the change in velocity is really strong.''

''Well, okay, then . . .''

''Report for duty, please, Rod.''

''Oh, all right. Now, let me see—where's *my* boss?''

Rod wandered away into the cubistic environment of the engine room. Fess boosted the gain on his microphones, to make sure he would be able to hear Rod if he was needed.

The light was dim but adequate, and all from ahead. Rod followed it, around shapes that he assumed had something to do with powering the engines. Then he began to hear the cursing. That made it easier—he simply followed the sound.

Whoever it was had a really remarkable vocabulary. Rod made mental notes of the more exotic terms, planning to ask for their definitions, after he got to know their author a little better. He rounded a large metal housing and saw somebody in a dirty, baggy coverall, hair tied back in a club, laboring over a machine with a wrench.

What was he supposed to do? Obviously, the guy thought he was alone. Rod swallowed, screwed his courage to the molly-bolt, and stepped forward, stiffening to attention and saluting. ''Recruit Rod d'Armand reporting for duty, *sir!*''

His new boss whirled, almost dropping the wrench, saw him, then relaxed. ''Hellfire, boy, don't *do* that! I thought I was alone down here.'' The engineer laid the wrench aside and stood, face coming into the brighter light of an overheard —and Rod caught his breath. The hair wasn't really clubbed, it was caught in a net, and the face under the grease smudges was oval and smooth, with delicate features. ''You're the new swabbie, right?'' The voice was a lovely alto, the eyes were large, green, and long-lashed, and Rod was in love.

"Uh-h-h-h—yes, ma'am. I'm your new engine-wiper. Where's the engine I'm supposed to wipe?"

"Over there." The engineer pointed to a bulging wall in the dimness at the end of the room. "Doesn't need any wiping, though. If it does, we're all in trouble. We just call you that 'cause it came down to us from ocean ships." She turned back, peering up at him. "Don't know anything about engines, huh?"

"Uh, no, ma'am. I want to learn, though!"

She groaned. "Defend me from the eager student! Why can't they send me someone who knows what he's doing?" She held up a hand to forestall the answer. "I know, I know—if she's learned that much, she's working on a better ship than this. Well, swabbie, I'm Gracie Muldoon."

"Rod d'Armand, ma'a—sir!"

"Better." Muldoon nodded. "And don't you forget it, swabbie."

"No, sir. Can I help?"

"Let's see." Muldoon pointed to the huge wheel she'd been working on, half-bared by an opened housing. It rippled with blades that looked uncomfortably like knives. "That's the backup turbine—and the threads on the last bolt are stripped, courtesy of the dirtside mechanic who overhauled it before I was hired; I'd never allow anyone to work on my engines without my watching."

Rod noticed the possessive attitude, though he doubted she owned the ship. He also noticed the correct grammar. Also the way her head tilted, and how fine her eyebrows were, though they didn't seem to be plucked . . . he hauled his mind back to the rotor. "How come it was the last bolt?"

" 'Cause when I found out it was stuck, I took off the other ones first."

"Oh." Rod felt his face heat up. "And when you try to turn the nut, the whole wheel spins?"

Muldoon nodded, watching him. "Not *spins*, really—it's pretty massive. But it doesn't stay put, either." She pointed to the wrench. "Give it a try."

Rod picked up the wrench and heaved at the nut. Sure enough, the wheel moved, but the nut didn't rotate. He nodded. "Any way to brace the wheel?"

"Yes, now that you're here." She knelt beside him, and his head filled with her aroma—female with a trace of perspiration. "Hand me the wrench, and take the Stillson . . . No, the *big* one."

Rod picked up the four-foot monkey wrench that lay beside her.

"Now, this is the brake lever." Muldoon hauled down on a stick to her right. "Watch the hub."

Rod saw a huge double cam rotate, pushing the edges of the hub out.

"But watch what happens when I lock it down." Muldoon made something click, and the stick stayed put—but the cam immediately snapped back ninety degrees, and the inner cylinder shrank.

"Another goodie, courtesy of that dirtside grease monkey who never should have come down out of the trees," Muldoon explained, "and *that's* why I was cursing."

Rod nodded, frowning at the huge nut in the center of the cam. "And I hold this still?"

"Yeah, after I put the brake on again." Muldoon released the stick, then pushed it down once more. Rod waited till the cam had stopped turning, then locked his wrench on and held fast. "What's the nut for?" he grunted.

"Taking the cam off—so push clockwise." Muldoon picked up her wrench, fitted it on the bolt, and heaved. The nut groaned, then began to move. Rod leaned all his mass on the wrench and pushed. Nonetheless, he felt himself beginning to move, and let go with one hand to grab the edge of the housing.

"Smart," Muldoon grated, and her wrench began to move more easily. Then it was going around and around quickly and smoothly, and the nut clattered off onto the floor.

"Success!" Muldoon crowed. "You can let up now, swabbie."

Rod let go of the housing and laid the wrench carefully aside. He was surprised to find he was panting.

"Good work." Muldoon stood up and came around to face the rotor. "Step back, now—these blades are sharp." Carefully, she lifted the rotor off its axle.

Rod scurried back out of the way, watching, amazed that a woman smaller than himself could handle a rotor bigger than herself.

She carried the wheel over to a workbench, mounted it on a

hub, and locked it steady. "Just one blade to replace. Know how to cut threads, swabbie?"

"Uh—yes, sir."

"Good. Do." Muldoon tossed her head at a huge rack of tools on the wall. "Take your time and do it right."

"Yes, sir." Rod got busy.

He was done before she was, but not by much. She took off her mask, racked the welder, and said, "Now. Let's see if you can put it all back together."

Rod swallowed and came over to unlock the rotor and take it off the mount. "Yes, sir."

Muldoon leaned back against the workbench, arms folded, watching while he worked. Occasionally, she made an approving noise. When he had all the pieces back in place, he turned to her and said, "Ready for inspection, before I lock them in, sir."

"Good idea. Glad I didn't have to recommend it." Muldoon came over and examined the fastenings. She nodded slowly. "Nice job—and a nice surprise. I thought you said you didn't know anything about engines."

"I don't. But I did learn a little basic mechanics."

"Why, rich boy?"

Rod sighed. "Everybody sort of assumed I'd go into the family business, when I grew up—so my father insisted I learn how to do *everything* needed in the robot factory."

Muldoon frowned. "I thought you technocrats had robots do everything from sweeping up to machining and growing circuits."

Rod shrugged. "Robots do the actual labor, sure. But people have to make sure they do it right."

Muldoon nodded slowly. "Smart again. Your old man has a good head on his shoulders."

Rod felt a flush of purely illogical pleasure, and pride in his father. For the first time, he was glad Dad had put him through all that boring training.

Then something clicked, and he began to wonder if maybe Dad hadn't figured the boredom might give Rod an extra reason to want to leave Maxima.

An unworthy thought, surely. Pater had only been trying to train Rod to be a responsible citizen, and a worthy member of the House d'Armand.

Surely.

As he finished tightening the housing bolts, Rod asked, "What's this turbine do?"

Muldoon grinned. "It kicks in if anything goes wrong with the main turbine."

"Sorry. Let me try again, sir—what's the *main* turbine for?"

"It runs the generator."

"Oh." Rod frowned. "Wouldn't it be more efficient to run a converter directly off the fusion plant?"

"Very good," she noted. "But you don't know anything about engines, huh?"

"I don't. That's electronics!"

"There is still a subtle difference," Muldoon admitted. "Well, it would be more efficient, yes—and we do use it when we go to FTL. But it's an extra drain on the plant, and we go sublight most of the time—we're a local freighter, running between Saturn and Mars. When we're sublight, we use water for reaction mass, and we're heating the water to steam and blasting it out anyway—so it might as well turn the turbine on its way. Effectively, we get our electricity for the cost of the turbine, and the company amortizes that over ten years."

"Oh." Rod nodded. "So the best way isn't always the best way, huh?"

"Well, not optimum, anyway." Muldoon smiled. "Come on—I'll give you the four-bit tour."

She turned away, beckoning, moving like a mermaid as she glided through the air. Rod decided he'd follow that wriggle anywhere.

Muldoon pointed to a massive door in a dull metal wall. "Lead, a meter thick. Behind it is the fusion plant."

Rod asked, "Why the lead? The plasma bottle is a better radiation shield than any metal could be."

She looked up at him, surprised, and nodded. "But if the bottle fails, there *could* be a brief burst of very hard radiation."

Rod gave a snort of derision.

"I know, I know—but tell that to the rest of the crew. And my hindbrain, for that matter—my prefrontal lobes may believe in science, but my cerebellum is superstitious." She put a hand over her tummy. "I still have hopes of having children."

Rod was suddenly acutely aware of his own vulnerability;

before radiation, we're all naked. In fact, we're downright transparent.

"I think you can figure out where the main turbine is, and the generator." Muldoon pointed to a large red toolbox on the floor. "That's the emergency kit. Small fire extinguisher, Geiger counter . . ." (her mouth twitched) ". . . basic hand tools, first-aid box, quick-patches in case we're holed, spot-welder, and steel patches. There's a box of quick-patches inset next to every hatch, and one in the middle of the longest wall in each room." She looked up at him. "You savvy?"

Rod nodded. "Maxima's only an asteroid, sir. We're very used to patches."

"Good. This ship has a good deflector field, mind you, and the signal officer—that's Weiser, the Second—"

"I met him," Rod grunted.

Muldoon flashed him a quick look, but went on. "We both spend a lot of time making sure the field generator and its connections stay sound. And the ship is double-hulled, with foam filling, ready to expand—but this is the asteroid belt, and some of the junk has a lot of punch. We still get holed once or twice each trip."

Rod grinned. "Ever taken a close look at the Maxima tugs, sir?"

Muldoon shook her head. "I don't usually get to a viewscreen while we're matching orbits with you."

"They have a *lot* of patches on them. All colors, too—and some pretty outrageous patterns."

Muldoon wondered, "Why colors?"

Rod shrugged. "Why not? If you're going to have to have patches anyway, they might as well be decorative."

Muldoon cracked a smile. "When you look at it that way, I suppose it makes sense. On with the tour."

She moved back toward Rod's bunk, and slapped the wall of rectangles. "Here's the accumulators, and . . . *What* the hell is *that?*" She stood rigid, staring at the corner.

"Oh, that's just Fess." Rod felt very sheepish. "He's my robot."

"You have your own *robot?*"

"Well, uh, I'd be lost without him, you know." Rod swallowed. "He's an heirloom, if you know what I mean."

"No, I don't." Muldoon was still staring.

Rod gulped. "Sorry about the surprise. I should have told you, sir."

"Yeah, you sure should have." Muldoon shook her head. "But I'll try to get used to it."

Rod almost went limp with relief. "Thanks. I mean, a lot, *sir*. Fess, come over here and say hello to my new boss."

The sculpture moved, turned its head, and drifted over to them with fluid grace. "Hello, madam. I am the old family robot." He held out his hand.

Muldoon accepted it gingerly, studying the joints and the structure. "Delighted. Solenoids, huh?"

"In the hands, yes, for better feedback in applying pressure. Most of my other joints are servomotors, though."

Muldoon nodded. "Good design. You'll have to take orders from me, too, you know."

Fess hesitated, and Rod said quickly, "Anything she says, Fess. Subject to your programmed restraints, of course."

"Oh, don't worry! I won't tell him to kill anyone."

"Certainly, Rod." Fess bowed to Muldoon. "It will be a pleasure to serve you, mem-sahib."

Muldoon actually blushed, but all she said was, "Does he always talk like that? The titles, I mean?"

"I'm afraid so," Rod sighed. "That's an heirloom, too. I cured him of it when he talks to me, but I forgot to tell him to hold off with other people."

"Don't bother." Muldoon grinned. "I kinda like it."

She turned away, heading back toward the workbench. Rod ventured. "You seem to know a bit about robots, sir."

Muldoon shrugged. "A machine's a machine. If it moves and has bolts, I can talk to it."

"Yeah, that's what I was wondering about. A robot's part mechanics, but it's mostly computer."

"And can I write a program?" Muldoon gave him a condescending smile. "An engineer these days has to know all the parts of a system, swabbie—including each type of subsystem. To be a specialist, you have to be a generalist."

Rod stood still, looking off into space. "You know, that's a very good way of putting it."

Muldoon said, "My first professor in college told us that. It stuck with me all the way through."

Rod focused on her again. "That's where you learned your engineering, then?"

Muldoon snorted. "The ideas and facts, or what to do with the wrench and the keyboard?"

"Both."

"I learned the book-knowledge in college, swabbie—but I learned how to do the job right here."

"You've got a bachelor's?"

"Only the degree."

"But if you've got *those* kind of qualifications, what're you doing aboard a little freighter like this?"

"Don't knock the *Murray Rain*," Muldoon snapped, "she's a good ship! And we all have to start someplace. I had your job, five years ago. Now I'm chief."

Which hadn't meant anything, Rod noted, until he had signed on. "But you could have moved on to a bigger ship."

A strange expression crossed Muldoon's face. "It's good enough here."

Rod glanced at her eyes, glanced away, and kept silent. For the first time, he began to understand what it meant to be adult, but insecure.

A chime rang; Muldoon looked up. "Chow time. Excuse me a second." She ducked into a closet and closed the door.

Rod suppressed a sudden urge to call out to Fess. If he'd been near the robot, he would have had a quick discussion of the day's events—but he couldn't bring himself to do it by yelling. Also, he'd been awake twenty hours now, and was beginning to feel it.

The door opened, and Muldoon came out wearing an officer's uniform with the same rank insignia as Weiser's. Rod goggled; the jacket was cut loose, but not loosely enough. Neither were the trousers. Also, the net was gone, and her hair floated in a cloud around her face.

She smiled at his surprise. "Well, thank you. Don't think it's a habit, though—we only dress up for dinner on this ship."

Rod glanced down at his own clothes, and his greasy hands.

"Don't worry, you're excepted until you're issued your uniform. You can wash up on the way." Muldoon set her cap on and tucked the strap under her chin. "Come on, meet your mates."

"Mates" had an unpleasant sound, suddenly. "Doesn't somebody have to stand watch?"

"The computer will, bucko. You wouldn't know what to look for yet, anyway." She turned away, and Rod couldn't help but follow—in uniform, her glide was even more a magnet.

As he passed Fess, the robot murmured, "Remember, Rod—swabbies should be seen, and not heard."

"Oh, don't worry, I won't make you ashamed of me," Rod grumbled. Just the same, he found himself making a mental note not to talk.

Apparently, he was the only one who didn't. Now he knew why they called it a "mess." He did think of adding his two cents' worth now and then, but every time he opened his mouth, Weiser caught his eye and, for some reason, Rod found himself shutting up.

They were gathered around the table. Rod started to sit, but a tall man with captain's bars cleared his throat, and Rod realized that the others were still standing. He pulled himself back up, surprised that he wasn't going to have to act proletarian to fit in, then remembered to salute. The captain returned it, then looked around at the others. "I hope you're all making our new crewman feel welcome." It was a remark certain to make Rod uncomfortable.

"Oh, yes, Captain! I've given him the full tour of the engine room, and checked his background." Muldoon was standing straight, shoulders back, eyes bright (maybe a little feverish), smiling. She seemed more reticent, somehow; the brassy lady projected shyness.

"Good, good. Well, let's see he meets everyone else, then. I'm Captain Donough." He was broad-shouldered, lean, handsome, and well-groomed. "The gentleman on my right is First Officer Jonas Whelk."

The first officer smiled and returned Rod's salute. He was skinny, balding, and sharp-featured.

"And I believe you've met Mr. Weiser, our second officer."

Rod saluted. Weiser returned it, narrow-eyed.

"Ah, you might ask to be excused, Albie," Donough murmured, and gave him the eye while he ran a finger over his own cheek.

Weiser's face darkened, but he muttered, "Asking the Captain's pardon."

"Of course."

Weiser left.

Rod wondered what all *that* had been about—but Donough was going on. "And this is Third Officer Noah McCracken."

Rod saluted. "A pleasure, sir."

McCracken returned it. His profile showed what free-fall could do for the figure—he was round as a ball from hip to shoulder, with another globe on top. No sagging; he was a perfect sphere. Rod wondered if he dared leave the ship on anything larger than Luna.

Weiser rejoined them, looking sullen but clean-shaven. Rod's eyes widened; then he remembered his manners and looked away, just before Weiser gave him a murderous glare.

"Gentlemen and lady," the captain said, "this is Spaceman Rodney d'Armand."

Weiser's eye lit with a wicked gleam, hearing Rod's full name. But the young man didn't care; just hearing the title from the captain's lips made his heart sing. He was a spaceman!

"However, as the junior member," Donough went on, "it falls to you to serve at table. Everyone else, please be seated."

Rod thought of mentioning something about his job description, then remembered how far it was to the nearest spaceport. Besides, Weiser had caught his eye again. And Muldoon was sitting down. Rod moved to hold her chair, but McCracken beat him to it. Not that it made any real difference—the seats were securely tracked, anyway. The other crewmen slid forward to lock themselves in place, and Donough said, "Stand by the autochef, Mr. d'Armand."

Rod looked around, identified the food synthesizer, and pushed himself over to it. He found himself really respecting Donough; any man who could keep his crew dressing for dinner, and even making some attempt at good manners, was pretty good. He was also pretty smart—it was a prime ingredient in maintaining morale.

It sure seemed to work on Muldoon.

"We'll begin with minestrone—key in I-C, please. And a plain salad, B-V. Dressings?"

"French," said Whelk.

"Russian," Weiser answered.

"Clavian," McCracken stated.

"None," Muldoon said.

"And I'll have Roquefort. Now, let's see the day's menu." He picked it up, pretending not to have it memorized. The others followed suit, except McCracken. Donough caught his eye, and the Third picked up the printout with a sigh.

The 'chef rang; Rod pulled cups out and started setting them in front of people.

"Thank you, Mr. d'Armand. Be seated, please."

Rod went to his chair, then stopped. He looked up and found the captain's eye on him, amused. "You might want to punch up one for yourself."

"Yes, sir!" Rod went back for another minestrone, brought it to his chair, and sat.

Donough picked up his cup, sipped through the spout, and set it down as he said. "I thought we did rather well at Maxima."

"Yes, sir," Whelk agreed. "Made a nice profit on the textiles from Terra."

"And the wines." McCracken smiled. "I never cease to be amazed that people will pay so much for fermented grape juice, when any decent autochef can synthesize it just as well."

"It's the status," Weiser grunted.

"And the link to the homeworld." Donough held his cup up, gazing off into space. "I remember when I was midshipman, on the Mars run . . ."

Whelk coughed politely into his fist and said, "Standing orders, sir."

Donough looked up, startled, then smiled with self-deprecation. "Yes, I have told that one a few times before, haven't I? Thank you, Mr. Whelk."

Muldoon glared daggers at Whelk, who carefully avoided her glance.

The captain pushed his almost-empty soup cup away, and everyone followed suit. Rod immediately rose and circled the table, clearing the cups, then went to the autochef and started serving again. The salads were just as easy as the soup had been, but he did have to try to remember which dressing went with whom. He didn't have much trouble with Muldoon, strangely.

Donough speared a tomato through the clinging film and lifted it through the surface tension as he said, "We should do well on Ceres. Not with the components from Maxima, of course."

"No, sir," Whelk agreed. "Coals to Newcastle, and all that."

"Very. But the people on Ganymede will pay through the nose for them, and Ceres should be a good market for the second-grade textiles." He looked up at a sudden thought. "We don't have any furs left, do we?"

"Two, I'm afraid, sir," Whelk answered. "The demand on Maxima wasn't quite what we thought it would be."

"Mm." Donough went after a cucumber slice. "Well, we certainly won't be able to unload *them* on Ceres."

Rod could scarcely believe his ears. All his life, "Ceres" had been synonymous with luxury and decadence—but here these men were saying that nobody on the big rock could afford anything nearly as good as the Maximans could!

And they couldn't be wrong. This was their living—and they were still alive.

When the salad dishes were cleared away, Donough said, "I think I'll have the ragout tonight—that's J-O. And I'll have a burgundy with it—A-A."

Rod pressed the pressure pads with the labels named, and waited. The others ordered, and he entered their dishes, then almost immediately started removing and serving. For a moment, he was tempted to mention that he had a robot who was really very good at this sort of thing, but he noticed Weiser's eye on him and changed his mind.

Finally they were all served, and Rod could punch in his own order and sit. They dug in, and he had to admit the first two courses had done the trick—he really wasn't all that hungry any more.

"I'm a bit worried about the political situation on Ganymede," Whelk noted.

Donough smiled. "We've known they aren't really a democracy for a long time, Number One."

"Yes, but this new president the Council has just, um, 'elected' . . ."

Weiser shrugged. "A dictator is a dictator. How's that going to affect trade?"

"Not at all," McCracken said, with finality. "I remember when we stopped at Triton, when I was a lad—little bit of a thing, scarcely two hundred pounds . . ."

The others all looked pained, but Donough leaned forward, all polite interest.

"They'd just elected a new Doge, and he was making loud noises about the 'Terran menace,' and glorifying home culture. But we landed with a load of Paris originals, champagne, Beluga caviar, and Cleveland cheeseburgers, and his agents bought two-thirds of the cargo. Then the locals climbed all over each other bidding for what was left. And all the while, he was spouting about the dangers of thinking anybody could make anything better than the Tritons could." He looked around with a hard smile that slowly slipped as he noticed his mates paying attention to their dinners. "I've told that one before, haven't I?"

"It was still fascinating," Donough said quickly, "and quite apt to the situation at hand. Now, Mr. d'Armand—if you would serve the sweet?"

Rod cleared, with a glance at the Second. He was startled; Weiser still looked ravenous. Rod wondered how he could have gone through such big portions and still be hungry.

Then he saw that the man was looking at Muldoon.

Alarm and anger flared in him, at the thought of that pig daring to even look at so ethereal a lady—but hard on the heels of it came a surge of sympathy; Rod knew just how the poor guy must feel, having to see the look on her face whenever she glanced at the captain.

Which made Rod terribly confused. He chucked his load in the recycler and went to punch in desert. Just serve the meal, swabbie—just serve.

"I push on the lower edge, right?"

"If the top edge is the outside, and if it operates as the locker does—yes."

"Okay, we'll try." Rod pushed in on the bottom line of the big rectangle on the wall, and the bed glided smoothly out and down. A stack of sheets and blankets lay in the middle; one end of the mattress bulged into a pillow. "Hmph! Well, here goes self-reliance." Rod picked up a sheet.

"I beg your pardon," Fess murmured, taking the sheet from him and shaking it out.

"Fess, *no!* If my shipmates catch you at it, they'll never let me hear the end of it!"

Fess paused in mid-shake. "Considering the evidence of Mr. Weiser's attitude . . ."

"Right." Rod took the sheet back, handed Fess the rest of

the stack, and started tucking. "I cannot believe Muldoon! She is a real beauty, and she doesn't seem to know it!"

Fess glanced back toward the engines.

"Oh, I'm not worried about her hearing—*she* has a cabin, and the door's closed."

"True—and she is beautiful," Fess admitted. "Still, she has not learned the graces of a true lady."

"Well, I never learned to be comfortable with 'em." Rod stopped in mid-movement. "Fess, when I saw her today, I felt a surge all through me."

"I was watching, Rod."

"And when it passed, I was still kind of light-headed, and the only thing I could think was, 'So this is what it's like to be in love!' "

"Yes," the robot murmured. "Yes."

"Did it show?"

"Only if you knew what to look for."

"Which she probably does." Rod's mouth tightened with chagrin. "Just as well she knows it, I suppose."

"A lady is always complimented, Rod."

"Yeah, I suppose so." Rod stood back, arms akimbo, proudly contemplating his handiwork. "There! I *can* make my own bed!"

"You have done well, Rod." Fess omitted saying anything about hospital corners, or smoothness.

Rod pulled out his duffel bag, took out pyjamas, and glanced around him. "If I can be sure that door stays shut . . ."

Fess boosted his audio gain, then reported, "She is breathing evenly and deeply, Rod."

"Asleep." Rod stripped quickly. "It still behooves me to move fast. Why the heck don't they give us at least a privacy curtain?"

"Possibly, Rod, because the designers assumed the whole crew would be of the same sex."

"Quaint." Rod yanked the pyjamas on, rolled into the bunk, and pulled the blankets up. "Of course, I suppose I should *want* her to surprise me in the buff."

"It would perhaps be premature, at this stage of your relationship."

"I'll take your word for it. I have to—I don't quite know how to act."

"Yes. You have never had such vivid feelings toward another person, have you?"

"But . . . Why?" Rod breathed. "When all my life, I've been surrounded by delicate ladies of high breeding, with all the graces and all the advantages—*why*?"

"Perhaps because Muldoon is of above-average intelligence."

"Well—maybe. But I don't remember anybody back home who had such a lovely face, either. Except Lucretia, and she's so neurotic it's a wonder she doesn't fall apart."

"I must say I'm delighted by your perception, Rod. Many men would fail to see Muldoon's beauty unless she used cosmetics in such a way as to make it overly obvious."

Rod's eyes flew open, staring into the darkness. He lay back, speculations running through his mind.

After an interval of silence, Fess murmured, "Good night, Rod."

"Hm? Oh. Yeah. Good night, Fess."

The ship shuddered, and Rod said, "Can I get up now?"

"Not yet," Muldoon called back.

"Shouldn't I have an acceleration couch?

"That's what your bunk *is*. So's mine. Everything has to do double duty, on a freighter."

So that was why she was staying in her room.

"Docking completed," Donough's voice said over the intercom. "Twenty-four-hour liberty commences *now!* Have fun in Ceres City, crew!"

They heard a cheer in the background, before the captain let the mike close.

Rod released his webbing and was sitting up before it had finished snapping back. He hopped down, pushed his bed up and into the wall, and headed for the passageway. Then he stopped, realizing that his footsteps didn't have an echo. He turned around and saw Muldoon with computerboard in hand, checking the bank of meters on the wall. "Aren't you coming?"

Muldoon shook her head. "Always something to do, here."

"But it doesn't *have* to be done, does it?"

"Have to or not, I'm doing it."

"But why?" Rod frowned, coming toward her. "You can't . . ."

And Muldoon burst into tears.

Rod froze, staring.

"Out!" Muldoon snapped. "Let me take care of my engines in peace! Now, get *out!"*

Rod got.

"But why didn't she want company?" Rod muttered.

"There are nuances in human relationships that are indecipherable without knowing the complex of ties involved," Fess answered, *sotto voce.*

"Which means we don't know enough to guess."

"A sufficiently accurate interpretation. And, if you'll pardon the comment, Rod . . ."

"It's none of my damn business." Rod lay back, waiting for the acceleration to pass. "But Fess, I *love* her."

"That does not give you the right to meddle in her affairs."

"I suppose," Rod sighed.

"But Rod, you have been worrying this problem for twenty-six hours now—and I am certain you scarcely noticed the sights of Ceres City."

Rod shrugged. "Ceres, I've seen before. Muldoon, I haven't."

The acceleration eased off, and the intercom announced, "Departure completed. We have set course for Ganymede. Duty stations."

Rod sat up, stood, and turned to push his bunk back into the wall. "Well, let's hope she's—"

A sudden raucous hooting echoed through the ship. Rod froze, recognizing the "loss of atmosphere" signal. "We're holed!"

If Fess said anything, it was to empty air. Maximan reflexes had taken over, and Rod was on his way to the emergency toolkit.

He yanked it up—it took quite a pull; the bottom was magnetized—and glanced up at the screen above it. An outline of the ship glowed there, with a red dot blinking in the forward hold. He turned toward the doorway, swinging the toolbox up as he sprang. Behind him, he heard Muldoon calling, but for once, it didn't seem important.

He shot down the passageway, ricocheted off the sides of the dog-leg, and hurtled past the entry hatch. Behind him, way behind, somebody was yelling, "Out of the way, swabbie!" But that didn't matter. He braced himself, wrenched at the grip on the hatch, and leaped into the forward hold, hitting the lights as he came.

It felt as though his face was trying to swell. He saw the puncture, an ugly, ragged hole with sharp edges pointing toward him, a good centimeter in diameter. He dove toward it, ripping the emergency box open and yanking out a temporary patch, then swinging the box down against the hull. The magnetic bottom clanked, hard, and Rod held onto it as he swung his feet up, went into a crouch by the hole, and slapped the patch on. He pushed against the box as he smoothed the edges, then swung his legs back to grasp the sides of the toolbox as he pulled an insulated glove on, then took out a steel patch and the spotwelder. Feet pounded up behind him, and Weiser's voice yelled, "What the *hell* do ya think y're doing? Out of the way, ya spoiled brat, before I push you through that hole!"

Rod gritted his teeth and ignored the man. He stuck the positive contact onto the wall, then held the steel patch over the temp. He pounded its center flat with the hammer end of the welder, then tilted the tip to the edge and pressed the button. Lightning spat from it, and the alloy edge of the patch flowed.

He traced the rectangle around the edges of the patch, then sat back on his heels and heaved a sigh. *Now* he could let the shakes hit.

And look up at Weiser.

He braced himself; he knew he had disobeyed a direct order. But the Second was studying the patch, and, slowly, nodding.

Rod felt limpness hovering. "I'm sorry, sir. I . . . ."

"Did what you should." Weiser still nodded. "Good job of welding, too. *I* should say, 'Sorry'; I didn't see you'd already put the temp patch on." He turned around to scowl down at Muldoon, who was coming up, panting. "Y' taught him fast."

Muldoon shook her head. "Not *that,* I didn't."

Weiser turned back to Rod. "Where'd ya learn, rich boy?"

Rod managed a thin smile. "I grew up on an asteroid, sir. Our buildings may not look like pressure domes, but that's what they are—and we're raised with puncture drills. I've known how to set a patch since I was ten."

" 'D ja ever really do it before?"

"Once. That was the only time I ever got there first."

Weiser nodded slowly. "Guess even an aristocrat can earn his keep. Well, the fuss is over. Back to stations, everyone."

*   *   *

Rod still served at mess that night, but Weiser didn't glare at him once. Rod's heart sang—he was proving himself!

And the topic of conversation had changed. The officers had some bragging to do.

"What were you trying to do in that restaurant, McCracken—eat the whole menu?"

"No, just everything on it."

Muldoon smiled thinly.

McCracken went on, "Too bad about the keg in the Fall Inn."

"What about it?" Weiser frowned. "I didn't see nothing wrong."

"Then why were you trying to outdo it?"

A laugh rounded the table; even Muldoon joined, and Weiser grinned. "Talk about me having the high old time! Whelk was out with his wife again."

"Which one this time?"

Muldoon's smile faltered.

"The Ceres one." The first officer smiled at Rod. "Entirely legal, Mr. d'Armand—on both Mars and Ceres. Not on Terra, of course—but I don't go there very often."

"Not unless he wants to wear his law suit," Weiser jibed.

"However, our gallant Captain must take his share of ribbing," Whelk said, with a sly wink at Donough. "That was a beautiful brunette we saw you with at Pastiche's, sir."

"Why, thank you, Mr. Whelk." Donough inclined his head, and Muldoon's smile disappeared.

"Brunette?" Weiser frowned. "She was a redhead!"

"No, that was the one at Malloy's," McCracken corrected him. "Cute as a button."

"In a pig's eye!"

"No, the one at The Pig's Eye was blonde."

"Hey, *I* was at Pastiche's, and she was a redhead!"

"Oh?" said Whelk. "When were you there?"

"Twenty-one hundred."

"Oh, the early shift. Well, I saw him there when we dropped in for a morning snack, about 0400. She was a brunette by then."

Muldoon had to look down at her plate. Rod felt a lump in his throat, and searched wildly for a way to change the topic—but all he could think of was Fess saying, "Swabbies should be seen and not heard."

"Gentlemen, gentlemen!" Donough smiled around at them, amused. "I'm afraid you have caught me out. Margot is my second cousin; she was waiting for me as . . ."

The hoots of laughter drowned out the end of the sentence.

"And I'll bet the blonde was your Aunt Greta!"

"No, she's the sister of a friend who asked me to take her to dinner, poor thing. She's very shy, never goes out . . ."

Weiser howled, then smothered it to a chuckle, glanced at Muldoon, and went silent.

"As to the other two," Donough said with dignity, "you'll have to assume prior acquaintance; there as no other way I could have arranged to meet them, ahead of time."

"No way at all," Whelk said, deadpan. "It's too bad you didn't have time to fully enjoy the company of any one of them."

McCracken tried to swallow a snicker.

"Social obligations must come before personal pleasure," Donough sighed.

"Yes, but personal pleasure should be considered." Whelk turned serious, and also turned to Muldoon. "You really must take shore leave now and then, Engineer. It's vital to your emotional well-being."

"Yes, Muldoon!" McCracken turned a genial smile on her. "Why don't you come along next time?"

"Yeah, Gracie!" Weiser said, with genuine concern. "You gotta quit moulderin' in that engine room! Get out an' live a little! You need it!"

"No," Muldoon said, very quietly, "I don't think so."

She was still very quiet as she led the way back to the engine room. Rod felt awkward as he followed behind her, knowing damn well that she wanted to be alone, but not seeing any polite way to excuse himself. He kept feeling as though he should make conversation, but knew it would do more harm than good.

As they came through the door, Muldoon muttered something about paperwork and sat down at her terminal. Rod drifted around the engine room, not knowing where else he could go, but not wanting to be in her way. She was punching at the pads as though they were mortal enemies. The silence stretched tighter and tighter, till Rod could almost hear it thrum.

Finally, he couldn't take it any more. "Uh, sir, I could take the watch, if you needed to do . . ."

Then he couldn't hear himself anymore, because she was sobbing.

Rod was terrified. Oh, he'd dealt with tears before, but these sounded *real*. His instincts moved him to her as surely as his glands, but he didn't know what he could do.

Finally, he gave in and dropped to one knee beside her. "It'll be all right," he murmured. "It all comes out okay in the end! It's not really *that* bad!"

"Oh, shut up!" she stormed. "You don't even know what you're talking about!"

Rod recoiled, stricken.

Muldoon saw, and broke up all over again. "Oh, I'm sorry! I didn't mean to be a beast when you were only trying to help. But it *is* that bad! He goes out and sees every pretty girl he can cram into twelve hours, because he knows he won't see one again for a month! And every day, he's sitting right across from me, seeing me every time he looks up! But *I'm* not pretty!"

"You *are!*" Rod protested.

"Oh, be quiet, you idiot! I'm as plain as they come! I'm *ugly!*"

"You are *beautiful!*" Rod stormed. "Underneath those smudges is the most delicate, entrancing face I've ever *seen!* Your figure takes my breath away! Your features are the kind men kill each other for! Your eyes are pools that a man could lose himself in!"

She stared at him, her sobs slackening. "Do . . . do you really think so?" She hiccupped.

"I swear it!"

"Well . . . You're a rich boy, you must have seen the best . . ."

"Best, my fandango! You're so far beyond them that you can look back at the galaxy!"

"But . . . but they've got those lovely dresses . . . and they're graceful, and refined, and . . ."

"They're as graceful as penguins on land! You move like a fairy princess!"

"You've only seen me in free fall . . ."

"Give me a chance to see you in gravity," he begged. "Go on shore leave. Believe me—the Maximan girls don't have an ounce of your beauty!"

"But . . . in the pictures on the screen . . ."

"What pictures? Oh—You mean those little clips they put in on the 3DT romances? Those're actresses, not real Maximans. Oh, sure, now and then you'll see a few shots of a real ball—but the camera's so far away that you can't really see the faces and figures at all."

"But they're aristocrats!"

"Yeah, and they look like it, too. All they have that you don't have is pretty dresses and makeup—and you can buy both of those."

"But I wouldn't know what to do with powder and rouge if I had it!"

Rod took a deep breath. "Trust me. I do."

He had studied the use of face paint through many an inordinately dull banquet—since he'd had to look at his table companions, he'd had to find something to keep his mind busy, so he'd started figuring out how they'd managed whatever effect they'd achieved. Then he'd had a few makeup workshops in the Maxima Amateur Theater Society, and he'd had a chance to study the process at close range, while the female Thespians labored with brush and liner.

"Yes, you *must* use a foundation! I *know* your complexion is perfect—I'd think you'd never exposed it to sunlight!"

"I didn't." Muldoon glared up at him. "I grew up in L-5. But I did have acne."

"Then you had one hell of a doctor. But skin is skin, and you're going to be a canvas!"

"Oh, all right," Muldoon griped, and sponged it smooth. Then she picked up a stick.

"No," Rod said, "not the pencil. Use the brush; shadow lines aren't really drawn with a ruler."

"But the pencil's so much easier!" Muldoon complained.

"Do you want ease, or results? Remember, it has to shade—chiaroscurro, just as in a painting. That's what you're going to be, when you get done—a work of art. Dust that color back in from the cheekbones."

*   *   *

"But I can't *move* with these things on!"

"Then you'll never be graceful in gravity. Those magnets should give you just about the same pull as one G—I had Fess design them. Remember, now, one foot at a time, and short steps."

"I'll never get anywhere, that way!"

"Where you're trying to get, isn't measured in meters. You can move fast if you take lots of quick steps. Okay, try it . . . Good! You've got the feet right. Now, keep your back straight, and your shoulders back a little."

"But that makes my—you know. Like I'm trying to show off."

"What's the matter—are you ashamed of them? No? Then walk as though you're proud—*that's* right! Now, tilt your chin up just a little . . ."

Rod's head swivelled from side to side.

"Give it up," Muldoon advised. "You can't see everything at once."

"I can try, can't I? Wow! So this is Ganymede!"

"Yeah, one big shopping mall, except for the spaceport. You name it, you can buy it."

"Oh, come on! There have to be *some* laws!"

"Don't tell the natives—they'll think you're swearing."

"Oh, wow-wow-wow-WOW!"

"Blink or your eyes will dry out," Muldoon grated. "We're here to look at dresses, not the lack of them!"

Rod pulled his eyes away with an almost-audible snap. "That is definitely not the right style for you!"

Muldoon scowled up at him. "How do *you* know what a woman should wear?"

"Sir, when it comes to beauty, I'm not just a consumer, I'm an addict! All I have to do is dress you like my dreams."

"I thought you said that *wasn't* the right style for me."

"Oh, doing your hair?" Rod popped in around the open cabin door. "Remember, now, you have to rat it before . . ."

"Shove off, swabbie," Muldoon muttered around a mouthful of hairpins. "This is something I *do* know."

"You do?" Rod couldn't help goggling. "Where'd you learn?"

"Before school, every day for thirteen years."

"Then wh—" Rod just barely managed to swallow the rest of it.

"Because when I got to college, I decided there was no reason to put up with the pain, and swore I'd never do it again. Will you get out of here?"

"But what about your oath?"

"I'm going to start using it in about three seconds. Now shove *off!*"

"Shopping!" Weiser chortled. "The little guy's going shopping! Hey, if ya see something frilly, take it in and have it filled, will ya?"

"Let him alone, Weiser," McCracken grumped. "At least he's getting Gracie to step out a little."

"Yeah. Nice move there, mister." Weiser throttled it down to a grin. "How come *you* know all about dresses, buddy boy?"

"Mr. Weiser," Rod said, in his loftiest manner, "I have always enjoyed studying dresses closely—after there's something in them."

"Oh, yeah? Did you learn anything?"

"A lot, about truth in packaging." Rod turned around at the sound of high heels. "Ready, sir?"

"You betcha, swabbie!" Muldoon floated up in a velvet dress, hair falling in gentle waves, makeup flawless, and a twinkle in her eye. "Let's go see Titan!" She hooked her hand through his elbow and charged out to do battle with the cash register.

Weiser's head pivoted on his shoulders as he watched her go by. He studied their retreating forms, mostly hers. "Y' know, that kid just might be smarter than he looks."

"Yeah, and maybe he's so smart that he's dumb." McCracken frowned at him. "I worry too much, Albie."

"D'Armand's Finishing School," Weiser chuckled.

"It'll finish you, if you don't stop snickering."

"I'm not snickering, I'm chuckling."

"Well, stow it, whatever it is—here she comes."

They tipped their hats as Muldoon breezed by. "Hi, Gracie!"

"Good to see you, Grace!"

" 'Grace' is the word," Weiser murmured, watching her retreating back. "Maybe the kid knows what he's doing."

"Maybe he does," McCracken agreed. "Pull your eyes back into your head, Albie."

"Ceres again," McCracken sighed. "Whelk goes off to his wife, the captain goes off with a crowd, and I go off to dinner."

"Whatever we're doing, let's *go*." Weiser had the fidgets. "Do we *have* to wait for the captain?"

"More a matter of him waiting for you." Whelk came up. "I understand he wants to give us all a sermon."

"For *liberty?*"

Donough came up with a smile. " '*Ten-shun!* Now, men, I know this is going to be something of a strain, but I understand we're giving the good ship *Murray Rain* a bad reputation."

"Bad rep?" Wesier squalled. "We've been angels! Well . . . compared to . . ." His voice trailed off.

Donough nodded. "Just what I had in mind, Mr. Weiser. Who ever heard of a sedate sailor, sea *or* space? Now, I do want dignity at all times—but see if you can't be a little wilder about it, eh? All right, now, out we . . . What are you staring at?"

All three officers were gazing past his shoulders with eyes like saucers. "Captain . . . Gracie . . ."

Donough turned to look, and looked again.

She came toward them with small quick steps, one hand on the bulkhead to keep her down to the deck, eyes bright, an eager smile, and a dress that clung to every contour.

Donough gasped as though he'd been hit, or at least smitten.

Weiser was the first to recover. "Hey, Gracie, I know this great little place . . ."

McCracken bowled past him. "Grace, would you consider dinner at the most fantastic restaurant . . ."

Whelk just looked unhappy; he had a wife waiting.

"Ten-*hut!*"

They all pulled a brace. The captain saw Gracie at attention, and took a deep breath himself. "Gentlemen," he said quietly, "for once, I'm going to pull rank. Ms. Muldoon, may I have the pleasure of your company for dinner tonight?"

"Oh, *yes*, Captain!" Muldoon fairly glowed as she took his arm and stepped out under the stars, gazes locked with Donough's. Weiser stood in the hatchway staring after them, muttering, "She's in love with him. I knew it, yeah—so why's it hit hard, now?"

"Maybe because he never realized she was a woman before," Rod said.

Weiser turned to him, narrow-eyed. "Speak when you're spoken to, Mister! If she gets a heartbreak, it's *you* I'll come looking for!"

And, for a moment, Rod didn't think Weiser was going to wait. He braced for combat, resolved not to lose his head this time. All he could say was, "She needed it."

"Yeah." There was no definite sign, but he could see Weiser cooling down. "I oughta hate you for it—but I can't. 'Cause I love her." He studied Rod for a long moment, then nodded slowly. "You, too, huh, kid?"

Rod swallowed and nodded.

Then Weiser's arm shot out—to slap him across the shoulders and turn him toward the hatchway. "Come on, swabbie—let's go get drunk."

And they did. Totally.

He woke to the sound of singing, croaked piteously, and tried to bury his head under the pillow, but it was fastened down.

"Oh, Rod, it was so *wonderful!*"

Rod rolled up enough to crack one bloodshot eye open. The ultimate vision of female loveliness sat down on his bed, and he was in no condition to do anything about it.

"The whole night, Rod! He spent the whole night, just with me! No taking me back to the ship and going off!"

"I'm s' happy," Rod moaned.

"First it was dinner, then it was dancing! Then we went to the first night club, and a gypsy came over and played a violin—just for us!"

Rod wanted to ask her to speak more softly, but he didn't have the heart.

"Then another club, and another, and I was hoping he wouldn't proposition me, 'cause I didn't know if I would've been able to resist—but he didn't."

Thank heaven for small mercies. Personally, Rod wished the ship would stop rolling.

Then he remembered it was a spaceship, and the waves were only in his stomach.

"No other women! No blondes! No brunettes! Just *me!*" Muldoon glided up into a pirouette. Rod caught his breath.

"We got drunk, but not terribly—we didn't need to. We had breakfast at Pastiche's and strolled back along the Boulevard Glazé, and I never realized before how beautiful the asteroids can be, like stars in a waltz! And he stopped in front of the church, Ceres' only church, and asked me to marry him!"

Rod stared, too horrified to make a sound.

"Of course I said yes. I didn't have to think about it—I already have, so many times! I said yes, and he took me inside and caught us a minister, and *he* helped us catch each other, and we stopped by a jeweler's on the way back to the ship, and here it is!"

She thrust a small glacier under Rod's nose. He goggled, staring at the iceberg and the slim gold band next to it, and felt his stomach sink, then lurch. But he managed to whisper anyway, "All best wishes."

"Oh, thank you, you darling! And I owe it all to *you!*" Muldoon seized his face, gave him a quick, warm, but thorough kiss, and said, "I'll never forget you for this." She bowed her head, suddenly looking terribly shy, and breathed, "Gotta go now. My husband is waiting."

Then she was gone, in a swirl of taffeta.

Rod moaned and rolled over on his bunk, hanging his head over the bucket beside it. "Fess—what have I done?"

"You have made a good woman very happy, Rod."

"But it wasn't supposed to work out this way!"

"How was it supposed to operate, then?"

"Oh . . . I dunno . . . But somehow, she was supposed to realize that I was the one who really loved her, and wind up with me!"

"You will have her eternal gratitude, Rod. You will have a friend for life."

"A friend is not quite what I had in mind . . ."

11

A low moan echoed through the hall.

The children were up in an instant, their hair standing on end. Gwen was sitting straight, glaring.

"Oh, no!" Rod groaned. "Not again!"

" 'T-'tis a spirit of another sort, Papa."

"I don't care *what* it is—we need our sleep!" Rod rolled over, sitting up to glare at Magnus. "Who did you wake this time?"

"I did not, Papa!" Magnus's voice broke. "Or if I did, 'twas unawares, from dreaming!"

"That's all we need." Rod held his head in his hands. "We're gonna be living in a haunted castle, with a son who calls up ghosts even in his sleep." He turned to the spectre. "Just who do you think you are, coming in here in the middle of the night and scaring my family half to death?"

The moan turned into words. "I cry thy pardon, gentle knight. I would not afright younglings an I had any other way to seek thee."

"How about catching me alone, when I'm on my way to the jakes?"

"I cannot, for 'tis thy son who doth give the power to bring me forth."

Rod glanced up at Magnus, eyebrow raised. "Settles that question, anyway." He turned back to the ghost, frowning, studying its appearance. The new apparition was a stocky suit of armor with a sword in its hand, clanking appropriately. "Have the courtesy to show your face, and tell us your name!" Rod growled.

"Thy pardon." The knight sheathed his sword and lifted not only his visor, but his whole helmet, too—and stopped looking frightening. He was balding, and had wrinkles in his kindly face, all in softly glowing outline. "I am Sir Donde L'Accord. I had not meant to afright, least of all little ones."

"We are no longer little!" Geoffrey snapped, but Gregory just stared.

"And I am Rod Gallowglass, Lord Warlock. This is my lady, and my children. What do you want with me?"

"A warlock!" The ghost's eyes lit with hope. "I cry thine aid, my lord! Have pity on a poor, troubled father, an thou wilt! Assistance, I prithee!"

"Father?" Rod was suddenly totally alert. "You wouldn't happen to have a daughter who roams this castle too, would you?"

"Aye." The ghost's expression darkened. "As will I, till I have found the means of my revenge!"

"Ah," Rod breathed. "Revenge on the man who wounded your daughter?"

"Aye, tortured her heart, then slew her! Would that he and I were flesh, that I might cast down my gauntlet and dash out his brains!"

"Not exactly a worthy thought, for one who presumably hopes to win to Heaven. How come you died so soon after your daughter's death?"

"I did not." The spirit stared. "Wherefore wouldst thou think I had?"

Well, so much for Holmes's methods; Rod wasn't scoring any higher than Watson had. "Had to be after, or you wouldn't have known how she died. Couldn't have been very long after, or you would have carved the villain's gizzard, and cheerfully gone to the block if you'd had to."

"Indeed I would have, an I could have." The ghost smiled sadly. "Yet I died ere she did, in battle. My spirit surged toward Heaven, yet slowed and tarried; my concern for her did bind me back to earth. Yet in all else I longed for the mede of the Blessed, and so I hung, poised between this earthly mansion and the one above, until at last her longing for me grew to terror, and drew me back to this castle—at the moment that her spirit stepped forth from her clay. Yet she could not see me, for her whole being was consumed with weeping, as it hath been ever since."

"The poor lass!" Cordelia cried, and Gwen said,

"Was her soul so filled with anguish, then, that she could not break free?"

"Aye, and ever hath been. I have slumbered by, for when death passed, her craving for my presence ceased; she was so filled with horror that there was room for naught else. Only now have I awaked—and I must needs find some way to ease my child's rest!''

Rod rolled out of his blanket and beckoned to his children. ''Up. Everybody up. Now it's *my* mission, too.''

''But their rest!'' Gwen protested.

''I think we'll have better luck sleeping during the day, dear. Fewer interruptions, you know?'' Rod turned back to the ghost. ''Name the villain.''

Fires licked at the backs of the spectre's eyes. ''The Count.''

''But I thought he whipped his son into line. Did he turn around and commit the same crimes himself?''

''Nay—he died. And the son became Count in his turn—the last Count Foxcourt, and the final scion of an evil line.''

''Evil line?'' Rod frowned. ''It sounded as though his father had *some* morals.''

''True, but only what was needful to bind his knights unto his service—and to be sure that none could have their will, save he.''

''Oh.'' Rod translated. ''So his son couldn't bundle the knights' daughters into bed, because that was Dad's prerogative—only Dad wouldn't do it, because he needed to have his knights stay loyal.''

''Aye, but his son had not so much wisdom. Bad blood will tell—and in him, it fairly howled. All his grandfathers had preyed upon the folk within their demesne, in all ways that they could, without inciting rebellion; they seized upon each chance for cruelty, every means of exploitation. Thus were they named as they were.''

''What—Foxcourt?'' Rod said. ''Doesn't sound all that evil.''

''Nay—that was but the sound the peasants gave it, till only we, whose forebears had been knights to that first Count, did remember its first form; for his neighbors dubbed him with the name that he, in insolence, took up in pride: *Faux Coeur.*''

The French vowel and ''r'' made all the difference; Rod's eyes widened. *''False heart!''*

''Quite false, in truth, for he was a man who would, for profit, swear to any oath, then be forsworn upon the instant. He would speak bravely as he led his troops out, yet would hang back behind while they did fight. Oh, false he was in words and deed, speaking fair and smiling sweetly, then wreaking every cruelty he could—and all his heirs were like him. Yet this last Count swore to outdo them all. He did not even deign to marry—what cared he for the future of his House?—but set out to seduce all women. Harsh-faced he was, but bore himself with a swagger, and spoke in honeyed tones, and wenches swooned when he came near.''

Rod nodded. ''Combination of a certain animal attraction, and money. Works on naive serving-wenches, every time.''

''Thou hast known the kind.''

''Yes—but I've also noticed their blandishments don't very often work on ladies of their own station.''

''Oh, he scrupled not to seek out other ways than wooing! By fair means or foul, he would seduce each lady that he could bring within his power, then spurn her from him, to dwell in shame—and several slew themselves. He only gloated.''

''Why, what a thorough villain!'' Cordelia said in indignation.

''And he used his tricks on your daughter.''

''Aye, for she was young, and very beauteous—and he, though a youth no longer, had taken womanizing as his foremost pastime. I sought to keep her from his sight, yet he did make a progress through his lands anon—I think more to espy out wenches than to be sure his bailiffs dealt honestly—and called in turn at each knight's house. He knew the number of my children, and summoned all before him—and when he saw her beauty, there was no restraining him.''

''You could have taken them and fled!'' Cordelia protested.

''Aye, yet I was bound by mine oath of fealty—the more fool I, for this Count did not feel bound by any oath of his! Yet when his man did come bearing his command to go unto his castle to attend upon him, and with all my family, I did say, 'Nay.' Within a fortnight, he did declare a war on Count Moline, and bade me forth unto the fray.''

''Ah!'' Geoffrey's eyes glowed. ''That command thou couldst not ignore, for 'twas the essence of thy knighthood!''

'' 'Tis even as thou sayest.'' The knight bowed his head. ''And he set me in the front rank, to be slain in the first charge—yet did not trust to fortune; for at the moment when my lance struck home 'gainst my opponent, a bolt did strike through mine armor 'neath my shoulder blade.''

"From behind!" Geoffrey cried. "Ah, what scurvy knave of an archer did that for him?"

"I know not, yet I misdoubt me an his pay was aught than death, for only a fool of a lord would chance his other knights' learning of such foul treachery. The barb pierced home, and I did swoon, and was mindful of naught else, till I did step forth from my mortal part."

"And went straight up to be caught between your duties and your rewards." Rod nodded. "So you don't even know what happened to your daughter."

"Only that she was driven to death by one means or another, and that my son was gone."

"Son?" Magnus looked up. "Nay, surely! He must needs be removed, or he would do all to prevent his lord from reaching to his sister!"

Cordelia turned to gaze at Magnus with a musing frown.

"Even so," the knight agreed. "He was a goodly lad, and would ward his folk from every harm. Nay, surely he must needs have been banished or murdered—and I have no doubt that his soul ascended on the instant of his death, for he was indeed a goodly lad."

"And thy daughter's spirit saw thee not?"

"Nay; she is ever incoherent in her grief. I did seek revenge and, I hoped, arresting of the Count's misdeeds, by haunting him; yet I had died without great anger, for I'd had little cause ere then, and my spirit lacked its fullest strength; and for his part, the last Foxcourt cared only for himself and his fleshly pleasures, and perceived little enough of others' feeling, and certainly naught of ghosts."

"Too insensitive to be haunted," Rod said, with disgust.

" 'Tis even so." Suddenly, the ghost was kneeling, with a spectral clanking. "I beseech thee, as one father to another—aid me! Find some means of bringing my child to the rest she merits! Avenge her murder!"

Rod's face hardened. "I don't deal in revenge."

"Art thou a craven? Why, then, pox upon thee! May thou forever be . . ."

"Nay, hear my father," Gregory said quietly, and, for a wonder, the ghost stilled at his words. He frowned down at Gregory, then looked up at Rod. "What means he?"

"He knows why I won't try for revenge," Rod said. "It bogs you down, keeps you from going on to make the most of yourself. The goal here is to give your daughter's spirit eternal rest, and her chance to finish her journey on the road to Heaven. If, in the process, the final Count finds himself on the receiving end of some of the cruelty he wreaked while he was alive—well and good; but that's only a byproduct.''

"Yet tell us this." Magnus stood, puzzled. "How may a ghost be hurt?"

The knight sighed and seemed to grow dimmer. "I know not.''

"The last Count is now but spirit," Gregory spoke up, "yet may feel spirits' pain. In truth, 'tis the agony of the soul that may yet redeem him, for if he comes to realize the pain that he hath caused, then may he yet repent.''

"The hour for that is past," the ghost said. "He is dead." But he turned to Rod. "What manner of child is this, who doth speak with the wisdom of a bishop?"

Rod winced. "Please! We've already been through that career plan.''

Far away, a rooster crowed.

The ghost's head lifted up. "The pregnant sky doth lighten with the dawn, and all the spectres of the night must slip away and hide themselves from light. I have overstayed my time. Farewell! Give aid to my child—and remember me!''

He faded as he said the words, and was gone, his last words echoing in repetition behind him: ''. . . Remember . . . remember . . . remember . . .'' Then the space where he had stood was empty, and the room was silent.

The children turned to look at one another, and Gwen sought Rod's gaze, but he still frowned toward the place where the ghost had been. She sighed, and turned away to stir up the fire.

Magnus stepped over to Rod, hand lifted, not quite touching. "Papa . . .''

"Yes." Rod looked up, then smiled. "Good morning, son. Feel like a little hunting?''

"How canst thou now, in the same chamber thou wast in before, read more of their tale now, than thou couldst afore-time, my son?''

"For that I now know whom I seek, Mama. 'Tis like to searching out a face well known within a crowd.'' Magnus was in one of the knight-and-lady chambers, fingertips tracing the wall. He frowned, shook his head, and turned to touch the bed. He stared then, and went rigid.

"What dost thou see, my son?" Gwen said softly.

"I see the wicked Count, Rafael Fer de Lance, ushering the Lady Sola and her mother, Dame Forla L'Accord, into this chamber." Magnus's voice seemed to come to them on a breeze, wafted from a great distance. "He is no longer young, and is harsh of face, yet with that sort of attraction for women that a snake hath for a bird."

Cordelia shivered.

"He is the last scion of an evil line," Magnus continued, "and is more evil than most, not even deigning to marry, but seducing every maid he can find, by fair means or foul, then abandoning each in her turn. Only the Lady Sola endures against his blandishments. She caught his eye, for she is very beautiful, and the daughter of one of his knights; so Count Foxcourt commanded Sir Donde to attend him with all his family. The knight refused, so the lord ordered him into battle, made sure of his death, and took his family into this castle 'for protection,' no matter Dame Forla's protests—for though her son Julius did succeed to his father's estates, he is too young to administer them."

"Here in his lair?" Cordelia asked. "How could the lady stand against him?"

"She had the love and support of her mother and brother when first she came, which did stiffen her resolve. Sin that she did resist his every blandishment, and her mother was the core of her strength, the Count did have the good dame poisoned."

The ladies gasped, and Geoffrey muttered darkly, but Gregory demanded, "Did the lady then find her own strength within herself?"

Rod glanced at his young son, then realized what he'd said, and stared.

"Not so," Magnus breathed, trembling, "for the Count did trump up a charge of treason 'gainst the brother Julius, but did intimate that the lady's acquiescence might save the lad."

"The villain!" Geoffrey cried, and Rod let out a long, low whistle.

"Then would the lady have yielded out of fear for her brother—but he contrived his escape, and came to her secretly to bid her stand fast. Then he laid a trail of false clues that led his pursuers to think him drowned by his own hand, and hid with a band of tinkers.''

"A shrewd lad, a clever lad!" Gregory clapped his hands. "Yet did not the Count suspect?"

"Aye. He did raise the hue and cry, and searched for Julius high and low, but never thought of disguises, and failed to find him. Yet he told the lady that the boy was imprisoned and would be tortured.''

Cordelia's eyes were huge. "How could she then hold against him?''

"The brother did contrive to bring his tinker-band hard by the castle walls, so that she saw him from her tower window, and heard him sing a song they'd shared in childhood.

Gregory sighed in admiration, and Geoffrey muttered, "The lad did not lack for courage.''

"The lady became obdurate again,'' Magnus went on, "and the lord did guess that someone in the castle had betrayed the secret that the boy was missing. He began a hunt for his supposed traitor, and confined her to her chamber, visiting her daily, and alone.''

"Oh!" Cordelia clapped a hand over her mouth. "He forced her, then?''

"Nay, for the chase had become too much a matter of pride for him. Yet he scrupled not to bring her wine mingled with a potent drug. She was wary, though, and knew the potion by its odor; she refused to drink—nor would she quaff too deeply of brandywine, though he did ply her with it.''

"A worthy lady," Gregory breathed, bright-eyed, "and a prudent one. Could the Count not see she was proof against his wiles?''

"Belike he did, for he lost patience, accused her of witch-craft, tried and sentenced her—and did attempt to have his rape of her be part of that sentence.''

"Would he not even then give over?" Cordelia said with some heat.

"He did,'' Magnus answered. "Not by any notion of chivalry, no, but by the clamoring of one and all, clergy and laity, who cried that he would have intercourse with the devil. When he discerned that they might topple him from his seat, he did give over, and had to be content with her burning at the stake.''

"Thus died a brave and valiant wench," Geoffrey murmured.

"Aye, and one whose life brought her only sorrow." Tears glittered in Cordelia's eyes.

"What of the lord?" Gregory breathed.

"The Count lived out his life as ever he had lived, in cruelty and depravity—yet was he more willing to resort to rape."

"And what of the lad?" Geoffrey demanded. "The bold, audacious brother? Sought he no revenge?"

"Aye, when he had come to manhood, and had claimed his right to knighthood. Then did he stride into Foxcourt's Great Hall and challenge the Count before all his company—with a score of King's knights at his back."

"There was no help for it, then." Geoffrey grinned. "The Count must needs have fought him."

"He did, yet with treachery and deviousness, as ever. He coated his blade with poison and did manage to nick Sir Julius, just as he was on the verge of slaying the lord."

"Ah, poor knight! What a base, depraved Count was this!"

"He was indeed." Magnus's voice finally hardened. "Yet he died in his bed, of no worse enemy than jaundice and gout—and he died without issue—or legitimate heirs, at the least."

"His line died with him, then," Gregory breathed.

"Even so. Oh, there was a cadet branch of the house . . ."

"Still is," Rod murmured.

". . . Yet they had too much sense to want the castle. Therefore hath it languished here, untenanted and grim, whilst centuries have rolled—and the Count's shade hath ceaselessly pursued the Lady Sola, whose ghost, ever lamenting the deaths of her mother, father, and brother, still haunts these halls, seeking some way to atone."

"Yet she hath no need!" Cordelia insisted. "There was no fault in her!"

But, "Hush," Gwen said, and reached out to take hold of Magnus's wrist, lifting his hand from the wall. The young man froze; then, slowly, his eyes came into focus again. He blinked, turning to look at Gwen. "Mother?"

"Aye," Gwen said softly. " 'Tis past, my son—hundreds of years past. Thou art with us again, as thou ever wast, with thy father, and myself, and thy sibs."

Magnus turned to his brothers and sister, blinking.

Cordelia whirled toward her mother. "There is no rightness in it, Mama! There is no justice!"

"The world is not always fair, my daughter," Gwen answered, her face grim, "and Heaven's judgement comes not till we are dead."

"Yet what justice hath Heaven given here, that the lass's ghost abides in torment, while the lord's is gone!"

"Gone where?" Geoffrey said, with a curl of the lip.

"Good point," Rod responded. "And for the damsel Sola— well, I can certainly understand why she lingers here, weighed down by false guilt for the lives of her whole family."

Cordelia turned, eyes wide. "Dost mean that, to free her, we have but to tell her 'twas the Count's guilt, and not hers?"

"No, we have to *convince* her of it—and with a good person, that can be very hard indeed."

Gwen eyed him narrowly. "Thou hast summat in mind, mine husband."

"Only a little demonstration," Rod said easily.

12

They slept for the remainder of the day. As the sun was setting, they were rising for a quick breakfast of porridge and water.

"Are we to fight spectres with naught but oatmeal?" Geoffrey demanded.

" 'Twill stay with thee, and give thee endurance," Gwen assured him. She glanced at Magnus, then looked again. "Didst thou not sleep soundly?"

"Aye, yet with many dreams. This Hall was the Count's prime place, Mama. 'Twas not the setting for his most shameful acts, yet 'twas filled with an abundance of petty cruelties and large humiliations."

"Thou hast awakened angry."

Magnus nodded. "I cannot wait to brace him!"

"Good," Rod said. "Good."

When darkness held the castle, and the only light came from the fireplace and a single sconce nearby, Magnus turned and strode to the dais where the count had sat, presiding over debauchery, two hundred years before.

The great chair stood there still. Magnus laid his hands upon it and called, "Rafael Fer de Lance, Count Foxcourt! Come forth to judgement!"

The evil laugh began once again, distant, but swelling closer, till it rang and echoed all about them—and Foxcourt was there, fully formed, even with faint colors glowing, so strong was his spirit. He was in his prime, his early thirties, his frame still muscular, his harsh features darkly handsome— but filled with sixty years of knowledge of human perversity, and delight in cruelty.

"Judgement?" he sneered. "And who will judge me, stripling? Thou?"

"That shall I! Yet I confess to wonder, that thou hast not yet been called before the greatest Judge of All!"

"I have been too much addicted to the pleasures of this life—most especially the delight of witnessing the suffering that I've caused." The ghost advanced on Magnus, slapping his palm with his riding whip. "I find the joys of cruelty too great, to wish to depart upon my final journey; though I'd have no choice, were there not foolish mortals like thyself, whose curiosity gives me an anchor with which to hold to this, the scene of all my pleasures."

Magnus stood firm, almost seeming to radiate a glow of his own. "Thou hast come to thy last journey here. Yet an I weaken, I have stronger spirits than mine, or thine, to draw on." He gestured toward his family. "Behold!"

An eldritch light shone about the Gallowglasses. Gregory started, but the others held firm.

The Count's laugh rang through the room. "What have we here? Two babes? And, ah! Two beauties!" He came down from the dais, advancing on Gwen and Cordelia. "One young, one in the fullness of her bloom—yet both fresh female souls!"

"Aye," Magnus said, from behind him. " 'Tis meat and drink to thee, to despoil the innocent, is it not?"

"Thou speakest well." He lifted his hand as he came closer to the women.

"Hold, foul worm!" Rod stepped in front of his wife and daughter, rage seething just beneath the surface of his face.

The count paused. "What have we here? A peasant, come to face a lord? Begone, foolish knave!" And he reached through Rod to caress Cordelia's chin.

Rod erupted into flame. White-hot flares licked out from him, searing the night, crisping the flesh on the spectre's form till spectral bones showed through. The Count's ghost screamed, whirling away, arms coming up to shield his face. Then Magnus's eyes narrowed, and the fabric of the spirit tore, and tore again, parting and parting like mist in a wind, as his shrieks rang through the hall, until his substance was shredded. Finally, Rod's flames withdrew, and darkness returned.

Out of the silence, Magnus asked, amazed, "Is that all? Is there no more to do than this?"

"Wait," Rod answered. "See his tatters, drifting? They're coming back together now."

And they were—swirling through the air like flakes of glowing snow, they pulled in upon themselves again, coalescing, returning to a form.

"I am ever proud when thou dost stand in my defense," Gwen said, low-voiced, "yet mayhap thou shouldst not have spent so much of thy power so soon."

"No fear—I've just begun to tap it," Rod answered. "Not that I had any urge to control myself, you realize."

"He comes," Geoffrey said, his voice hard.

The Count was there again, though without color now, only a pale and glowing form, but one with fury contorting his features. "Foolish mortals, to so bait a ghost! Hast thou no sense of caution? Nay, I shall be revenged on thee!"

Magnus was eyeing him narrowly. "He hath less hair, and more belly."

The Count whirled, staring at him in rage. "Avaunt thee, stripling! Up, men of mine! All mine old retainers, out upon him! Men-at-arms, arise!"

Magnus stepped down and over to his parents. "What comes now?"

Rod shook his head. "Can't say. Let's see if he can bring it off."

But the Count was succeeding. With drunken laughter, his retainers appeared—men-at-arms with ghostly pikes, and knights in spectral armor. But they were only outlines, and their laughter sounded distant.

"The lesser evils," Rod muttered.

"To horse, and away!" Count Foxcourt called—and suddenly, his knights were mounted on ghostly Percherons, and his men-at-arms advanced not with pikes, but with sticks and horns, blowing a hunting call.

"The game is up!" the Count cried. "Ho, bearers! Drive them from the covert!"

The men-at-arms came running, eyes alight, shouting with laughter and glee, thrashing at the Gallowglasses with sticks while the Count and his knights came riding, seemingly from a great distance.

"Avaunt thee!" Magnus shouted, and a wall of flame encircled the family.

"Oh, be not so silly!" Cordelia sniffed. "We must banish

them, not hold them back!'' And the sticks writhed in the spectres' hands, growing heads and turning back on the men-at-arms, becoming snakes which struck at their holders. With oaths, the soldiers dropped them. Instantly, the snakes coiled and struck, then struck again, and the men-at-arms fled shouting in disorder.

''A most excellent plan, my daughter!'' Gwen cried, delighted, and the hunting horns grew limp, then swung about, their bells turning into gaping jaws, glowing eyes appearing behind them as they sprouted wings, and dragons drove at the men who had them by the tails. The soldiers yelled in fear and fled, pursued by instruments of destruction.

Then the whole band of soldiers ran headlong into the advancing wall of knights.

Their masters rode them down with curses and galloped toward the Gallowglasses, faces filled with hungry gloating, their mounts' eyes turning to coals, flames licking about their outthrust jaws.

''This, then, is mine!'' Fess galloped out between the family and the knights and, suddenly, he seemed to swell and grow to twice his normal size, bleaching into a pale and giant horse with mane and tail of flame, glowing coals for eyes, and bright steel teeth that reached out past the Percherons' heads to savage their riders as he screamed with insane, manic glee.

'' 'Tis a pouka, a spirit horse!'' Gregory shrank back against Gwen, and even Geoffrey had trouble holding his ground. ''What hath possessed our good and gentle Fess?''

''The same thing that possesses him every time someone tries to hurt us,'' Rod said grimly, ''and the foe are of his own form, this time.''

But the horses were fleeing now, ghosts overawed by ghosts, while their riders saved face by kicking and cursing at them, as they dwindled into distance.

''The false cowards!'' Cordelia stormed. ''They were as struck with fear as their mounts—nay, more!''

The pouka had faded, darkened, and dwindled, and it was only their own, old Fess who came trotting back to them—albeit with a ghost of glee in his plastic eye.

''When did you learn how to do *that* trick?'' Rod asked, fighting a grin.

''I have been considering its feasibility for some time,''

Fess said, with airy disregard. "I had wondered if I could exert the same ability to project illusions as you could. Indeed, use of psionic amplifier . . ."

"Aye, wherefore not?" Gregory said, eyes alight as he stepped away from Gwen.

"Yet would real folk see the seeming?" Geoffrey frowned. "Ghosts are illusions themselves, and would certainly hold another such to be as real as they. Folk of flesh and blood, though, might not."

"Yet 'tis ghosts we fight at this time and place," Gwen reminded, "and Fess's devising is most puissant with them."

Magnus's lip curled. "Assuredly, we shall have no difficulty with so tattered a band."

"We won't have any trouble with his lordship, either," Rod said, "except that he'll come back every time we tear him apart. We need to banish him, not kill him."

"How will that aid the damsel Sola?"

"It will not." Gwen touched Rod's shoulder. "Hurt his pride."

"Of course." Rod lifted his head with a grin. "He's nothing but egoplasm, now—where else would he be vulnerable?"

The Count had rallied his courtiers now, primarily by banishing their horses. "Slay them!" he screamed, pointing toward the Gallowglasses.

The ghosts turned to look, then began to march with low, gloating laughs.

"Show me how he looked when he was old," Rod suggested.

Magnus frowned, concentrating—and, at the head of his troops, the Count began to age visibly. His hairline receded, then crept down the back of his head as his belly grew, and his whole body began to swell. His cheeks thickened as liver spots bloomed all over his skin.

His courtiers began to mutter among themselves, pointing. Someone giggled.

The Count halted, his lascivious leer turning into a scowl. He turned to look at his retainers, saw the pointing fingers, and turned to look back at the Gallowglasses. His face had swollen with fat and sagged into jowls.

"Is this how he truly looked at the end of his life?" Gwen asked.

Magnus nodded. "So say the stones."

"What kind of illnesses did he have?" Rod asked.

Magnus grinned.

The Count took another step, and howled with pain. "My gout!"

"Thou art no longer young," Gwen informed him. "Thou art an aged fool!"

But the malice in those eyes was anything but foolish.

"Didn't you say something about jaundice?" Rod muttered.

Magnus nodded, and His Lordship's skin gained a pale yellowish cast.

"Summon Sola," Gwen ordered.

Sweat beaded Magnus's brow, and the ghost-girl was there, wailing, "Wherefore hast thou brought me forth?"

The Count looked up, aghast, trying to balance on one foot while he cradled the other.

"Behold," Gwen called out, "thy tormentor's triumph! Old age!"

Sola turned, her weeping slackening. Her eyes widened, her lips parted. Then she began to laugh.

"Be still!" the Count commanded, alarmed.

Sola laughed the louder.

"Now!" Rod said to Magnus. "The pratfalls!"

The Count's remaining foot skidded out from under him, and he landed flat on his back with a howl.

Sola howled, too.

His courtiers stared, astounded.

The Count scrambled to rise, but he was too heavy. He roared in anger, trying to turn over, but even then, he had to kick a few times before he could finally work up enough momentum.

Someone in his court began to snicker.

"I—I shall be . . . revenged!" the Count panted, getting his feet under him, and treating his courtiers to a great view of his expanded backside. They began to laugh openly. He looked back at them, startled, then managed to heave himself to his feet and turned on them, his hand going to his sword, crying, "Be still, dolts!"

"The sword," Rod muttered. Magnus nodded.

The Count tugged at his hilt. He tugged again, then frowned and looked down. It was still there, all right. He set himself and gave a mighty pull—and the blade flashed out, describing a glittering arc through the air, heaving him around. His feet tangled, and he fell again.

The courtiers bellowed with mirth.

Livid, the Count tried to scramble to his feet once more, giving Sola the posterior vista. She howled the louder. "I should . . . not . . ."

"Nay, do!" Gwen encouraged. "Thou dost owe him far more!"

Sola's eye gleamed.

The Count struggled to get his knees under him.

Sola stepped forward, her dainty foot swinging hard in an arc.

The Count slammed down on his face again, and the Great Hall rocked with hilarity.

"Husband, this is humor of the lowest," Gwen said, trying to contain her laughter.

"Not quite." Rod turned to Magnus. "Aren't there always dogs under the tables, at these feasts?"

And the dogs were there, sniffing at the Count and wrinkling their noses in disgust. One fastened its teeth in his pants, then let go with surprising haste, hacking and coughing as it backed away. The rest of the curs gave a snort, turned their backs, and scratched dust into his face. He was roaring, of course, but nobody could hear him any more.

"Nay, let me join this mirth," Gwen said, and, suddenly, a duplicate of the Count appeared, advancing toward Sola, but with his rum-blossom nose a bit more swollen, the malice in his face somehow become foolish. "Behold, milord!" Gwen called, and the Count turned about, on hands and knees, and looked up to see—himself.

Himself, as others saw him, waddling toward a pretty girl with a swollen paw outstretched, burbling, "Nay, my pretty, dost thou wish advancement?"

"Why, aye, my lord," the ghost-girl responded, and stepped aside. The doppelganger blundered on by, groping about, finally managing to stop, while Sola watched it, giggling. There was nothing threatening about it now—it turned back, still groping and loosely grinning, merely an old, ugly, coarse, and foolishly leering dotard.

But Count Foxcourt laughed, too. "Why, what old fool is that?"

"Who?" Cordelia cried indignantly. "Art thou so blind? Nay, then, here's thy mirror!"

And a full-length cheval glass appeared in front of Foxcourt, right next to his doppelganger. He could not help but see, and blanched, turning to stare at the co-walker, then back to stare at the mirror, glancing from one to the other as his visage slackened.

Then rage contorted his features. "Nay, thou shalt not mock me! All men of mine attack! Or wouldst thou yet be banished?"

The laughter died as though it had been cut off, and the ghosts stared, horrified. They all knew what awaited them.

"Now!" the Count howled, and they started forward, faces grim.

"Remember, all they can do is scare you," Rod said quickly to his children. "Everybody take a dozen or so, and keep them from being scary."

"Like this, dost thou mean?" Gregory chirped, and Sir Borcas's ghost slipped, skidded, and flopped floundering down.

"Yeah, that's the idea! Keep it up!"

Sir Dillindag hauled out his sword, and found it was a daisy. A man-at-arms chopped with his halberd, and it kept on going, spinning him around and around in a circle while he howled.

"Good idea," Rod grunted, and another halberdier went spinning, but this time rose up slowly, his halberd acting as a helicopter rotor, until he dropped it, screaming with fright.

Then Fess reared, his whinny a scream of fury as he whirled and struck out with his forehooves at advancing knights.

It was a mistake; this, they could understand. The knights descended on Fess shouting, englobing him in seconds, a melee of flailing swords and ghostly battle axes.

"Get away from that horse!" Rod shouted, humor forgotten in the threat to his old friend, and he waded through the knights, struggling to reach his companion.

He got there just in time to see Fess go rigid, knees locking; then his head dropped to swing between his fetlocks.

"A seizure," Rod groaned. "Too many enemies, too fast."

"Who is elf-shot?" cried a treble voice.

" 'Tis the horse!" answered a crackling baritone. "Yet who did fling the shot?"

" 'Twas none of us," answered a countertenor, and Rod drew back, staring in disbelief—for miniature ghosts were climbing out of chinks in the walls and coalescing out of thin air, translucent and colorful, and none more than a foot high.

"Mama," Cordelia gasped, "they are ghosts of elves!"

"Yet how can that be?" Gwen marvelled. "Elves have no souls!"

" 'Tis he hath done it, mistress!" An elfin dame pointed at Magnus. "He doth call up memories of such of us as once did dwell here."

"Yet what can have slain thee?" Gregory wailed. "Elves are immortal!"

"Not when we're pierced by Cold Iron—and so cruel were this Count and his men that they did hunt us out to slay us!"

" 'Twas good sport," said Foxcourt, with a feral grin. "And it shall be again, if thou dost not take thee hence!"

"Indeed it shall," chuckled a pretty elfin damsel, "yet 'tis we who shall make sport of thee! Gossips, what use is a count?"

"Why, for numbering," answered a dozen voices. "Shall we tally all his bones?"

And a skeleton grinned in the dark, a foolish thing that busily ticked off each of its own pieces—and somehow bore Count Foxcourt's face.

"How dost thou dare!" the Count cried, livid with rage.

"Why, for that thou canst not slay us now, foul count," said a larger elf, grinning with malice, "for we are dead. Now ward thee from the wee folk!"

People were laughing again, and in the gloom, a ring of merry elfin faces was appearing—faces crowned with caps and bells, forms bedecked in motley. The fools and jesters had come to take their turns in the audience.

Foxcourt couldn't stay on his feet; the floor kept sliding out from under him. At one point, he was actually bouncing about on his head, while Sola laughed and laughed, one hand pressed to her mouth, tears streaming down her cheeks.

Behind him, his court were chopping frantically with swords that sprouted wings and chicken's heads and fluttered, squawking indignantly. Knights kept grabbing at armored pants that kept slipping down, and men-at-arms kept skidding on squashed fruit, as overripe pears and plums flew from the jesters and clowns all about them, and the manic laughter made the whole hall shake.

"What ails thee, milord?" a voice called. "Hast thou a bout of gout?"

"Good night, bad knight!" another cried. "When thou canst not prevail, thou must needs take to thy bed!"

"Yet he'll not prevail there, either," a third voice answered.

A fourth called, "In what cause hast thou fallen, Sir Borcas? Art thou down for the Count?"

"Why, he doth flounder!"

" 'Nay, a flounder's a fish!"

"And so is he—he's found his *fin!*"

"Hast thou downed the Count?" a new voice cried; and another answered,

"The Count is down!"

"Nay, Count up!"

"He doth not count at all!"

"Then he is of no importance?"

Pale with humiliation and rage, the Count was inching back within the ranks of his courtiers. But, "Nay," Gwen said, "how unseemly of thee, to depart ere the festival is done!" And the audience of fools seemed to curve around as the howling, cursing mob of courtiers faded, leaving the Count encircled by jeering grotesques, pointing and laughing.

"Be damned to you all!" he shouted, despairing, but the audience only laughed the louder and cried, "Brother, will he seek to step?"

"Nay, he'll step to stoop!"

"An he doth stoop, he'll never stand up straight again!"

"Why, gossip, he hath not been upstanding since he came to manhood!"

"Aye, nor hath been upright since his birth!"

"What, was he born?"

"Aye, borne in triumph! See his noble stance!"

Which, of course, was the cue for the floor to slip out from under him again.

"Away!" the Count screamed. "Avaunt thee, monsters!"

"Doth he speak to himself, then?"

"What, shall we show him the true shape of his soul?"

"Nay, do not!" the Count cried in panic. "Go leave me! Get thee hence!"

"Why, I have hence, and roosters, too."

"And so have I. Wherefore ought we seek more?"

"To give us eggs."

A pale spheroid flew through the air and struck, breaking open on the Count's head and oozing down over his cheeks. He howled in dismay and turned to run—but he could only run in place.

"There is only one direction in which thou mayest go," Gwen said, her voice hard.

"Any! Any way is good, so that it takes me from these loons!"

"What—a loon, doth he say?"

"A loon he needs, for he doth weave."

"Hath he a woof?"

"Nay, for they did spurn him."

"Then must he have a warp!"

"Aye. Now see him take it."

And the ghost began to diminish, shrinking into the distance as he bumbled away in a limping run; though he stayed in the same place on the dais, he grew smaller and smaller, with his crowd of hecklers hard on his heels, till they all shrank away to nothing, and were gone.

The Gallowglasses were silent, listening.

Faint, ghostly laughter echoed through the castle, but it was hilarity now, not the wicked gloating they had heard before.

"We have won," Magnus whispered, unbelieving.

Rod nodded. "I had a notion we could, if we just kept from being scared. Embedded memories aren't going to hurt you, you see—they can only make you hurt yourself."

"Yet if they're naught but memories, how could we best them?"

"By making new memories to counter them," Gwen explained. "Now, if the Count's wickedness should echo within thy brother's mind, these scenes of humiliation will arise, to make him slink away again. For look you, all that he did truly seek in life were pride and power—pride, gained by shaming those about him; and power, by giving hurt wheresoe'er he could. 'Twas that which was his true pleasure—the sense of power; his fornicating and his cruelty did feed that sense most vividly, for him."

Cordelia's eyes lit. "Yet here, he was himself held up to ridicule, which did shame him unmercifully."

"Aye, and at the hands of a victim, too."

"And he found he had no power, to strike back! Nay, small wonder that he fled, even if 'twas to his just desserts!"

"If 'twas truly his soul." Magnus frowned. "If he was only memories embedded in the stone, brought to seeming fullness by my mind, then what we have seen may have been but illusion."

"And if it was," said Gregory, "his soul's been frying in Hell these two hundred years."

"Gregory!" Gwen gasped, shocked at those words coming from an eight-year-old.

Gregory looked up at her, wide-eyed. "The good fathers do speak such words from the pulpit, Mama. Wherefore may not I?"

Rod decided to save her from an awkward answer. "I think it's time to revive Fess."

"Oh, aye!" Cordelia leaped to the horse's side. "Do, Papa! How can I have not have thought of him!"

"We were a little busy," Rod explained. He stepped up to Fess and felt under the saddlehorn for the reset switch—an enlarged "vertebra." He pushed it over and, slowly, the robot raised its head, blinking away the dullness from its plastic eyes. "I . . . haddd uh . . . seizurrre?"

"Yes," Rod said. "Just wait, and it will pass."

"More quickly for me than for a human," the robot said slowly. It looked about at the empty chamber, and the small boy building up the fire again. "The ghosts . . . are . . . ?"

"Gone," Rod confirmed. "We embarrassed them so much that they decided to seek out new haunts."

Cordelia winced. "The elfin ghosts have affected thee, Papa."

"Ghosts of . . . elves?"

Magnus nodded. "I, unwitting, served for thee to bring them forth."

"*I?* But how could I . . ."

"The folk hereby do think a seizure's brought by elf-shot," Gregory explained, "so when thou didst seem to be so shot, the elves came forth to seek the slinger."

"But elfin ghosts could be nothing *but* illusion!"

" 'Tis even as thou sayest," Cordelia agreed, "yet were the Count and his men any more?"

"Yet if the ghosts are but illusion," Geoffrey said, frowning, "how can this battle we have held banish them?"

"By counteracting them," Fess answered. "Believe me, Geoffrey—it is a process with which I am intimately familiar."

Rod looked up, surprised. He had missed the analogy between the computer's program, and the interactive loop between psychometricist and stored emotions—but of course, they were much alike.

"Then Sola's ghost was not truly her soul?"

Gwen spread her hands. "I cannot say. Yet soul or dream, I think she's freed for Heaven."

"Still," Rod mused, "it wouldn't do any harm to have Father Boquilva over for dinner. He understands computers, and he carries holy water."

Faint in the distance, a hoarse, raw masculine scream rang out one last time, diminishing into the fading echo of dying laughter. Then, finally, all was quiet.

"Is it cleansed now?" Gwen asked softly.

Magnus frowned, went to Foxcourt's chair, and grasped the wood firmly with both hands. After a moment, he nodded. "Not even a trace doth linger—naught of him, nor of any old angst or melancholia."

And, suddenly, she was there, radiant in the darkness before him, glowing with faint colors, vibrant, alive, and more beautiful than she had ever been. " 'Tis done—thou hast wrought famously!"

Magnus could only stare, spellbound.

So it was Cordelia who asked, "The wicked lord is fled?"

"Aye." Sola turned to her, glowing in more ways than one. "Foxcourt saw that he would be forever mocked, if he dared to linger here—so he hath fled to try his fate in the afterworld, convinced it cannot be worse."

Rod asked, "Didn't he ever have a hellfire-and-brimstone preacher?"

"Aye, and therefore called a priest, and confessed his sins, when he foresaw his death—yet that part of him that lingered here did seek to turn again to some pale shadow of its old delights."

"Foul!" Geoffrey glared, indignant. "Is there no justice in Heaven, either? Will he not be dealt with as he did deal?"

"Not so." Gwen's hand was on his shoulder. "For, though he may yet be redeemed, he must first come to know his guilt, and to believe in it, in his heart of hearts; then may he make reparation. He shall be long in Purgatory, son—if he doth win to it at all. He may not have been truly repentant when he was shriven.''

Geoffrey still didn't look content, but he was silent.

''Justice, I desire,'' Sola admitted, ''yet I'll be content with his wickedness ended. Thanks to thine aid, good folk, none shall ever again suffer from the cruelty of Count Foxcourt. Thou hast proven the worth of my father's death, and my brother's; thou hast given their chivalry meaning, and vindicated my mother's suffering. Thou hast made their fates worthwhile by encompassing the downfall of a villain!''

Rod looked around at his family. ''You'll pardon me if I feel a certain sense of satisfaction about that.''

''As well thou shouldst.'' Sola stepped forward, arms outstretched as though to embrace them. ''I thank thee all, most earnestly; thou hast rescued me from ancient suffering.'' She turned to Magnus. ''Yet most greatly I thank thee, good youth, for I do know 'twas thee who did most earnestly press to aid me. 'Tis thou hast ope'd the way for me, that I may leave this mundane sphere, and commence my journey up toward Heaven.''

''I . . . I was honored . . .''

''As I am honored by thee! Be sure that, if I do gain the Blessed Mede, thou wilt ever have a friend in the hereafter!''

Then she turned, lifting a hand. ''Farewell, good friends— and pray for me!''

Then she was gone.

The hall lay dark and still, except for the murmuring of the flames on the hearth.

''Pray I shall,'' Magnus murmured, gazing at the space where she had been, ''and may thy journey be brief and blessed, beauteous lass.''

But a friend, Rod noted, was not what he'd wanted.

The hall was quiet, and Cordelia and the younger boys were finishing straightening the furniture that had been tumbled about in the wake of the ghosts. Geoffrey, of course, had complained before, during, and after. ''Wherefore hath Magnus not aided, too, Mama?''

''Hush,'' Gwen said. ''Let thy brother alone awhile, to let the pieces of his heart join together again.''

Cordelia looked up, startled. "Was he heartbroken, then?"

"Let's just say that his feelings had become too thick on one side, and too thin on the other," Rod hedged. "He needs to get them into balance now."

"It makes no sense," Geoffrey grumbled, and went off to Fess, in search of sanity.

Gwen looked out the nearest of the high, thin windows, and just barely espied the small, antique cemetary outside the castle walls.

"What do you see?" Rod said softly.

"Our lad," she answered, equally hushed. "He doth stand quite still, gazing upon a tombstone."

"Ah." Rod nodded. "Sola's, no doubt. Poor kid—I know how he feels."

Gwen turned to stare at him, startled. "Dost thou so!"

Rod gazed deeply into her eyes before he let the smile lift the corners of his mouth. "Why, of course, dear," he said quietly. "You know you had to heal my heart, when you found it."

She gazed back at him, then slowly smiled, too. She turned to wrap his arms about her, her back to his chest, resting her head against his shoulder as she gazed out at the youth confronting death below them. "Will he, too, find one to heal him?"

"We can only hope," Rod breathed, "hope that he, too, will someday meet a woman who will make all his previous wounds unimportant."

She looked up into his eyes, and hers held stars.

Across the hall, Cordelia watched them, pensive and thoughtful. "Fess?"

"Yes, Cordelia?"

"Was Mama the only lass who ever fell a-love with Papa?"

"I have spoken to you before, about asking personal questions about your father's past." Fess was instantly severe. "Such information is definitely confidential. You must ask your father to tell you."

"But he will never tell me of these things that truly matter, Fess!"

"Then neither shall I, Cordelia."

"But are we never to learn more of Father's wanderings?" Gregory asked.

Fess was still a moment, then said, "I cannot say, children. It will depend on your father's permission, of course . . ."

"And he will never give it!" Geoffrey said, in disgust.

Fess stood mute.

Cordelia noticed, and said, "Dost thou think he might, good Fess?"

"One can never tell, Cordelia. Even I cannot tell what your father will agree to, when the time and the circumstances are correct."

"There may be more tales, then?" Gregory asked hopefully.

"Oh, certainly there will be more stories! You had many ancestors, children, and not all of them lived dull lives. Whenever you wish, you have but to . . ."

"Now!"

"Another ancestor, Fess!"

"They are ours, after all!"

"Tell!"

"Well, not immediately," the horse temporized. "Even I feel the need of rest and reflection, after the upheaval of our confrontation with Count Foxcourt."

"At bedtime, then?"

"At bedtime," Fess agreed, "or perhaps another day."

"Tomorrow," Cordelia said brightly, "*is* another day."

Epilogue

Jose rose to go report to his supervisor. It meant his job, but that was better than having a robot go wild and kill somebody because of a programming flaw.

He knocked on the door. "Al?"

The door was open. Al looked up and smiled. "Hi, Jose. What gives?" Then he saw the look on the younger man's face and straightened. "Come on in. Need to sit down?"

" 'Fraid so, Al." Jose sat down carefully, feeling old.

"So what happened?"

"I copied the Declaration of Independence into a robot brain along with the operating program."

Al just sat very still, his eyes growing very, very round. Then he said, "You copied the WHAT?"

"The Declaration of Independence."

Al erupted into guffaws.

Jose stared, then frowned. "It's not funny, Al! We've got to catch it before it's installed!"

"I—I'm sorry," Al managed. Then his face split into a grin, and he was off again. He leaned back in his chair and held his belly, whooping with glee.

Jose sighed and waited for it to pass. Illogically, he began to feel there might be hope.

Finally, Al got himself under control and leaned forward, grinning. "I'm sorry about that, Jose—but you have to admit, this is a new one. How'd you manage *that?*"

Jose spread his hands, the picture of forlornness. "I called it up to check something that was bothering me, then left it on scroll when I went to help Bob. By the time I came back, it was off the screen, and I'd forgotten about it."

"But it was still in memory." Al shook his head with a grin. "Who else would get so upset about something in the Declaration?"

"It was an argument," Jose muttered.

"On the other hand," Al answered himself, "who else would come report it right away, instead of trying to cover up?" He finally managed to look sympathetic. "You're right, Jose, this could be bad. What kind of program was it?"

"One of those new ones—the FCC series."

Al smiled. "Well, at least, if you had to do it, you used one that's just into production." Then he turned thoughtful. "Wait a minute, though—maybe it's not a total loss."

Jose felt a surge of hope and tried to ignore it. "How?"

"That's the 'Faithful Cybernetic Companion' series. The program's for extreme loyalty, as well as the usual total obedience." Al turned to his screen and called up the program. "It just might be strong enough to counter the Declaration."

Jose frowned. "How could it . . ." Then his face lit up. "Of course! If the robot's extremely loyal to you, it can be totally independent, and still be on your side!"

Al nodded. "Independence might counter an inclination toward obedience, but loyalty would make the robot do what his owner said to, anyway—unless there was a damn good reason not to." He shrugged. "But all our programs have overrides for illegal or blatantly unethical commands, anyway."

Jose felt excitement building. "Then the robot might not have to be destroyed?"

"And you might not have to be fired." Al nodded. "I'm routing this whole snafu over to programming to be checked. I don't think there'll be any problem, though—this time." He turned back to Jose, suddenly totally serious. "But don't let it happen again—okay?"

Jose stared straight into Al's eyes and nodded slowly. "Never, Al. My word."

"Who was the argument with, anyway?"

Jose swallowed. "My wife."

Al turned grave. "Not much you can do about that. But next time, if you're upset, don't come in. All right?"

Jose nodded slowly. "I promise, Al. Better not here at all, than not all here."

Al grinned. "You got it. And you still have your job."

But Jose's attention had drifted again. He was thinking that, if a robot could be independent down to its most basic programming and still be intensely loyal, maybe a person could, too. And if that was so, maybe it was possible to be really independent but still be married, after all. He whistled, and went back to his work.